Maggie Russell—legal assistant by day, horror writer by night—gets the scare of her life when she wakes up in a strange café without any idea of how she got there. But if she tells anyone about her sleepwalking escapades, she could lose her grandmother's house, and she'd fought so hard to keep it.

Dean Parker is a private investigator whose office is next door to Maggie's law firm. He's been eyeing the pretty brunette ever since she started working there, but getting involved with anyone isn't in his game plan. When he finds out she's been having sleeping problems, he suspects her money-grubbing cousin is involved. Instead, he discovers something worse: a ghost is living with Maggie and it appears another may be possessing her.

Dean is determined to help Maggie rid her home of the uninvited guests. He just never figured his attraction to her would be reciprocated. Keeping his distance is no longer an option, though. If he fails, Maggie could very well be possessed forever.

Books by Stacy McKitrick

Ghostly Encounter series:
Ghostly Liaison
Ghostly Interlude

Bitten by Love series:
My Sunny Vampire
Bite Me, I'm Yours
Blind Temptation
A Vampire Wedding

Short Stories in the Following Anthologies:
Home for the Holidays
Love's a Beach

Ghostly Interlude

(Ghostly Encounters #2)

Stacy McKitrick

Mythical Press * Dayton, Ohio

MYTHICAL PRESS * DAYTON, OHIO
www.mythicalpress.com

Cover designed by Maria Zannini of Book Cover Diva
http://bookcoverdiva.blogspot.com/
Edited by Piper Denna and Stephanie McKitrick
Formatted by Enterprise Book Services
http://www.EnterpriseBookServices.com/

This story is a work of fiction. Names, characters, places, and incidents are either products of the authors imagination or are used factiously. Any resemblance to actual events, locales, business establishments, media title, or persons living or dead, is entirely coincidental.

Published in the United States of America
First Electronic Edition: February 27, 2018

In loving memory of my father
Harold Gregory Thurber
1925 - 2017

Chapter 1

Something poked Maggie in her shoulder and she swatted it away. Time to have a serious talk with her cousin about boundaries, and if that didn't work, she would finally install a lock on her bedroom door.

"Ma'am, wake up. You have to go."

Ma'am? That didn't sound like Erica because, well, Erica wasn't a guy. So what was a guy doing in her bedroom? Maggie bolted upright and blinked as the bright room came into focus. Better question: Where was her bedroom?

Keep calm. Keep calm. You've just been sleepwalking. Again.

The mantra did nothing to keep her heart from racing. Probably because every other time it had happened she'd woken up at home. Not at some strange café.

Dirty dishes littered the table before her. God. She was eating in her sleep now? Should she be thankful she wasn't wearing her pajamas? She apparently had the sleep-sense to put on a sweater and jeans.

The person who'd poked her was actually a waiter, and a young one at that. He couldn't be more than twenty. "Here's the check. I have to close up."

"What day is it?"

"It's seven. We're closing."

She grabbed his arm. "Not time. Day. Day!"

His eyes widened and he shrugged free. "Sunday?"

"Sunday?" No. No-no-no. That couldn't be. She'd lost two days. Two freakin' days! Who sleepwalked for two days?

"Are you okay?" he asked, taking several steps backward.

She was far from okay, but spooking the waiter wouldn't improve her situation. "Sorry, I got confused." Maggie scooted away from the table and found her purse on the floor. Thank God she had her wallet, and money. She paid the young man and stood on unsteady legs. "Can I use the restroom before I go?"

He nodded while he bused the table. "Just be quick. I want to go home."

Home. That sounded good. But how far was she? Her eyes scratched with each blink and she practically stumbled to the ladies' room. Why was she so tired? If she'd been sleepwalking, wouldn't she be rested? She splashed cold water on her face but instead of shocking her awake, it only made her shiver. Great.

She pulled out her phone. Maybe it would show where in the world she had ended up. She pushed the on button and was faced with a blank screen. She shook it as if it would do any good. Dead. Figured. Now she'd have to make a bigger ass out of herself and ask that waiter where she was. He probably already thought she was high on something.

At least she didn't look high. Tired, definitely, but not high or drunk. She ran a brush through her hair and headed back to the dining room.

Had she driven over here? If she had, she certainly wasn't in any condition to drive home, even if she lived close. God, she hadn't left town, had she?

"What street is that?" she asked the waiter, praying for a familiar name.

"North Dixie?" he answered, as if she should know.

She sighed in relief. Local. Finally, some good news. "May I use your phone? Mine died."

The request did not sit well with the young man as he rolled his eyes, but he showed her the phone by the register. "Just be—"

"Quick. I know," she finished. "I will." She found her cousin's business card—and it was a good thing she had it; she wasn't sure she'd remember the number in her current state—when she spotted the number to a cab company written on a piece of paper attached to the register. Erica would want some answers. The cabbie, not so much. Maggie called the cab company. The address to the café was listed on the menu and she gave it to the dispatcher.

After hanging up, she found a five in her wallet and handed it to the waiter. "Sorry for being a bother."

"No bother." He shrugged but took the money. "Kind of surprised the guy left you like that anyway."

Guy? Oh great. Not only was she having strange meals in strange cafés, she was having them with a guy now. Asking for a description was tempting. So…so…tempting. But who didn't remember their dining mate? Or what day it was?

Clearly, she was suffering from more than sleepwalking. Could dementia hit early? Grandma had been a little whacky at times, but she'd been old. Not twenty-eight.

Maggie stepped outside and was hit with a blast of frigid, February air. Before she had a chance to wonder if she'd brought a jacket, the waiter tapped her shoulder and held out her coat.

"I think you forgot this."

At least her crazy mind had remembered to dress warmly before leaving the house. "Thanks."

The young man shut the door and locked her out. Guess he wasn't too worried about her well-being after all. Not that she was in a horrible part of town. Wasn't exactly pristine, either.

A couple of motels littered the street. Unknown, unbranded, and certainly nothing she would feel safe in. She leaned up against the brick building and did her best not to slump to the ground.

She pulled out her keys and pressed the panic button on her fob. All was quiet, which meant her car wasn't parked close by. She looked to the sky. "God, please let it be at home." She could only imagine what she would tell the police if by some chance it wasn't.

Twenty minutes later, the cab arrived. So much for speedy pickup. She climbed into the warm vehicle and gave the driver her address. Weariness settled over her, and she leaned her head back.

Her house was a welcome sight. She paid the driver and stumbled to her front door. All she had to do was make it to her bed. If she was lucky, Erica was out on a date and wouldn't notice Maggie's arrival until morning.

As she fumbled with the key in the lock, the door swung open.

"Oh my God!" Erica wrapped Maggie up in a bear hug. "Where the hell have you been? I've been worried sick."

Maggie offered a weak smile. Should have called her cousin and saved the cab fare, since it seemed she was answering questions tonight after all. But not the truth, because the truth was she didn't know where she'd been, and if she admitted that, Erica would probably whisk her straight to the hospital. And then all the work she'd gone through would be for nothing.

She couldn't—wouldn't let that happen.

Chapter 2

Dean Parker sprinted inside his office and yanked off his knit mask. Jogging in the fall had been pleasant. Winter in Dayton, Ohio? Not so much. Even during lunch. Just because the sun was shining didn't mean it gave off any warmth.

His assistant, Bridget Gentry, smiled behind the counter. "You know, if you bought a treadmill, you wouldn't risk frostbite."

"Maybe, but they're boring." And what's a little frostbite if he could get a glimpse of Maggie, the employee next door. Not that she took her lunch outside during the freezer months. Still, he'd hoped to catch her coming or going, but no such luck this week. He tugged off his thermal shirt, baring skin, and spread his arms wide. "Besides, then I wouldn't be able to traipse in front of you like this."

He'd lost quite a bit of weight in the past months and was pretty proud of the results. Took him long enough to finally believe his doctor: that his surgery had been a success, that running wouldn't cause another incident. Too bad his scar hadn't disappeared behind his newly formed muscle. He'd told Bridget his near-death experience was caused by a heart attack, requiring surgery, because it was the one excuse he could use and not be questioned.

She smiled. "Like I care what you look like."

Dean clutched his chest. "Ouch."

She laughed. "You know what I mean. You know I only have eyes for my husband."

"Well, I don't," Peter said.

Dean spun around at the sound of the ghost's voice. Tall, lanky, and perpetually forty-three, Peter McDermott came with the building, an apparition Dean hadn't known about until after his own "death." Who knew being brought back to life would also give him the ability to see spirits when he was alone? He'd thought he'd been a freak until he'd met Bridget and her husband, Rob. They had both technically died—in different ways—and survived, and they also shared the same ghost-seeing ability. Good or bad, that meant Dean could see the spirits when they were in the room, too.

"I have to say," Peter said, "you're not turning out to be such a slob anymore. I could get used to seeing you like this."

"Do you mind?" Dean asked, holding the shirt up to his chest, which had nothing to do with Peter being gay—okay, maybe it had a little to do with that—but mainly because Peter was one nosey-assed ghost. "I knew I should have showered at home."

Bridget laughed at Dean's embarrassment. "You could always move."

Peter's eyes widened. "Don't do that! I'll be good." With that, he vanished.

"Damn ghost," Dean muttered.

"Ahh, Peter's okay. But he's right. You are looking pretty buff there. Not that I noticed."

"Thank you. I think."

"You might want to get cleaned up. Maggie's due here in about thirty minutes."

"What? Why didn't you say something before my run?" Then he might not have run, or better yet, would have gone home and cleaned up. His good clothes were there, as well as his razor. He ran a hand over his scruffy face.

"Because she made the appointment while you were out. Is there a problem?" She cocked her head and batted her eyes.

Damn. She didn't suspect anything, did she? And wouldn't that make his life miserable if she did. Bridget had already tried fixing him up a couple of times—that they'd been disasters was saying it kindly—he didn't need her knowing he had a little crush. She might never stop then.

"No. No problem." Thirty minutes? Shit. He couldn't have Maggie see him all sweaty. Plus, his deodorant had given out a couple of miles ago. But showering at work meant… "Can you keep Peter busy?"

"Peter's not going to bother—"

"Yeah, yeah, I know." Which Dean certainly did not know, especially after Peter's earlier remark. "Can you?"

"I'll do my best. But if someone comes in—"

"Yeah, yeah, I know. Peter!"

"What?" the ghost snapped as he appeared behind Bridget, who jumped out of her seat.

"Hell's bells! Not nice," she said, rubbing her belly. "You want to put me in labor?"

"Oh, sorry, Bridget. I keep forgetting."

How could Peter forget? The woman was as round as a basketball. She and Rob hadn't wasted any time in starting that family, having been married less than a year. Heck, they hadn't even really known each other all that long before they got hitched. Dean was happy for them, for sure, they were great people, but no way would he get sucked into domesticity. Single thirty-five years and counting. Besides, no one deserved a defective old heap like him, anyway. And he certainly wasn't passing on his genes.

"How would you like being solid for a few minutes?" she asked Peter, doing that eye-batting thing again.

Peter's face lit up. "You mean it?"

Damn, she was good. Dean nearly kissed her. Whenever someone of their kind were alone and touched a ghost, the ghost became corporeal. Of course, once they became corporeal, some had exhibited feats of strength. Peter hadn't shown that skill, if he even knew he had it. But Bridget and Dean kept that knowledge to themselves. Why give a ghost an opportunity to hurt them?

Dean rushed into his office, causing some loose papers on his desk to flutter to the floor. No biggie. He waved them off, grabbed his spare clothes out of his desk, and sprinted to the bathroom. His offices had previously been a residence, but when the street had widened and the property rezoned, most of the homeowners had moved out and sold their homes to businesses. Before his operation and near-death experience, Dean had spent a night or two a week in the building. It basically had three bedrooms and a full bath. But after discovering Peter, it felt downright creepy staying, knowing the ghost could pop into his shower, or his bed, at any moment. Not that Peter had, but still…

All clean and dressed, Dean ran a comb through his hair before sticking his head out the door. Peter wasn't with Bridget any longer. Which meant either someone was in the room or...

"Just because I'm gay doesn't mean I'm a pervert."

Dean nearly pounded his head into the door jamb. Bridget might have something about that moving bit. Except moving meant he might never see Maggie again. He wasn't willing to risk that.

"No one said you were a pervert." Although weren't most ghosts? What else was there to do when sight and sound were all one had left? And most people—those who couldn't see ghosts— wouldn't know one was hanging around, watching...everything. A draft of cold air was all they'd feel whenever a spirit hovered about.

"Oh really? Then what was that bit with Bridget? Don't get me wrong, I love being solid. Wish you'd do it more often. But to distract me so you could take a shower? Please. Your body may be looking better, but you're really not my type."

"You have a type?"

"Yeah. Someone who's into me."

"Forgive me for not believing you, because there's no way you'd know if someone was into you since you can't be seen by the general public. And just to be clear, again, my aversion to you has nothing to do with your sexual preference and everything to do with you being a ghost." Dean headed for his office. He picked up the documents that had landed on the floor earlier and started straightening up his desk. Oh, who was he kidding? There wasn't much he could do to make it neater. Papers were papers and would always look messy. He should probably go digital, and maybe he would when it became impossible to get hacked.

"Why haven't you moved?" Peter asked. "I mean, I'm glad you haven't, but you seem to hate me so much. Or better yet, find out who killed me and then I'd move on."

Dean did not want to have this conversation again. Why did Peter keep insisting someone killed him? No one had forced him to swallow the sleeping pills.

The intercom buzzed, followed by Bridget singing, "You decent?"

"Very funny. Send her in." Saved by Bridget. Well, actually Maggie, someone who couldn't see ghosts. Didn't mean the conversation was over; Peter was nothing if not determined. Dean stood behind his desk. As soon as she came into view, Peter misted away. Dean smiled. "Hey, Maggie."

With hair the color of milk chocolate and eyes like emeralds, she smiled back and he nearly lost it. Damn, she was stunning. Then again, she was always stunning.

Too bad he could never have her.

* * * *

Smiling took more energy than Maggie ever imagined. Maybe because she'd been plastering on a fake smile all morning. Make that all week. She might have woken in her own bed for the past four mornings, but it didn't mean she'd gotten any rest. Every morning she woke more tired than the night before. Problem was, she couldn't remember not sleeping.

But her body woke right up after seeing Dean's friendly face and smile. Heck, his size alone made her all gooey inside. All that running had really hunked him up, not that he was bad looking to begin with. Standing at six-foot-three with the widest shoulders she'd ever seen, he could probably wrestle a bear and win. But a bear wasn't responsible for her problem. Not that she'd ask him to help with that. She couldn't ask anyone without sounding crazy, and she wasn't all that sure she wasn't crazy.

Since she started clerking for the lawyers next door—a job that paid the bills and nothing more—this was the first time she'd actually been in Dean's office. She'd usually e-mail the information if any work was needed. But she had to get out and move. Now that she spied the brown vinyl couch that hugged the left wall, moving didn't seem all that important. The couch practically called to her.

"You're welcome to sit on it, but it's not really all that comfortable. Plus, you'd be all the way over there."

For him to notice her staring, she must really be out of it. "Your office isn't that big."

"Big enough. So where's it gonna be?" He gestured between the couch and chair.

She took the chair, smoothing her skirt in the process. "Thanks for seeing me on such short notice."

"Not a problem. You know, you didn't need to come over here. You could have called."

"The office was kind of closing in on me." And she'd fallen asleep at her desk at least four times this morning alone. Maybe Dean was the fix she needed. Coffee certainly wasn't helping.

"Spring can't get here soon enough, huh? So, what do you have for me?"

"Tom needs you to locate a witness." She started to place the folder on his desk and nearly choked. Holy crap. Every available surface was covered in books and paper and folders. He must be on an important case. Or was he just a slob? Her fingers itched to organize the mess while she continued to hold the folder over the desk. "Are you going to be able to do this? You look a little...overwhelmed."

Laughing, he took the folder from her. "I won't lose this. I promise."

"So, your desk always looks like this?" Oh, she could never work in such conditions. It would drive her nuts.

"Actually, it used to look worse. I have Bridget to thank for cleaning it up a bit." He moved some paper around. Before she could cringe at the unorderliness of it all, he uncovered a novel displaying her pen name: M. L. Detrick.

He was reading her book. *Hers.* She'd never seen anyone read her book before. Well, except her cousin. But relatives didn't count.

Maggie had taken her grandmother's maiden name because using her mother's maiden name made her think of her cousin Eddie, and that bastard didn't deserve his name on the book. Plus, she really didn't want anyone to know she wrote horror novels. Or wrote novels at all. It was her sanctuary and her business and it made sense to keep it away from family. Especially her mother's side.

"You like horror novels?" she asked.

"Yeah, I do. The scarier, the better. This one's pretty good. It's about this guy who can change into a doppelganger and is...well, I don't want to spoil it for you. Want to borrow it when I'm done?"

"Thanks, but I'll pass."

"Not a fan of horror, huh?"

She just smiled back at him. Ha! If he only knew. But he wouldn't. Not if she could help it.

He opened the folder and frowned. "Did you forget something?"

"Forget?"

He turned the folder upside down, but nothing fell out. The papers. She'd forgotten the papers.

"Oh my God. I'm so sorry." What was that, the third time she'd forgotten to do that this week? As tears threatened to leak from her eyes, she stood. "I can't believe I did that. I'll go get them."

"Hey." Dean stood and came around the desk, grabbing her arm to keep her from leaving. "Your eyes are all bloodshot. What's the matter? Aren't you feeling well?"

"I'm fine. I just haven't been sleeping well. I guess it's catching up with me."

He pulled her over to the couch and sat beside her. "Is it Eddie? Has he started harassing you again?"

If only it were that simple. Unfortunately, her bastard of a cousin was innocent for once. "I haven't heard from him since he last contested the will."

A will his mother had screamed "fake" since Eddie wasn't even mentioned. Maggie had thought that was strange, too, because she'd never told anyone what he was capable of, but then maybe Grandma had seen the real Eddie. A person who would do anything to get what he wanted. Seemed he took after his mother after all. Aunt Gina's temper tantrum after the reading had brought Maggie a little solace after losing her grandmother.

"Then what's the matter?" He placed his arm along the back of the couch, within inches of her shoulders.

He made her ache, and not exactly in a bad way. How easy would it be to just lean against that hard body of his? Let him take care of her problems? Too bad he couldn't. No one could. "Nothing's the matter." Maggie stood, breaking the connection she was too willing to succumb to. "I just forgot to put the papers in the folder. I'll go get them."

Well, it was settled now. She was officially going nutso.

* * * *

Dean reached out to grab her arm, but she was fast out the door. "Maggie, wait!"

Something was definitely wrong with her. He'd never seen her look so tired. If Eddie was no longer bothering her, then who was? Dean rushed out to the reception area hoping to stop her, but she'd already gone outside.

"Is everything okay?" Bridget asked.

"I don't know." Forgoing his coat, he dashed outside. The cold air was a mere nuisance as he easily caught up with Maggie before she could disappear inside the lawyers' building. "Why didn't you wait for me?"

"I didn't mean to put you out. I'm sorry."

"Will you stop apologizing? It's only papers. I wish you'd tell me what's wrong."

"I told you. I haven't been sleeping well. Maybe I'm coming down with something. You should stay away from me."

Like hell he would. She reached for the door, but he beat her to it and followed her inside. Maggie's doppelganger stood as they entered the office.

Doppelganger? Okay, he should probably lay off the horror books. The lady was most likely Maggie's sister. Or…twin? Gee, what were the odds?

"There you are. Did you forget we were going out for lunch?" For as much as this woman resembled Maggie, she didn't sound like her at all. At least his dick didn't think so.

Maggie covered her mouth. "Was that today? Oh God, Erica. I'm so sorry."

"What are you talking about? I reminded you this morning." Erica glanced at Dean and smiled. "Of course, I can maybe understand why you'd forget if you were with him."

"Who?" Maggie turned around as if someone else besides Dean was behind her. "Oh. This is Dean Parker. From next door. Dean, this is my cousin, Erica Russell. Excuse me while I go hunt for those papers." She headed down the hall and disappeared into a room.

"Cousin? Wow, you two look like—"

"Sisters?" Erica finished. "That's because our fathers are identical twins and our mothers are cousins. Freaky, huh?"

Maggie's father was a twin? Again, what were the odds? "I wouldn't say freaky. Unusual, maybe."

"Yeah, it's unusual, all right. So, you're the investigator, huh? She's mentioned you."

"She did?" He couldn't help but smile. He'd gotten the impression Maggie had never really noticed him before.

"Yeah. Said you were a big help in that stupid case Eddie filed against her. Which reminds me. Is it possible he could be doing something to her? Especially last weekend? She hasn't been right since we moved into the house. I'm worried about her."

"What happened last weekend?"

"She disappeared. I woke up Saturday and there was no sign of her until late Sunday evening. After apologizing profusely, she said she had a date that turned into an overnighter and that she would have called, except she had no phone service."

Disappointment almost cinched his chest—Maggie was dating someone?—except Erica's tone implied otherwise. "You didn't believe her."

"No. She doesn't date anyone, no less an overnighter. Unless... Was she with you?"

Dean shook his head. He wished, boy did he wish.

"Then I'm wondering if Eddie did something to her."

"Like what?"

"I don't know. Can someone be hypnotized or drugged and not know it? She's been sleepwalking."

Sleepwalking could possibly be a reason for Maggie's tiredness, but hypnotized? Drugged? Erica officially crossed over to the overreacting relative. "That seems a little far-fetched, but I can do some checking. See what Eddie was up to last weekend."

"Thanks." She smiled and looked so much like Maggie. Yet Maggie was the one who made his heart sing. Erica didn't affect him at all.

Tom emerged from his office and waved. "Hey, Dean." When he passed the room Maggie had entered, he looked inside and stopped. "Maggie? What's the matter?"

"I can't find the papers I made copies of," she said. "I'm sure I left them in here."

"You did. I put them on your desk, nice and neat, just the way you—hey, are you okay?"

Erica dashed to the room and Dean followed. Maggie was on her knees, sobbing.

"I think it's time to see a doctor." Erica turned toward Tom. "She's been sleepwalking. I think the stress of the house has gotten to her."

"I'm not feeling any stress," Maggie muttered. "I'm fine."

"You're not fine," Tom said. "I saw you asleep at your desk a couple of times today."

She looked up with shock on her face. "I'm so sorry. It won't happen again."

"I'm not scolding you, but I think Erica is right. You don't look well."

"But the papers."

"I'll take care of them. Go on. Get some rest. And take tomorrow off, too. We'll see you Monday."

Erica went to work grabbing Maggie's coat and purse while Maggie stood, staring at the floor. Maybe Erica wasn't over-reacting. Maybe something weird was going on. An urge to hold her came over Dean hard and fast. But then Tom was talking and Dean had to let her leave. God, he hoped she was all right.

* * * *

Maggie shrugged free from Erica's arm as soon as they were outside and out of sight. "I'm not feeble. I'm just tired."

"Yeah, well, you keep it up and you *will* be feeble. Not sleeping isn't good for you."

"But I am sleeping. I go to bed at night and I wake up in the morning."

"No. You go to bed at night and wake up an hour later. Sometimes less. I hear you moving around."

"And you're just now telling me this?" Oh, God. It was worse than she'd thought.

"I should have insisted you go to the doctor Sunday night. I knew you weren't out on a date. You never date. You're always writing."

The excuse had sounded good at the time.

Erica ushered Maggie to her car.

"What about mine?"

"We'll get it later. You're in no shape to drive. Plus, I'm not so sure you'd drive to the doctor."

Erica was probably right. Something must be seriously wrong if Maggie didn't remember waking up during the night. Hopefully it was something simple, like a brain tumor. Those could be fixed, right? Being crazy, not so much.

As they drove out of the parking lot, Erica said, "You never told me Dean was a hunk."

Jealousy pinched Maggie's heart. Was Erica interested in Dean? Not wanting to give anything away, Maggie rolled her eyes. "I don't tell you a lot of things, but what does that have to do with anything?"

"Do you like him? Because he sure likes you."

Okay, that was unexpected, and a little relieving. "What are you talking about? We have a professional relationship."

"Yeah, right. That's why he looked at you the way he did."

How had he looked at her? Why hadn't she noticed? Maybe because her brain had flown the coop? Not that it mattered. Until she got her life figured out, men were off limits. "Again, what does that—"

"I'm just saying, when this is all over, when you're all better, you might want to ask him out. I'd bet he'd say yes."

"And you're living in Fantasy Land again. He's been nothing but professional with me. If he likes me, why hasn't he asked me out, huh?"

"Maybe he's shy. I bet you could butter him up real easy-like. You need to at least try to have a love life."

As if love would fix a broken mind. "I think you should worry about your own love life before you go worrying about mine."

Erica stopped at a light. "There's nothing wrong with my love life. I've had sex four times in the past month. How about you?"

"No comment." Maggie would not admit to her cousin that she was still a virgin. She'd never hear the end of it then, if Erica didn't see fit to remedy the situation. And probably with Dean. God! Best to let her cousin think she was going through a dry spell instead of never having dipped into the well. Or was that being dipped? Whatever.

"That bad, huh? Still, I think Dean could be the one for you. You two would make beautiful babies."

"Babies?" Maggie groaned. Erica never let up.

* * * *

Dean returned to his office, holding the papers Maggie had meant to give him earlier.

"So what was that all about?" Bridget said. "She didn't look well."

"I think the stress from the lawsuit has finally gotten to her. She hasn't been sleeping."

"She's schizo," Peter said. "Which explains things."

Dean stared at the ghost. "Explains things how?"

"Besides falling apart over some lost papers? She was glowing earlier. If that's not a sign of being schizo, then I don't know what is."

Glowing? If anyone was crazy it was Peter. "She's not schizo. How many times do I have to tell you not to snoop?"

"You just don't like me snooping on her." He cupped his hand along his mouth and leaned toward Bridget. "Because he likes her."

Bridget snorted. "Like that's a secret?"

Dean glared at her, hoping to stop the abuse. "Don't you have work to do?"

"Sure. While you were next door, Greg Parker called. I didn't know you had a brother."

So now Greg had resorted to calling the office. That's what Dean got for ignoring the phone calls. And the e-mails.

"I didn't either," Peter said. "What gives?"

Dean ignored the ghost and turned toward Bridget. "Did he say what he wanted?"

"No, just that it was important and for you to call back. He gave me his number, thinking you didn't have it." She held out the note. "Do you need it?"

"I got it, thanks." No way would he call back, though. He talked to Mom every Sunday. If anything was wrong, she would have said.

As Dean headed toward his office, Peter placed his palms together and widened his eyes at Bridget. She frowned and shook her head.

He knew he would regret asking, but he did anyway. "What's going on?"

Bridget slumped in her seat. "Would it be okay if I looked into Peter's death?"

"Oh no. Not you, too."

"I'll only do it when I'm not busy. Plus, it'll give me some experience."

"Rob is not going to want you traipsing around town in your condition. He'll kill me."

"I don't plan on traipsing. If any footwork is required, I'll talk to you first. Promise."

Dean rubbed his face. Maybe having a second opinion would get Peter off his back. "Fine. But real work comes first."

Peter wrapped Dean in a cold hug. "Thank you, thank you, thank you."

Ghostly Interlude

What was that bit about moving again? Tempting, tempting, tempting.

Chapter 3

Eddie froze as his front door swung open, revealing one angry wife.

"Where were you last Saturday night?" Veronica glared at him with those baby blues, her hand on her hip.

Answering the question would have to take some finesse, since he didn't want her to know the truth, so he settled on a joke. "Why? Did my girlfriend call?"

Her eyes widened. "You bastard. I told that woman she was mistaken. How could you do this to me? First the gambling and now a woman?"

His mother rose from the couch. Of course she'd be witness to this. She never left the living room except during meals or bed. "Eddie, don't you know what happens to men who poke their dicks in too many women? They tend to get them cut off."

"What are you talking about? I was only joking." He tossed his computer bag on the couch and grabbed his wife's shoulders. She was the only bright spot in his otherwise dull life and he couldn't afford to lose her. "Ronnie, baby, you're my only girl and I promised I wouldn't gamble anymore."

And he'd eventually keep that promise as soon as his mother was out of his life. But what kind of man kicked their dear-old-Mom out? Ronnie's opinion of him meant everything and she wouldn't tolerate him doing such a cruel thing. Until then, he was stuck going to the Racino because it was the only place he could think of to escape to where no one would notice. Plus, gambling had to be way cheaper than drinking. And man, if he wasn't tempted to drink.

"Then why would someone call and tell me they saw you at the Racino with someone who wasn't me?"

Shit. Someone saw him? And who the hell had he been talking to at the time? "Ronnie, I swear. It wasn't me. I went to Butch's to fix his computer. You can ask him."

Unless Butch was the one who'd ratted him out. What was the world coming to when he couldn't even count on his friends anymore? Was everyone out to get him?

Why, oh why did he let his mother move in with them? Oh yeah. The estate. An estate she'd been so sure he'd inherit. She'd promised she'd stay only until he received ownership. Even after their last failure, she insisted they continue to fight for it. And, of course, he went along. Because that's what good sons did, right?

What might his life have been like if she'd been the parent that died?

* * * *

Dean pulled alongside the curb in front of Maggie's house and killed the engine and headlights. Situated in an older part of town, the two-story, white-paneled home featured a lit porch with a sea green-painted railing. Traffic was practically nil since the garages in this neighborhood were located in the back of the houses and accessible through the alley.

An old wooden swing stood in the corner, with a view of the street. He bet her grandmother had sat many a warm summer night on that swing. He would if he lived there. Preferably sitting beside Maggie.

He really needed to stop thinking about things he could never have. It would only get him in trouble.

Maybe he shouldn't have come—a phone call would definitely suffice—but after her little breakdown he needed to see for himself that she was okay. So what if he used the ruse of informing Erica what his investigation had uncovered? Erica most likely didn't want Maggie to know she'd asked him to investigate, and since he didn't have Erica's number... Yeah, it was a lousy excuse, but the only one he could come up with. If only he'd found something incriminating regarding Eddie.

The man's wife insisted he'd been at home on the weekend in question—thanks to a call from Bridget implying maybe Eddie was somewhere else. Didn't mean he couldn't have visited Maggie after his wife went to sleep.

Still, why would Erica think Eddie was responsible for Maggie's sleeping disorder? He was a computer person, not in the medical profession. Probably hadn't even been close enough in proximity to Maggie to do any harm. Still, Dean could take a look around the house and see if anything was out of place. But since the sun had set, that plan of action was no longer feasible. Guess he'd have to come back tomorrow.

Like that would be a hardship.

He climbed out of his car and trotted up the steps. Three light knocks and a moment later a sparkling Erica in the process of slipping on her coat opened the door. How many sequins did that dress have?

Erica blinked a couple of times. "You're not Trevor."

"No, I'm not."

She laughed. "Sorry. Should have known he wouldn't knock. Come on in."

"Hot date?" he asked as he stepped inside the warm interior. No formal foyer here. The entrance led him straight into the living room containing a worn couch, two chairs, and a smallish high-def television. A light blue rug covered the wooden floor, giving it a homey touch. Matching carpeted stairs to the upper level disappeared through the back wall.

She shut the door and hung her coat back on the hook. "I wish. So, how are you doing? Find out anything?"

"Is Maggie home?" God, what if she had a date, too? It *was* Friday night.

Erica placed a hand on her hip and raised an eyebrow. "Oh, so you came to see her, did you?"

"What? No. I just thought you didn't want her to know about your request."

She patted him on the shoulder. "Sure you did, Dean. Sure you did."

Crap. Did everyone know he liked Maggie? Was it written on his forehead?

She strolled through the tidy living room toward the back of the house and waved him along. "Come on."

"Where are we going?"

"To Maggie."

Good, she didn't have a date. Not that he was worried or anything.

He passed through a small hallway and entered a country-style kitchen where an old wooden table with four chairs stood in the middle. His nose was in heaven. Cinnamon and vanilla scented the air. Maggie was bent over the oven door—those jeans of hers displaying one fine ass—and pulled out a tray of...cookies. Man, he'd love to sample her baking, among other things. One of these days he'd have to get it over with and ask her out. Nothing like a rejection to force her out of his head.

Except he wasn't so sure he wanted her out of his head.

When she spotted him, she smiled wide. Her eyes practically sparkled. Not a trace of the crazy, tired Maggie remained. "Hi, Dean. What are you doing here?"

Truth or the ruse? Ah, he couldn't lie to her. "I came to see how you're doing. You look a lot better."

She placed the tray on the stove and removed the potholder mitt. "I feel great. I haven't baked in weeks. It's been a wonderful day. I guess a night in the hospital was exactly what I needed."

"You spent the night in the hospital?" Damn, he wished he'd known. He would have visited her. Boring was a nice word for those places.

She transferred the cookies to a cooling rack. "Yeah. They tested me for sleep apnea or whatever. I guess I passed. I slept the night through."

Erica reached for a cookie, but got her hand slapped for her effort. "Why make them if I can't eat any?"

"You can have one after they cool."

"By then I'll be gone."

"I promise to save you some, okay?"

"Yeah, whatever." Erica sat at the table, sulking. "You get any writing done today?"

"You write?" he asked.

Erica grinned. "Yeah, she writes. She didn't tell you?"

Maggie's eyes widened. "It...uh...never came up. I'll probably try tonight. I wanted to celebrate and was in the mood to bake."

"Guess if I come home and see the light on in your office, I'll know you're really writing this time, huh?"

"What are you talking about? When was the light on?"

"Couple of nights ago. I just assumed you had insomnia or…"
Before Erica could finish, Maggie rushed to a room at the end of
the kitchen.

Dean followed her to a small office. If this was an office, where
were the filing cabinets? The papers? Then again, maybe she was
the kind who did everything digital. Inspiration posters covered
two of the walls of a room that barely had space for the desk. A
pretty empty desk. No note pads. No knick-knacks. Just her laptop
sat on top. Only other piece of furniture was a bookcase, where he
did a double-take. Several copies of the book he was currently
reading were stacked on one of the shelves.

Holy shit. She'd never said a word.

* * * *

Maggie ran her finger over the mouse pad on her laptop. When
the screen lit up, her stomach dropped. "It's on. It shouldn't be on.
I turn it off when I'm finished."

Dean came around the desk and stood beside her. "Maybe you
forgot."

That was possible. The recent events had been pretty stressful.
But she hadn't been in this room all week. At least, not that she'd
remembered. Then she spotted the bookcase. "Erica, have you
been messing with my stuff again?"

Erica looked at the case and straightened the books. "That
wasn't me. I swear."

"You can tell someone moved your books?" Dean asked.

"She hates disorder. Didn't you know? Hey!" Erica snapped her
fingers. "Maybe Eddie was in here."

Maggie looked up at her cousin. "Eddie? Why would he be
here?"

"Because he wants this house and he's trying to make you
crazy."

"And making me think I'm going crazy is going to give it to him
how?"

"So he could set it up to look like a suicide. Just like this case I
read about last summer. Some local woman was murdered, but the
murderer set it up to look like a suicide by drug overdose. People
do all sorts of things for money. Eddie's no different. You die, he
gets the house."

Dean cleared his throat, or was he coughing? "Let's not jump to
any conclusions. Did you give Eddie a key to the house?"

"No," Maggie said. "Which just goes to show how crazy Erica's theory is." She wagged her finger at her cousin. "You've been reading too many murder mysteries."

"It's not a crazy theory. He could have gotten through a window. Or the basement. Are there even locks on the windows down there?"

"Now you're just trying to freak me out." And was doing a rather bang-up job of it, too. Maybe her cousin should be the horror writer. Erica was always thinking the worst.

Dean gripped Maggie's shoulder. His touch, his presence, reassured her. "Now, we can't have that. Why don't I go check and see if they've been disturbed recently? Where's the door?"

"This way." Erica waved over her shoulder and Dean followed.

Even if Eddie had managed to get into the house, why mess with her laptop? Maggie displayed a list of recently opened files. The first one was unfamiliar and she clicked on it. "What the—"

"What is it?" Erica asked.

Maggie hadn't noticed her cousin's return. "Are you attempting to write your own book? Like, maybe, erotica?"

"If I was, I wouldn't use your computer. I have my own upstairs." Erica came around the desk and read the screen. "Oh my God. 'She bent over the kitchen table while he pounded his hot rod into her'? That's not erotica. That's porn. It's got to be Eddie. He's trying to make you think you're crazy by writing this shit."

Right. Or her brain had turned to mush and she'd written it during one of her sleeping episodes. So much for thinking this was a great day. A headache struck her temples and she rubbed them.

Dean returned. "If he came through the basement, he walked through the walls. Those windows haven't been opened in ages, if ever."

Erica snapped her fingers. "Wait a minute. Did you change the locks after you were given the house?"

Maggie shook her head. "No, because I was told I had all the keys." Didn't mean she did. "You think Eddie has a copy?"

"I think you should probably change the locks and install a security system," Dean said. "Just to be safe. I can recommend some places."

That made sense, but what if the intruder lived inside her head? How would any security system detect that?

* * * *

23

Laughing so hard she brought tears to her eyes, Lindy floated along the ceiling inside the small office that used to be Mom's sewing room. These bozos didn't have a clue as to what was happening, which was fine by her. Watching them scramble was entertaining. She hadn't had this much fun in years.

Strike that. She'd never had this much fun.

If they ever actually figured things out, her life—or unlife—would go back to being unbearable. And that was unacceptable.

A car honked outside.

"Now *that's* Trevor," Erica said. "You gonna be okay?"

"Yeah," Maggie said.

"I'll see you in the morning, then. Bye, Dean." Five seconds later Erica was out of the house.

Maggie stood and wiped her hands on her jeans. "I don't know about you, but I could use some cookies and hot chocolate. Would you like to join me?"

Lindy followed the couple into the kitchen. She could only imagine how good the place smelled. Mom used to bake. Some of her concoctions had been edible, too. If Erica was any indication, Maggie hadn't inherited her baking skills from Mom.

"Sure, thanks," Dean said. "So, when were you going to tell me you're M. L. Detrick?"

Maggie pulled out a plate and transferred some cookies from the wire rack. "Figured it out, huh? Guess there's a reason you're a private investigator."

P.I.? Shit. He could be trouble. He could ruin everything. Except… Apart from his little investigation, he didn't act like he was here on P.I. business. Not with the way he'd been mooning at Maggie. Even Erica had teased him about his arrival. So what was he doing here?

"Is he your boyfriend?" Lindy mused aloud, not that anyone could hear her. "No, not a boyfriend. You two are too formal for that. You barely even touched." Although Maggie had done her share of staring, too. Lindy hovered between the couple. "I know. A potential boyfriend! Is that it? Kind of old, isn't he?"

But in all honesty, he was rather buff, even for an old man. What was he, in his thirties? Still, a boyfriend might spice things up—teach her a few things—and with the way he was ogling Maggie, that could very well happen.

Ghostly Interlude

Lindy smiled. To think she'd been out looking for fun when she only had to wait for it to walk through the door.

Chapter 4

Dean drove past Maggie's house for the umpteenth time. Not the way he'd planned to spend his Saturday night, but something was going on with Maggie and that house and he was determined to find out what. Even if that meant reconnaissance work on the sly. Because he was pretty sure Maggie would insist on paying, or stopping him altogether, and neither was going to happen.

He'd investigated the grounds during the day to see if there'd been any sign of an intruder but had come up with nothing. If Eddie, or someone else, had walked on the frozen grass, there was no sign. And if Eddie had a key, why would he sneak in through a window? He'd walk up to the porch or come in through the alley and take the path from the garage.

All this driving gave Dean the munchies. And he wouldn't mind munching on some more of Maggie's cookies. There was definitely a difference between store bought and the delectable ambrosia that had gone on in his mouth. He had to quit after eating two because any more and he'd not only have to run farther, but his mouth might join up with his dick and convince his brain that he should make a move toward Maggie.

But being with Maggie would be selfish. She wasn't someone he could have a fling with. She was the real deal. Thankfully, she didn't show an interest in him. But whoever captured her heart would be happy for the rest of their life.

So why did that thought make his chest hurt?

He turned onto her street again, but this time it wasn't deserted. He pulled over before Erica could spot him. She was getting into the passenger side of a car. A date two nights in a row? Well, someone was getting lucky.

About thirty minutes later, his phone vibrated. Holy shit, it was Maggie. She hadn't seen him driving around, had she? He answered the call while willing his racing heart to calm. "Hey, Maggie. Everything okay?"

She laughed uneasily. "Yeah. So far," she added as an afterthought so quiet he almost didn't catch it. "Didn't mean to scare you."

"No problem." Embarrassed was another matter. Thank goodness she hadn't caught him surveying the neighborhood. "What's up?"

"Can you come over? Or is it too late? I mean, if you're on a date—"

"I'm not on a date." Hell, there hadn't been a steady girlfriend since his operation. And no one since he'd met Maggie last summer. God, his life was pathetic.

"Then would you please come over? I need to talk to someone and I don't want to do it over the phone."

"What about Erica?"

"Even if I could talk to her, she's on another date. So what do you say? I have some cookies left."

Oh God. Cookies. His mouth took over. "I'll be there in a few."

* * * *

Maggie placed her phone on the kitchen table and cradled her head. Hopefully calling Dean wasn't a colossal mistake, but she needed an impartial sounding board.

She'd gone to bed at her normal time last night. But when Erica knocked on her door at ten in the morning asking when she'd get the breakfast she was promised, Maggie woke up groggy. Like she hadn't slept at all.

She'd almost cried.

Whatever the cause of her fatigue, she made sure to contact the security firm Dean had recommended and silently cheered when told they could do the install that day. By the time they left, Maggie could no longer fake looking alert and had closed herself in her office. Someplace Erica wouldn't dare bug her. Writing was out of the question, but she'd turned on her computer anyway, hoping some social media fun would get her rejuvenated. No such luck. The insistent knocking on the door woke her.

"What?" she yelled.

"Sorry," Erica said. "But you've been awfully quiet. Everything okay in there?"

Maggie stared at the monitor. A document she didn't remember opening or even writing stared back at her. She gave Erica her standard answer. "Yeah. Just doing a lot of thinking."

"Well, you might want to think about dinner. But don't count on me. I've got plans."

That had been when she'd glanced at the clock on the monitor. She'd spent three hours in her office, most of it sleeping, or something, and she hadn't felt rested at all.

Now with Erica gone, fear set in. Going to bed was not an option. What if she went to sleep and had another episode? Who would stop her from leaving the house? And why did she think Dean could help her? She couldn't very well ask him to babysit her.

A knock on the front door happened sooner than she'd expected. She rushed to the front of the house and peeked through the panel window—could never be too careful—and grinned at Dean's smiling face. That big bruiser of a guy made her feel safe and he'd done nothing but stand on her porch. Too bad he didn't live next door.

Maggie turned off the alarm and opened the door, letting in the frigid air. "Wow. That was quick."

"I wasn't far when you called."

Should she consider that a good omen? She could use some good about now. The fact he'd come at all was also good. He was someone she could count on and that knowledge brought her relief. He stared at her and she smiled. How had she never noticed his eyes before? They were the color of steel. Strong, just like the rest of him.

He gestured toward the living room. "May I? It's kind of cold out here."

Oh God. Could she be any ruder? "Yes. Sorry. Come on in. I'm sorry if I'm spoiling your night."

Rubbing his hands together, he stepped inside. "Trust me, you're not." He pointed at the alarm pad. "I see you took my advice."

"Yes. Thank you for the reference. I can't believe how quickly he got it installed." Now if it only made her feel secure. After resetting the alarm, she took his coat and hung it on the rack beside the door. "Would you like some hot chocolate to go with your cookies?"

"You know, you're wreaking havoc on my diet."

"Oh." She hadn't thought about that. "I guess my comfort food's not very nutritional. I'm sure I have some fruit."

"Are you kidding? I want those cookies. But I'll just have some water to go with them." He followed her into the kitchen and took a seat at Grandma's old dining table. "So why do you need comfort food?"

"Just worried, I guess." She put the kettle on to make some hot chocolate for herself. What did it matter if she gained ten pounds? At her rate, she'd end up in a mental ward eating gruel, or at least really bad meals. Might as well take advantage of the good stuff for now.

"About someone breaking in?"

She shrugged. If only that was it. Could she tell him everything and lift this burden from her mind? Or would that be asking for a room at the mental ward?

"No one can get in here without your knowledge. You know that, right?"

She nodded. Problem was, the thing she was afraid of most likely lived in her head. No alarm system could defend against that.

He leaned back in his chair. "So, what did you want to talk about?"

Ah, the moment of truth. Thankfully, the kettle whistled and she busied herself making her hot chocolate. Eventually he'd want an answer, but what could she say that didn't sound...crazy?

Maggie took the plate of cookies and his water to the table. After grabbing her mug, she sat in the chair beside him. When she still couldn't find the right words, she took a cookie and bit into it. Who talked with their mouth full?

He took her hand and the coldness left her extremities. "You didn't sleep last night, did you?"

God, he nailed that one. She swallowed. "I thought I did, but Erica didn't mention any sleepwalking." Didn't mean she hadn't, though. "Do you think Erica's theories have any substance?"

"Which one? That someone is pulling a gaslight number on you or that someone is drugging or hypnotizing you?"

"What? She thinks I'm being hypnotized?"

"I admit, it's far-fetched."

"Far-fetched? Don't you mean impossible?" She couldn't even imagine how anyone could do something like that without her knowledge, which left crazy. She was going crazy.

"I don't know if someone is involved, but you have to admit, you've been under a lot of stress. Erica's concerned." He rubbed the back of her knuckles with his thumb. "I'm concerned."

His touch might have been soothing if he hadn't implied what she was already thinking. She jerked her hand away. "You think I'm crazy."

"No. Not even. And the doctors didn't think you were, either, or they wouldn't have released you. What happened last weekend? She said you were gone without a word."

Maggie took a sip of her chocolate and felt the warmth flow to her stomach, giving her a little more courage. He might not think she was crazy *now*... "The short story is I went to bed Friday and came to Sunday night at a café across town."

Well, he didn't laugh at her. That had to be good. Right?

"And the long story?"

Yeah, the long story. Better to get it over with and lay it all out in the open. Otherwise the anxiety was bound to crush her. "Don't tell Erica, but...it's not the first time it happened. I mean, that's the first time I lost two days and came to someplace other than home, just not the first time I lost...time."

"How long has this been going on?"

She lowered her head and muttered, "Since I moved in."

"What? Maggie! That was a month ago."

Twenty-eight days to be exact. "Yeah. I've lost a few Saturdays. The other days I wake up...groggy, which blows your stress theory. I'd already won the case, so what was there to stress about? Now it's gotten where I'm afraid to go to bed. Why bother? I'm not getting any rest anyway."

Could she crawl in his lap and try, though? To be in his arms and sleep, now that would be heaven.

"Did you tell your doctor any of this?"

"No. I slept fine at the hospital. I figured it was over. But then I come back here and... Oh God. Maybe Erica's right." Because why would she just be crazy at home? Wouldn't she have been crazy at the hospital, too?

"Sounds like something or someone is messing with your sleep cycle."

That sure sounded a whole lot better than going crazy. "How can we find out?"

"Aside from watching you 24/7? I don't know." He picked up a cookie. "Is that what you want? Someone to watch you?"

He raised an eyebrow while staring at her with a kind of…longing. Damn, was he volunteering? Or was her tired mind hallucinating?

"Like a babysitter or like a bodyguard?" She laughed, because really, this whole conversation was insane. "Either one, I'm sure that would look normal to Erica. *Not.*"

"I was thinking along the lines of installing security cameras. She already suspects someone is breaking in."

"True. Except they wouldn't prevent me from walking out the front door. Now would they?"

He shook his head. "No, they wouldn't."

She took a sip of her hot chocolate. What he must think of her. A grown woman, needing a…babysitter. If she could only fill up her empty hours with a man. A man like Dean. Why stop at a man *like* him? Why not *him*?

"You sure Erica doesn't know what's going on?"

"Oh, I'm sure she suspects something. But I don't want to confirm it. She'd never leave me alone and that wouldn't be fair to her. She has her own life to live." Of course, asking Dean to stick around wasn't very fair to him. What the heck was she doing? And why wasn't he ready to scram as far away from her as he could get? Maybe she wasn't crazy, but she wasn't normal, either.

"Want me to stay until Erica gets home?"

Yes, please. "I can't ask you to do that."

"You didn't. Got a DVD player? I could order a pizza and we could watch a movie. But first I'll take a jaunt around the property and make sure no one's watching."

And just like that she fell a little in love with him. Too bad he only saw her as some damsel in distress. It might help if she stopped acting like one, though.

* * * *

Dean glanced Maggie's way several times during the flick, each time she laughed or shifted or stifled a yawn. Oh hell, sometimes he looked at her even when she wasn't doing all that.

She'd nixed the pizza he suggested and fixed them hamburgers instead. Man, they'd been the best burgers he'd ever eaten. And her French fries? They weren't from her freezer. No, she'd cut and fried her own. The night turned out way better than he'd imagined and was probably the closest he would ever come to dating her. Except this wasn't a date. He was here as a friend, and the sooner he got that through his thick head, the better off they'd both be.

Instead of mooning over her and her food, he should figure out what was going on. During the contest of the will, he'd never noticed her act any differently than before her grandmother had died. If she experienced any stress, she'd hidden it well. What was happening to her now, though, she couldn't hide. Having her sleep cycle disrupted since moving in did point to Eddie a little—he hadn't been happy about the loss—but could he really have done something so outrageous? Would he have the means? The knowledge?

The movie ended and still no sign of Erica. Maggie got up and removed the DVD.

"Is it like her to be out all night?"

"Yeah, but you can go. You've done enough already. I'll be okay." She fidgeted with the DVD box and made no move to put it away.

"I'm okay with watching another movie if you want."

She shook her head. "I want to go to bed, but…"

"Then go. I'll stay until she gets here."

"I can't do that to you. Well, maybe if I hired you. How much do you charge?"

He stood. "I'm not going to charge you."

"Why not? It's not fair I ask you over and—"

"I'd like to think you asked me over because I'm a friend. I certainly came because of that."

Her eyes shined and she blinked several times. "You did?"

"Maggie, I can stay here until Erica gets back if it'll make you feel safer. And if she doesn't return, I'll sleep on the couch."

She looked down at the floor. "That's not necessary."

Maybe it wasn't necessary, but he wasn't leaving her like this. He grasped her shoulders. "Trust me. No one will get to you tonight. And I won't let you leave. Okay?"

She hugged him. "You're a good man, Dean Parker."

Should he hug her back or not? Her breasts pressed against him, bringing his dick to attention. He settled on not. How good of a man could he be if his thoughts centered on stripping her bare and taking her on the floor? To pound all the uncertainty out of her head. To make her forget about everything but him.

Shit. As if that would ever happen. He needed to get it together. Which meant no hugging.

She brought him a pillow and a comforter then wished him good night. After he ensured all the doors and windows were secured, he kicked off his shoes and sat on the couch. Sure beat driving around her neighborhood. Not only warmer, but more comfortable. He pulled out his phone and checked his e-mails.

Thirty minutes later he turned off the phone, stuffed it in his pocket and settled along the length of the couch. He was longer than the couch, so he propped his head on one arm and his feet on the other. The lamp by the front window gave a soft glow and created interesting shadows along the walls and ceiling. Like some kind of abstract art. No artwork adorned these walls, though. Only a few family pictures sat on the fireplace mantle.

The floorboards on the stairs squeaked. Dean sat up. Maggie appeared on the steps, clutching the thin robe she wore.

He stood. "You forget something?"

She shook her head and stepped closer. When she was barely six inches away, she opened her robe and let it fall to the floor. Naked. She stood there naked.

Every inch of her was glorious. Her breasts jutted out, waiting to be held. Her nipples pebbled, waiting to be licked.

"Maggie?" He thought he'd been hard for her during the movie, but that was nothing compared to what was going on in his pants now. Had he gone to sleep? Was this a dream? If it was, it would end up being a wet one.

"Don't just stand there. Kiss me. I know you want to."

Oh, hell yes, he wanted. Had wanted ever since he'd met her. Besides that hug, she'd never shown any interest in him. What changed now?

She extended her hand. The moment she touched his cheek, her eyes rolled back and her legs buckled.

"Maggie!" He caught her before she hit the floor.

She blinked. "Dean? What are you doing in my room?"

"Um, I'm not in your room."

"What?" She looked around and then saw her state of undress. Her cheeks reddened.

"Ah shit." He closed his eyes while she steadied herself. "Your robe is on the floor."

"Oh God! It *is* me!"

Footsteps pounded up the stairs while Dean slowly opened his eyes. Yeah, she was gone. What the hell happened? Could she have been sleepwalking? Whatever, he needed to make sure she was okay.

A slight pressure pushed against his ears as if he dropped in altitude. This pressure used to give Bridget a tremendous headache, but then she'd been under stress at the time. He'd never been anything but annoyed at the experience.

He ran up the stairs. If he'd learned anything from Peter it was not to let a ghost know it could be seen or heard. But damn. A ghost. A freakin' ghost was in Maggie's house. As if this night wasn't bizarre enough.

* * * *

Maggie leaned against her bedroom door clutching her robe. What had she done? How could she ever look at Dean again? He must think she was some kind of slutty nut.

God. How many times had she done this? Nothing had happened at that café, but that didn't mean it hadn't happened elsewhere.

"Maggie. Are you okay?"

"No. I mean yes. I'm fine. You can go home now."

"Maggie, let me in. We need to talk."

"I really don't think we have anything to talk about."

"Nothing happened."

"What do you mean nothing happened? I was naked, for Pete's sake."

"But you woke up as soon as we touched."

"And that makes it better, how?"

"I'm coming in."

"No!" Shit. Why didn't the stupid doors lock? She had nothing to barricade it with, either.

The door opened and he stepped inside.

She clutched the robe even tighter. Even if she'd covered herself with her comforter it wouldn't diminish the fact he'd seen her naked. "You don't think I've been humiliated enough for one night?"

"I'm not looking to humiliate you. Get dressed. I need to take you away from here."

Take her away? "You mean you want to put me away, don't you? Well, I won't let you."

"I don't want to put you anywhere. I just want to talk to you before...Erica comes home. That's all."

Like hell that was all. He was lying about something. "Did you ever think that maybe I don't want to talk to you?"

"Please, Maggie. Just get dressed." He turned and faced the door.

So not only was he not leaving, she couldn't either. Not without shoving him out of the way, and with his size that would be an impossible task. Besides, where could she go dressed, or undressed, as she was?

"And if I don't? Do you plan to stand there all night?"

"If that's what it takes, sure. And then when Erica comes home, she'll wonder what we've been up to. I doubt she'll believe the truth."

"Oooh. That's not fair."

"Then get dressed and come with me." He was playing dirty and knew it. Maybe he wasn't planning on taking her to a hospital yet. Didn't mean he wouldn't later on.

How did her life get so messed up? She sat on the bed as tears slipped from her eyes. "Why should I?"

"Ah, Maggie. Don't cry." He knelt in front of her and wiped her tears. "We're friends, right? I won't do anything to hurt you. I promise. Please trust me."

"Friends? Do friends go and make sexual advances toward one another?"

"That wasn't you. I know that. Now hurry up and get dressed so we can get out of here before Erica shows."

"It's highly unlikely she'll even come home tonight. Can't we talk downstairs?"

"I'd prefer to get you out of the house. To someplace…neutral."

"Neutral? You mean a hospital."

"Not a hospital. I promise."

He seemed sincere. God, if she couldn't trust him, who could she trust? "Fine. Then wait in the hall while I get dressed."

"Ummm… I think I'll wait here, if you don't mind." He turned back toward the door. "I won't look. I promise."

What was his problem? Well, he wasn't budging so she grabbed her clothes and squatted behind the bed to get dressed, just in case he decided to take another peek.

Chapter 5

Bundled up in a sweater, coat, knit cap, and scarf—although she could wear a tent and still feel exposed—Maggie followed Dean out to his car, their breaths hanging in the air like some kind of contrail. Dang, it was freezing. Why'd they had to leave her nice, warm house? It wasn't like he had pranced naked in front of *her*.

Although, if he had, she certainly wouldn't want to leave the house.

He opened the passenger door to the blue Honda. Papers covered the seat. Papers filled the footwell. Papers even hung from the visor. He cursed softly. "Sorry about that. I keep forgetting to take these inside."

"Bridget must really love you." How did he manage to keep anything straight with that mess?

He ignored her statement and shoved the papers into the back seat, giving her a nice view of his butt. And what a nice butt. It was probably his best feature. Next to his chest and biceps and... Oh heck, there wasn't anything wrong with him. If only she wasn't destined for a mental ward, she would have eventually taken Erica's advice and asked him out. Maybe.

She bounced in place, hoping to generate some heat. "So, what did you want to talk about?"

He threw the last bit to the back and crawled out of the car. After a glance at the house, he said, "Not here."

He'd been acting strange ever since he barged into her bedroom. Even after she'd gotten dressed, he'd stuck by her side, almost as if he were afraid to be alone. What was his problem? She was the one who most likely needed a doctor.

"In you go." He held the door open and she climbed inside.

Clearly he had an agenda, so she kept quiet. The heater hadn't even had a chance to kick in when he parked at a bar. In fact, they were barely a mile from her house.

"Why are we here?" Although, where else would he take her? His place? That had to be worse than her house.

"I just thought it would be private. And I could use a drink about now. How about you?"

A drink certainly couldn't hurt, not that she'd ever had one before. That would have required a social life, something she'd just never got around to having. Erica had tried to get Maggie out a few times, but being alone with her writing always seemed like the better option. Could getting drunk help her forget this night happened? Well, maybe not the entire night. She'd enjoyed cooking dinner for Dean and watching a movie with him. It was the stuff after that she wanted to purge from her head. "Sounds good."

The place was small and dark, and surprisingly smoke free. Sure, it was against the law to smoke in a restaurant or bar in Ohio, but it didn't mean every establishment followed those rules. She'd read the paper.

Dean led her past the bar, where a couple of men sat quietly, to a booth in the corner. "What would you like to drink?"

"Um…" Okay, now there was the problem. She didn't know one booze from another. So she picked what Erica always drank. "A rum and Coke?"

He went up to the bar and ordered. One of the men they had passed looked her way and squinted. That was her cue to turn around. Thankfully her seat sat facing away from the bar. A couple of minutes later Dean returned with her drink and a beer for himself.

She twirled the straw in her drink, making the ice clink against the glass. "So what was so important you couldn't say at my house?"

He leaned over the table. "Actually, I thought a change of scenery would help you forget what happened."

"Not possible." Maggie sucked on her straw and practically downed her drink. Whoa. No wonder Erica ordered these. They were good.

Dean grabbed the glass and stopped her from emptying it. "Easy now. I didn't bring you here to get drunk."

"Why shouldn't I? I'm certainly not in my right mind."

"There's nothing wrong with your mind."

She bounced her knee out of habit. "How can you say that after what I did? What if you aren't the first one I did that to? What if I'm having sex? I'm not on the pill, so I not only have to worry about an STD, there's a good chance I could be pregnant?" She clutched her stomach as that possibility roiled through her head. "I think I'm gonna be sick."

He slid beside her and took her hand. "Maggie. You're over-reacting. Nothing happened."

"Am I? Just because nothing happened with you, doesn't mean nothing happened with someone else." Like that guy at the café. Although, if they'd had sex, wouldn't he have stuck around?

"You would have noticed if you had sex."

Would she? She wasn't exactly experienced in that area. Maybe her other persona was good at cleaning up. "I'm not so sure. I don't notice any of the other strange things I'm doing. For all I know I've been banging the whole neighborhood."

He winced briefly before taking a swig of his beer. "Now you're just being silly."

Maybe she was, but it didn't make her feel any better. What did make her feel better was Dean sitting beside her. It'd been nice when he held her hand, too. Too bad nothing could ever happen between them. Kind of hard to date when you're living at a mental institution, and she was pretty sure she was headed there. Maggie took her drink back and sucked down the rest. A nice fuzzy sensation came over her. Yeah, she would definitely need to get this drink again before they carted her away. A bunch of them. Then maybe she wouldn't care.

The man who had squinted at her from the bar earlier appeared at their table. "Well, hell. I never thought you'd show your face here again."

She blinked at the guy, trying to focus. "Excuse me? I don't know you."

"Oh, so you're playing that game, huh?" He turned toward Dean. "If I were you, sir, I'd leave this one alone. She'll only knee you in the gonads once you show an interest."

Dean shot out of the booth as if she had cooties. "Is that so? And you know this how?"

"She was in here last week. Asked me to buy her a drink. Said she wanted to go back to my place. Then she had the nerve to..." He glanced down at his crotch. "Well, before she zipped out of my apartment."

She hugged herself. Oh God. That made two strange men she'd been with. Could it get any worse?

"You say she was here last week? When?"

"Friday. About this time."

That would be the famous lost weekend. Just how many men had she hit on?

Dean clapped the man on his shoulder. "Sorry, man. She's right. You got the wrong woman. She was with me."

The man bent over and looked her in the eye. "No shittin'? Man, she sure looks like the woman."

"They say everyone has a twin somewhere. Guess hers lives in Dayton, huh?"

"Right. Whatever." The confused man walked away.

Dean slid back beside her. "You okay?"

"You lied to him."

"Did I? How do you know he wasn't with Erica?"

"She wouldn't have gone with him if she wasn't interested. It was me. It had to be." She shook her head. "This can't be happening."

He put his arm around her shoulders and squeezed. "Hey, look on the bright side. Nothing—"

"If you say that one more time, I'm gonna smack you." She resisted the urge to lean into his side, although he'd make a pretty sweet pillow. That drink not only made her head fuzzy, it made her more tired. As if that were even possible.

Why'd he put his arm around her anyway? Afraid she might crack? Or run off? She couldn't easily slip away anyway, not unless she slid under the table. On a yawn, she rested her head on the cool table top. "I wish I could be transported into one of my books, then I could say I was possessed."

If only that were possible. No, she had to face the fact. She was going crazy. Completely. Bat-shit. Crazy.

* * * *

Dean reveled in the softness that was Maggie. When he'd slid in beside her, he was only trying to offer her comfort. Instead, she'd woken up his body. One part in particular. Even her threat of smacking him got him hot. The smart move would have been to keep his distance, return to the other bench, except the head above his shoulders wasn't doing the thinking. Not until she uttered a word that set off alarm bells—possessed.

He removed his arm from her shoulders. "Why would you say that?"

Maggie sighed. "Does it really matter? I'm not living in a fictional world."

Yeah, it mattered. She had a ghost in her house. Could it have been possessing her? Could they even do that? But if he told her he actually saw ghosts, she'd probably drag them both to the hospital. Before he blabbed all that, maybe it was best to rule out everything else first.

"Are you sure the stress of the lawsuit isn't getting to you?"

"Why would I feel stress when I won? If anything, I should feel less stress."

He nodded. She had a point there. "Okay. Then could it be possible that maybe you feel...guilty?"

She lifted her head and frowned. "Guilty? I didn't call anyone a thief."

"When did Eddie call you that?"

"He didn't. His mother did. At the reading of the will."

Ah yes, the reading. Tom had mentioned that fiasco. Something about Eddie's mother throwing a chair after the reading. He hadn't elaborated and Dean hadn't pushed, but now he was curious.

"What did your grandmother leave Eddie?"

"Nothing but a chance to get the estate. If I'm dead, of course, or if I fail to meet the requirements of the will—"

"There are requirements?"

She leaned back and nodded. "Nothing too restrictive. I can't be gone for more than a week out of each quarter of the year for five years. It's not like I go anywhere anyway."

No, but someone trying to get her to break her requirements could make that happen if she had to be hospitalized. She was already down one day.

"So Eddie didn't get anything. Didn't that surprise you?"

She shrugged and stirred the ice in her glass with her straw. "I never asked for the house. Grandma gave it to me," she said, pointing at her chest. "If she had wanted him to have it, if she had wanted him to have anything, she would have said so in the will."

"But you weren't surprised. Why? What do you know?"

"I know I'm tired. Can I go home now?"

He probably should let her go home, but she was hiding something and his investigator sense kicked in. "Let me finish my beer first, okay?" He made sure to sip slowly. "You don't like Eddie too much, do you?"

"He's not on my list of favorite people."

"Before or after the lawsuit?"

She propped her head in her hand, elbow on table, and raised an eyebrow. "Mr. Parker, are you interrogating me?"

Maybe a little. "I'm just trying to determine if Eddie has a beef with you or your grandmother."

"Does it matter? He can't do anything to Grandma."

"No, but he could do something to you. Besides gaining the estate, is there another reason he might be after you?"

"You still think Eddie is doing something to me? You don't think I'm going crazy?"

Again, she skirted his question. What the hell was she hiding? Or maybe she wasn't hiding anything and was just too exhausted to think straight. There was one possible way to get his answers, not that he relished the thought. But first he needed to comfort Maggie some more. Because he really didn't think she was crazy. At least no crazier than he was. He hugged her across the shoulders once again and willed his dick to relax, not that it ever listened to him. "Crazy people don't think they're crazy."

She laughed until tears flowed. "Then what's happening to me?"

"Ah, Maggie, don't cry." He wiped the tears from her face. "We'll figure it out. I promise."

And it was a promise he would keep, even if it meant talking to a ghost.

Chapter 6

Dean opened the door for Maggie and she rushed to the security panel. Whether or not it was needed any longer—it certainly wasn't designed with ghosts in mind—it seemed to give her comfort. He couldn't very well deny her that.

"You think Erica's home yet?" If she was, that might make his job a little more difficult.

Maggie shook her head. "Light's still on. But if you want to go—"

"No, no, no." He hung his coat on the rack by the door. "You go on up to bed. I'll stay until Erica comes home."

"And if I come back downstairs again?"

If only he could reassure her, but he wasn't ready to share his ghost-seeing ability with her now, if ever. Because if a ghost wasn't involved, he would have blabbed for nothing. And then what would she think of him? Instead, he smiled reassuringly. "I'll cover you in a blanket. All while closing my eyes. I promise."

She covered her face. "I still can't believe I did that."

"Hey." He pulled her hands down, fighting the urge to wrap her in a hug. "Stop it. That wasn't you. You have nothing to be ashamed of."

She touched his cheek. "You're a sweet man, Dean Parker."

"If you want to give a guy a compliment, don't call him sweet." Her fingers were heaven. How easy would it be to turn his head and kiss her palm? Oh, who was he kidding? Forget the palm; give him those lips, those sweet, luscious lips. He stifled a groan. If he didn't stop those thoughts, he'd end up with a boner for life.

"No? What should I call him?"

Mine. As if that could actually happen.

She snapped her fingers. "I know. How about my rugged hero? Would that work?"

It worked at getting his dick's attention—again. God, if only he could kiss her and make her forget everyone and everything. So why didn't he? Maybe kissing her would get her out of his head. Or her slap would. She'd slap him for making such a move, wouldn't she? Yeah, she would. Decision made, he pulled her in and kissed her.

Instead of repelling, she molded into him.

Instead of flattening her lips, she opened up.

Instead of stopping what could amount to be the biggest mistake of his life, he dove in for more.

He grabbed the back of her head and angled to get deeper inside her. He couldn't remember ever kissing lips this soft. Or tasting a mouth as sweet. He devoured her as his heart raced. His dick was more than hard now.

She put her hands on his chest and slightly pushed. What the hell was he doing? Thank God she'd finally come to her senses, because he was fairly sure his had left the stratosphere. He gripped her shoulders and backed away, preparing himself for her slap. He should apologize, except he wasn't sorry he'd kissed her. It was the best kiss of his life. Figured.

"I like you, Dean, but shouldn't we wait until this is sorted out?"

He blinked. She liked him? How would he ever get her out of his head? At least she'd stopped him now. Later, he would have to hurt her, but at least it wouldn't be tonight. "See? You used logic. Crazy people aren't logical."

"Right…" Tears filled her eyes and shot darts into his heart.

"Hey, it'll be okay." But her tears were not okay and like the idiot he was, he held her close. Because that was saying *We'll wait to sort it out*, now wasn't it?

Her breath hitched. "I'm scared."

The protector in him surged. "I know you are, but I'm here. You don't have to face this alone, okay? Now, go on up to bed. I'll stay until Erica comes home. I promise."

"Thank you." Maggie headed up the stairs. As soon as she was out of sight, his ears crackled.

The ghost appeared in the corner. Damn, she was just a kid, too.

* * * *

Lindy sat up when Maggie climbed the stairs. If her bed was still in the corner of the living room, she would be sitting on it, or as close to sitting as she could get. Instead, she floated in the air over where her deathbed used to be. Ever since Dean zapped her, she'd barely been able to move.

At least she could move now. Dean remained standing by the door. She crossed her arms. She knew that bastard was trouble as soon as she'd discovered he was a P.I. and shouldn't have let his potential involvement with Maggie sway that decision. But to zap her out of Maggie's body the way he had blew her mind. Exactly what kind of power did this man have? Whatever it was, Lindy needed him out of the house.

Could she scare him away? She'd scared her mom a couple of times by moving the knick-knacks on the mantle. But that's as much as she'd done. Now, if she could move furniture like that crazy ghost, Rhonda, could, that might scare him away. But no matter how hard Lindy had tried, the furniture never moved. And she doubted moving a tiny trinket would scare that big bully away.

Stupid man! He was ruining everything. As she floated toward the staircase she stuck her tongue out at Dean.

He laughed.

At her.

What the?

"Yeah, I can see you," he said.

No way. She moved to the right. She moved to the left. Each time, Dean's eyes moved in sync. "How is that possible?"

"It just is," he said. "Can we talk?"

Out of all the people who lived in this house, why'd it have to be him who could talk to her? Was that his super power? Is that what made it possible for him to zap her out of Maggie's body?

"Have you seen me the whole time?"

He shook his head. "Didn't even know you were here until after Maggie bared it all, which I'm assuming you saw."

He said saw, not possessed. So he didn't know what she'd done? What he'd done? Hmmm… "So how come you can see me now and not before?"

"It was the first time you've been in a room I was alone in. What's your name?"

Oh no. She wouldn't divulge that information. Why make his job easier?

He sighed. "Listen, I'll find out who you are eventually. But I'd like to call you something other than 'Yo, Ghost.'"

"And you think I'll answer to that?"

"I don't care what you answer to. I was only trying to be nice."

He'd been keeping his voice low. So his ability to see and talk to her was most likely a secret. If she got him mad enough, would he blow his cover? Probably not. He probably had an answer for everything. Still, she was curious about what he wanted to talk to her about. Didn't mean she had to play nice. "You can call me L."

"El? As in Ella?"

"No. As in the letter, dumb shit. What do you want to talk about?"

He moved over to the couch and sat. "Are you related to Maggie or were you a neighbor?"

"Does it matter?"

"Not really. I just thought if you were a family member, you'd be more inclined to help Maggie."

"If I were to help anyone, I'd help myself."

"Are you the only ghost in the vicinity?"

"Of course not. Don't you know? We sit around and play bridge every night."

He stood and paced. "Come on. I'm serious. Who's been possessing her? Is it you?"

Shit. He knew about the possession. Probably one of his super powers. It's how he woke Maggie up, right? But if he knew Maggie was being possessed, how come he didn't know who was doing the possessing? Maybe his super powers weren't all that super. All the more reason to play it cool. "Don't I wish. Then maybe *I* could have a little fun."

He scrubbed his head and muttered, "Shit. I was right?"

Crap! He'd been fishing and she just bit the bait. Didn't mean she had to tell him any more, though.

"Who's doing it?"

"You think I'm a snitch, is that it? Well I'm not. I don't have a lot of friends anymore. Certainly don't want to lose the ones I do have."

"But she's ruining Maggie's health. Doesn't that mean anything to you?"

"How do you know it's a she?"

His eyes widened.

"Yeah, you think about that. See ya!" She waved goodbye and eased out of the room while he pleaded for her to stop. Yeah, no, she wasn't going to stop. She'd said enough already. Had Dean bought it? Or was he going to be more determined? Unless he told Maggie he could see ghosts, he was going to have to be tricky about it.

Well, she could be tricky, too.

* * * *

Dean collapsed on the couch, leaned over, and held his head. Damn. He was right. Someone was possessing Maggie. And just thinking some guy was doing the possessing made Dean want to punch a wall. But did it really matter whether the ghost was a dude or a girl? Maggie was being possessed and he had to stop it. There were a lot of homes—old homes—in this neighborhood. It could take forever to search the records of every one. How would he ever find out who was behind it all?

He couldn't very well follow Maggie while she was possessed. For one, he wouldn't allow that to happen if he could help it. And two, his identity wasn't much of a secret to the possessing ghost.

One thing he could do: find out who this L really was. Then maybe he could work his way from there. Or at least show her what he was capable of and get her to talk. Then what? What if she still wouldn't say anything?

He straightened up. Bridget. She could help. No way would she be awake now, but he texted her that he'd stop by in the morning. Maybe by then his head would be clear of thoughts of Maggie.

Except...his thoughts were all he had left, and giving those up seemed unconscionable. He relived every second he'd been with her. How she'd fit in perfectly beside him in the booth. Her soft fingers against his cheek. The silkiness of her hair. The curve of her back. And that kiss. Oh yeah, definitely that kiss. He sank into the cushion and smiled.

* * * *

Lying under the covers, in the dark, Maggie touched her lips. She still couldn't believe Dean had kissed her. Actually kissed her!

And man, did that guy know how to kiss. No one had ever gotten her so…excited before. Instead of pushing him away, she'd nearly ripped his shirt off.

No wonder she couldn't sleep. He'd woken up her sex drive.

Of course, that kiss happened after she'd bared everything to him. Had she only revved up his testosterone, or was he really interested in her? He seemed to care. And he said he wasn't charging her for the work he would be doing. Why would he do that if he didn't care about her?

Damn it. Maybe she should have ripped his shirt off. Life was too short to put off living, right? Who knew how much longer she'd have her freedom anyway. She should go back down there. Tell him she'd changed her mind. If he wanted to be with a crazy girl, she wasn't going to stop him. She'd worn the virgin title long enough. Dean was the one.

She whipped off the covers and turned on the light. First, clothes. Sexy or not? Okay, maybe not sexy. She didn't own any tops that showed cleavage, anyway. T-shirt and jeans it was. Next, bathroom to freshen up.

Teeth brushed. Face washed. Hair combed. Makeup or not? Maybe lipstick. She found the pink and put it on. No, that screamed *Innocent!*, and while she was technically innocent, she didn't want it advertised. She wiped it off. She found some red and put it on. God, so not her. Rubbed it off. Ugh! Her lips were red from all the rubbing. Hmmm… That kind of worked. After several deep breaths, she opened the door and headed for the stairs.

The front door opened and closed. "Oh, hey, Dean. What are you doing here? Is Maggie okay?"

Damn it. Erica would have to come home now. Maggie leaned against the wall to the upstairs hallway and held her breath.

"Uh, yeah. She thought she heard something and called me. False alarm. I told her I'd stay until you got home."

She could kiss him right now for not mentioning her…what should she call it? Her episode?

"You telling me a hunky guy like you didn't have a hot date?"

"I'm…uh… What?"

"You know she likes you, right?"

Maggie closed her eyes. Oh, Erica. No!

Dean coughed. "I'll see you later. Have a good evening. And don't forget to code the alarm."

"Oh shit. Yeah. Thanks!"

Once the front door shut, Maggie moved to the top of the stairs and waited. A few moments later Erica appeared on the landing, her shoes dangling from one hand. She stopped when she saw Maggie.

"'You know she likes you'? Really?"

Erica grinned and climbed the rest of the way up. "Hey, Maggie. I didn't know you were still up."

"What were you doing?"

"Well, hey, I just thought he should know. I mean, I suspected he liked you before, but now I know he definitely likes you."

Maggie wasn't about to fuel her cousin's fantasies. What went on between her and Dean wasn't anyone's business, so she did her best to play it cool. "What are you talking about?"

She pointed at her crotch. "I caught him with a bulge going on down there and a smile on his face. I'd say that was like. Okay, maybe lust. Same diff. So what were you doing up here and him down there? You two should have been to-geth-er." She then proceeded to make a circle with her thumb and forefinger and stuck her other forefinger through the hole, dropping her shoes in the process.

"I think you've had too much to drink. I'll see you in the morning." Maggie went back to her room.

"Hey, I'm just saying it could happen if you let it."

Maggie shut the door, silencing her cousin. She placed a hand over her racing heart and smiled. Dean had been hard. For her? If she hadn't taken so long to get ready, could they have? Would they have? Ugh!

How the heck would she get to sleep now?

Chapter 7

Dean stifled a yawn as Bridget opened her door. Barnaby jumped up, wagging his tail. The chocolate Lab searched for a kiss. Dean leaned down for a few slobbers.

"Wow. You look like shit. Want some breakfast?"

"Yeah, that would be great." Tossing and turning all night, thinking about Maggie and that ghost, made for little sleep. He'd almost staked out her place, but what good would that do? There was no guarantee he'd see any ghost, no less the one possessing Maggie. All it took was one set of non-seeing eyes and all ghosts became invisible to him.

He followed Bridget to the kitchen and breakfast nook while Barnaby weaved around his legs. Dean nearly tripped over the creature.

Rob got up from the table and grabbed the dog by the collar. "Barnaby, sit." Once he got the animal settled down, he returned to his seat. "Sorry about him. He doesn't get many visitors."

"Ah, he's okay." A waffle iron sat on the counter next to a pitcher of batter. He smiled at Bridget. "Ooh. You're making waffles? I love waffles."

Bridget laughed. "You sound like that donkey on *Shrek*."

Dean shrugged. What could he say? He did love waffles.

"I shared your text with Rob. Hope you don't mind." She poured the batter and it steamed and hissed as it hit the hot waffle iron.

"Hey, the more heads the better." Because his alone was doing a half-assed job. Dean plopped on the seat and rested his head in his hands. "I can't believe a ghost is possessing Maggie."

"I didn't even think that was possible. Are you sure that's what's happening?" Bridget asked.

"I only have another ghost's word."

"Which you never take at face value," Rob said. "So why now?"

"Because it makes sense. I'm pretty sure I caught Maggie in the midst of a possession. When I touched her, she woke up, well, more like fell asleep. She only woke up when I caught her. But it was like I ripped the spirit from her. That would make sense, wouldn't it, since I can touch ghosts?"

"Yeah, I can see that happening." Bridget removed the cooked waffle from the maker and slid it, and some bacon, on a plate. When she handed it to Rob, Dean slumped in disappointment. "I did a little research on Maggie's family, at least those that lived in that house. Her aunt died there in 1973. She was sixteen."

"Sixteen sounds about right," Dean said. Barnaby glanced at Rob, who was busy eating his waffle, and inched his way toward Dean's chair.

Instead of going back into the kitchen to make another waffle, Bridget went into the family room. One look at her retreating figure and Barnaby scampered to Dean's side. Unable to resist, Dean scratched behind the dog's ears and earned a head in his lap.

Bridget returned with a photo. "Look familiar?"

Dean snatched it out of her hand. "That's L. She's the ghost I spoke to. How'd you get this so fast?"

"You think she sleeps all night?" Rob asked.

"I can't help it if the baby wakes me." Rubbing her belly, she kissed Rob on his cheek and headed for the kitchen. "Her name is Linda Steele. I'd like to talk to her. See what's keeping her here."

Rob dropped the fork onto his plate, splashing syrup. "Oh, no you don't. The doctor said no outside stimulants." He turned toward Dean. "She's already had a couple of false alarms. It's too soon."

"I only want to talk to her."

"And she might want to do more than talk. Not all ghosts are friendly. You know that."

Dean interrupted. "Rob's right. And Linda seems rather belligerent."

"Well, wouldn't you, too, if you were a sixteen-year-old who'd been a ghost for over forty years?" Bridget poured more batter into the waffle iron.

"I don't care about Linda, okay? I want to help Maggie."

"What does she think about all this?" she asked.

"I haven't told her yet." And if he could help it, he never would.

"What? Don't you think you should?"

"How will my telling her help her? It'll just freak her out. I want to stop this ghost, but I have to find it first."

"Maggie might be able to help. She knows the neighborhood."

"She doesn't know it that well. Remember, her grandmother lived there, not her."

"Dean..." Bridget drew out his name as if he was some petulant child. "Maggie has a right to know what's going on. It would have to be a relief to know she's not going crazy."

"Unless she thinks I'm crazy telling her." And why wouldn't she? Who went around blabbing that they saw ghosts?

"Then we'll all tell her. She can't think we're all crazy."

Rob groaned. "Do you think that's wise, Bridget? She'll think we're ganging up on her."

Dean pointed toward Rob. "Yeah, that. I'm not telling her. And you aren't either."

"How do you expect her to move out of her house without a valid reason?"

He rubbed his hand over his face. "It won't matter. She won't move out. She can't if she wants to keep the estate, and I know she does."

"I doubt she'd want to live there if she knew she was being possessed."

Dean ran his fingers between Barnaby's eyes. Why couldn't his life be normal? Ever since he'd come back from death, life had been anything but. Maggie made him feel normal because she didn't see him any differently and he really didn't want to lose that feeling. "I can't tell her. Not yet, anyway."

"Then what do you propose we do to protect Maggie?" Bridget slid a plate to him.

Ah, waffles. And bacon. He breathed deep and took in their scent. His mistake was thinking on an empty stomach. He'd come up with something once he filled his belly.

* * * *

"Are my red shoes down there?" Erica yelled from upstairs.

"No," Maggie yelled back from her perch on the couch. Maybe if her cousin bothered to clean her room more than once a week, she might find her shoes a lot easier.

"Never mind. I found them." A minute later, Erica came down the stairs wearing a short black skirt and her sparkly red top. The shiny, red, four-inch heels decorating her feet seemed more appropriate for a date than meeting a friend.

"Was there a dress code I missed?" Dean had said he'd meet them at the local family diner. Not some swanky restaurant.

"What?" Erica looked down at her outfit and laughed. "Oh. No. I'm meeting the boss later."

"Since when do you dress up for him? And on a Sunday?"

"Since he wants to schmooze with a client. Apparently I'm the eye candy." Erica turned in a circle while shaking her hips. "Looks appealing, doesn't it?"

"He's pimping you out? And Trevor's okay with this? Maybe you should get another job. And a boyfriend."

"He's not pimping me out and Trevor isn't my boyfriend. He's just a friend with benefits, you know? Besides, I'll only go out with this guy if I want to. And if he's good looking, why wouldn't I want to? I'm just glad I found my shoes. Don't know what they were doing in your closet."

"Those shoes were in my closet?" Maggie's heart pounded as she stood and pointed at Erica's feet. Only one explanation as to why any of Erica's clothes would be in Maggie's room.

"I know, strange, huh?" Erica's eyes widened. "I mean, I'm sure I probably put them there by mistake when I was cleaning."

The absurdity of that statement alone made Maggie snort, which was probably better than breaking down into a puddle of sobs. "Don't you mean I probably put them there after one of my escapades?"

Escapades. Sleepwalking. Split personality. No matter what they called it, it all came down to one thing—losing control. At least she'd slept fine last night. Well, she assumed she'd slept well. She'd woken up rested for once.

"I'm sorry. I wasn't thinking, okay? If it makes you feel any better, I don't think you wore them. Number one, they weren't scuffed. Number two, I'm pretty sure you'd have fallen on your ass, which would have woken you up. Right?"

Erica's grin brought out the giggles in Maggie. "I guess you have a point there." Didn't make her feel any better about losing control, though.

"You sure Dean said for both of us to come? You're not using me to keep from being alone with him, are you?"

She might have in the past, but not with Dean. "He said he wanted us both there. That it had something to do with my *case*."

"Uh-oh. Why do I get the feeling that's a bad thing?"

"Because you said... Oh, never mind." Being a case certainly didn't sound all that good. Sounded formal. After last night's kiss, and the fact Erica had said he was interested, she expected more. Probably just as well nothing had happened last night. Heck, nothing would have happened. Not if she was just a case.

"I'm sure he didn't mean anything by that."

If he didn't mean anything by it, why'd he say it? "Whatever. You ready to go?"

"Do you mind if I drive? It'll be easier to drop you off than switch cars after." When Maggie nodded, Erica grabbed her coat. "You sure you want to wear that?"

Maggie looked down at her sweater and jeans. "What's wrong with—"

"Maybe you should freshen up your makeup."

"Why? Do I look—"

"And your hair. You can't go out like that."

What was wrong with her hair? Maggie ran up the stairs, Erica's laughter fading behind.

"See? I knew you cared. Sure you don't want to change while you're up there?"

Maggie looked in the mirror. There was nothing wrong with her hair or her makeup. And if Dean didn't like her in jeans, well, that was tough. She was just a case, anyway. She strolled down the stairs. "Was that fun for you?"

Erica shrugged. "Just trying to prove a point. You like him."

"Of course I like him. He's a friend." Maggie slipped on her coat.

"No, I mean you *like* him, like him. Why don't you just admit it?"

"Because it's pointless and you know it."

"Nothing is pointless if you want it bad enough. And he's not exactly running away, now is he? I told you, he likes you."

"No, he doesn't. I'm just a case to him."

Erica laughed. "Yeah, right."

While traveling to the restaurant, Maggie received a text from Dean saying he was sitting in the back. Not a phone call, but a text. Why did that bother her so much? Why did anything he did bother her? They weren't dating. They weren't anything. And they couldn't be, either. She should be glad he was being so distant. So why wasn't she?

As they entered the restaurant, Maggie took in the smell of freshly baked bread. This place teased her palate more than any other restaurant by placing the ovens by the entrance. She was such a sucker for hot rolls.

Dean was sitting in a booth situated in the far right corner of the restaurant. He stood and waved when he saw them. Her heart leaped in joy. Stupid heart. Didn't it know she was just a case to him?

He smiled broadly as he gazed at her. Not Erica. Her. And he kept staring. And grinning. Most likely reliving her naked exhibition. That was why he'd kissed her. That was why he'd had a boner. She'd given him a free burlesque show. Heat spread across her cheeks.

"Hello, Maggie. You look lovely tonight."

"Told ya," Erica whispered with a little snicker as she slid in the booth. "So nice to see you again, Dean."

Erica had it so wrong, but no way would Maggie explain that to her.

"You, too, Erica. Another hot date tonight?"

"You don't think I dressed up for you?"

Maggie slid in beside Erica. If only she'd brought along some duct tape. It would fit nicely over her cousin's mouth. "Ignore her. Why are we meeting here instead of my house?"

Dean sat down. "It's possible your place is bugged. I didn't want to take a chance—"

"Bugged?" Holy crap. He really did think someone was behind it all. "Don't you have equipment to check for that kind of thing?"

"Not on hand, no. And I won't be able to get anything until Monday. But if someone is using a long-distance listening device, there's no way for me to know that regardless."

"So Eddie has been eavesdropping on us?" Erica asked. "That son of a bitch."

"I don't know, actually, but it is a possibility. It could be how he's making Maggie think she's going crazy."

"No thinking about it," Maggie muttered.

The waitress brought over a basket of rolls and took their drink order. Maggie placed her hands in her lap. The rolls were no longer enticing. Bugs. In her house. When had she started living in a spy movie?

Dean opened his menu. "I don't know about you two, but I haven't eaten anything since breakfast. Go ahead and find something. It's on me."

"Aren't you sweet?" Erica grabbed a roll while she perused her menu.

Dean didn't correct her for saying that, like he had with Maggie the other night. Then again, he hadn't seen Erica naked. She flipped through the menu, but nothing appealed to her. When the time came to place her order, she settled on soup.

"That's all you want?" Erica asked.

"I had a big lunch." Maggie placed the napkin in her lap. "So, what's the plan? If you have one, that is."

"Oh, I have one. And it sounds crazy, but this should put a stop to the sleepwalking. At least until we find out how it's happening." He dug into a satchel that was beside him on the seat and pulled out a chain with a leather cuff of some sort attached at each end.

"Whoa, Dean. You into some kind of kinky shit we should know about?" Erica said.

"What is that?" Maggie asked.

"Looks like something someone into BDSM would own."

Dean blushed. "I know it looks bad, but it was the best I could find on quick notice. And something that won't hurt you, Maggie. When you go to bed, wrap this around your ankle, lock it up and then lock the other end around something in the bathroom. Just in case you have to use it during the night. The chain should be long enough. Then make sure the key is out of reach."

"You want to chain me to the house? What if there's a fire?"

"That's where Erica comes into play. If it's an emergency, like a fire, Erica will free you. However, if you ask her to release you, she should wait for the code before freeing you. And it's a code you can't come up with at the house. Which means, if you do use the code, you'll need a back-up, so you might want to make a list. Just make sure not to mention them at your house. And don't write them down."

None of what Dean said made any sense. Why so covert over sleepwalking? Apparently, Erica felt the same way.

"Why the covert act over sleepwalking?" she said. "Won't Maggie know all that whether she was awake or not?"

"She might. It's just a precaution."

Maggie shivered. He meant if she wasn't actually sleepwalking but had a split personality instead. If he was trying to make her calm, he'd failed miserably. "How long will I have to wear that to bed?"

"Until you start waking up rested."

With that thing around her ankle, that might never happen.

* * * *

Their meals arrived and they pretty much ate in silence. Reassuring Maggie was top on Dean's list, but how could he do that without telling her the truth? Even as he'd heard himself explain everything to the two women, he wondered about his own sanity.

"Listen, I hate to eat and run, but I have to be someplace," Erica said. "Could you take Maggie home?"

As much as he enjoyed Erica's company, this news came at the best time. Alone time. With Maggie. "It would be my pleasure."

"You don't have to do that," Maggie said. "I can leave now."

Erica grinned. "Sorry, but I don't have time to take you home."

For some reason he didn't think Erica was sorry at all. Maggie scowled, though. Why? Had he done something wrong? "It's not a problem. Really."

"See?" Erica said. "He doesn't mind. So what code should we use for tonight?"

"How about prisoner, because that's what I'll feel like," Maggie said.

Her acerbic tone wrenched his heart. Dean leaned over. "I know it seems that way, but do you really want to go out walking again at night?"

She lowered her head. "No."

"Prisoner might not be a good word. You're liable to use it. How about pickle? And if you have to use it tonight, then your back-up code is stereo. You'll need to figure out more, but remember, not at your house." Because Linda knowing the codes would defeat the whole purpose of tying Maggie to the house.

Erica nudged Maggie, who scooted off the bench. "Cheer up, cuz. Pretend we're playing spy games, or you're researching for your book. Hell, you'll probably use all this information for one anyway. See you later, Dean. Take care of my cousin."

She hugged Maggie and whispered into her ear before taking off. Maggie slid back onto the bench and proceeded to stir her soup. She'd barely eaten any of it; it had to be cold by now.

"Do you want to order something else?"

She looked up from her spoon stirring. "Do you really think someone's behind this or are you just trying to soften the blow?"

Dean leaned over. "I don't think you're crazy."

"I'd have to be crazy to think that someone else is responsible for me walking out of the house without my knowledge."

Would telling her someone else, some ghost, was responsible really make her feel any better? No. If anything, she'd think he was nuts. "Give this a try. If you are sleepwalking, it's possible your subconscious will know you can't go out if you're tied to the house."

"And that's the solution?" She pointed to the bag.

He placed his hand over hers. "No. It's only temporary. If this doesn't work, we'll try something else."

"You mean, you'll admit me to the hospital." A tear rolled down her cheek and wrenched his heart.

He got up and slid in next to her. Wrapped her in a hug. "Ah, sweetheart. I won't do that to you. That'll have to be your decision, okay?"

She tensed in his arms. "What are you doing? Do you hug all your clients?"

"Client? Is that what you think you are?" Although she had a point. Why was he hugging her? He released her and scooted away.

"I don't know what to think anymore."

"Well, I don't think of you as a client." He never would have kissed a client. And he wanted to kiss her again. In a bad way. But if the hug irritated her, he could only imagine what a kiss would do. Not that he should be kissing her. She'd been right to call him on the hugging.

Except...she felt so right in his arms.

"But you called me a case."

Okay, color him confused. She'd been into that kiss last night, but irritated he'd hugged her. Now hurt because he'd referenced her dilemma as a case? Maybe he didn't deserve her, but she certainly didn't deserve not knowing how much she turned him on.

"Force of habit. It helps me to focus. To make sure I didn't miss anything. Doesn't mean I think of you as a client." He leaned into her. "FYI, I don't kiss my clients."

She stared at his lips and his cock surged. "You don't?"

He shook his head. "And I want to do it again."

Shit. He hadn't meant to say that out loud. Apparently his dick was controlling his mouth.

She nodded. "Okay."

Okay? Hot damn. Mustn't disappoint the lady. He leaned down and kissed her. One lick of her lips and she opened up for him. God, she tasted better than last night. And just like last night, she molded against his body. A perfect fit.

Someone cleared their throat and Dean broke the kiss. The server placed the bill on the table. "Is there anything else I can get you?"

How about a hotel room? Damn, he was hard. He smiled at the waitress. "No, thank you." He turned back to Maggie and brushed a wayward strand of hair away from her face. Anything to keep touching her. "Well, that was awkward. Hope I didn't scandalize you."

She laughed. "I'm good. I don't eat here much anyway. I prefer my own cooking."

Couldn't argue with that, not after eating those burgers. He pulled out his wallet and placed the credit card on the table. "You okay with tonight's plan?"

"I don't see why I have to tie myself to the house. I slept fine last night."

Hmmm… Maybe Linda was telling the truth that the ghost was out of commission because he'd knocked it out of Maggie. Didn't mean the ghost was out of commission now.

"That's good, but I don't see how it can hurt. Wouldn't it be a relief knowing you can't wander the streets?" It would certainly help him rest easier knowing she couldn't get out. And if his plan worked, that ghost would show and then maybe Dean could put a stop to it.

"I suppose. I know Erica will be relieved to know I won't be using her shoes anymore."

He didn't understand her, but her laughter lifted his heart. Hopefully, this little experiment worked quickly. He didn't relish staking out Maggie's house for more than one night. It wasn't exactly summer weather out there.

* * * *

Hovering in the living room, Lindy watched TV with Maggie, who was curled up on the couch. In another hour or so, Maggie would head on up to bed and then Lindy's fun would begin.

Only one little snag—Dean—but she could deal with that easy enough. As if staking out the front of the house would prevent Maggie from being possessed. He wasn't inside the house and he wasn't watching the back, so what did he hope to achieve? Maybe he wasn't as bright as she'd thought.

The door opened and Erica entered. She went over to the panel.

The code. Shit. Lindy popped over in time to see Erica punch in the numbers. Whew. Too close. Wouldn't want the fun to end before it even began.

"I can't believe you set me up," Maggie said.

"How else was I going to get you to see you were more than just a case?" Erica turned from hanging her coat and strode through Lindy.

Shit, shit, shit! Lindy closed her eyes and shuddered. Not that she felt anything, but what if she opened her eyes and saw that person's innards? Gross. Most of the time she'd skedaddled out of the way, but she'd been too busy memorizing the code. That would teach her not to pay attention.

Erica plopped onto the chair and rubbed her arms. "Damn. What do you have the heat set to? Forty?"

"It would serve you right if I did." Maggie grabbed the afghan from the back of the couch and tossed it to Erica. "You could have warned me."

"What fun would that have been?" Erica huddled under the blanket just as Lindy entered the room. "I swear, the heat is leaking out of this house. All I ever feel are drafts."

The only draft Erica felt was from Lindy. Mom had felt the same draft. Neither Maggie nor Dean felt it, though. At least they didn't complain. Wonder why that was?

"The house is plenty warm. Maybe you're coming down with something."

"For a month? No, you've got a leak somewhere. Lots of leaks. If it weren't for your inheritance, I'd say give the house to Eddie. He deserves the cold."

"You don't have to live here if you don't want to."

"Neither do you. I bet your books take off before you can even touch that money."

"I'm not living here because of the money. I *want* to live here. Mom grew up here. I love sleeping in her room. Makes me feel a little closer to her."

Lindy placed a hand on her chest and puffed out a breath. Damn, that was close. The money stipulation was meant to be an enticement. It hadn't occurred to Lindy that Maggie might not need it. Who didn't need money?

"Plus, you don't want Eddie to have the house. I wonder why he wants this place so bad. I can't imagine he wants a connection with his father. Plus, he seems like he needs the money now, not five years from now. Did your grandma hide jewels or gold coins?"

Lindy bent over, laughing. Jewels? Gold coins? Wouldn't that be something? The only thing her mother left behind were years of junk and papers to fill several garbage cans. All stored in the attic, which these two women hadn't even bothered checking out.

"If she'd hidden anything, wouldn't she have left me a letter or something?"

"I suppose. Maybe the land is worth something."

"Yeah, right. That's why there are for sale signs everywhere. So what are you doing home early? Decided not to go for it?"

"The client was a skeeze. And married. Didn't even hide that fact. I feel sorry for his wife. And how was your night? Did my little plan work? Did you and Dean..." Erica wagged her eyebrows.

Maggie shook her head and rolled her eyes, but Lindy knew better. Those two had performed a little kissy-face before he drove off. It hadn't been ten minutes when he'd returned, though. Probably didn't want her knowing he was staking the place out and he'd certainly not mentioned his ghost-seeing ability.

"I think I'll head to bed." Maggie picked up the bag that she had placed on the floor after Dean had dropped her off. "I can't believe I'm going to do this."

"But if it works..."

If what works? Lindy followed the duo up the stairs into the bathroom. Maggie placed the bag on the floor and pulled out a chain that contained two little buckled belts on each end. "What is that?"

Maggie opened up one of the belts. "This is too short. It won't fit around the sink pedestal."

"Give it here." Erica looped the chain around the pedestal, grabbed a small padlock from the bag, and locked the chain together. The little belt dangled. "See? That works."

They dragged the chain into Maggie's room.

"Make sure you don't trip on the chain going down the stairs," Maggie said.

"I doubt I go downstairs before you. Here's the lock for your end. I'll put the keys in my room." She fingered the plushy part of the belt. "At least they're soft. Hell, when this is all over, maybe you could have some fun with these with Dean."

That earned a smack from Maggie. "Would you stop talking about my sex life?"

"You mean your non-existent sex life?" Erica plopped onto the bed. "Seriously, though, you've gotta know you're more than just a case to him. He's into you. Even knowing about all this shit. If he makes a move, I hope you don't turn him away. You deserve some fun."

Lindy hovered along the ceiling, keeping her distance. Why couldn't those two just say what the chain was for? Dean probably knew, but asking him was out of the question. He'd want to know why she cared.

"I'll keep that in mind. See you in the morning." Maggie ushered her cousin out and then rearranged the chain so she could shut the door.

While Maggie prepared for bed, Lindy lowered to the floor. About damn time. Wonder how long it would take for Maggie to fall asleep? She'd gotten enough rest the night before, so she probably wouldn't crash right away. So, maybe thirty minutes until the sign? Whatever, it couldn't come fast enough.

Maggie climbed onto the bed and picked up the little belt. She wrapped it around her ankle and secured it with the lock.

"What? No!" Lindy screamed. That man was ruining her life!

* * * *

Dean leaned his head back when Maggie's bedroom lit up. His plan had to work, and soon, or she could easily crack under the pressure. He would. Hell, he didn't even have will power around her anymore. Every time he'd told himself he shouldn't kiss her, he'd ended up kissing her. Certainly didn't help when she'd kissed him back.

But was it really so wrong to kiss her? Especially when she didn't stop him? She was an adult. She could have said no. And it was just kissing. She'd probably been kissed a lot, not that he liked to think about that.

Maggie's light went out. Shouldn't be much—

"What the hell are you doing?"

Even though he'd been expecting the visit, her arrival still made him jump. "Hello, Linda. Linda Steele, right?"

"If you were any good at your job, you'd know my name is Lindy. Now tell me what you're doing."

"I'm sitting here minding my own business."

"Like hell you are. You got Maggie to chain herself to the house. You're ruining my life!"

"You mean death, right? You're dead. What do you care anyway? You're not the one controlling her. Are you?" He'd bet his last nickel she was, though. She didn't seem like someone who cared about anyone other than herself.

"No, but my friend will not be happy with this. They'll blame me."

"I doubt that. You, or any other ghost, can't exactly stop Maggie. But hey, tell your friend to come see me and I'll clear you of any wrongdoing."

"God, you're frustrating!" She swung out and struck him.

He winced and rubbed his arm. Damn, why did ghosts have to be so stinkin' strong?

"I touched you. I can touch you?"

Oh shit. Where were people when he needed them? He reached for the door handle, but she grabbed his arm and held him captive.

"Holy shit! What are you?"

He took a calming breath. Her grip wasn't hurting. Yet. "Just someone you can touch, okay? Now, will you let me go?"

"No. Not until you get Maggie to take off that chain."

"Fine. Let's go inside, shall we?"

"What do you think I am, stupid? You can call her."

"Lindy, face it. I know there's no friend. Why are you doing this to her?"

She shook her head. "It's not me."

"Be that way. Then your friend isn't going to get their way. And whether or not they blame you, I couldn't care less. Maggie is my concern. Not you."

"How about your wellbeing? Do you care about that?" Maggie grabbed Dean by the neck and squeezed. Damn it. Why'd he have to egg her on? No amount of pulling or punching affected her in the least. A crushing sensation enveloped his chest and spots marred his vision. He wheezed out a breath.

Not again. No.

＊ ＊ ＊ ＊

Lindy squeezed Dean's neck. She'd show him who was in charge here. Messing with her plans came with a price, especially now that she knew she could touch him. "Not so tough now, are you?"

His face turned a nice shade of purple and his arms went limp. Crap! What was she doing? She only wanted to scare the guy, not kill him.

When she released him, he slumped against the door. She slapped his face. "Dean? Come out of it, Dean. Wake up. I'm sorry. I didn't know I was that strong."

How could she get help? What could she do? Was he having a heart attack? When she leaned down to listen to his heart, she grabbed the steering wheel and the horn honked.

Wait a minute. Everything became solid when she touched him. She could signal for help. Grabbing his shoulder, she turned and slammed on the horn. Please let it work. Please let it work.

A few seconds later her hand went through Dean and the steering column as she became incorporeal. Either someone saw her or…he died? Crap!

＊ ＊ ＊ ＊

A long honk came from the front of the house.

"Who the heck is out there honking this time of night?" Maggie snapped the covers back and maneuvered the chain so she could reach the window. As soon as she peered outside, the honking stopped. Dean's car was parked down the road and it appeared Dean had fallen asleep. Or worse. Had he honked the horn? "Oh shit."

"Erica, get me loose!" When she got no response, she continued to scream her cousin's name.

Erica opened the door. "That was quick. What's the code?"

"Dean's out there. I think he's in trouble." Or he would be if she didn't wake him up.

"I'm not falling for that. If you want out, you have to give me the code."

"Pickle! Pickle! Now undo me!"

"Hold on. Let me get the key."

While Erica was gone, Maggie grabbed her robe and slippers. Why hadn't Dean mentioned he was surveilling her house? She would have checked on him, then. Oh sure, if her house was bugged, someone would have listened, but they could have come up with some kind of plan around that. Instead he was outside, most likely suffering from hypothermia. Stupid man!

Erica barely returned when Maggie snatched the keys from her cousin's hands. As soon as she unlocked the restraint, she hurried down the stairs as fast as her scared little mind would let her— thank God it was dark—but as soon as her feet touched the first floor, she practically flew out the door.

Holy ice cubes, it was freezing. Her slippers didn't do a damn thing to keep her feet warm, either. Doing her best to ignore her discomfort, she ran to the car and yanked the door open. He nearly fell out of the car.

"Dean? Wake up."

But he hadn't stirred. Were his lips turning blue?

"What's the matter with him?" Erica asked.

Propping him upright, Maggie placed fingers along his neck. It was worse than she'd thought. "There's no pulse. Call 9-1-1. Hurry!"

Erica ran back to the house. Maggie grabbed Dean under his arms and pulled. Damn, he was heavy, but if she had any hope of getting his heart started, she needed him lying flat. As she cleared his butt from the car, he slipped out of her grasp. His head hit the pavement with a sickening thunk.

"OhGodohGodohGod!" She lifted him again and dragged the rest of him out of the car. Now would be a bad time for someone to drive down the street, but nothing she could do about that. She folded her hands together and started CPR. Red markings in the shape of handprints ringed his neck. Someone had choked him? Who would do that? Who else? Eddie. Was he still lurking around?

Dean took a wheezy breath, but she checked his pulse to be safe.

"Oh, thank God." She fell on top of him. Sure, she probably shouldn't have done such a stupid thing, but so what. He was alive and she cried.

Chapter 8

Lindy hovered in the yard next door to her house. Eventually that old crony would make her way here; she loved nothing better than protecting her bubble. Lindy could only hope the ghost would answer her questions, if she was willing to talk at all.

The last time Lindy had ventured into Rhonda's territory had ended badly. Dean's zap was nothing compared to that ghost's fury.

Either it was her trespassing or the flashing lights of the ambulance that eventually got the old ghost's attention. Lindy waved as she stepped back into her own yard. "Rhonda! Can I talk to you?"

Wearing the long nightgown she'd died in, Rhonda drifted over slower than molasses dripped down a tree. "Thought I told you to stay off my property, little girl."

Technically, it was Lindy's property, too—being in both their bubbles—but now wasn't the time for that argument. If ever. "I need to know something, then I'll leave you alone."

Rhonda crossed her arms. "What's in it for me?"

"Are you serious? What can I give you? You don't want my company."

"You're right. I don't. So maybe if I help you out this one time you'll stay the hell away from me. Forever."

"Fine." It wouldn't be a hardship, either. "Do you know what would happen to me if I accidentally killed someone?"

"I thought you were too weak to hurt anyone before you died. How could you have killed someone?"

"I don't mean before I died. I mean like the way I am now. As a ghost."

Rhonda laughed. "Did you finally figure out how to move furniture? Is that it? Did you clock someone in the head?"

"No. I choked someone." Lindy pointed to the commotion on the street. "Him."

"Not possible. We can't do that. Trust me, I tried."

"But my handprints were showing around his neck."

"Wait. You touched someone?"

"Isn't that what I just said?"

"No, you said you choked. How did you touch this guy?" Rhonda moved toward the scene in the street, but stopped before going too far. Another foot and she would have popped back to her place of death. Of course, it wouldn't have kept her there for long.

"I don't know. He told me he can see ghosts. But I was mad at him and I might have killed him. Does that mean I'll go to hell?" That was if she could ever leave Earth. She still hadn't figured out how to do that.

"What, you don't think living here is hell? I've got news for you. It is! But I want to know more about this guy. Can you bring him to me?"

"I just told you I probably killed him!" Geez, had the woman lost her hearing along with her compassion?

"He's not dead yet. So if you didn't, can you bring him to me?"

Rhonda was right. Dean was still alive. They wouldn't give air to a dead guy, would they? This time Lindy crossed her arms. "What's in it for me?"

Rhonda floated side to side while tapping her lips with her finger. "I'll give you three free passes into my territory. How about that?"

There had to be a trick to that. There usually was. "How long would my passes be for?"

"Two hours."

"That's not enough time."

"Fine. Four hours."

Wow. Negotiation actually worked? Rhonda must really want to see Dean. Three passes at four hours each, without fear of being zapped, would be nice. There was still a lot of territory she hadn't been able to explore. Of course, she'd have to bring Dean to Rhonda first. A moot point if he died.

Lindy would have shook on the deal if she thought Rhonda would only shake her hand. "I'll do my best. But what if he dies? Do you think I'll go to hell?"

Rhonda shrugged. "I have no idea. But if you do, it'll be quick."

And most likely painful. She'd heard the cries of the guilty. Shit.

* * * *

Eddie pulled into his driveway, ready to crash for the night. He hated leaving Ronnie with his mother, but he couldn't stand to listen to another word that woman said. If only he could get rid of her, but what kind of son would he look like then? Ronnie's opinion of him meant more than anything.

He grabbed his laptop bag and climbed out of the car just as a flashing police car blocked his driveway. Now what?

The cop opened his door and stood. "Edward Steele the third?"

That didn't sound good. No one called him that. "Yes. What can I do for you?"

"Where were you at ten-thirty this evening?"

Veronica chose that moment to step outside. "Eddie? What's going on?"

"It's okay." He waved her off. "Go back inside." But of course she wouldn't. Even worse, his mother joined her.

"What do you want with my husband?"

Shit. Couldn't she go inside for once?

"We need to know his whereabouts this evening."

"He was at his friend Butch's. Weren't you, honey?"

Lie to the cops or face divorce court? Neither sounded promising. "What's this about?"

"Do you know a Maggie Russell or a Dean Parker?"

His mother piped in. "Maggie Russell is a thief and a liar and has been a pain in our sides since his grandmother died."

For once his mother got something right. Maybe his luck was changing. Maybe they came to tell him Maggie had died. Life would be a whole bunch better then. "She's my cousin. I don't know who this Parker guy is. Why do you want to know?"

"Mr. Parker was attacked tonight and Ms. Russell claims you're responsible."

"What! It couldn't be me. I was at the Racino. There have to be cameras…" He realized his mistake too late.

Veronica glared at him. "You were where?"

"Eddie, Eddie, Eddie," his mother said, followed by several tsks of her tongue.

Fuuuuuck! Wasn't it bad enough Maggie had his inheritance? Now she wanted him in jail. And he hadn't done anything wrong. Well, if she wanted a war, she'd get a war.

* * * *

Dean woke to the sounds of beeps. Steady beeps. He looked up at the heart monitor. How'd he end up in the hospital?

"Hey. You gave us quite a scare." Sitting in the bedside chair, Bridget slid her smart phone inside her purse.

"What am—" Pain pinched off his words. Damn. What happened to his throat? And his voice sounded like he'd gargled with acid. Hell, it didn't feel too far from that, either. He swallowed gingerly and took in a slow breath. "What am I doing here?"

"Don't you remember? Maggie found you in your car."

Car… Maggie's… Lindy! Damn ghost tried to kill him. It all came back and he slapped his forehead. "Is she okay?"

"Physically? Yeah. She's out in the waiting room with Rob. Scared shitless, I might add. She's been here all night."

All night? At least that meant Maggie wasn't at home with one angry ghost. He could only imagine what Lindy would do to her. "And you're here because…"

"You made me your emergency contact even knowing how much I loathe hospitals. When did you do that?"

"Oh, did I forget to tell you it was part of the job? Figured you'd be on my side when it came to getting out of these places." Which he wouldn't mind doing right away. He sat up. Street and parking lot lights were the only things illuminating the outdoors. "What time is it?"

"A little after five. What happened? Who tried to strangle you?"

The truth would only set Bridget on a path he had no intention of her taking. "No one. I must have had another heart attack."

She shook her head. "Not gonna fly. You have hand prints around your neck, so the police are interested. Maggie insists Eddie is responsible."

He touched his throat. Hand prints? Police? Shit. He shook his head, albeit minutely. Lindy had done a number on his neck and, besides being painful, it had become stiff. At least he was still alive, so she'd failed in killing him. For now. "If I tell you, you have to promise not to do anything stupid."

"You mean more stupid than being strangled by Eddie? How'd he get the drop on you, anyway? He didn't seem like the stealthy type."

If only it were Eddie. Dean could have sat on the guy and squished him. "Eddie didn't do this. It was Lindy. Lindy Steele."

Bridget's eyes widened. "Hell's bells. What are we gonna say? We can't very well tell the police a ghost tried to kill you."

"I'll say I don't remember. That I had another attack. It's true, isn't it?"

"Except you have hand prints around your neck due to being strangled. How am I supposed to keep the police out of this? Maggie told them that Eddie did this."

"But there's no way she saw him. I'm the only witness. Don't worry, I'll take care of it." Thank God he had friends on the force. He really didn't want them snooping around. If only Lindy hadn't left marks. Shit. "How'd Maggie find me, anyway? I didn't tell her I was surveilling her house."

"She said you honked the horn."

Honked the horn? Wouldn't he have remembered that? "That wasn't me. Huh."

"So then Lindy honked the horn? If she did, then that means—"

"She wasn't trying to kill me," he finished. "There's a first." Didn't mean Lindy wouldn't try again.

"Not all ghosts are evil, you know. But what'd you do to her?"

"Took her fun away. She's the ghost possessing Maggie."

"She admitted that?"

"No. She still claims someone else is involved. But there's no way. She's only out for one person—herself—and I pretty much told her I didn't give a damn."

"And you think *I* take risks with ghosts. I gotta talk to her now."

"Oh, no you don't. This is why I didn't want to tell you. Lindy is dangerous and Rob would fillet me alive if I let you get near her. Promise me you'll stay away."

"But, Dean. She's mad at you. Not me."

"She's mad at everyone and I don't trust her."

"You don't trust any ghost."

"You shouldn't either. Especially in your condition."

Bridget rubbed her belly and sighed. "Fine. But you have to tell Maggie. She deserves to know the truth. If not for her, you'd be dead. Do you understand? D. E. A. D. Dead."

"What? Afraid I didn't leave you the business?" When that didn't bring a smile to Bridget's face, he back-tracked. "I get it, okay? I owe her my life." And he'd thank Maggie later. As for telling her… Yeah, that wasn't happening. But right now he only wanted one thing. "Can you disconnect me from this machine without them thinking I died?"

"I shouldn't, but your heart rate seems fine." With her pregnant belly in the way, she took several struggling moments before she could stand. A few pressed buttons later, the beeping stopped.

"Thanks." He removed the clip from his finger then yanked the IV from his arm. Okay, that might have been a stupid move. It not only hurt like the blazes, blood trickled onto the sheets.

"Hell's bells. What do you think you're doing?"

He grabbed some tissues from the box on the side table and applied them to the needle hole. "Getting out of here. What else? Do you have a Band-Aid?"

"Damn it, Dean. I should get a nurse."

"I thought you were a nurse." Well, she used to be. Just because she wasn't practicing anymore didn't mean she couldn't help.

Instead of helping, she glared at him.

"Never mind. I'll find it myself." He tested standing, found the room only tilted a little and then headed for the bathroom. As he passed her, he kept the opening of his gown from her view. There were some things an employee shouldn't see. Their boss's ass, for one. "Would you get my clothes, please? I would prefer wearing something less revealing."

"You're impossible." She stormed out without giving him his clothes. And after he'd said please, too.

The toilet paper was thin, but at least it came in a strip instead of little pieces. He wrapped his arm and blood spots bloomed through the paper. His coat would cover that. If he had a coat. Shit. He opened the closet. Eureka! His coat hung from the hangers and a plastic bag sat on the floor. Ah, his clothes. He'd barely gotten his pants on when Bridget returned with reinforcements. Thank goodness he still wore the nightgown. Maggie didn't need to see his scar.

"What are you doing?" Maggie said, her forehead furrowed. "You should be in bed."

For someone who basically had a heart attack, he managed to become aroused at the sight of her. Not that she was wearing anything revealing. The flannel shirt and jeans kept her pretty well covered. She just looked damn good in them. If it weren't for the fact she was mad enough to toss his ass on the bed, and that they had an audience, he'd kiss her. Or at least attempt it. "I'm fine." And he might have been more convincing if his voice didn't sound like it'd been rubbed with sandpaper. "My throat's a little raw, but it'll get better."

"You're not fine. Your heart stopped."

"Even I'm surprised you can move around as if nothing happened," Rob said.

"Whose side are you on?" Dean asked.

"There are no sides," Maggie said. "We're all here for your best interest. Now sit your butt on that bed. You're not going anywhere."

"Whoa, she told you," Bridget said.

Rob grasped her arm. "Come on. Let's go. I think she's got this."

"Just so you know, I'm going into work late," Bridget said over her shoulder. "And I better not see you there, either."

"Good luck, Dean," Rob said.

"Luck? Why would I need luck?" But his answer came at the couple's retreating backsides. He turned toward Maggie.

With hands on hips, she glared at him. Damn. Did Bridget teach her that or did all women learn that in school?

"You need to get back in that bed," Maggie said.

"No. I need to leave." He pulled his shirt out of the bag. Probably better if he dressed in the bathroom. His scar would only worry her more.

She picked up the buzzer. "Do I have to get the nurse to restrain you?"

"You wouldn't."

She hovered her thumb over the button. "Try me."

Shit. He couldn't very well tackle her for it. Number one, he didn't want to hurt her. Number two, he didn't want to hurt himself. He was sore enough. Giving up, he threw the shirt on the bed and sat in the chair. "I was hoping to have this discussion someplace else, but I guess here is good as any. I certainly don't want to talk at your house."

She sat on the bed, facing him. "Why? Is my place unsafe? Should I call Erica?"

"Erica isn't having problems living there, now is she?"

"No, but if Eddie tried to strangle you, what's to stop him from doing the same to Erica?"

"Eddie didn't strangle me."

"No, thank God. But he came pretty damn close. I made sure the police knew it, too."

"Yeah, about that."

But she kept right on talking. "I hope they caught him and put him in jail. He can't get away with this."

"Maggie, stop. It wasn't Eddie."

"What do you mean? Of course it was Eddie. Who else could it have been?"

He couldn't say ghost. Not here. "The same person responsible for your night adventures."

"But I'm... I mean..." Her eyes widened as he shook his head. "Not Eddie?"

"Not Eddie."

"Oh God! I did this?"

"Oh hell, no." She would go there. "You were chained to the house, or did you forget that?"

A nervous laugh escaped her. "Yeah, but maybe I napped before Erica came home. It's possible."

"I promise, it wasn't you. Okay?"

"So, when you tell the police, this will all be over with? I'll be able to go back to things being normal?"

Hope. She had it. He would crush it.

Chapter 9

Maggie stifled a yawn but couldn't help but smile. Her sleepless nights were finally behind her. Dean had seen the perpetrator, he could press charges, and then it would all be over. Life would go back to normal. Finally. If she weren't so tired, she'd jump up and dance.

"I'm sorry, but I can't tell the police," Dean said.

And just like that her jubilation deflated. "You can't or you won't?"

Before he could answer, the door opened and a nurse walked in. "Mr. Parker! I thought I heard voices down here. You really shouldn't be out of bed. And who are you?" she said to Maggie. "No visitors until eight. You have to leave."

Maggie stood. "But I was keeping him from leaving."

"That's all well and good, but you can't be here. Out, out!"

"I'm leaving, too." Dean picked his shirt off the bed. "I'll meet you in the hallway," he said to Maggie.

"You'll do no such thing. Look at the mess you made. Who said you could take that out? Now get back in that bed."

Maggie backed into the hallway as Dean argued with the nurse. What should she do? Stay and wait? Or abandon him? He couldn't very well leave if he didn't have a ride. At least, not easily.

But just the idea of stranding him pinched her heart. Maybe she could talk him into staying. Promise him something, anything. If only she had something he wanted.

Dean emerged from the room, wearing his shirt and coat. He grabbed Maggie's arm. "Let's go."

Or she could let him steamroll over her. She seemed to be good at that. "Are you sure that's a good idea?"

The nurse trailed after them. "Don't make me call security."

"Please, Dean. I don't want you to get in trouble."

"She's bluffing. They can't do anything to me. Let's go get something to eat, shall we?"

Eat? How could he think of food at a time like this? "At least get cleared by a doctor first."

"To eat?"

"No. To make sure—" Her thoughts derailed when he dragged her past the elevators and headed toward the stairwell. "Why aren't we taking the elevators?" She could deal with small spaces a whole lot better than a bunch of steps.

"It'd be my luck she *does* call security and that would be the first place they'd look. I don't need the hassle."

That made sense. Sort of. But they were on the third floor. And the stairwell was probably open, and high. "How about I meet you down there? It's just that I'm really beat and—"

He put his hand up, silencing her. "You're right. I'm sorry. I'll see you down there."

He disappeared into the stairwell and she pushed the down button. She hated lying to the man, although she hadn't, not entirely. For someone who had nearly died a few hours ago, his energy rivaled that of a power plant. Whereas she had the energy of a sloth.

She rode the elevator down. When it opened on the ground floor, sure enough, a security guard loitered in the area. He glanced inside the elevator and, after finding it empty, proceeded to pace. He didn't pay her any mind at all.

She strolled around the corner to the stairwell. Dean had beaten her down and eased her against the wall, out of sight of the security guard. "I hope you brought your car."

"You're just now asking?" Maybe he was more tired than he let on.

He shrugged. "So sue me."

As they headed toward the side exit, little drops of red landed on the floor.

"Are you bleeding?"

He lifted his hand, where a line of blood trailed down his index finger. "Ah, crap. It's from the IV. Wait here." He dashed into the men's room and came out less than a minute later. "Ready?"

"Dean, please don't do this. What's it gonna hurt if you stay here one day?"

"I'm glad you're concerned and all, but honestly, I'm fine. How about the Pancake House? Is that okay with you?"

She must have nodded. Next thing she knew, he'd grabbed her by the elbow and ushered her outside. Once they got to her car, she figured he'd take the keys and drive, but instead he opened the driver's door and waited for her to get inside.

Maybe he wasn't as fine as he let on.

As she buckled herself in, he slid into the passenger seat. His size and the compactness of her car made for one sizzling atmosphere. If he hadn't nearly died, and she wasn't ready to crash onto the nearest bed, she might have jumped his bones. She certainly wouldn't mind kissing him again. Which only proved she was existing on fumes. And she had to be at work in three hours. Seemed she was destined to take more naps at her desk.

Thank goodness the Pancake House wasn't far. She pulled into the empty parking lot while the world was still dark and most people could probably be found asleep in their homes. Something she wouldn't mind doing, if only for an hour.

The temps outside could bring a freezer to shame, but inside the restaurant was nice and toasty. While Maggie removed her coat, Dean asked for the corner booth. Probably for the privacy, not that the place was crawling with customers.

After ordering them coffee, he slid in beside her instead of across the table as she expected. His closeness nearly did her in, but then she wasn't completely with it, either. He turned toward her and spoke softly. "Listen, what I have to say isn't going to be easy for me. Hell, it took me a long time to get used to the idea, so I'll understand if you think I'm crazy. But I'm not, okay?"

If he was crazy, what did that make her? She'd been the one sleepwalking for days on end. Who was she to judge? "Does this have something to do with why you won't tell the police about who attacked you?"

"It's not like that."

He stopped when the waitress returned with two empty mugs and a carafe. When she asked for their order, he went with the huge combo meal—pancakes, eggs, bacon, and potatoes—and Maggie settled for a waffle.

Dean poured the coffee. "Do you believe in ghosts?"

"I don't know. I never really thought much about them." She picked up her filled mug and took a long sip. Ahhh. Caffeine. She might need an IV of the stuff later on. "What does that have to do with who strangled you?"

"I'm getting there. Have you ever noticed sudden chills in your house?"

If he was getting there, he was taking the scenic route. "I don't see what that has to do with your attack."

"Just humor me and answer the question."

With her tired mind and his near death, she'd had enough. So her answer might have come out a little snarky. "It's an old house. It's drafty."

He didn't seem to take notice of her snippiness. "I'm sure it is, but I mean in one spot only, like walking through a refrigerator. Or freezer."

"I haven't, but Erica complains about that all the time. Then again, she's always cold. And whines. A lot." Oh great. She moved from snarky to whiny. Just call her Erica.

He chuckled. "Maybe so, but she has a valid reason to whine. And I guess it makes sense you don't notice it."

"Nothing you're saying is making sense." But the coffee? Yeah, the coffee was making lots of sense. It kept telling her to drink it. So she took another long sip.

"Sorry. I know this is confusing. But what Erica is experiencing is what most people feel when they walk through a...ghost."

The mug slipped through her fingers, but she caught it before it spilled. "Excuse me? You're saying my house is haunted? What are you? A Ghostfacer?"

"A ghost what?"

"You know. From the television show 'Supernatural'? They're paranormal hunters." Although maybe she should have said Ghostbuster. Those Ghostfacers were a bit inept.

He closed his eyes briefly. "Oh God, no. I'm no hunter. But I *can* see and communicate with them."

He may not have heard of the show, but he sure sounded like one of the characters. She must've given him a concussion when she'd dropped him from the car. "You sure you don't need to go back to the hospital?"

"I told you you would think I was crazy. But please hear me out and know I'm not any crazier than you."

"So you *do* think I'm crazy?" Although did it matter what a crazy person thought? Gosh, she was giving herself a headache. More coffee. She needed more coffee.

"No." He shook his head. "Neither one of us is crazy, okay? Four years ago, I died, but—"

She nearly choked on a half-swallow. "What? You died? How?"

"That's another story. What's important is that I was brought back to life. With an ability I didn't possess before. An ability to see and communicate with ghosts."

"For real? You're not just saying this to make me feel less crazy?" As wild as it sounded, believing him was better than thinking they might be roommates at the sanitarium.

"For real. And you're not crazy, so quit thinking you are."

"And there's a ghost living in my house."

"Yes. Do you remember a family member by the name of Linda Steele?"

"My grandmother is haunting me?"

"No, no." He shook his head. "Not your grandmother. Your aunt. Lindy."

Lindy? Now there was a name from the past. She was Mom's older sister and had died when Mom was thirteen. Maggie took another long sip of coffee. Too bad it wasn't spiked. Maybe then their conversation wouldn't seem surreal. "Why would she be haunting me? I never even met her."

He took her free hand, his warmth enveloping her suddenly cold hand. "Maggie, she's doing more than haunting your house. I don't know how she's doing it, but I believe she's been possessing you."

"Wait a minute." Heck, she'd only been kidding about being possessed. Now he was telling her it was possible? "You said the person who strangled you—"

"Was responsible for your night adventures."

She let that sink in for a microsecond. "You were strangled by a ghost?"

"Yep."

79

The waitress chose that moment to return with their order. Probably just as well they'd been interrupted. Because what could she say to that? "Sucks to be you"? Of course, she was the one being possessed, so who had it worse? Ghosts possessing. Ghosts strangling. What else did ghosts do? According to the movies, they could throw stuff around. Her ghost hadn't done anything like that. Yet.

And why was she thinking the ghost was hers? Ugh.

What little appetite she'd had disappeared. Maggie picked at her waffle. Even Dean didn't eat with the gusto he'd shown the other night.

"So ghosts can touch you." Just how much danger was he in?

"When I'm alone with them, yeah. That's the only time I can see them, too. I've been spared seeing ghosts in the presence of non-seers."

"And you can communicate, how?"

"I can talk to them just as I'm talking to you. Again, provided I'm alone with them."

"Did she say why she's been possessing me?"

"Well... Technically she hasn't admitted she's doing it. But she sure got angry when you chained yourself to the house. Why would she be mad if she wasn't the one doing it?"

Suddenly all that spy stuff—keeping secret codes away from the house—made sense. "You set her up."

"That was the plan."

Maggie put her fork down while Dean continued to eat. Even with the bruising around his neck. Bruising caused by hand prints. "But instead of confessing, she got mad and tried to kill you."

He rubbed his neck. "I know it looks that way and I had thought the same thing."

"So why are you thinking differently? Have you seen your neck?"

"Well, for one I would probably be dead if she wanted me dead. But she's the one who honked the horn. Not me."

"You didn't honk it?" Now that she thought about it, he'd been slumped over by the time she'd looked out the window. Plus, the honking eerily stopped at that same moment, too.

"Nope. She did it after I passed out."

She banged her fist on the table. Didn't he realize how close he came to not having breakfast with her, or having breakfast at all?

"Don't act like you had a case of the vapors. You died. Your heart stopped and you stopped breathing."

"I'm sorry. I don't mean to upset you. I should be thanking you for finding and reviving me. I know I owe you a lot for that."

"You don't owe me anything. Any decent person would have done the same. I just don't want you to think this isn't serious."

"Trust me, I know how serious this is. But not to me, to you. Any other time I would agree she set out to kill me. Ghosts only care about themselves. But I have to wonder why she would honk the horn if she wanted me dead. I'm guessing she needs me for something and realized her mistake before it was too late." He shook his head and chuckled. "Man, she's super strong. Gotta remember not to egg her on again."

How could he sit there and laugh about it when she was on the verge of breaking down and crying at how close she came to losing him? "This isn't funny. You almost died. She almost killed you."

"Maggie…" He wrapped his arm around her. "But she didn't. And I'm okay."

So he kept saying, but his pale complexion gave him away. As did the sheen on his forehead and his rapid breathing. His near death was catching up to him, but he was "okay." Sure he was.

He slid his arm along her shoulders, setting off a spark of desire. If only they were on a date instead of discussing possession and strangling.

"So, have you come up with another brilliant plan?" That had come out snarkier than she'd intended. Coffee. She needed more coffee so she'd sound sane. Or saner. She still wasn't on board about being sane in the first place.

His chuckle accompanied a wonderful squeeze on her shoulder. "Yeah, my plans have pretty much sucked, haven't they? And until I figure out something that'll actually work, you can't go back home. Lindy is unpredictable and careless. If she had any kind of control over possessing you, or if she were trying to be stealthy, you'd have never woken up anywhere but in your bed. It's almost like she's practicing, and with each possession she gets stronger. I don't like the thought of that."

"How strong can she get if I keep chaining myself to the house? She'll lose interest, right?" She wouldn't necessarily enjoy doing that, but better than being walked out of the house. And if she continued to lose sleep at night, she could always nap during her lunch break.

"Or she'll continue to possess you until she figures out how to get you loose."

"I'll take that chance. Certainly I can handle one ghost now that I know she's there."

"I'd rather you didn't have to deal with her at all. And I'm not talking permanently. Only until I can help her move on."

"Move on? You think it's fair for her to possess someone else?"

"Not that kind of move. I'm talking about heaven or wherever it is ghosts go. The ghosts I've run across are here because they committed suicide or have unfinished business. Since Lindy didn't commit suicide, there's something personal keeping her around. When I can find out what, then maybe I can help her get it. Once she moves on, you'll be safe living in your house. But until then…" He shook his head. "She scares me, Maggie. I was able to get her to leave your body that one time when we touched, but what if she gets stronger? What if she fights the influence I now have over her? What if she can eventually control her possession and never lets go?"

That sent chills across her skin. "You think that's possible?"

"I'm beginning to believe anything is possible. Four years ago I'd have told you ghosts don't exist. Or at least no one actually saw them. They're spirits, for Christ's sake. I shouldn't be able to see them, but I do."

And she was being possessed by one. Could life get any stranger?

* * * *

Dean wiped his sweaty brow. When did the restaurant get so hot? Or was it his seatmate making him warm? Mmmm… Maggie. He would never tire of being in her presence. Sitting beside her and having breakfast was a dream he'd never even imagined. So what if the circumstances weren't ideal? None of this would be happening if they were. He wasn't her date, though, so he probably should stop acting like one.

Reluctantly, he removed his arm from her slender shoulders and continued eating a breakfast he wasn't sure he could finish. Whatever made him think he could eat all this food? Whether from nearly dying or removing the IV the way he had, not only was his stomach on the fritz, a headache bloomed behind his eyes. But if he showed any sign of weakness, it would only spur her to send him back to the hospital. And that wasn't happening. Better to keep her mind busy elsewhere.

"At least you know you don't have a split personality." When she raised her eyebrows, he gave her a shoulder bump. "Yeah, I know you were thinking it." Hell, even he'd wondered. "You just have a night visitor in the form of a ghost."

"You mean hijacker. Why me, though?"

"Rotten luck?" He laughed, but she shook her head and picked at that poor waffle. Maybe he should have gotten one of them. He'd have finished eating by now. Maybe.

"That's me. Lucky." She shoved the plate away and leaned back against the seat cushion.

"I know it doesn't seem like it, but in a way you are lucky. Lucky to have someone who can get to the bottom of all this. And I will do that."

"You've helped other possessed people?"

"Actually, you'd be the first. That doesn't mean I can't help you, though. Which means helping Lindy. What did she die of?"

"She had leukemia. My mother said she couldn't even go to school during her last semester. She was in and out of the hospital."

"Did she have a boyfriend?"

"I have no idea. What does that matter?"

"He could be the reason she's sticking around. Find him and solve the problem. Do you have a family member who might remember if she had a boyfriend?"

She shook her head. "Grandpa died in '83. Uncle Ed died in '93, Mom died in 2003."

"Damn. Every ten years?"

"Yeah. Grandma was sure they were cursed, but 2013 came and went without anyone we knew dying. Guess fate just waited. Makes me wonder if 2023 is my—"

"Don't. Don't. It's just a coincidence."

She smiled and patted his arm. "I know that. The only other person who might know is Mom's cousin, Erica's mother, but Mom said they weren't close until after Lindy's death. Wouldn't it be easier to ask Lindy?"

"She won't even admit she's possessing you, so no."

Maggie yawned and covered her mouth. "I'm sorry. I had hoped the coffee would have kicked in by now."

Dean closed his eyes. What a colossal idiot he'd become. Their conversation certainly could have waited until she was more rested. "Bridget told me you were at the hospital all night and here I am being a pig. You must be exhausted."

She shrugged. "No different than any other day. I know you don't want me going home, but that's where all my clothes are and I have to get ready for work."

"You're not in any shape to go to work." He'd find a way to keep her home. Well, not her home, but somewhere. Anywhere else but her house. He would not let her go back there. After tossing some money on the table to cover the check, he stood and the room spun, sending him on his ass. Seemed she wasn't the only one unfit for work.

Chapter 10

Maggie held on to a wobbly Dean as they headed for her car. A few more minutes of this and she'd be wobbly, too. His size. His scent. His warmth. Each second that passed, her body clamored for more. She really shouldn't be desiring him now, but her head was losing that argument. "I should take you back to the hospital."

Her heart was still trying to get over seeing him fall. He could have been seriously injured.

"I'd just leave again," he said.

Of course he would. Why would the man think the hospital could help him? Sometimes she wanted to smack some sense into the guy. "You're kind of pigheaded. Anyone tell you that?"

"Only everyone I've ever met." He grinned. Oh great. Now her insides turned to goo. There should be a law against being that sexy.

Doing her best to ignore her tightening nipples and throbbing sex, she helped him to the passenger door and left him to fend for himself while she hurried to the driver's side. After starting the car, she grabbed the ice scraper. Even the short amount of time they'd spent in the restaurant hadn't prevented the windows from icing over.

"I can do that." He stopped mid-buckle and reached for the door handle.

"If you even try getting out of the car, I'm taking you back to the hospital." She shut the door on his protests and proceeded to scrape away the thin coating of ice. The cold air, and lack of his proximity, helped cleared her head. The issue at hand wasn't her desire for him, but for his well being. If he wouldn't go back to the hospital, then she'd have to make sure he stayed at home. But how? It wasn't like she could call his boss.

By the time she finished clearing the windows, her nipples were still hard, but for a completely different reason. Too bad she hadn't scraped long enough for the car to warm up. She shivered as she belted herself in. "I should have gotten some coffee to go."

"You won't need coffee at all if you stay at my place today."

"Stay at your place?" A tingly sensation raced across her body. Damn nipples. They might never get soft.

"Sure. You want me rested. You need rest. And you can't get it at your house. Or work."

Well, she *was* looking for a way to keep him at home. But rest with him, as in sleeping at his place? Now her heart rate was getting some action. "Is that a new pick-up line?"

"It can be whatever you want, as long as it works."

While spending the day resting sounded tempting, she did have obligations, as well as bills to pay. "I can't take off work like you can."

"Sure you can. Call Tom. He'll understand."

She shook her head. "I'm not calling Tom. I've missed enough work as it is."

He pulled out his phone. "And you say I'm pigheaded."

"What are you doing?"

Dean held his forefinger in the one-minute signal. "Good morning, Tom. Listen, Maggie needs another day off."

"No, I don't." She slapped her hand over her mouth. Had Tom heard her? Whatever would he think?

"Oh, she'll tell you she's fine, but another day of rest will really benefit her. Great. She'll see you tomorrow, then." He disconnected the call. "You're all set."

Except now her boss would think she'd slept with Dean. Why else call at oh-dark-thirty in the morning? But if she brought that up, Dean would think she had sex on her mind. And while that was true, he needed to stay home and rest. If that meant staying with him, she'd do it. She put the car in drive. "Fine. You won this round. Where to?"

He brought up a navigation app on his phone, all the while smiling as if he'd won the lottery. "Just follow the young lady's directions."

The drive barely lasted fifteen minutes and Dean wisely kept quiet. Maggie turned into a huge apartment complex and parked where he indicated. A dozen buildings, each three stories tall, surrounded a pond. And every building had multiple sets of stairs. Stairs that were on the outside of the buildings. Oh, that didn't look good. That didn't look good at all. "Which apartment is yours?"

Please be on the first floor. Please be on the first floor.

"Over there." He pointed to a set of stairs. "Top floor."

Of course it was. She climbed out of the car as Dean did. "Where's the elevator?"

"There isn't one."

Of course there wasn't. Why, oh why, did the stairs have to have open slats? And the hand railing. All it would take was one wrong step and then…splat.

"You okay?" he asked.

If okay meant being on the verge of a heart attack, then she was peachy. "Did they forget you lived in Ohio? Who builds the stairs outside the building? Won't they be covered in ice?"

"They have rubber treads to keep from slipping."

Rubber treads weren't even close to the carpet on her stairs. She grabbed hold of Dean's arm and took the first step.

He looked down at her hands. "Holding a little tight there, aren't you?"

"I don't want you to slip." *Or me fall to my death.*

"Okay. Whatever." He might have chuckled. Or cursed. She couldn't tell. The sound of her blood rushing pretty much drowned out everything else.

Still, she managed to let up on her grip a little and kept her focus on Dean and the wall. But when they reached the half-landing, she'd not only lost her wall, a gust of wind nearly knocked her over. Oh shit. She wrapped her arm around his waist and turned her head into his side.

Can't look down. Can't look down.

Dean placed his arm across her shoulders. "Guess it got a little windy, huh?"

"Just a little." At least she had the wind as an excuse.

They pivoted to the next set of stairs. It was the longest pivot of her life. Why was she doing this, again? Because there really wasn't any sane reason she would put herself through this.

Dean stopped to catch his breath on the second floor. "You're probably right about that slipping thing. Thanks for being my crutch."

Okay, there was one sane reason: Dean. She never would have been able to live with herself if he'd fallen on her watch. But he got it wrong. He was *her* crutch. "Glad I could help."

With a little prayer up the last set of stairs, they successfully arrived at his door. But her heart continued to flail against her sternum. The wind whipped even stronger on the small balcony.

He stuck his key into the lock and turned. "I don't remember what condition I left this in, so if it's bad, it's not usually like that, okay?"

"How about I don't judge you on it." *And how about you just open the damn door already?* Every second they stood on this death trap was a second too long.

"That works, too." He opened the door and ushered her in first.

Her breaths came easier once she crossed the threshold. At this point darkness was her friend. What she couldn't see couldn't hurt her. He shut the door and flipped on the light. His apartment wasn't in that bad of shape. No dirty dishes were scattered anywhere. Trash can by the kitchen wasn't overflowing. In fact, the place smelled nice and clean. There were, however, piles of paper and envelopes on the coffee table and dinette. "I'm beginning to think you have a thing for paper."

"Oh, that's just junk mail. Mostly."

"Mostly? You don't know?"

"I'll get to it when it's time to pay the bills." He plopped down on the couch and leaned back.

She knew some people didn't go through their mail daily. Erica wouldn't if not for Maggie. Not knowing that there might be something important would drive her nuts. But this wasn't her home. Wasn't her mess. Wasn't her problem. As long as the guest room didn't look the same.

"Help yourself to whatever you want to drink. I might have some beer."

"Beer? It's not even seven a.m."

"Oh, yeah. The darkness is kind of throwing me off a bit. In that case, I might not have much for you."

More like his near death was throwing him off a lot. "Doesn't matter, I'm not thirsty. Where's your guest room?"

"I don't have one. You can use my bed."

"What?" He couldn't seriously mean they were sharing a bed. Unless that was the way he operated. And really, would that be so bad?

"I won't be in it, of course. And it's clean. I promise, no papers."

Surprisingly, disappointment that he wouldn't share the bed stung her heart. "What about you?"

"I'm not tired."

"You can barely stand. And you said you would rest."

"Sitting is resting and I can stand just fine." He stood, although slowly, as if he didn't believe his own words. "Come on. I'll show you where."

He led her down the hall, past a bathroom and a room that contained exercise equipment, to his bedroom. She stopped at the doorway. That was one large bed. But then, he was one large man, why would he own differently? And it was made. Wow. A man who made his own bed. According to Erica, they didn't exist.

He turned back the covers, the white sheets a stark contrast to the dark green comforter. "Take off your shoes and climb on in."

It was so tempting. Not just to sleep knowing there wasn't a threat of being possessed, but to sleep knowing he had slept in that bed. Heck, it probably smelled like him—dark, dangerous, and sexy.

He must have sensed her hesitation. He came back for her, took her hand, and pulled her to the bed. Before she had a chance to miss holding his hand, he took her purse and placed it on the nightstand. Then gripped her shoulders and pushed her onto the mattress. "See? That wasn't so hard, was it?"

"I don't want to take your bed. Just get me a pillow and some blankets. I can sleep on the couch."

He crouched in front of her. "Humor me, okay?"

His close proximity set her heart off again, and when he gripped her calves and gently removed her shoes, she nearly swooned. How might she react if he touched other parts of her body? The intimate parts?

He stood and wavered. As she reached out for him, he plopped on the bed beside her. "Damn. Gotta stop getting up so fast."

"Ahh, Dean. You're not well. You should go back to the hos—"

He placed his fingers against her mouth. "Don't you go saying that word. It's not allowed here."

His fingers were warm against her lips and she closed her eyes. As badly as she yearned to kiss him, he really wasn't in any shape to do anything but sleep. Heck, she was about ready to crash, too. "Fine. But I can't take your bed when you need it more than I do. I'll be okay on the couch."

"No, you won't. It's not all that comfortable and I'd never forgive myself if I let you take it."

"Don't you believe in buying comfortable couches?"

"I believe in it, just haven't done it yet. But if it'll make you feel less guilty, I'll sleep on the bed with you. Fully clothed—can't have you molesting me." He bumped shoulders with her and smiled. "Even better, I'll stay on top of the covers while you're under them. How's that?"

Sleeping together? Parts of her body partied at what that might entail, sleep being way down at the bottom of that list. Except neither one of them were really capable of much more than sleeping at the time. "I suppose I could do that."

"Thatta girl."

She removed her flannel shirt, leaving the t-shirt on, and slid under the sheet. He covered her with the blanket. Even tucked her in. She smiled on a deep breath. She was right. The bed smelled like him: heavenly. Turned out she had no problem sleeping beside him.

* * * *

Stifling a yawn, Eddie shuffled into the empty kitchen wearing his pajamas. Good, no sign of Mom. But then that really wasn't a surprise. Ronnie wasn't cooking anything.

For all he knew, she'd never cook again. At least, not for him.

He'd barely gotten any sleep last night. After the police left, Ronnie had wanted to hear the whole story, but with Mom standing there being the pest that she was, he'd said he couldn't talk it. That was when Ronnie had stormed off to their bedroom and slammed the door. Which was followed by the slowest damn hour of his life.

Giving her time to fall asleep before crawling into bed with her, he'd sat on the couch and waited. Mom had decided to wait right along with him. But would she remain quiet? Hell, no. She proceeded to tell him how much of a disappointment he would have been to his father. When really, he was more of a disappointment to her.

And frankly, he wasn't giving much of a shit about that anymore.

He refused to be a disappointment to Ronnie, though. All night he'd tossed and turned wondering how he could make it up to her. But short of telling her the truth and letting her see what a horrible son he'd become, he didn't know what he could say. Well, he could start by making her coffee. Bring it as a peace offering. But by the time he started the coffee pot, Ronnie walked into the kitchen wearing her robe.

She slid onto a stool at the counter. "How bad is it?"

He looked at the coffee maker. "I don't know. It's barely started dripping. But I made it strong like you—"

"Not the coffee." She sighed and placed her head in her hands. "Your gambling."

Okay. Color him embarrassed. His head really wasn't screwed on tight enough this morning.

"I don't have a gambling problem." More like a Mom problem, but how could he tell Ronnie that? What son didn't love his mother?

"Then what are you doing every night? You lied about being at work. And you said you weren't cheating on me. Was that a lie, too?"

He sat on the stool beside her and took her hand. "Ronnie, I swear, I would never cheat on you. Never. And I only gambled a little. You do the bills. Wouldn't you have noticed a lack of funds?"

"Then what's going on?"

Lie, lie, lie! That little voice inside his head said it was the only way out of this mess. "It's just stress. Between the lawsuit and work, it's really getting to me. I thought if I blew off steam at the Racino, I wouldn't bring it home with me."

"Oh, Eddie." She cupped his face in her hands. "Don't you know I'd help you through anything?"

His heart ached less with her sincere statement and knowing she still cared about him. "I shouldn't involve you at all. This is not your mess."

"When we got married, my messes became yours and yours became mine. We're a team. So starting today, you'll come home after work and we'll talk it out."

Hard for him to treat them like a team when it was all one-sided. She didn't have any messes. "Why do you stay with me?"

"Because I love you." She kissed him on the mouth. "Why'd you make the coffee the way I like it?"

"Because I love you." He ran the back of his fingers against her cheek. "More than anything."

"Good. Now, go get ready for work and I'll fix breakfast."

Eddie slid off the stool as she went to work in the kitchen. He'd love nothing more than to be a team with her, but this problem was his and he would fix it. Or at least get more information. For some reason Maggie had it in for him. Bad enough she'd won the lawsuit, now she was accusing him of assault. Was she trying to ruin him, too? Maybe it was time to have a talk with this Dean Parker.

Chapter 11

Dean opened his eyes to blinding light and quickly shut them. That's what he got for not closing the stupid curtains, not that he was ever in here during daylight hours. He rolled onto his back and winced. What was with the back of his head? There was a lump the size of Kentucky and it hurt. He sat up and froze. Shit. He'd forgotten Maggie was in bed with him.

During their sleep, she'd uncovered herself and the blankets were bunched up between them. Every curve of her luscious body was exposed; her t-shirt and jeans were doing a lousy job at hiding her assets.

What was he thinking, letting her sleep here? He wasn't, that's what. But she was so tired and he did not want her going back to her house, it seemed the logical place. Sure, he could have given her his business to use—there was a bed and a shower—but he didn't trust Peter. If one ghost could possess Maggie, couldn't another? It certainly wasn't anything he wanted to mention or discover. One ghost was freaking her out enough as it was. Hell, one ghost able to possess at all was freaking him out.

God, she was beautiful, though. Wouldn't mind waking up to her every morning. But that would require more than he could give. Of course, it was probably long past morning. What time was it anyway?

Her purse blocked his clock. He leaned over Maggie and pushed it out of the way.

"Good morning," she said.

"Actually, it's afternoon." As he rolled back he was met with one set of beautiful green eyes. And a nice, lush mouth. He'd joked about her molesting him when he should have promised not to molest her. But kissing wasn't molesting, was it? It certainly wasn't a commitment.

"Is it?" she said on a sigh. A pretty sexy sigh. "And how do you feel?"

"Pretty good. Guess your prescription of sleep was just what I needed." He could think of other things he needed—like his mouth against hers.

"Yeah?" She looked at his lips. Invitation accepted. He moved toward her as she brought her hand up behind his neck and pulled him down.

Was this for real or was he dreaming? She opened up for him and he dove in for a taste. Propped up on one arm, he used his free hand and found her breast. One perfectly sized mound.

A gentleman would stop. But she tasted so good and damn, he was getting hard.

A gentleman would ignore his dick. Ah hell, he never claimed to be a gentleman. He wanted to splay her out and taste every morsel. Then feel the heat as he entered her.

He moved from kissing her mouth to nuzzling her neck. Could he have casual sex with her? Because that's all it could be. Just sex.

Probably really good sex, too.

He wouldn't know unless he tried. If she said stop, he would stop. But if by some chance she said yes...

Slowly, he slipped his hand under her shirt and then nudged the bra out of the way. Instead of stopping him, she arched into his hand. Then she let out the sexiest moan. If that wasn't encouragement enough, the clincher? Her nipple hardened.

Not as hard as his dick, but hey, it was a sign. A very good sign.

* * * *

Maggie closed her eyes as ripples of desire floated over her. And all it had taken was for Dean to rub his thumb over her nipple. If she had known what that simple touch could do, she wouldn't have stopped him the other night.

Heck, she would have made moves on him a long time ago.

While nuzzling her neck, he slid his hand down her waist, to the top of her jeans, and found the button. "May I?"

"Yes." A needy ache bloomed in her sex as he released the button and then slowly unzipped her jeans. Was this really happening? Oh yes. Yes, it was.

He ground his erection into her thigh and she boldly ran her fingers along the ridge in his pants. So long. So hard. He inhaled sharply at her touch. A sense of power came over her—she made him do that. What else could she make him do?

He found her soft folds and fingered her clit.

She gasped. Holy crap. No wonder he'd reacted. Having him touch her there was a thousand, no, a million, maybe a billion times better than touching herself. "Oh God. That feels…awesome."

Which seemed so inadequate to say since there were no words for what she felt.

"Good. Hate to think I was doing it wrong."

No, he definitely wasn't doing anything wrong. In fact, he could continue to do whatever it was he was doing…forever.

His mouth covered hers again. His tongue went deeper, like he couldn't get enough of her. He lit a fuse inside her; she could explode at any minute. And they hadn't even done "it" yet.

"Maggie, I want to be in you so bad, but if you're not ready…"

"I was stupid to stop you before. I want you, too."

"Then let's get you out of these clothes." Grinning, he straddled her legs and pulled her upright. He grabbed the bottom of her t-shirt and yanked it off. Instinctively, she moved to adjust her bra, but he held her hands. "Don't. God, you're beautiful."

Nerves struck. Should she tell him before or after? Before. Definitely before. It was the right thing to do. She hoped. But with him sitting on his knees and grinning as if she was giving him a show—and man, she'd never get enough of that smiling face—she knew if she didn't say it now, she never would and then what would he think of her? "I'm not on the pill."

Okay, that wasn't exactly what she wanted to say.

"So you said the other night. Don't worry. I've got condoms." He ran his finger along the ridge of her bra. All kinds of warmth followed his touch.

Tell him, tell him, tell him! She closed her eyes as he reached for the clasp in back. His body heat nearly melted the words from her brain. "Just so you know, I've never done this before."

He kissed her while he slid the straps down her arms. "What? Having sex *after* sleeping at the guy's house?"

A nervous chuckle escaped. They were kind of doing it backward, weren't they? "Yeah. No. I mean both."

"Both?" He stilled while his forehead scrunched up in confusion.

"I'm a virgin."

She'd never uttered those words to anyone, so wasn't sure what to expect. Laughter? Possibly. Compassion? That would have been nice. Him scrambling off the bed as if he'd been burned? Not even close.

"You're a virgin?"

Suddenly self aware, she tugged the blanket up to her chin. "Is that a problem?"

"How old are you?"

"Why does that matter?"

He went from standing stock-still to pacing. "It doesn't. I'm sorry. It's just...I mean...I'll think more clearly if I hop into the shower. Don't leave. We need to talk."

"Talk?" The bathroom door shut on her question. If he'd heard her, he was ignoring her.

Tears leaked out of her eyes and she brushed them away. She should have never said anything. Just let things happen. He probably wouldn't have even noticed.

Instead, he didn't want anything to do with her. When did a virgin status garner such...disdain? Well, she wasn't going to sit around and wait for him to yell at her. Or worse—stare at her like she was some kind of alien. As she hunted for her clothes, the shower turned on. Good, he wouldn't hear her leaving.

She quickly got dressed, slipped on her coat, and grabbed her purse. When she opened his door to the bright midday sun and the ground below could be seen through the slats, her heart seized. She closed the door and slunk to the floor. Oh God. She was trapped.

* * * *

The cold water shocked the desire right out of Dean's body. Remembering the pain on Maggie's face had helped, too. How could he leave her like that? What was he thinking? He wasn't. He'd panicked. "Great going, turd-face."

Now he had to go out there and face her. Hell if he knew what they would talk about. How could he take her virginity? This was Maggie, for Christ's sake. If she'd been holding onto it this long, wouldn't she be holding it out for a future husband? He certainly wasn't husband material.

Technically, he shouldn't have even been born.

The right thing to do would be to let her go to find someone else. Except that left a bitter taste in his mouth. Why couldn't he stay with her a little while longer? At least until he solved her problem? Just without the sex. He didn't want to lose her. Not yet, anyway.

He stepped out of the shower and dried off. First, he'd apologize to her. But as he got dressed, all he could do was stare at the door. Okay, maybe first he'd comb his hair, then he'd apologize. After every hair was in place, he took two steps toward the door and stopped. Teeth. He should brush his teeth.

His dentist would have been proud with the amount of time he'd spent cleaning them. He rinsed and stared at the door. Wiped his mouth and stared at the door. Nothing left to do now but face his fate, whatever that might be. He put his hand on the cool doorknob, took a deep breath, and opened the door.

The bed was empty. Disappointment stung his heart. What did he expect? That she'd stay after he'd pretty much insulted her? Well, he could find her at home and then he'd apologize. He headed toward the living room and froze.

Sitting on the floor against the front door with her legs pulled up to her chest, Maggie rested her forehead against her knees. She hadn't moved when he entered. Either she was asleep or, even worse, crying.

"Maggie?"

She jerked and opened her eyes, but kept her head down and her sight trained on her feet.

"I'm surprised you're still here," he said, but awfully glad. Helping her with her ghost problem while at odds with one another would have been difficult.

"I was going to leave. But then remembered your car is back at my place and I thought you might need a ride."

"I would have taken a cab." Was she for real? He basically rejected her and she wanted to give him a ride to his car? Or was there more to it? Whatever, she stayed and that was all that mattered. He walked over to her. "What are you doing on the floor?"

"You said the couch was uncomfortable."

"And the floor isn't?"

She shrugged, but still wouldn't look at him. He crouched in front of her and lifted her chin. She yanked her head away. The tear running down her cheek just about killed him. He'd done that to her.

"Ah, Maggie. I'm sorry."

She stared at him with red-rimmed eyes. "For what? For me being a virgin or for you almost bedding one?"

That stung, not that he didn't deserve it. "Neither. You caught me off guard and I reacted horribly. There's nothing wrong with you."

"Yeah, right." She swiped at the tear as if it were a traitor and lowered her head to her knees.

"It's true. There isn't. It's me. All me."

She lifted her head and hit him with a you've-got-to-be-kidding-me look. "Don't tell me you couldn't get it up. I felt you."

And her touch had been ecstasy. "It has nothing to do with my desire for you. I just didn't think I'd be your first. I've never been anyone's first before."

"What does that have to do with it?"

"Most women I've talked to think their first time was a mistake."

"So you're saying I should go do it with someone else first?" She shoved him away, sending him on his ass, and stood. "What kind of sicko are you?"

"Oh God, no. That's not what I meant." Even the thought of her with someone churned his stomach. He slowly got to his feet.

"Then what did you mean?"

"I don't want to be a mistake." Again. Couldn't forget that part. "Especially since you've been saving yourself."

A laughing snort escaped her mouth. "Even if I am saving myself, and I'm not saying I am, I like you. A lot. I don't see you as a mistake."

Damn, she made it sound like he was the one—*her* one. "You might want to know me better before you go saying that."

She crossed her arms and paused in thought. "Okay."

"Okay, what?"

"Okay, I'll be your girlfriend. It's what you meant, right?"

Wow. His mind hadn't even gone there. But it'd be one sure-fire way to protect her. He'd have a reason to be with her all the time. That wouldn't be so bad, would it? "You want to be my girlfriend even knowing I won't have sex with you?"

She shrugged. "You want to get to know each other better first. I'm good with that."

First, as if there would be sex later. Yeah, that wasn't going to happen once she realized he wasn't right for her. Hopefully she'd come to that conclusion soon, or as soon after he solved her problem, because rejecting her again just might kill him. If his blue balls didn't do the trick first.

Chapter 12

In all the years since her mother's death, Maggie hadn't felt the loss as deeply as she did now. Sure, she could talk to Dad, except he was in Florida and she didn't really think he'd be all that keen on talking about her first love.

Because, yeah, she loved Dean.

Maybe if she had talked to Mom about a certain incident that happened with Eddie, Maggie wouldn't have escaped from the world in her writing. She might have gone out more. Dated more. Okay, dated, period. And maybe one of those dates would have led to sex. She hadn't saved her virginity for marriage, but it was kind of sweet that Dean thought she had.

Then again, wouldn't losing her virginity with someone she loved—Dean—be better than with some fling? Guess she'd never know, because he was the only one she wanted to be intimate with. Why couldn't he just forget about the no-sex thing? Figured when she found the right guy he'd be all moral about it. Somehow she'd have to get him to change his mind.

Telling him she loved him would not be the way to do that. He'd freaked out over her virgin status, she could only imagine how he'd react if she uttered the L word. It would help to know exactly where he stood when it came to the two of them, though.

"So we're doing this boyfriend-girlfriend thing...exclusively?" she asked.

"There's no one else I want to date. You?"

She shook her head. Why was her heart beating so fast? He gave the right answer.

"Good." Dean approached her and she nearly stepped back. Which would have been silly. He wasn't going to hurt her. And while she was wondering what he was up to, he leaned down and kissed her. Just a simple little brush of his lips against hers, but the contact alone lit her up again. Before she had a chance to grab him by the neck and plunge her tongue inside his mouth, he stepped back. "There. Sealed with a kiss."

Well, it wasn't a commitment, but it was a start.

"Ready to go?" Dean slipped on his coat. "We'll get you checked into a hotel and then get my car."

And just like that she went from elated to deflated. "Hotel? What are you talking about?"

"About getting you out of that house. You're entitled to vacation time, right?"

"I'm not taking a vacation. I've been away from work long enough."

"No, no, no. You misunderstood. I meant vacation from the house. You get a hotel room and stay there a week while still going to work."

"I'm not spending money on a hotel I don't need. You're not even sure she's possessing me."

"Oh, she's possessing you. I'd stake my life on it."

"I'm not having a ghost chase me out of my own home. I'll just continue to chain myself to the house."

"That won't stop her from possessing you. That'll only stop her from taking you out of the house. Please, give me until Saturday."

"And what would you have me tell Erica? I'm guessing not everyone knows you see ghosts."

He lowered his head. "No, they don't."

His dejection hurt her heart. Would spending a week in a hotel really be all that bad? Yes, it would. Why should she spend her hard-earned money on something she didn't need to? The ghost certainly wasn't going to reimburse her for that expense and neither would Dean. She'd make sure of it. "I don't see why you can't talk to Lindy."

"Talking to Lindy won't do any good. She'll say what I want to hear and then do what she wants to do. Same as every other ghost."

"How many ghosts do you know?"

"Enough." He opened the door. "I'll think of something to tell Erica. Let's go."

Oh God. The steps. With palms extended and eyes downcast, she shut the door with them still inside. "This isn't settled. I'm not getting a hotel room."

Heck, she may never leave his apartment. How long before the sun set?

"Then you leave me no choice. I'll just move in with you."

Move in? But Lindy... "You would do that knowing she almost killed you?"

He shrugged. "I don't know how else to keep you safe."

She'd never felt so loved before. That he would put her safety before his own. "I don't know about you, but I think better on a full stomach. Why don't I fix us some lunch here and we can discuss it further? Figure out all the pros and cons."

Then maybe afterward she'd get the nerve to go down those stairs. Even better, the sun set in about four hours. Could she delay them that long?

"That would be a good plan if I had any food. There's a place around the corner we can go to."

So much for prolonging the inevitable. "I don't really want to talk about this in public, do you? I have food at my house. Lindy can't hurt either one of us if we're together, right? Then maybe if she hears us talking about it, she'll have a change of heart."

"Hardly," he said on a snort. "But you're right. I don't necessarily want to talk about this in public. So, we can go now?" Raising an eyebrow, he put his hand on the door knob.

Oh crap. Do or die. After a nod from her, he opened the door. One deep breath later, she stepped outside and kept her back to the railing and impending death, her focus on the side of the building.

Mustn't.

Look.

Down.

He locked up and stared at the spot where she was gazing. "What are you looking at?"

"Nothing. Just thinking. About a scene. In my book." A lie, but it was possible. Erica had caught her staring off into nothing many times.

He offered his arm. "Is that so? Can you share?"

How many times had she wished to share her ideas with Erica, but every time Maggie started talking about her latest project, Erica's eyes would glaze over. Figured he'd be interested. Why did all his good traits come at the wrong time?

"I'd rather not. Bad luck." Maggie grabbed onto him with one hand and the rail with the other. If only there was an idea to share. Then maybe she could stop thinking about falling.

"Bad luck? How so?"

"My muse gets mad." Which was a boatload of crap. She didn't believe in muses. And she'd give anything to think of an idea to discuss. Anything to distract her from impending death.

They reached the first half-landing and the parking lot came into view. Her vision swirled and her heart skipped a few beats. When did two-and-a-half floors become so darned high? If she had seen this coming up, she never would have made it to Dean's apartment. Not conscious, anyway.

"So how do you come up with ideas? Just think of scary events?"

And just like that she got the distraction she needed. She'd kiss him if it was even remotely safe. "Scary events help."

Scary, like heights. Boy, could she work with that one now.

Discussing books in general helped her climb down the stairs without throwing up and by the time they reached the bottom, she nearly kissed the ground.

"You're shaking. Are you thinking about that scary scene again?"

Scary scene? Oh, the book. "Nah, just cold. What is it? Twenty degrees out here?" She pulled her keys out of her purse with shaky hands. Good thing it was freezing out. "Should have brought my gloves."

"Want me to drive?"

Oh God, yes. "You feel up to it?"

"My neck is only a little sore. Other than that, I'm fine." He held the door and waited for her to climb into the passenger seat. When he squeezed behind the steering wheel, he scraped his head in the process. He rubbed the offending site. "Okay, maybe I have more pain. But for the life of me I don't know how I got this bump on my head."

Guilt burned Maggie's cheeks. "Oh, well, that would be me. I kind of dropped you when I dragged you from your car. Sorry."

His laughter filled the interior and lightened her mood. "Glad that mystery is solved. I'm surprised you were able to get me out of the car at all. Hell, I have trouble getting out of that thing."

After he adjusted the seat, he took off for her house. Once the heat kicked in, his scent filled the enclosure. All musky and male, it sent her libido in overdrive. If sitting this close to him got her motor running, how might it be if he was living in her house? He'd said no sex. She'd never had it and wasn't sure she could survive being so close and not sampling. What kind of willpower did he have, anyway?

He pulled his phone out of his pocket and handed it over. "Can you read that text for me?"

It was from his employee. "Sam says he still needs to talk to you about the Mitchell case and wants to know if he can stop by your place."

"Tell him I'll be in the office by three. That should give us enough time to discuss all the pros and cons, won't it?"

"Right. Pros and cons." Pro for staying at home: Dean lived at her house. Con: Lindy still possessed her. Pro for staying in a hotel: Lindy didn't possess her. Con: Dean didn't live at her house. Okay, maybe it wasn't a valid con, but it was a con all the same. The future discussion seemed hopeless. Maggie texted the information back to Sam and returned the phone to Dean.

She directed him down an alley to the garage behind her house. While he shut off the engine, she put her hand on the door handle and hesitated opening it. A ghost lived here. Not just any ghost, but her late aunt. Staying at a hotel was starting to sound good, regardless of the cons.

But what she couldn't see couldn't hurt her. At least not while she was awake.

She climbed out of the car and led Dean up the path through the backyard to the backdoor. She pulled out her key. Her hands shook once again and not from the cold or from heights, but because her Aunt Lindy could very well be standing beside her. Maggie shuddered.

"You okay? Want me to get that?"

"I got it." She steeled herself and unlocked the door. Nothing seemed any different. No cold blasts. But then, she'd never felt them before so why would it start?

"I'm surprised you haven't heard from Erica. Is your phone dead?"

After punching in the security code, Maggie walked through the kitchen to the living room and placed her purse on the table beside the couch. "No. I texted her from the restaurant. Kind of led her to believe that I was taking care of you at your place. So if she happens to act giddy around you that would be why. She seems to think we'd make beautiful babies." Shit. Now why'd she go and blurt out that?

He choked as if something had gone down the wrong pipe. Most likely her words. "She what?"

"She didn't mean anything by it. I don't mean anything by it. I'm going to go upstairs and freshen up and then I'll fix lunch." Babies? Now that would be kind of hard to do with the whole no-sex thing. And why was she obsessed with sex anyway? She should be more worried about the ghost possessing her body. Sure could be an excellent excuse for her big mouth. Sheesh.

* * * *

As Maggie climbed the stairs, Dean pictured her heavy with child. Yeah, that was the thing. She would make a great mother whereas he wasn't about to spread that bastard's genes around. He couldn't do that to his mother. Or to the man he'd considered his father.

He returned to the kitchen, where a ghost slammed into him and hugged him tight.

"I'm so glad you're not dead!" Lindy said.

Dean tugged on her cold arms—it'd be his luck if she cracked a rib or three—but she held on tight. "Ease up, ghost. I can't breathe."

"Oh, sorry." She released him and stepped back. "You feel kind of good, though. Warm."

"So I've been told."

"I didn't mean to hurt you. Last night, that is. You gotta know that. I didn't even know I was that strong."

"Yeah, I kind of figured that out."

"I only meant to scare you, but scared myself instead. If I kill someone, I might be stuck here forever, huh? So you don't have to worry about me, I won't hurt you again."

"That's nice to know." Not that he believed a word of it. "But what about Maggie? Are you going to stop possessing her?"

"I never said I was possessing her."

"Oh, cut the crap. We both know it was you. I don't see any other ghost here."

"Fine. So I'm possessing her. Big deal. You don't know what it's like being stuck in a bubble for forty years. I just wanted to have some fun."

"Fun? You call rape fun?"

Her eyes widened. "What are you talking about? No one got raped."

"What do you call that little seduction you performed on me the other night?"

"Are you telling me you wouldn't have enjoyed it? 'Cause you sure look interested."

Could she really be that dense? "You think because you want to have sex, or you get some unsuspecting guy to want sex, that it's not rape? Well, what about Maggie? She hasn't given you permission to use her body to have sex. She hasn't given you permission for anything. That, in my book, is called rape."

Lindy lowered her head. "I didn't know. But if it makes you feel any better, nothing happened."

"And nothing better. Maggie doesn't need to lose her virginity because you're looking for fun."

"Virginity? But-but, she's old!"

He couldn't blame Lindy thinking that. Hell, he'd thought the same thing. Still, it wasn't his business why Maggie was saving herself. Only that she was.

"You stop possessing her and I promise to find a way to help you." Oh, why did he even bother? Like a ghost could be trusted to keep a deal. At least Maggie's virginity was intact, if he could believe Lindy about that.

"Promises mean shit, you know that?" Lindy popped out of the room.

"Wait!" Ah, shit. She was gone.

"Wait for what?" Maggie stopped in the entrance to the kitchen. "Oh. You've been talking to her, haven't you?"

"Yeah. She kind of apologized for attacking me."

"Better than attacking you, huh? What about possessing me?"

"She hasn't exactly said she'd stop."

Maggie pulled out foodstuff from the fridge and placed it on the counter. "I can't believe she wouldn't, not if we explained it to her. Mom always said Lindy was selfless."

"Maybe when she was a naïve sixteen-year-old. Being stuck as a ghost for over forty years can change a person." Somehow he had to get Maggie and Erica out of the house without Erica finding out the real reason.

The old cabinets caught his attention. Old, wooden cabinets. Could that be the answer? He opened up one of the doors. Yeah, really old wood.

"What are you looking for?" she asked.

"I'm thinking you might have termites."

Maggie dropped the knife with a clatter. Mayonnaise splattered. "What? Where?"

He fingered the old nicks in the wood. "I'm no expert, but this could be their handiwork. We'll need to get a fumigator in here to be sure. Could take a week."

After inspecting the spot he pointed to, she narrowed her eyes at him. "Are you saying that to get us out of the house?"

Guess he couldn't pull one over on her, but there was a reason he always won arguments. "What do you think Erica would say if I mentioned termites to her?"

She yanked a paper towel free and wiped up her mess. "You know, I'm beginning to see a pattern with you, Dean."

First it was the fire in her eyes when she suspected he was manipulating her. Then it was the jiggle of her ass as she cleaned. Damn, he was getting hard. Good thing he could get her out of the house. If he had to live here—and he would if she remained stubborn—he might have a permanent boner.

She tossed the towel into the trash can. "Do you think the fumigator thing will work?"

"It'll work to get you and Erica out of the house. Whether or not you need to be treated for termites is for the fumigator to say. Just leave it to me, okay? Now, are you going to finish those sandwiches? I'm starving."

She patted his stomach and smiled. "I have a feeling you're always hungry."

Maybe not for food, but he sure was hungry for her. That little touch only increased that appetite, too. Yeah, it was a good thing he was getting her out of the house. From Lindy and him. It was the only way to ensure she stayed pure.

* * * *

Maggie and Dean ate their lunch while Lindy hovered in the kitchen. So her sister thought she was selfless. Yeah, maybe she had been, back when she was alive. Death was a whole 'nother matter. If she didn't look out for herself, no one else would. Not even Dean.

He was out to get her. Why else get the girls out of the house? And what did he hope to achieve during a week? Maybe he expected to convince her he could help. Ha! As if that was even possible.

His accusation still stung. She'd never even considered what she was doing came close to rape. And he had to be lying about Maggie being a virgin. Besides, Maggie wouldn't even know what was going on, so there was no way she could be traumatized even if she was a virgin, which she wasn't. Couldn't be. It didn't make any sense. The woman wasn't ugly. But with Dean keen on Lindy's plan, she'd have to figure out a way to convince him she'd go straight. Guess she had a week to do it, too.

Damn. Another week of misery. If only she hadn't gotten cold feet. First that guy at the bar, then the guy at the café. But they weren't really into her. They hadn't looked at her like Kevin used to. Or like Dean had the other night. Not even like Eddie had, back in 2000. Now that would have been perfect.

On that fateful day the sun had been shining and Eddie was mowing the lawn. Caroline and her husband had dropped thirteen-year-old Maggie off for the day. Maggie followed Eddie around like a little puppy, or a girl who had a crush on an older boy. So when he snuck out to the garage for a toke, she managed to find him.

He tried to get her to leave. She said she would tell on him if he didn't let her try one. Eddie was a wimp, plain and simple. He handed the weed over to Maggie. After a few tokes and several coughing spasms, she glowed.

Intrigued, Lindy hovered closer and felt a tug. Similar to being dragged into the water when someone close had jumped in. A few more inches closer and Lindy had gotten sucked straight into Maggie's body. Startled, Lindy was able to pop out, but it only took a few seconds to realize what a wonderful thing had happened. She moved toward Maggie and let the invisible string pull her inside.

First thing she noticed: the heat. Wonderful, glorious heat. Next thing she noticed: the air was filled with the scent of freshly cut grass mixed in with the pungent smell of marijuana. She moved Maggie's hands and feet and touched the ground. How was it even possible?

Eddie laughed. "Feeling it now, aren't you?"

Feeling it? Oh. He thought she was high. And in a way she was. She stared at the boy beside her. Technically, he was her nephew, but not by blood—a secret Lindy had overheard years before. Maybe if he were a blood relative, she wouldn't have gone as far as she had, but that possessing thing had really shocked the shit out of her.

He'd been about her age—sixteen—and while Eddie was no Kevin, he was cute, even if he was a little chubby. His eyes were glassy and he was probably stoned out of his mind, but she wasn't about to blow this miracle. She kissed him.

What a rush. It had been so long since she'd kissed a boy.

When he groped her boob—well, actually, Maggie's boob, and maybe, when she thought about it now, he could have been pushing her away—Lindy spurred into action. She shoved her hand down his pants and grabbed his penis. He gasped and widened his eyes, but didn't pull her hand away. In a matter of moments, he grew hard.

Her dream was coming true. She would finally have sex. The only thing that would have made the moment perfect was if the boy was Kevin. But hey, she wasn't going to refuse this miracle.

She quickly got undressed and, lying there naked, she managed to convince him to get his pants off, although he fumbled for a bit. Then bad luck struck. Either she lost control or the weed had worn off. Pop! Lindy had been shoved out with such a force that she'd flown through the wall.

Maggie had screamed rape.

Eddie had screamed tease.

Lindy wanted to cry. The tug was gone. Gone! So close. So damn close.

If she hadn't lost control and had gone through with it, would it really have been rape? Good thing Dean didn't know about that incident, then. He might never let Maggie move back. That man took the fun out of everything.

But that experience had taught Lindy something: her existence could be fun once again. Because that night? Maggie had glowed. The tug had returned. Lindy had wasted no time and set in motion what had taken her years to see accomplished. She wasn't about to let Dean ruin it all.

Maybe she should take him to Rhonda. Bet that ghost could do some damage to him and get him out of the way. Lindy smiled. That might work. And anything that scary ghost did would be on her, not Lindy. Now to figure out a way to do all that.

Man, why couldn't death be easy?

* * * *

Eddie drove into the little parking lot that bordered the two businesses. Figured the private investigator was next door to *those* lawyers. Was everyone in cahoots against him?

Police said he had no right to retaliate against Maggie's false claim. That no one had been hurt in the process. Well, what about him? He'd nearly lost his wife over this. Maggie had only mentioned Eddie's name to the cops for revenge. Plain and simple.

Well, if she wanted revenge, she should have gone after the real culprit—Mom. She'd been insistent they file the suit in the first place—that grandma had promised his dad he'd get the house. Mom had heard it with her own ears. Or so she kept saying.

Except Dad was dead and Mom was…Mom. She and Grandma never had gotten along very well. A lot could have happened to change Grandma's mind. Didn't seem fair he'd gotten short changed, though.

But he wasn't here about that failed lawsuit. He was here about Maggie's false claim. To make sure this Dean Parker wasn't in on the scam. Being as he was neighbors with the bitch's lawyers, it wasn't looking good for the P.I.

Another car pulled into the parking lot. Dean Parker. Eddie slunk down in the seat. Should he confront the P.I. in the parking lot or his office? Keep it unofficial or make it official?

While Eddie pondered his choices, a pregnant woman came from Parker's office and approached Dean as he climbed out of his car. "Well, you don't look all that much worse for wear. How's Maggie?"

The car honked once—causing Eddie to jump a bit—and Dean pocketed his keys. "I finally talked her into moving out, with a promise to take her to dinner tonight."

"Dinner? Ahh, so you're dating now?"

The man actually blushed. "I guess you could say that. So where are you headed?"

"Um… Getting some coffee for Sam? We weren't expecting you until three."

"There's coffee in the supply closet."

"There is?"

"You know there is." Dean took her arm and shook his head. "You were going to buy some more M&M's, weren't you? Good thing I came back when I did, huh? Let's go."

"But Dean…" Her words faded as he escorted her out of sight.

Eddie sat up. Shit. It was worse than he'd thought. Maggie and Parker were fucking dating. And he didn't look like he'd suffered any attack. What exactly were they up to? Were they so petty they had to take revenge on him because of a stupid lawsuit? A lawsuit they'd won?

But wait. Maggie was moving out? This was great news. She was breaking the will and breaking the will meant the house went to its rightful owner—him. The day just got brighter. Peace was in his future.

Chapter 13

Dean leaned back in his chair and rubbed his eyes. Computers would definitely be the death of his eyesight and force him to buy glasses—*shudder*—but it was a small price to pay for the convenience. Without the Internet, he'd be driving around conducting his search, a feat that would have taken way more than ninety minutes to accomplish.

But glasses? Maybe not such a small price. He'd always prided himself on having excellent vision, because he certainly didn't have an excellent heart. Man, technology was the pits. Or was he just getting old?

Nah, technology. Definitely technology.

At least a headache hadn't accompanied the eye strain, which surely would have occurred if a certain ghost hung around to bug him. But Peter had been scarce; probably more interested in seeing what Bridget discovered in her search than being a pest. If Dean had known that was the trick in keeping the spirit away, he would've suggested the investigation months ago. It'd been too long since he'd enjoyed a quiet afternoon.

An afternoon he could have spent with Maggie. Would have spent with her if only she wasn't a virgin. Thank God she'd said something before it was too late. If he'd gone through with it, he'd never be able to face her again. Because a person didn't have casual sex with a virgin. And he definitely wasn't worthy enough to be her first. She might have expected more out of him. More than he could give her. She deserved better than that.

Which reminded him, he still needed to find a fumigator. Not that Maggie's house had termites, but if they were going to use the excuse, better make it legit. He didn't want to cause Maggie any more grief. Plus, he'd promised.

As Dean opened the search engine on his computer, the office phone rang. And rang and rang. Where the heck was Bridget?

"She's in the bathroom," Peter said upon materializing, as if Dean had asked the question aloud. "That woman sure has to go a lot."

"Comes with the pregnancy." Dean answered the call, "Parker Investigations, how may I help you? Hello?" A click sounded over the line and he returned the handset. "Guess they got the wrong number."

"So. Is it true? You're finally dating the crazy chick next door?"

Dean shook his head. He should have known his quiet afternoon wouldn't last. "Don't you have someplace else to be?"

"I'm just saying, she must be crazy if she's dating you." Peter's cackling excuse for laughter was interrupted with the sound of the toilet flushing. "Oh good. Back to work." He floated over to the door, but when he reached the hallway, he misted away.

Ha-ha! Someone must have entered the building. Served him right.

"Hello. Can I help you, sir?" Bridget asked. "Wait! Dean!"

Dean grabbed the baseball bat leaning against the wall. The first time someone barged their way inside, he'd nearly gotten clocked. Subsequent times he'd fared much better, not that he would have used the bat. But it sure made a nice statement.

He rounded the desk to confront his visitor and froze in mid-step. The one person he'd hoped to never see again appeared in the doorway.

"Do I need to call the police?" Bridget asked.

If only it would be that easy. "No. It's okay. I know him. Thanks."

"Okay. I'm headed to my doctor's appointment. See you tomorrow."

Bridget left and Dean faced his brother.

His twin brother.

Not that Bridget would have known; they didn't look anything alike. Fraternal twins, they were called. Made for a handy explanation—especially since Dean was six-three, built like a line

Stacy McKitrick

backer, and had sandy brown hair, while Greg was slimmer, dark-haired, and only five-eleven. Dean had grown up assuming Greg had taken after Dad and he'd taken after Mom, but the truth was they had different fathers. A realization that had hit Dean after the fiasco with his damaged heart—a trait no one in his mother's and supposed father's family carried. But Greg didn't know the truth and Dean preferred it stayed that way.

"You gonna hit me with that?" Greg pointed to the bat.

While Dean had never intended to see his brother again, it wasn't because he'd disliked the guy. Who wanted to see the truth every day? He returned the bat to its home. "Sorry. Habit."

"Habit? I thought your cases were non-violent."

"They are, but when a client barges in…" Dean shrugged.

"Is that what happened to your neck? An angry client?"

"Something like that." Dean adjusted his shirt. Damn it. He should have worn the turtleneck. "What are you doing here?"

Greg sat in the chair and propped his right ankle up on his left knee. "Looking for you. You don't return my calls. You don't answer my e-mails. You don't even answer my letters. I don't know what the hell I did to you, but you have to come home."

Dean sat in his chair. Home? Cleveland had stopped being home four years ago. "Sorry. Ain't happening. I'm busy. I can't just up and leave."

"Even for Mom?"

"What are you talking about? Mom's fine. I talked to her last weekend." And he called every weekend, just as a dutiful son should. It was easier to deny the truth—or ignore the lies—when you couldn't see the person's face. He had his assumptions and didn't wish to get them confirmed or denied, because denial would only make matters worse.

"That's just it. She sounds fine, but she certainly doesn't look it. But whenever I suggest she see a doctor, she poo-poos me. I'm scared, Dean. You need to come home and see for yourself. She'll listen to you."

Dean nearly laughed at his brother's attempt at flattery. Maybe she'd listened to him in the past, but not now. Definitely not now. "Trust me, she doesn't want to see me."

"What are you talking about? She complains about you not visiting all the time."

114

That wasn't really a surprise. What mother wouldn't complain about their son not visiting? She'd probably only did it so no one would question why she wasn't complaining. Dean shook his head. "Can't you call Aunt Di?"

"Please, Dean. I'm begging you. I don't know what I did to piss you off four years ago, but I don't need you hating me because I didn't force you to see her. I pray to God I'm overreacting, but what if I'm not? Do you really want to take that chance?"

No, he didn't. Damn it. Guess he was going to Cleveland. But picturing the hatred in his mother's eyes made his stomach churn.

* * * *

Eddie parked around the corner from his grandmother's house—he refused to think of it as Maggie's—and walked down the darkened alley where the garages to all the homes were located. Still no lights shone from inside the house. When he'd driven past he'd kind of hoped someone was home because he really didn't want to do what Mom had asked him to do.

It was his own fault for telling her that Maggie was moving out. Instead of being happy with the news, Mom had announced that now was the time to break in and search the attic. Well, that was news to him. He hadn't even known there was anything of value in the house. But when he argued to wait until they won the suit, she'd insisted now would be the perfect time to get what was due them.

Them. Not him. Oh sure, he wanted the stupid house for her, but only to get her out of his own. Not once had she ever mentioned this supposed valuable object.

"What is it?" he'd asked.

"It's probably in a photo album, so just get them all."

"*What's* in a photo album?"

Her silence had been a slap in the face. After everything he'd done for her, she still didn't trust him with the details. Before he could tell her to go screw herself and get the damn photo albums herself, Ronnie had entered the room. Her timing was perfect, as usual.

So, like a good son, he'd departed to follow her crazy plan. Although why she thought Maggie wouldn't have found this valuable object already was beyond him, but if he'd voiced that opinion it would have only caused another argument. Good sons didn't argue with their mothers.

He walked around the garage and let himself in through the gate. He'd spent many a summer here mowing Grandma's lawn and helping out however he could. He'd loved the old woman and thought she'd loved him back. If Grandma had issues, why couldn't she have talked to him instead of leaving everything to Maggie? It just didn't make sense.

Unless... Had Maggie told Grandma about that summer? No, she couldn't have. Grandma would have said something either to him or Mom. And neither had said a word. Besides, he and Maggie were stoned out of their minds. She would have gotten into just as much trouble if she'd admitted anything, and he was pretty sure he'd scared her into keeping her mouth shut.

He climbed the steps to the back door. He fished out the key his mother had given him. As he slid it in the lock, the sign on the window caught his attention. He quickly removed the key.

Alarm? The house had an alarm? Since when? Shit. And he'd almost triggered the stupid thing.

Oh, great. Just what he needed. Another reason for his mother to yell at him. Would anything ever go his way?

* * * *

At nine o'clock, Dean's stomach objected to missing dinner—a dinner he was supposed to have had with Maggie. God, he'd hated breaking that date. He'd been afraid she'd go back to the house. But she promised she wouldn't. Instead, she and Erica were staying at Erica's parents' house.

Not perfect—he'd no idea if ghosts hung around there, too—but at least she was away from Lindy.

He pulled onto Mom's driveway alongside Greg's car and shut off the engine. Opening the door would be the next logical step, but Dean couldn't bring his hand to the lever. Why, oh why did he come here? He should start the car, back up, and head home where one wonderful woman was waiting for him.

Greg stopped those plans by opening the door. "Thanks for not turning around. I almost expected you'd do that."

"And have you hunt me down again? No thanks." Resigned to his fate, Dean climbed out of the car. "It's late. Do you think she's up?"

"She's up. I sometimes wonder if she sleeps at all. I think she still misses Dad. Is that why you haven't visited? You know you're not to blame."

Maybe not directly, but the semantics didn't matter. Dad—correction: Greg's dad—wouldn't have been on the road at all if not for Dean. And Mom wouldn't have lost the love of her life. He knew better than to hang around and become a constant reminder of all the things that shouldn't have happened. "I haven't visited because I've been busy. You think running a business is easy?"

"What happened to you, Dean? It's like the doctor cut out a part of your heart instead of fixing the hole. Ever since then you've been…different."

Yeah. Knowledge tended to do that to a person. "I'm tired, okay? Let's get this over with."

"Aren't you gonna get your bag?"

He'd only packed it to placate his brother. "I don't plan on staying here."

"Yeah, right." Greg opened the back door and grabbed the bag. "You really think Mom's going to let you stay in a hotel? Think again. Besides, how do you expect to convince her to see a doctor if you're not here to see how she is?"

"I don't need to spend the night to see her." He swiped for the bag as Greg pulled it away. "Give it back, you little twerp."

Greg grinned. "Make me."

It'd probably been ten years since Dean last tackled his brother and that grin only egged him on. "You are so dead."

"Dean? Is that you?" Mom stood on the porch for a second, then came bursting into the yard.

"You didn't tell her I was coming?"

"Hell, no," Greg whispered before smiling at Mom. "Look who I found wandering around Cleveland."

The woman who hugged Dean tight was not the vibrant woman he'd left four years ago. She was only sixty, but looked ancient. She looked…breakable. "Oh, my baby. You've come back. You've really come back."

Dean attempted to unhook his mother's arms, but she held on tight and he didn't want to hurt her. And returning the hug didn't seem…right. Not anymore. If his biological father had only left her alone, then he wouldn't have been conceived. Wouldn't have been born. And then her husband wouldn't have died in a stupid car accident on his way to the hospital to visit a man he thought was his son. He'd still be here with his family.

"Mom, let's go inside where it's warmer," Greg said.

She finally released Dean and looked at Greg. "Oh yes. Inside would be good. Would you like some hot cocoa?"

Hot cocoa brought on memories of Maggie. He'd have to call her tonight and tell her...something. Especially if he was stuck here awhile.

Greg stared at Dean for a beat then handed the bag over. "Sounds good, but I can't stay. Just wanted to make sure the old brute didn't get lost. I'll be back in the morning to take you to breakfast, though. You too, Dean."

"What time do I need to be here?" Because there was no way Mom would want him to spend the night, regardless of what Greg thought.

"What are you talking about?" Mom asked. "You're staying the night."

Okay, that totally didn't make sense. Unless it was for Greg's benefit. Then, maybe it did.

Greg nudged Dean. "Told ya."

She hugged Greg and kissed him on the cheek. "I love you."

"I love you, too, Mom."

As Greg drove off, Dean followed Mom into the house. Sweat broke out on his brow and upper lip and it had nothing to do with nerves. "How high do you have the heat on?"

"I don't know. I turn it up until I'm comfortable."

God, her heating bill must be enormous. How did she afford it? He dropped the bag on the floor and hung up his coat on the hook by the door. Beside another, familiar coat. A sharp pain stabbed his chest. How many more memories would he stumble across?

A lot, it seemed. The couch was against the same wall as ever and Mom's latest knitting project covered one of the cushions. He still owned every scarf she'd ever made him and probably would have kept the sweaters if they'd still fit. And had anyone used Dad's recliner since his death? Dean could almost see him sitting in the chair, reading his paper.

Dean rubbed his chest as he headed into the kitchen. Whether it was phantom or real, the pain felt the same. How much pain did his mother suffer? "You still have Dad's coat?"

She lit the burner under the kettle. "Well, it's my coat, now. I find it's the warmest. So, what brought you to Cleveland? You didn't mention a trip when we talked last."

No use lying to her. "Greg did. He's worried about you and I have to say, he has good reason. You don't look well."

She shook her head and joined him at the kitchen table. "No, I look old. And that's because I am."

"You're only sixty. That's not so old."

Her eyes widened. "What happened to your neck?"

Ah, damn it. Dean adjusted his collar. "A run-in with a client. I'm fine."

"Did you see a doctor?"

"Yes. Have you?"

"There's nothing wrong with me."

"Mom..."

"There isn't."

"Then what's the problem? Go to the doctor. Let him tell us you're perfectly healthy. Then we can stop worrying about you."

She sighed heavily. "Fine, I'll go. But only if you promise not to stay away so long."

"We talk on the phone every week." Seemed she was going to put on airs for him, too. Why couldn't she just be herself and kick him out of the house?

"That's not the same as seeing you. Dayton's not that far away. You can spare a weekend every now and again, couldn't you?"

"I work on the weekends, too."

"But not every weekend." The whistling kettle spurred her into action. After turning off the stove, she pulled out cups, saucers, and the cocoa mix. "I don't care if it took Greg's wheedling to get you up here. I'm so happy to see you."

Dean smiled for her, but it didn't reach his heart. Apparently, she was sick and living in Fantasy Land or she was just being polite. Still, it was nice feeling her love again, even if it was fabricated.

Chapter 14

Maggie stared at the calendar. Tuesday had turned into Wednesday, which morphed into Thursday, finally crawling into Friday. No sooner had Dean promised to talk to Lindy than he'd gotten a case that took precedence.

Sure, he had to make a living, and sure, she was safe as long as she stayed away from her house, but that didn't mean she was happy about it. How long did it take to talk to a ghost anyway?

And no, her foul mood couldn't possibly be attributed to the fact she hadn't heard from Dean since Monday evening, when he'd called to cancel their date.

She'd expected to hear more from him—especially about the fumigators—but when her third call went to voicemail, she'd stopped calling. Either he was too busy to talk or he was avoiding her. If he didn't want to have a relationship, why'd he agree to date? The man made no sense.

With the weekend looming ahead, Maggie wasn't sure what to do. She couldn't stay with Erica's folks indefinitely. Besides, Erica was going stir-crazy having her every minute watched and wanted to know how much longer before the fumigators were finished. The only good thing about the week: not once had Maggie fallen asleep at her desk. She'd been getting rest every single night. But her week was up and she needed to move back. She'd like to do it with Dean's okay.

A man bundled up in a parka walked into the office. "Maggie Russell?"

"Yes?"

"You've been served." He pulled an envelope out of his satchel and placed it on her desk. "Have a good day."

"Wait. What?" But when she looked up, he'd already gone out the door.

Served? No way. She ripped open the envelope and nearly cried. Sued. Again. It was just like Eddie to pull this stunt on a Friday afternoon. The lawyers were all gone for the day. The only reason she wasn't, too, was because she'd hope to see Dean.

She stood and jerked on her coat. None of this would be happening if Dean had done what he'd said. She grabbed her purse from the drawer and slammed it shut. If he wouldn't take her calls, then she'd get Bridget's help. After locking the doors, Maggie stormed over to Parker Investigations.

She yanked the door open to a startled Bridget.

"Hi, Maggie. What's—"

"Where is he?"

Bridget smiled. "On his way in, actually, but he may be a while. Is everything okay?"

Maggie wagged the papers while frustrated tears threatened to fall. "No, everything is not okay. I'm being sued. Again. And Tom isn't in...and..." Damn it. She couldn't say the rest. Bridget didn't know about her case. Did she? Maggie collapsed on the chair and wiped her eyes.

Bridget sat in the chair beside her and wrapped her arm around her shoulder. "And what?"

Maggie wanted to divulge it all, but it wasn't her place to share Dean's ability. "Doesn't matter. He's busy. I understand."

"Maybe I can help. What's this about being sued?"

Okay, the house part she could share. "My cousin Eddie. He apparently found out I'm not living at the house. I can lose it, that's if I haven't lost it already."

"Oh crap. Dean was supposed to talk to Lindy, wasn't he? Guess I'll have to do it instead then."

"You can talk to..." Damn. Just how many people saw ghosts?

"He didn't tell you?" When Maggie shook her head, Bridget smiled. "Wow. That was sweet of him. But yeah, I have the same ability and I know all about your case. So let's go over to your place and see what we can find out. Then when Dean gets back, and he finishes yelling at me, he can take over."

"Am I getting you in trouble?"

"No, of course not. He's just protective of my condition and maybe a little scared of Lindy." Bridget rubbed her belly. "But we're tough and I don't believe Lindy will hurt me. I didn't piss her off."

"I don't know…"

"Come on. What do we have to lose? And if there's a real problem—and I don't expect there will be—you come into the room and she'll vanish."

Bridget made a valid point. Maggie nodded. "Okay."

If Dean had bothered to do his part, she wouldn't even need to go to this extreme, so if he got mad, he got mad. It wasn't his life that was on hold.

Bridget slipped on her coat, then grabbed her purse and a vase containing a dozen pink roses.

Maggie couldn't help but sniff the buds. "Mmmm… Pretty."

"Aren't they? They're from Rob, my husband. It's our first Valentine's Day."

Valentine's Day? Oh, right. That was tomorrow. Maggie had almost forgotten. Not that she cared about the stupid holiday. But Bridget was, what, seven or eight months pregnant? Maggie couldn't have heard her right. "Your first?"

Bridget looked down at her expanded belly and laughed. "Shocking, huh? Who knew condoms don't work so well in the pool? Oh, don't get me wrong. Even without the accident, we would have tried, just not quite so soon. We both want a big family."

A large family sounded wonderful to Maggie. Growing up an only child had been kind of lonely. Erica had been a godsend after Mom died, but she'd still lived too far away for regular visits. It took a driver's license before they'd become really close.

"I'll follow you, okay?" Bridget asked.

Follow? Oh yes. Maggie hugged the woman. "Thank you. I really appreciate this."

"Hey, I haven't done anything yet."

Maybe not, but it was more than she'd gotten from Dean.

* * * *

Dean pulled into the small parking lot he shared with the lawyers. He turned off the engine and sat there while the shadow of trees from the low-hanging sun danced before him on the wall of his building.

He wiped away a tear.

Cancer. That word had been floating around in his head since the doctor uttered those words.

The shock ranked up there with the day he discovered that Greg was only his half-brother. Just because he didn't want to see Mom didn't mean he wished her dead. Although she might think differently now. As soon as he'd gotten her settled at home, he high-tailed it out of there. It was one thing being cordial to him when she thought she was fine, but he wouldn't let her continue with her masquerade when she should be concentrating on getting well. So he left her to her sister and brother-in-law. And Greg. They would take care of her and she wouldn't have to exert any energy at pretending she cared.

He climbed out of the car and a gust of wind hit him in the face. A slap from his mother? Or maybe his brother? Either way, he probably deserved it.

The lot was empty. Damn, what time was it anyway? His phone indicated it wasn't even five, yet. Well, he'd told Bridget not to stay all day. Nice to see she'd finally taken him up on his offer. And Maggie must have left when the lawyers did. Why else stick around?

God, she must really hate him. He should have returned her calls, but he really didn't know what to say to her. It wasn't like he could talk to Lindy over the phone and solve her problem.

Time to suck it up. After he checked his mail and messages, he'd give Maggie a call and take her out to dinner. Then later tonight he'd head on over to her house and see about talking to Lindy. Didn't know what good it would do, but he had to start somewhere.

He entered the building and was bombarded by Peter. "Not now."

"Maggie was here."

"Is that so?" The news perked him up—maybe she didn't hate him after all. All the more reason to see her.

"That cousin of hers is suing her again."

"What? Why?" Poor Maggie. He should have been here for her. Looked like he would need more than a dinner out to make it up to her.

"Because she's not living in her house, why else, idiot? Sheesh. But hey, don't worry. Bridget is off doing what you couldn't. How is your mom, anyway?"

"Bridget's doing what?"

"Talking to Lindy. To help her move on."

"Oh shit. No." Dean locked up and rushed to his car. If anything happened to Bridget, Rob was so going to kill him.

* * * *

Lindy hovered over her house. On a nice day she would go up high like a bird; the view could be something. But the encroaching dreary clouds would obliterate any view today. The clouds pretty much summed up how she was feeling, too.

She'd seen no sign of Maggie or Erica, or even Dean, since Monday. Guess she only had herself to blame for that fiasco. Eventually Maggie would come back. She wanted the house. Didn't she?

Two vehicles pulled up to the curb. Lindy dropped down to the lawn to get a better look. Well, well. Maggie was here. She greeted some pregnant chick and the two of them walked up to the house. Lindy followed them in the open foyer, not that they could see her.

Maggie disabled the alarm and hung her coat—along with the pregnant chick's—on the hook. "Where should I go?"

The pregnant chick waddled to the stairs and looked up. "If I yell, can you hear me up there?"

Maggie nodded. "You sure you'll be okay?"

"I'll be fine. Don't you worry about a thing. We'll get this settled."

Settled? What did the pregnant chick hope to get settled? And why would Maggie need to go upstairs. Unless…

Maggie climbed up the stairs. When she disappeared from view, the pregnant one turned to Lindy and smiled.

"Hi. Lindy, right?"

Lindy shook her head. Another ghost-seer. "Damn. How many are there of you?"

"I have no idea. My name's Bridget and I work for Dean."

Of course she worked for Dean. He probably employed a whole group of ghost-seeing people. "Is he afraid of me now? I apologized for choking him."

"He's not afraid of you. He's been out of town and it's come to my attention that he meant to talk to you this week. Will you talk to me instead?"

Maybe now there was a chance at getting Maggie to come home. Bridget seemed a lot less agitated than Dean. Lindy put on her biggest smile. "Sure. What about?"

"About what's keeping you here."

Well, that was a new one. She'd thought for sure the chick was going to harp on the possession thing. "You're not very smart, are you? I'm stuck here because I died here."

Bridget smiled and sat on the couch in that weird way pregnant women sit. "I know you're stuck in a quarter-mile radius. What I meant was why you're here on Earth. Unless you committed suicide—and I know for a fact you didn't—souls don't stick around without a reason. Tell me your reason. Maybe I can help you fulfill it."

There was a reason she was stuck here? Why didn't Rhonda tell her that? Or Dean? "What kind of reason?"

"I don't know. It's different for everyone. Is there someone you wanted to say goodbye to, but didn't get a chance?"

"All my family is dead, so...no."

"What about a friend? Or a boyfriend?"

Could this lady actually find Kevin? And then what? Talk to him? The only way Lindy could do that would be through Maggie, and Dean certainly wouldn't go for that. Lindy had to face it. There was no help and she'd been stupid to think there was. "And what good would that do? It's not like anyone's going to hear me. Hell, you can't even see me if Maggie is in the room."

"Just because they can't see and hear you doesn't mean you can't get closure by seeing them. If you have a request I can—"

"Save your breath. There isn't anyone or anything you can help with."

"But you've been possessing Maggie. Is she the way you can get what you need?"

"Maggie was only a means to get out of my bubble, but since Dean told me what I was doing constituted rape, I won't be doing it anymore." God, this chick was buying it, wasn't she?

"If you want to be free, you can. You only have to move on."

There was the move word again. What was it with her? Did she have a bead on heaven? "Oh yeah? You know that for a fact?"

"Well, no."

Just what she'd thought. "If you really want to help me, you can help that freak, Rhonda. She's taking up a good portion of my territory and she scares the shit out of me."

Bridget pulled out a pad of paper and a pen "Do you have a last name or an address?"

"Don't know her last name or where she died exactly, but I see her across the street. That's the edge of her boundary. Don't go looking for her on your own. She's been dead a lot longer than me and I think it's gotten to her." Lindy tapped her head to make the point.

Could this be the way to get Dean off her back? He'd be interested enough to check out Rhonda for himself, wouldn't he?

"I'll see what I can do. I really wish you'd let me help you—" Bridget gasped and clutched her stomach.

"Whoa. Are you okay?" Instinctively, Lindy placed a hand on Bridget's arm and solidified in the process. Gravity took over. Her feet touched the ground and the scents of the house came alive. What a rush.

* * * *

Dean parked behind Bridget's car and prayed he wasn't too late. He raced up the porch stairs and barged in without even a knock. The sight that awaited him nearly took his breath away. Lindy was holding onto Bridget, who was doubled over.

"Get the hell away from her!"

Lindy snapped her hands away. "She just—"

Her words cut off as she misted away, leaving Bridget teetering by the couch.

Dean ran to Bridget and grasped her shoulders. "You in labor? Do I need to call Rob?"

Maggie appeared at the foot of the stairs. "What happened?"

Bridget waved him away. "No, don't bother him. It's just those stupid Braxton Hicks. I'll be fine. Lindy was only helping me up."

"You're okay, then?" Maggie asked.

"Yes, I'm fine. Thank you."

How could she be fine? She'd been accosted by a ghost. Dean turned toward the person responsible. "What were you doing bringing her here?"

Maggie glared at him as if she had a right to be mad at him. He wasn't the one who'd brought Bridget here to get hurt by a ghost.

"Now, Dean," Bridget said. "Lindy didn't do anything to me and Maggie was just a yell away."

He ignored her and kept his sights on Maggie. "You know Lindy is a threat, yet you come here anyway?"

Bridget grabbed his arm. "Stop it."

Maggie placed her hands on her hips. "If you had done what you said you would I wouldn't have needed her help. Besides, I didn't ask her. She volunteered."

"And you should have declined the offer."

"And do what? Wait for you? I've been waiting all week long. You don't take my calls, so what am I supposed to think? And now I'm getting sued. So thank you very much for that." She sat on the bottom step and looked up at the ceiling as if she could see the ghost hovering around. "You hear that, Lindy? Looks like my cousin will get this house. Have fun possessing him!"

Shit. Maybe he had overreacted a little. Dean crouched in front of her. "Maggie, no one's getting your house."

She lowered her head. "You don't know that."

"I know they'll have to go through me first." And he'd do his darnedest to make sure she didn't lose it. He turned toward Bridget. "Are you really okay?"

"Yes, worrywart. Just a little cramp. I'll go head on home." She held her palm out. "Yes, I can drive, and if you call Rob I'll sic Peter on you."

As if Peter needed any help in that department. Dean stood and examined her. Color returned to her cheeks and she was standing straight. Well, as straight as a pregnant woman could stand. He snatched her coat from the rack and held it out for her. "Text me when you get home, okay?"

"Will do, but I'm fine. Really." She slipped her arms in the sleeves. "See you later, Maggie. And don't take any gruff from him. He doesn't always know best."

After smacking him in the arm with a smile, Bridget left.

"Who's Peter?"

"An irritant." He turned toward Maggie. This wasn't the reunion he'd hoped for. Man, he was screwing up all around. "I'm sorry for snapping at you."

"You're forgiven." Maggie stood. "Where have you been? Erica wants to know what's taking so long with the fumigator. I know that was the ruse, but you said you'd get one anyway and I haven't heard anything and I don't know what to tell her anymore."

"Oh shit!" He grabbed his head. "I'm so sorry, Maggie. It completely slipped my mind." God, he really messed up, hadn't he?

"I can't be away for another week. Not after being served."

No, of course she couldn't. Damn it. Guess he'd have to work quicker, then. "Do you have the legal documents with you?"

"They're in the car. I can't believe I have to go through this again."

Dean grabbed her coat and held it out. "What did Tom say?"

"He wasn't in and I didn't call him." She looked at her coat. "We going somewhere?"

"Yes. Out of here." Because this discussion didn't include a certain ghost. "Let's get something to eat and I'll look over the documents."

She put on the coat. "Is this a date? Because I'm not so sure I'm in the mood."

"We'll just call it dinner." At least she hadn't kicked him out of the house. That had to be a good sign. "I'm sorry about the Houdini act. I'll make it up to you. I promise."

A promise he would keep. She deserved no less.

Chapter 15

Maggie leaned her head against the passenger window. It'd been sunny when she and Bridget left work. Now an hour from sunset, dark, thick clouds had rolled in and made it appear like twilight.

The houses passed by in a grey blur as Dean drove down the street. He wanted to eat. She wanted to talk. But being new to the relationship scene, she was unfamiliar with what was appropriate and inappropriate to ask a significant other. She didn't want to come out sounding like a nag, but didn't she have a right to know where he'd been? If only to find out if they still had a relationship? She turned toward him and tried to smile, to look confident. Too bad she wasn't feeling all that confident inside. "So, where were you all week?"

Dean stopped at a signal and his whole body sagged. Even the air within the vehicle seemed to thicken with his sadness. "In Cleveland. To see my mother. How does Mexican sound? Or would you prefer something less spicy?"

Redirection. Must be bad. Probably worse than her situation with a ghost, because she'd like to believe he wouldn't have forgotten about her over something silly. "Mexican's fine. Is everything okay? With your mother, I mean."

He swallowed. "No, not really. I'd rather not..."

"I'm sorry. Didn't mean to pry." She looked down at her lap. It was bad. So bad he couldn't talk about it. At least that explained why he'd forgotten about her. Guess she'd put family members under the inappropriate column. She didn't remember her high school dates being this…complicated. Not that she'd dated all that many boys. Okay, boy. She'd dated one boy.

"You didn't. It's hard to talk about right now." He looked at her as if he debated on saying more when he grabbed her by the neck and pulled her in for a kiss. She opened her mouth in a gasp and he took that as an invitation to explore. His tongue was scorching hot and oh, so sexy. She nearly melted in her seat.

A horn honked from behind and he broke free. Her lips tingled, as did other parts of her body. Holy crap. Where had that come from? Not that she was complaining. No sir, no complaints from her.

He drove through the intersection. "I realized I hadn't properly said hello to you."

"Oh." With hello kisses like that, he could say hello all day long.

The rest of the drive went by in silence. He was the perfect gentleman, though. Held the door to the restaurant open for her. Helped her with her coat and chair. Even when the waiter placed the chips and salsa on the table, Dean offered them to her first.

The waiter handed them menus and took their drink order: a beer for Dean and soda for her. No drink-drinks this time. She could easily down several and she wasn't in the mood to get drunk. Okay, maybe she was in the mood—she'd love to forget about ghosts and lawsuits—but getting drunk didn't seem sensible.

Dean sat cater-corner to her and, after stuffing a chip in his mouth, pulled the documents from the envelope. Seemed he was back to business when she'd rather he go back to him kissing her. She opened up the menu, but nothing really appealed to her. Well, that wasn't true. Dean appealed to her. That kiss in the car appealed to her.

"How many times did you sleep over at your grandmother's before you inherited the house?"

"Just once. Why? Oh God. Do you think Lindy possessed me then?"

"I don't know. Do you?"

All she remembered of that horrible day was Eddie and his marijuana. To think she used to worship that guy. She'd had such a headache when she went to bed that night and had woken okay, but had she slept? "I really don't know."

"When was this?"

"Saturday, July 22, 2000." A date she wouldn't mind forgetting. "I was thirteen. My parents drove to Kentucky to attend a funeral of a friend of my dad's. They didn't want to leave me home alone and I didn't want to go, so I stayed with Grandma."

"Wait. July 2000?" He rubbed his jaw in thought. "Holy shit. How'd she do it?"

"How'd who do what?"

"Lindy. Get your grandmother to change the will."

"What makes you think Lindy was behind it?" She didn't have to ask how. If Lindy was behind it all the only way she could have done it was by possessing Maggie. Unless Grandma could also see ghosts and found out about Eddie from Lindy.

"Because your grandmother changed her will less than three weeks after your visit. Tell me that's a coincidence. I bet she discovered she could possess you and somehow got your grandmother to change the will."

The waiter returned with their drinks. Maggie took a sip of her soda. Maybe she should have ordered a drink-drink, and nearly did so when she placed her food order. But booze couldn't fix the past.

"If Lindy used me to get Grandma to change the will, why wouldn't Grandma say something to me later, to confirm information? She never said anything to me to indicate that we'd ever spoken about a topic I was unaware of."

"Good point." Dean took a drag of his beer and his eyes widened. "That little shit. I bet she possessed your grandmother, too."

"Then why would it matter if *I* got the house? What's in it for Lindy?" When he couldn't answer her, she continued, "It's probably a coincidence. Aunt Gina could have easily done something to piss off Grandma. They never did get along." She didn't even want to think of the implications if that wasn't the case. She'd rather think about Dean. And how far his body was from hers. Too far for an indiscreet kiss. If they'd sat at a booth, would he have sat beside her? Would he have snuck in another kiss?

"I suppose." He scooped up some salsa on a chip and stuffed it in his mouth. Such a wonderful mouth. A mouth she longed to have against her own. Probing. Wanting.

She grabbed a chip while shooing the image from her head. All this rest seemed to have made her horny for the guy. She needed to focus, because resolving the lawsuit and getting Lindy out of the house should take precedence. Dean could be the prize at the end.

"What about your mother? She's not mentioned in the will, either. She died after it was written up."

"I assumed Grandma discussed it with Mom beforehand."

"That's possible. But then wouldn't she have told Gina she changed the will? You know, rub it in her face?"

"Not necessarily. Grandma loved her practical jokes, and to string Gina along would have been a whopper." Would have been nice to have been clued in, though.

"Really? Huh." He stuffed another salsa-dipped chip into his mouth and looked at the lawsuit. "So your grandmother could have told Gina there was something valuable in the house. In essence, rubbing it in."

"There's something valuable in the house?" Maybe it was time to check the attic. But that would require getting a ladder. And then climbing… She nearly shuddered at the thought.

"I don't know. But they must think so. Why else go through all this trouble? I understand he's pissed he was left out of the will, but the estate really isn't worth all that much, at least not worth all these trips to court."

Their meals arrived and the rich spices made her stomach rumble. Seemed she was hungry after all. She dug into her enchilada.

Dean picked up his taco. "There's only one problem with the practical joke theory: Eddie is the one who got hurt. Did your grandmother have something against him?"

Damn. Why'd it have to keep coming back to that summer? The only way Grandma could have known about Eddie was if Lindy had told her, and that wasn't possible. Okay, maybe it was a little bit possible; Lindy could have possessed Maggie to do it. Which meant she could have possibly talked Grandma into leaving the house to Maggie. But then why didn't Grandma say anything to her later? It didn't make sense.

Maggie shook her head while cutting another piece of enchilada. "She must have, right? I could talk to him. Or Aunt Gina. Find out what went on between them. Then maybe—"

"No, no, no. I don't want you near them."

"But if I can get this settled—"

"Let me do a little checking first, okay? And then let Tom take care of it. They seem a little unstable and I don't want you getting hurt if they happen to get physical."

"Physical? They're not going to hurt me."

"People do strange things for money. Now, if only money worked for Lindy." Three bites and his taco was history. Certainly nothing wrong with his appetite.

"I'm surprised Lindy doesn't possess someone else, not that I want her to do that."

"Me, too. Guess I got my work cut out for me this weekend."

"I could help. I'm pretty good at research."

He smiled. "I'll keep that in mind. But Bridget's gotten pretty fast. I might not need you. Hopefully I'll get this all settled by Monday."

"Monday?" She lowered her fork to the table. "I can't put Erica off anymore without lying and I won't do that. Can I tell her what's happening? Please? I'll make sure she promises not to tell anyone else."

He sighed. "I guess that's the least I can let you do. I'm so sorry for dropping the ball like this."

"Thank you." That was one load of many off her mind. Now maybe she could ease into his problem. She picked up her fork and toyed with the enchilada. "Just so you know, I missed you. Bridget led me to believe you were on a case."

"Because that's what I told her."

"If you need someone to talk to, I have these ears. They listen pretty good."

He took her hand—his warmth so welcoming—gave her a reassuring squeeze, and smiled. "I'll keep that in mind."

And she would keep in mind that for now, he liked being around her. And as his hand warmed hers, that thought warmed her heart.

* * * *

Dean dropped Maggie off at her car with a kiss that ended way too soon and a promise to call her later. And apparently no time was too late. He wasn't sure if that was a good thing or a bad thing. He liked her company, and he couldn't get enough of her kisses, but was he being fair to her?

Probably not, but he couldn't very well stay away. She needed his help and there wasn't anyone else she could go to. If only he possessed some willpower, but every time she was near, his little head did all the thinking—willpower be damned. He could only hope that maybe she'd finally come to her senses, see him as being all wrong for her, and end it herself. Because he wasn't so sure he could let her go.

A visit to Bridget didn't garner much. Seemed Lindy's pigheadedness wasn't only aimed at Dean. That bit about Rhonda was new, though. And if he thought for one minute she was a threat to Maggie, he'd check that ghost out. But damn, to have her across the street? He'd have to be careful where he parked from now on.

He positioned his car alongside the front of Maggie's garage, climbed out, and took a deep breath. He was crazy coming back here alone. Just because Lindy said she didn't want to hurt him didn't mean she wouldn't. Rob had offered to accompany him, but after the close call with Bridget, Dean didn't want her to be alone, either, in case she really had a contraction.

Using Maggie's key, he opened the back door and stepped inside. Flipped on the light. The kitchen seemed eerie without Maggie in it cooking something.

"I wasn't hurting her," Lindy said from the archway.

"So she said." Even admitting that much grated on him. Bridget was still a softy when it came to ghosts, even after the unfortunate incident with Mary Alice at the river last summer. Talk about a crazy ghost! He shut the door, punched in the code, and then headed to the living room where he sat on the couch. Was this going to be a waste of time or would Lindy actually admit to anything? Would he be able to tell if she was lying or not?

"Is it true Eddie can get this house?" Lindy asked.

Nice to know she cared about something. Too bad it wasn't Maggie. "If Maggie loses the lawsuit, yeah."

"So that's why he was poking around here on Monday?"

"Son of a bitch! He was in the house?"

"No. He saw the alarm sign and then left. But he did have his key and probably would have come inside if you guys hadn't changed the locks."

Dean sighed in relief. Thank God Maggie got the alarm. Eddie could have easily broken in otherwise, even without a working key. But what did he want? Lindy seemed more chatty than usual. Dean would take advantage of that. "Did you witness your mother telling Gina that there was something valuable in this house?"

"No, but Mom wasn't here all the time. And if she did tell Gina that, I can't imagine it being true. I never saw Mom stash anything of value. She loved her paper, though. Attic is full of the stuff."

"Attic?" He looked upward. Maggie had never mentioned the attic. Could that be the answer? "What else is up there?"

"Probably lots of stuff. Mom didn't throw out anything. Not even after Dad died. It's creepy up there, so I stay away."

Dean nearly laughed. "Creepy? To a ghost?"

"Hey, even this ghost has her limits. There are these dolls up there... I swear they're looking right at me."

Dean shuddered. Okay, maybe that could be creepy. He never did like dolls.

"So what are you going to do about Eddie?"

Seemed she did not want her nephew in this house. Almost comical if she wasn't so dangerous to Maggie. "Why do you care? You're not going to possess Maggie again, so why does it matter who is living here?"

"Because my mother obviously wanted her to have it."

"Bullshit! I think you possessed your mother and—"

"Ewww. I did not! That would be gross."

For some strange reason he believed her. That could also be a reason she didn't want Eddie to have the house—she didn't want to possess a man. "But it wasn't gross possessing Maggie, was it?"

"She's not old and wrinkly, so no. But if it'll help, you should know that Eddie shouldn't get the house because he's not a family member."

Well, that came out of nowhere. What kind of game was she playing? "Really? He's your brother's son. That makes him a blood relation."

"No, he's not. Gina cheated on Ed."

If that were true, it would certainly solve Maggie's lawsuit problem. "You have proof?"

"Proof, like in writing?"

"That would be proof."

"I'm a ghost. How would I get that? But I overheard Gina talking when she thought she was alone."

Figured it was a conversation. Why couldn't anything be easy? But if Lindy knew, had she used Maggie back in 2000? "How did your mother find out?"

"She…uh…okay. Fine. I possessed Maggie and told Mom."

Damn, and he didn't even have to twist it out of her. "You possessed her back in 2000? When she spent the night here?"

"I did. But I didn't even know it was possible until then. Saw an opportunity and took it. Someone had to tell Mom. Gina certainly wasn't going to do it. I only did it for Caroline and Maggie."

Laughing, Dean sat back on the couch. "Oh, that's a good one. Got any more stories for me?"

"I'm telling you the truth."

"If that were the case, your mother would have told someone. She would have had it investigated. She would have needed proof."

"She did tell someone. She told Caroline. Maybe she got the proof."

"How convenient. Did she tell anyone who's still alive?" When Lindy only rolled her eyes at his question, he shook his head.

"I'm sure you could have some tests done. Confirm my story. Then Eddie won't be able to get the house, right? It would belong to Maggie."

She had a point, not that he'd admit it to her. He could have Eddie's DNA matched to Maggie's. If there wasn't a link, it might be enough to convince the court that Eddie wasn't a blood relation. Dean rubbed his head. At least it was something to go on, which was more than he had before he came here. Still didn't resolve Maggie's problem with Lindy. "Say we're able to get this all straightened. Where does that leave you? You gonna start possessing your neighbors now?"

"I can't possess my neighbors, doofus."

"You can't or you haven't tried?"

"I've tried. It doesn't work."

Holy crap. Why didn't he see it before? "It's the house, isn't it?"

"What's the house?"

"You can only possess people in this house."

"That's a good theory. Do you write books for a living, too? I told you I didn't possess my mother."

"Because you said that was gross."

"What about Erica? She's not gross, but you don't see me possessing her."

"Or you are and you've gotten better at it since messing up with Maggie. But if Eddie got the house, you're screwed, because possessing Eddie would be gross. So you came up with this story of Gina's infidelity and told your mother. And for some reason she believed you. Or should I say, believed Maggie."

"You think you know everything, but you know nothing. It's not me. It's not this house. It's your girlfriend. She's the one who sucked me into her body. You want to blame someone for this mess, blame her."

Okay, now he'd heard it all. Lindy was like every other ghost he'd met—a lying pile of horse manure—and he'd been a fool to even believe a word out of her mouth.

* * * *

Lindy waited while Dean processed the information. She hadn't meant to admit that it wasn't her ability, but rather Maggie who created that ability. If another ghost got wind of that, Lindy might never be able to possess Maggie again, and despite what Dean thought, Lindy would. Going about it was a whole 'nother issue. Still, maybe now Dean would see that Maggie wasn't safe from any ghost and having her back home would be the best.

"Maggie sucked you in?" He practically doubled over in laughter. "That's a good one. And to think I almost believed you about Eddie."

Damn it. What would it take to get this guy to believe? "I'm not lying about Eddie or anything. Listen, I heard it with my own ears. Gina was sitting in her car right out front, talking on that newfangled mobile phone of hers. This was before my brother died. She was screaming at someone, probably Eddie's real father. Gina was freaked out. By the time I got close enough to listen, I heard her say she was afraid they'd find out."

"Who? Find out what?"

"I don't know. I couldn't actually hear what the guy said. She had the phone too close to her ear. But Eddie doesn't really resemble Ed. I figured Gina cheated on him."

Dean chuckled and shook his head. "That's it? You heard a one-sided conversation? For all you know Gina owed her bookie money and didn't want anyone to find out."

No, no, no. It had to be the other. Otherwise she'd kissed her nephew. Almost had sex with her nephew. Ewww. "Why do I even bother talking to you? You don't believe anything I say."

"Because what you say doesn't make sense. All you do is spin stories so you'll get your way. Why don't you do us all a favor and move on?"

"Don't you think I would if I could?"

"You can. You just don't want to. All you have to do is let go of what's keeping you here."

"You're starting to sound like Bridget. She thinks I have some unresolved issues." But the only unresolved issue she could even think of involved her mother, so where did that leave Lindy? Stuck here for all eternity? Why couldn't Dean—or someone with his ability—have come along when there was hope of getting it all fixed? But he hadn't and Maggie was her only chance now.

"Because you do, or you wouldn't still be here. So what is it? What's keeping you here? You need to tell me so I can fix it or you need to let it go."

"I can't."

"You mean you won't. Well, at least I can keep you from getting Maggie. Now what are you going to do?"

"I was doing fine until you showed up. Why'd you have to ruin everything?"

"I didn't ruin anything. I saved Maggie. But you don't care about her, so move on. But do it soon. The longer you stay, the harder it will be to get what you want."

"You've already told me I can't have what I want."

"Using Maggie for sex? Yeah, you're not getting that. But I can't believe that's what's keeping you here. She wasn't alive when you died."

"What if I want to use her to talk to someone?"

"If you want to talk to someone, tell me who. But you are not going to possess her again. Are we clear?"

As if she'd let him talk to Kevin for her. "You could at least ask Maggie if she would let me."

"How many times do I have to say no? You're not possessing her."

"Then we're through here, aren't we?" Lindy popped out of the room and onto the roof. Damn it. Somehow she would get around Dean. He couldn't be with Maggie all the time, now, could he?

Chapter 16

Maggie stood frozen at the opening to the closet where a ladder sat under the attic access. She could probably climb it easily enough. That wouldn't require her to look down. And it did seem sturdy enough since Erica and Dean made it up without a problem. But once she needed to leave... Shit. No one knew about her fear and she'd like to keep it that way. Somehow she didn't think that was possible any longer. She swiped the sweat from her brow.

Erica poked her head down the opening. "You coming up?"

"Yeah, sure." Maggie offered a smile, yet she was far from happy. She could do this. If only Dean was up there giving her a reason to climb, but he'd left to find a better light and had come down before she'd had a chance to go up. She took a deep breath and focused on the rungs as she climbed into the dimly lit space.

"I can't believe you never told me about the attic." Erica blew dust off a box. "Ugh."

When Dean had called Maggie asking about the attic, she'd known her days of denying its existence were over.

"What was there to tell? I thought it was empty." At least she'd hoped it was empty. Certainly would have made the lie easier to say. But of course it wasn't empty. The space was packed better than a storage unit.

Thankfully, she wasn't too tall for the low ceiling. She meandered around the boxes to the other side, as far away from the opening as possible, and sat on the dusty floor.

Erica fanned her face. "I guess heat really does rise. It's warm up here, isn't it? I figured it would be cold."

Maggie breathed in relief. She'd thought the same thing. Maybe it wasn't her fear causing her to sweat. "Me, too. Guess I didn't need the sweatshirt."

Dean hefted that scrumptious body of his through the opening. The muscles in his biceps strained against the sleeves of his t-shirt and the sight nearly caused her to swoon. Which was a much better reason than fainting from heat or fear.

He stood and bumped his head on the low ceiling. "Damn it."

Erica giggled. "You'd think you would have remembered doing that the last time."

"You'd think." He squatted over to the middle of the room, attached the light to one of the beams, then plugged it in. "Let's see if this works better."

The lamp lit up the attic and brought to life the years of junk that had been hidden in the dark. It would take days to get through all the stuff. Maggie nearly groaned. Could she manage the ladder for that long? She purged the thought from her head and concentrated on the work. And Dean. He more than made up for her fear of heights. Well…almost.

Dean picked up one of the dolls from a box. "Oh my God. Lindy was right. These things are creepy."

"They're just dolls," Maggie said.

"Yeah, whatever." He put the doll back, face down.

She dusted the top of the closest box and opened it. Paper. Lots of paper. "What am I supposed to be looking for?"

"I wish I knew." He handed over a green trash bag. "Here. If we don't separate the junk from the questionable, we'll never get through this mess."

"You know, Dean. I never took you for the supernatural type," Erica said. "Except your name is Dean, so maybe I should have. Do you have a brother named Sam?"

He scrunched his forehead. "Am I supposed to know what that means?"

"Dean Winchester. You know, from 'Supernatural'? The television series? Although you're not as hunky as Jensen Ackles. No offense."

"Ignore her," Maggie said. "She not only reads too many mystery novels, she watches too much TV." And Erica was totally wrong about Dean. He was way hunkier than Jensen Ackles.

"I think it's cool you can see ghosts. Not so cool one is possessing Maggie, though. Do they all do that?"

"God, I hope not," he muttered as he weaved around the boxes. "So, what do we have here?"

Maggie smiled at Dean's sly way of changing the subject. "Lots of paper. You should feel right at home."

He laughed. "Touché."

"There are some old yearbooks over here." Erica held up a stack. "Which relative was in high school in 1972? Damn, what's with the cold air? Is there a window I missed?"

"You're feeling cold air?" Dean crawled over and grabbed the book from Erica.

"Wait. Are you saying that's the ghost? That your Aunt Lindy is doing that?" She smiled and waved. "Hey there!"

Maggie would rather smack Lindy than wave to her.

"This was Lindy's," Dean said. "Do you mind if I take it?"

"You can do whatever it takes to resolve this mess." Except he wouldn't sacrifice the virgin—her—now would he? Okay, maybe Erica wasn't the only one who had to stop watching TV.

Dean crumpled a paper and tossed it toward the garbage bag.

"What are you doing?" Maggie asked.

"Uh oh," Erica said. "You're in trouble now."

Dean scrunched his forehead, clearly lost as to the great offense he'd taken. "Why? What'd I do?"

Maggie got up and retrieved the crumpled paper, then proceeded to smooth it out. "Wadded up paper takes up more space."

"Plus, it's messy," Erica said. "To *her*."

Yeah, there was that, too, but she didn't want to sound like a total freak. "This will all go into the recycle bin. Flat fits better."

"So she always says. So what's the dealie-o with moving back?" Erica asked. "Apparently I'm safe, but will Maggie have to continue to live elsewhere?"

"I'm not living somewhere else. I can't."

Dean looked up from perusing his stack of papers. "Why do you think you're safe?"

"Because I always wake up in my own bed. And I'm not tired like Maggie. Plus, a few of my things have ended up in Maggie's room. Why would Lindy do that if she could go straight to the source?"

"Well, shit. That just blew my theory out of the water. I assumed Lindy could possess anyone in this house."

"Or maybe only family members," Maggie said. "Or maybe I have some funky gene that lets me be possessed like you can see ghosts."

"Well, technically, I'm related to Lindy, too," Erica said. "Just a first cousin, once removed, or some shit like that."

"Because your mothers were cousins," Dean said. "Which side? Detrick or Steele?"

"Detrick. My grandfather is Maggie's grandmother's brother."

"So, it's the funky gene, then?" Maggie said.

"It's not a funky gene," Dean said. "But I hadn't thought of the family member tie. It would make sense. If Lindy can't possess Erica, and she certainly would have done that once you were chained up, then maybe it's because you're family via the Steele line. Said she didn't even know she could possess anyone until you. If you can believe her."

"Lucky me, huh?" She grabbed her throat. Fresh air would be great right about now, but of course there wasn't a window in sight. And going back down the ladder wasn't an option.

"You don't like ghosts much, do you?" Erica said as she pried open the box beside her.

"Because they lie. They lie about everything."

"Sounds like some of my old boyfriends." She wiped her brow. "You know, that light is making it even hotter up here. I'm gonna change my shirt and get a bottle of water. Anyone else want one?"

"Good idea," Dean said. "Why don't you bring up a few? And some more trash bags." Once Erica disappeared, he turned toward Maggie. "Hey, you okay? Is the heat getting to you, too?"

"I'm fine. Just throwing a little pity party, but I'll get over it."

"This is not your fault. It's Lindy's."

"Maybe so, but she couldn't do it without me. At least she told Bridget she'd stop. So I'm moving back."

"No. You can't. I don't trust her. It's not safe for you to stay here."

"It's not safe in the streets, either."

"Maggie... You're not going to end up in the street."

"That's right, because I'm staying here. I'll continue to chain myself to the house, but instead of using a key and depending on Erica, I'll get a combination lock and memorize the number."

"Or you can stay with me. I'd be a perfect gentleman."

That he would—regardless of what she wanted—but it still wouldn't solve her problem. And there were all those steps. "You know that's not a solution. I have to come back or I will lose this house. Lawsuit or not."

"I don't trust Lindy."

"I know you don't. But she did make it possible for me to have this house. And if that means living with her, then I'll live with her. At least I can keep her from taking me out of the house."

"I'll do my best to get her out of here, too." He ran his fingers against her cheek and she closed her eyes. "I promise I won't let her hurt you."

What was it about this man that got her motor running? She was about to pull him in for a kiss when he grabbed her by the neck and beat her to it. His tongue explored her willing mouth and she sagged against him. If Erica hadn't chosen that moment to return, would he have lost control and done more than kiss? Guess she would never know.

But damn. There was the non-gentleman she craved. Somehow she would break that moral barrier of his.

* * * *

After two hours of sitting in a dusty and warm attic, Dean had had enough. His legs needed a stretch and the ceiling was too low for him to stand straight. He'd already bumped his head twice. Didn't want to go for that charm.

"I'm done," Erica said as she neatly placed another stack of papers in the garbage bag. "So far all I've seen were old billing statements. God, these things go back forever. Didn't she realize she could throw them out after seven years?"

"You can?" Dean asked.

Maggie laughed. "Well, that explains a lot. Do we need to come over to your office next?"

He was glad she could joke, even if it was at his expense. He didn't know how else to lighten the mood.

"You two yuck it up," Erica said. "I'm going to take a shower and then do a little reading before bed. In my own bed." She stood and stretched. "So glad to be back. Even knowing there's a ghost in the house. Good thing I'm not shy or taking a shower might be…awkward."

Maggie's eyes widened. "Oh crap. She can't be that bad. Can she?"

"She's a ghost," he said. "Of course she's that bad." And he had a prime example of one: Peter. But Dean wasn't going to admit he had his own ghost problem. Maggie might not believe he could help her, then.

Erica stepped on top of the ladder. "She's a ghost who's probably bored. I know I would be. If I were her, I'd be peeping. See ya later."

Maggie shook her head. "Just when I was feeling comfortable about sleeping here…"

His hopes rose, albeit temporarily. "You don't have to."

"I'm not giving up this house because of one nosey ghost."

"I'm sure she's seen everything by now, anyway." He wouldn't mind seeing all of Maggie again, either. Damn it. Now he was getting hard.

"Is that supposed to make me feel better?"

"Just pointing out the facts. My offer still stands, though. If you can't stomach it here, you can always stay with me." He'd end up with blue balls for sure, but if it meant she was safe, it would be worth it.

"If I can't stomach it here, then I'd gladly give up the house. But I won't know until I stay."

Why'd she have to be so stubborn? And why'd he care so much? It was her life; she should be able to do what she wanted. All he could do was make sure she stayed safe and the chain would do that. He stood and dust flew. "I do like Erica's idea about a shower. I can't imagine how many years' worth of dirt is up here."

She held her hand out for a help up, which he gladly gave. "You're welcome to use ours."

"Uhh…"

"Gotcha. See, it's different when it's you, huh?" Laughing, she brushed the dust off her pants. "You want some milk and cookies before you head on out of here?"

Oh God. She knew exactly how to snag him. "When did you make cookies?"

"Well, they're store-bought. And I'm not even sure if the milk is still good."

"Then I'm in for whatever you have." It beat going back to an empty apartment, in any case. Crouching, he followed her for a few steps, then backtracked to grab the yearbook and unplug the lamp. When he headed toward the opening, he nearly tripped over Maggie. She was on her hands and knees, but she wasn't moving toward the exit. She wasn't moving at all. "You okay?"

"Would you go down first and hold the ladder, please?"

"Oh, sure." He dropped the yearbook to the floor below and climbed down. When he reached the bottom, he steadied the ladder.

Slowly, she descended, giving him a nice view of her ass. Was she purposely torturing him with the slow movements? Or was he torturing himself because she was off limits? And if she was off limits, why did he continue to kiss her? Again, his little head liked to be in control whenever she was near, like talking him into kissing her. And if Erica hadn't returned when she did, that little head might have talked him into doing more than kiss, because kissing her was heaven.

With her shoulders level with the opening, she tentatively reached inside, causing the ladder to wobble for a bit. She grabbed onto the rungs. "I can't get the cover."

"That's okay. I can get it."

"Thanks." As she reached the bottom, that wonderful ass rubbed up against his crotch and growing erection. "Tight quarters, huh?"

Oh, he didn't mind. Not in the least. But he couldn't answer her on account he was sure his voice would come out all squeaky.

She stepped out of the closet. A sheen of sweat had covered her pale face and she was practically panting.

"You okay?" Maybe he was getting her all hot and bothered, too.

She nodded. "I think the heat got to me."

Yeah, heat. Sure. Heat wasn't his problem. Except the desirous kind. Damn woman was going to melt his resolve if he let her. But would that really be a bad thing? She'd basically given him the green light. So why did he stop? She hadn't asked for any commitments. He'd only assumed. But how could she not want a commitment? Why else wait to have sex?

145

He climbed up, secured the opening, and came back down. Two nightstands and a dresser filled the room, but no bed. "So whose room was this?"

"Grandma's."

"Didn't keep her bed?"

"Well… We found her in it."

"We?"

"My dad was visiting from Florida for my birthday. We were all supposed to go out to dinner, but when she didn't answer the door…"

"Yikes. Some birthday, huh?"

"At least she died peacefully. Can't really ask for more than that. Why don't we go get those cookies, now?"

"Sounds good." He picked up the yearbook and followed her out. "So what time do you want to start on this tomorrow?"

"You don't have to come over. I've taken up so much of your time already."

"Time I don't mind spending with you." And wasn't that the truth. He wrapped his arm around her delicate shoulders as they headed for the stairs. "Why don't I pick you and Erica up for breakfast so we'll have more energy to tackle that mess? How does ten sound?"

"Like way too early for Erica. How about I let Erica sleep in and you come by for breakfast here?"

"You want to cook me breakfast?" Something he'd envisioned after a night of sex. Which would never happen if he had any say.

"Well, you don't want to take my money."

Or her virginity. Had she implied that?

As he passed the downstairs bathroom, his bladder spoke up. He told Maggie he'd wash up and meet her in the kitchen. No sooner had he unzipped his fly when Lindy's face appeared in the wall above the toilet. He jumped back and covered himself. "What the hell?"

She laughed. "Man, you should have seen your face."

He turned and zipped back up. "Not funny, Lindy."

"Says you. What are you going to do with my yearbook?"

Figured he'd done something to bring this about. "I'm gonna find out which one of these students knew you when. Especially the male ones."

"Why do you have to keep poking into my life?"

"Funny question coming from you. And it's not really a life anymore, is it?"

"Ooo, you think you're so smart."

"I try. Now, are you staying for the show? Because I really gotta go." He unzipped and waited a beat. If she watched, she watched. He couldn't have her control his life. But if he read her right, she was all talk.

Her eyes widened and she poofed out of the room.

Thank God. He wasn't sure he could have peed with her watching.

Chapter 17

Eddie stabbed his eggs, but couldn't bring the fork to his mouth. His appetite had left the moment his mother sat her fat ass at the table.

She had no trouble wolfing down the stack of pancakes heaped before her. Using her fork, she pointed at his plate. "You need to eat. You're much too thin."

Thin? His mother packed extra poundage so everyone was probably thin to her. Sure, he'd been thirty pounds overweight back before he dated Ronnie. That she'd even been interested in him then was a miracle in itself. But his weight was perfect now and he aimed to keep it that way.

"It's that house, I know it. But we'll get it back for you, and then you'll be able to put that weight back on." Mom shoveled another stack into her mouth. "I don't know why you didn't empty out the attic during the week, while the bitch was gone."

"You want me to go to jail?" What had he ever done to deserve her? He should go over to that house and burn it to the ground, then maybe she would stop harping at him. Too bad a stunt like that would only add to his problems. Until he could afford a separate place for her—and it appeared he sucked at gambling, so no luck there—she was stuck living with them. All because he was an only child and didn't know how to kick her out into the street and still keep Ronnie.

"She only put the sign up to discourage burglars."

"And I was supposed to test that theory? No thanks."

"You have a key. You wouldn't have been charged with anything. Really, grow a set." She turned toward his wife. "Veronica, sweetie, be a dear and make me some more. I don't know what's gotten into me, but I'm still famished."

"Oh sure, no problem." Ronnie stood, even though she hadn't taken but two bites of her own food.

"Ronnie, no. Mom can wait until you've finished eating. Can't you, Mom?"

"It won't take her that long to make them," Mom said.

"It's okay. I don't mind." Ronnie went to the griddle. "How many more?"

"Same as last." Mom slurped at her coffee, dripping some on her flowery robe, which was splattered with older food stains along with today's syrup. He wasn't about to suggest she get it washed because he knew who would end up doing it. "You've got yourself a fine woman there, Eddie. I knew from the moment I met her she'd take care of my boy."

More like take care of her, but Eddie kept his mouth shut. How had Dad put up with her? Or maybe she'd been different when he was alive. Eddie certainly didn't remember being the center of his mother's universe until after Dad's death, but then he was only nine at the time.

She rubbed her chubby hands together. "You did good work, Eddie, getting those papers served to Maggie yesterday afternoon. I hope she squirms all weekend. No one rips off our family and gets away with it."

The compliment surprised him. The fact she labeled herself "our family" did not.

Eddie leaned on his elbows. "Besides the house, what exactly has she ripped us off with? I can't imagine pictures in a photo album are worth all that much."

"Better than pictures. You find that photo album and we can stop the lawsuits."

"You're still not going to tell me what's in them?"

"Everyone knows you're the weak link. That Parker fella would probably only look at you funny and you'd tell him everything. It's best you don't know."

The fact she thought so little of him was also not a surprise. Still stung, though. "So how do you know Maggie hasn't already thrown out everything in the attic?"

"She doesn't strike me as the kind of person who throws stuff out without inspecting it first, especially from her precious grandmother."

"But will she recognize the value?"

Veronica returned with a stack of six pancakes. "Here you go, Gina."

"Oh, such a dear. Such a dear." After Mom slathered butter on every cake and drenched the whole thing with syrup, she cut a wedge and shoveled it into her pudgy mouth. "Maggie doesn't have a clue what's in that house, you mark my words, which is all the more reason we need to get over there and empty out the attic."

That *we* was most likely *he*, and he really had no desire to haul crap out of that house. "How come you never got it before Grandma died? Why didn't Dad?"

"Your father didn't believe it was worth bothering your grandmother about, and after he died, well, she became difficult. She never did like me."

Eddie couldn't imagine why. His mother oozed contempt.

Syrup dripped down her chin and landed near the other syrup stain as she shoved another wedge in her pancake hole. "I thought I could just wait her out. Guess that's what I get for thinking. But don't you worry, we'll get what's coming to you."

He stabbed at his egg. Would this item bring him peace? Because he'd really like a part of that.

* * * *

Sitting beside Dean at the breakfast table, Maggie smiled as he polished his plate. He certainly loved his food, even simple scrambled eggs and fried potatoes, and she loved cooking for him. If she had paid attention to the calendar earlier—heck, *he* probably didn't even realize it was Valentine's Day—she would have created something more elaborate.

Maybe it was true that the way to a man's heart was through his stomach. She never would have pegged him to be old fashioned, but then she never thought he'd say no to sex, either. Well, if she could weaken him with food, then food it was. Because she really did want his heart.

The sex would be a bonus.

He grabbed a popover from the basket and devoured it. "What are these called again?"

Okay, maybe she had gotten a little elaborate. A yummy treat for all of his help. "Cinnamon popovers. I take it you like them?"

"Like 'em? I love 'em. I'll have to run extra to burn the calories off, but it's so worth it." He bit into another one and closed his eyes. "I swear, I've died and gone to heaven."

"You act like you haven't eaten in ages."

"What can I say? I love your cooking."

"Thanks." Nice to know she'd already won over his stomach. How much longer before she lassoed his heart?

Maggie took his empty plate and her equally empty coffee mug to the kitchen. "So, what are you going to do with Lindy's yearbook?"

"I gave it to Bridget so she could track down Lindy's friends. She's better suited for that kind of work."

"Why do you say that?"

He leaned back in his seat. "Because she has more patience when it comes to ghosts. Speaking of which, how did you sleep last night?"

"Fine." If fine meant that she woke up as tired as she'd been when she went to bed. But if she told him that he might drag her out and chain her to a hotel. If only they were a real couple—one who slept together—then there'd be no issue. But the chances of that happening were as likely as Erica joining the convent.

"Really? Or are you just saying that?"

"I can't tell if she possessed me, I can only go by how I'm feeling. Plus, the restraint was still attached." Sure, it had kept her in the house, but had done nothing to deter one pesky ghost. Tonight she'd have to make sure not to have anything interesting within reach.

"Yeah, well, that doesn't mean she didn't or won't later. Maybe you should get a dog. From what I hear they can see ghosts."

"Can a dog eject a ghost from my body?" *Like you do?* Maggie nearly concluded, but she wouldn't put that kind of pressure on him. Even if it was a solution. It didn't seem all that likely he'd come up with that idea on his own if he was thinking about dogs.

"I don't know, but what do you have to lose? I can ask Bridget and Rob if you can borrow Barnaby. You know, before you go buying your own dog."

Maggie poured more coffee into her cup. Dogs wouldn't solve her current problem, but caffeine certainly could and she took a long sip. If only there was a way she could help Lindy move along. And quickly. She wasn't sure how much longer she could dodge Dean's observation.

"Good morning, everyone," Erica said as she strolled inside the kitchen, wearing a thin robe over her t-shirt and pajama pants. Her eyes lit up when she spotted the basket. "Ooo, popovers." She plopped down on the chair across from Dean, grabbed one out of the basket, and took a bite. "Mmm. It's like a little party inside my mouth. You know, Dean, she doesn't make these for just anyone. I always have to beg."

"Is that so?" He stared at Maggie and smiled, sending a thrill through her system. It was stuff like that that made her think he did want her, regardless of what he said.

Maggie diverted her attention to her cousin. "If I made them every day, then they wouldn't be special, now would they?"

"Don't know," Erica said between bites. "Why don't we give that theory a test? I'm game."

Dean burst out laughing. God, even his infectious laughter turned her on. He was so full of life and she wanted to be a part of it. And while she was now, in a way, didn't mean it was permanent. Once Lindy left, would he leave, too? She'd have to figure out a way to make him want to stay.

Erica propped her slippered feet on Maggie's vacant chair. "Do you mind if I bail on the attic today? I was invited to an ice skating party and that sounds like more fun."

"Anything sounds like more fun than the attic," Maggie said. "But this invitation seems awfully convenient. Why didn't you mention this yesterday?"

"Because I didn't know about it yesterday. I don't always open my e-mails, especially if it looks like work."

"And you thought work-work would be better than attic work?" Dean asked.

"You got that right. Turns out it wasn't even from work, she just used the work e-mail. But it's all on the up-and-up. I'll even show you my e-mail. You can both come, too."

"I'm surprised you don't have a big date tonight," he said.

"I do. After the ice skating party."

Maggie carried her coffee over to the table and knocked Erica's feet from her chair as she took her seat. "What time is this party?"

"Well... Not until three, but—"

"No buts. We can still do some work upstairs. I'm sure the party will make a good break."

"Then we'll be too tired to go to the party."

"We're not lifting heavy weights. We're just sifting through papers."

Erica leaned over to Dean and shrugged. "I tried."

He laughed. "Why don't we make our job easier? We'll bring everything down so we can go through it more comfortably. It's gotta come down anyway, right?"

"Right..." Maggie took another sip of her coffee. She was all for easy, but not if it meant climbing up and down that ladder. And with a box! Oh God. She could already hear the sirens from the ambulance.

"You expect us to carry boxes out of the attic?" Erica said. "Who do you think we are? Wonder Woman?"

Maggie could kiss Erica and her laziness right then and there.

"Actually, I expect to hand them down to you," Dean said. "You can handle that, can't you?"

Guilt oozed its way into her chest. What was she doing? He wasn't her helper. "You don't have to go to all that trouble. I can hire someone to do that."

"Are you kidding? After eating these," he said, grabbing another popover, "I could use the exercise. It's not a problem. Honest."

He was making it harder and harder not to love the guy. "Okay, then. Sounds like a plan."

"Well, apparently I'm not going to get out of working at all, so yeah, I can handle that," Erica said. "You're still invited to the party. That's if you want to go."

"It's been a while since I last skated, but I'm game if Maggie is."

Maggie fought the grin that threatened to take over her face. Skating with Dean? Yeah, baby. Heck, she'd do anything with him. "I guess you can count us in."

"Great. Now, what are you cooking for breakfast? Because as much as I love them, I apparently can't live on popovers alone."

"But you can try, right?" Dean asked.

"You got that right."

Maggie headed for the kitchen. As a yawn threatened, she turned her back to Dean and Erica and gave in to the attack. Albeit, discreetly. At least with the prospect of physical activity, she'd have an excuse for being exhausted. Hopefully not too

exhausted to go ice skating. Dean might have to hold her upright.
Hmmm… That wouldn't be such a bad thing, either.

* * * *

Hot chocolates in hand, Dean stepped away from the snack bar,
which was decorated in a zillion red hearts. How had he not known
it was Valentine's Day? And neither Erica nor Maggie had uttered a
word. Some boyfriend he turned out to be.

Not that Maggie was up to any kind of date. He'd lost count of
the times she'd yawned during their trips around the rink, and she'd
clung to him more for support than anything romantic. Not that he
minded. He took any excuse to hold her. Or kiss her. Or just be
near her.

Whatever happened to that man who'd been happy to like her
from afar? Gone, that's what. He could never go back to being that
person once this fiasco with Lindy finally ended. Maggie was a
drug. Plain and simple. And when it all blew up in his face—and it
would eventually, once she knew about the real him—he'd find a
way to deal with the pain. Until that day, he would enjoy what time
he could have with her, because it would be the best time of his
life. There would never be another Maggie.

As he approached the bench they were sharing, she smiled and
covered up another yawn. His heart ached. She was physically
exhausted—no thanks to his brilliantly stupid idea about emptying
the attic—but had insisted on coming out anyway. Would she get
any rest tonight? He still wasn't sure Lindy hadn't possessed her
last night.

He handed her one of the hot chocolates and sat beside her.
"I'm afraid this is the only Valentine's gift you're gonna get from
me today."

"I don't think we've been going out long enough for gifts, do
you? But thank you." She stifled another yawn while opening the
lid.

"I feel bad working you so hard today."

She sighed. "You didn't. I have a confession to make. I woke
up tired."

Damn it. Why couldn't he be wrong for once? "Please
reconsider staying in a hotel tonight."

She wrapped her gloved hands around the Styrofoam cup. "I
know you mean well, but I wish you'd stop asking me to do that.

Yes, I believe she possessed me last night, but it was my mistake. I won't leave the books within reach again."

"What do books have to do with—oh, she's reading. When are you going to realize she's not going to stop?"

"She'll stop when she has nothing to do. I'll make sure there won't be anything around to tempt her, so I should be able to sleep."

"I wish I could say that would stop her, but she'll keep at it until she wears you down, gets the combination, and vamooses you out of the house."

"Then I'll try the dog thing. I'm not spending another night out of that house until this whole lawsuit thing is dealt with."

"Yeah, about that. I know what I said, but now I'm thinking the dog thing won't work. Barnaby can see ghosts, but he can't make them solid." Which meant the only sure-fire way to keep Lindy away until she was gone for good was for him to touch Maggie while she slept, requiring that he…sleep with her. Could he do that and not jump her bones? Oh hell. She probably wouldn't even go for it anyway. But if she did… *Oh God, kill me. Kill me now.* He swallowed the lump in his throat. "I could sleep with you."

She looked at him with widened eyes. "What?"

"Nothing sexual. Just sleep. You wear a chastity belt to bed, right?" He laughed and nudged her, but she didn't even smile at his joke.

"I don't want you doing something that makes you uncomfortable."

She shouldn't be thinking about his comfort; he'd rather have blue balls than see her suffer. "I'll be fine. Honest."

"Even knowing Lindy will be able to see…everything?"

"I'm sleeping over, not living there. I'll come over before your bedtime and go home on the way to work. So what if I'm late? I know the boss."

Thank God that got a laugh out of her. He was beginning to doubt his ability to lighten the mood.

"I don't even know how I could possibly thank you enough for this. Except…." Maggie grabbed his arm and smiled wickedly. "Wanna prank a ghost?"

She told him her idea. Man, she was definitely a girl after his heart. Oh heck, she had a part of it already. He almost didn't mind, either.

155

* * * *

Lindy floated from room to room, passing all the stuff she'd like to use but couldn't, especially that stack of books beside Maggie's bed. The book she'd started last night was downright steamy and she couldn't wait to get back into it. She would have loved to have kept control until she reached the end, but Maggie had set the alarm and Dean was due to come over. Lindy wasn't going to risk getting caught. Or zapped. Then it'd be another day before she could possess again.

At 8:07 p.m., according to the TV box, Maggie walked through the door, but with Dean in tow. Figured she'd bring him. Didn't the guy have his own apartment?

Lindy swung her fist through Dean's head. "Why can't you just go home?"

She was more than ready to possess. But instead of leaving, he insisted on moving the boxes from Mom's bedroom to the dining room, since they'd planned on sorting through all that junk tomorrow.

Even Maggie helped carry those dusty boxes, much to Dean's dismay. Hey, whatever made her sleep faster was fine by Lindy. But the clock sure did seem to move slowly.

After stacking the last box, Dean stretched. "I don't know about you, but I'm beat. Do you mind if I crash on your couch tonight? Then I can help get an early start on this."

"My couch is always available for you," Maggie said. "I just wish I had an extra bed. I'd give you Erica's if I thought she'd be out all night."

Oh great. The man was staying. But as long as he stayed downstairs, he'd never know what was going on in Maggie's room. He wouldn't go up there to investigate without reason, so Lindy wouldn't give him one. She'd be as quiet as a ghost. Ha-ha!

"Couch will be fine. I've slept in worse places."

"Lindy's not going to bother you?"

"I'd rather she bother me than bother you. But I'll call you if she starts to strangle me."

"Ha-ha, very funny."

Lindy swore. If she didn't bug Dean—even a little—he'd wonder what was up. Nothing like postponing her fun, as if she had all that much time to begin with.

Maggie and Dean headed upstairs, grabbed some bedding from the hallway closet, and then returned downstairs. After they made up the couch, Dean pulled her into his arms.

"I had fun today. Thanks for being my Valentine."

"You're a strange man to think moving boxes is fun."

"We ice skated, too."

"Did we? I remember falling a lot and you catching me. That couldn't have been fun."

He laughed. "Well...it might have had something to do with the company." He took her face in his hands and kissed her.

Lindy almost looked away. Kevin had never kissed her like that. Of course, he was only seventeen at the time. He probably kissed better now. Not that she'd ever find out. Without Maggie's body, she'd never experience anything like that. And she wanted to. She wanted to very much.

She also wouldn't mind someone having a bulge in their pants for her.

"Goodnight, Maggie."

"You sure you don't want to come upstairs?"

Shit. No!

"Maggie...I thought we talked about this. I'm not comfortable with her...watching."

"Her?" Lindy asked. "Who the hell is—oh. Me! Thank God." Her breath released on a giggle. That was too close.

"I know. Can't blame a girl for trying. See you in the morning." Maggie smiled and headed up the stairs.

Dean turned around and grinned at Lindy. "Did you enjoy the show?"

"Were you doing that for me? Won't Maggie be hurt to know that?"

"And you're going to tell her how?"

Oooh. Could she hate another man as much? She didn't think so. "Why are you staying the night? Aren't you afraid I'll strangle you in your sleep?"

"I thought you heard. I'm helping to go through your mother's stuff. You do want Eddie out of the picture, don't you?"

"Sure, sure." Had she lingered here long enough? Oh hell. Maggie probably hadn't fallen asleep by now anyway. Maybe another minute or two...

He sat on the couch. "What do you really want, Lindy? Before you realized what you could do with Maggie, what did you want? What kept you here?"

This again? The man truly was a broken record. "Let's say something or someone kept me here. Up until meeting you, I had no reason to believe anyone could help me. So why would that keep me around? Maybe there isn't anywhere for people to go."

"If that were true, where's your mother?" Dean shook his head. "The only thing keeping you here is you. And your insane desire to possess Maggie. You have to stop doing that or you'll never move on."

"You kind of put the kibosh on possessing Maggie, now haven't you? As long as she continues to attach herself to this house, what's the use? I have more fun hovering around. So thanks so much for that."

"My pleasure."

Smug bastard. She'd like to give him the pleasure of her fist. Instead, she stuck her tongue out and poofed away, right into Maggie's room. Hopefully that was enough to keep Dean from growing suspicious.

The light was out, but Maggie hadn't fallen asleep, or relaxed enough. It took another ten agonizing minutes until she glowed enough for Lindy to slip inside. Not that she was counting.

She turned on the bedside lamp and grabbed the book she'd started the previous night. Before she got comfortable and lost in reading, she checked the alarm clock. Good. Not set. Except it wasn't all good. Maybe Dean was the alarm clock. Shit. Well, she should be safe until at least six-thirty. Dean didn't appear to be the kind of guy who woke up early.

A knock sounded at the door. Lindy froze.

"Maggie?"

Dean? What did he want? "Yes?"

The door opened. "Where do you keep the aspirin?"

"Uhhh…" *Think, think.* "In the kitchen?" Shit, she didn't mean to make it sound like a question. She needed to distract him from that. "Too much ice skating today?"

"Nah. Too much ghost." He walked over to the bed and sat down.

Lindy shifted Maggie's legs away so they wouldn't touch. Why couldn't he just stay downstairs?

"You okay? I thought you were going to sleep."

"I needed some relaxing time, first. You know, reading." She held up the book to make her point.

He leaned into her, but still not touching. "I know a way to relax you."

"Yeah?" She swallowed. What was he doing? He'd made it clear he wasn't interested in doing it here. "But you said—"

"Forget what I said." He took Maggie's hand.

No, no, no! Electricity ripped through her body. Not a moment later, Lindy found herself floating above the living room floor, zapped of all her strength.

Footsteps pounded down the steps and Dean appeared. "Glad to see I still have the touch."

She didn't even have enough in her to shout obscenities at him. And she would have. A lot of them.

He disabled the alarm, went outside, and returned with a gym bag. He reset the alarm and headed for the stairs. "Just so you know, Maggie is the one who decided to get back at you." He lifted the bag. "And if you couldn't tell, I'll be sleeping in her bed from now on, so you can kiss any future possessions goodbye. You better think about another way to get what you need to move on, because you're not getting it through Maggie. Good night."

Damn it! This wasn't fair. She hadn't asked to be a ghost. She hadn't asked for anything. Maybe it *was* time she asked for some help. She certainly wasn't getting it on her own. But the thought of asking Dean for anything made her want to hurl.

* * * *

Maggie tugged the covers up as Dean walked in her room. "I was right, wasn't I?"

Only way to explain having suddenly seen Dean sitting on her bed holding her hand. Lindy had taken control. Maggie fisted the covers as tears came to her eyes. She didn't want to give up this house to Eddie, but if Dean didn't succeed, what choice did she have?

He tossed his bag on the floor and kicked off his shoes. "Yeah. I have a feeling she won't be back up here for a while. And not because she doesn't want to. I think I weakened her considerably. She didn't look all that well. For a ghost."

"Good. Glad to know I'm not the only one."

"Why do you say that? Did she hurt you?"

"Didn't feel a thing. I'm sure I would have in the morning, though."

"That's true," he said, staring at the bed. The double-sized mattress really was kind of small for the giant, not that he was supposed to sleep away from her. For this to work, they'd have to touch. All night.

She still couldn't believe he'd actually suggested it. But now, with the way he was staring at the bed… "Are you changing your mind?" She wouldn't blame him if he did. Sleeping with a woman without the benefits of sex had to be a man's worst nightmare. "If she's as weak as you say, she probably can't even try anything tonight."

He shook his head. "I'm not taking that chance. Just wondering what is the best way."

"Best way?"

"To sleep and not touch you anywhere inappropriate."

"You won't insult me if you happen to touch my boobs. It's just sleep, Dean." But she wouldn't mind at all if he copped a feel. She snuggled under the covers and turned on her side, facing the edge. "And that's what I'll be doing. Sleeping. Good night."

Would he snuggle or place his back against hers? Would this even work if he was a mover during sleep?

The bed dipped with his weight and he snuggled up behind her. However, the blanket tightened around her.

"Dean, you're not under the covers. You'll get cold."

"That's okay. I don't need them."

"Don't be ridiculous." She turned around. "You still have your clothes on? I thought you were going to wear your sweats."

"I changed my mind. Go to sleep."

What was his problem? He'd just said Lindy wasn't moving anywhere to even sneak a peek of him changing his clothes. Would she ever understand that man?

"I can't sleep knowing you'll be uncomfortable." She climbed out of bed and headed for the door.

"Where are you going?"

"To get you a blanket. It's on the couch."

"I can get it."

"No. I'm already up." She shook her head as she descended the stairs. Sheesh. How could she get it through his head that she didn't care about being a virgin anymore? She grabbed the blanket and froze. According to Dean, Lindy was here, since this was the place of her death. Maggie would love to throttle her neck, except if it weren't for Lindy, Dean wouldn't even be in Maggie's bed. It certainly wasn't the perfect way, but maybe she'd be able to finally break down that wall of his.

She looked around the empty room, but nothing seemed out of the ordinary. No ripples, or whatever a ghost might project, if anything. "I'm not sorry for the stunt we pulled on you. You kind of deserved it. But I am sorry you're stuck here, and I really wish you'd move on. Don't you want to see your family again? I know Mom would love to see you. She talked about you often. Life, your existence, whatever, has to be better for you elsewhere. I know mine would be if you left."

Or would it? Because if Dean left with the ghost, her life would be empty.

* * * *

Dean lay back on the bed. This wasn't going to work. Why in the hell did he suggest sleeping with her? He was going to stay awake all night with a boner, he was sure of it.

Maggie returned with the blanket and shook her head at him. He couldn't blame her for that. He was looking kind of stupid lying on top of the covers, fully dressed. Well, nearly. He had taken off his shoes.

And as for the cold bit—he could stand to be cold. Maybe it would keep his libido at bay.

Ah, who was he kidding? He could be in the middle of Nowhere, Alaska right now, standing in sub-zero temps, and if she were beside him, he'd have a boner.

She tossed the blanket over his body. "You can still change your mind."

He could, but she needed rest. If he kept his mind there, thinking about her wellbeing instead of his dick, he could do this. Hell, he might even get some sleep. "I'm fine. Get in bed."

"Are you sure you don't want to wear your sweats?"

And have his desire exposed for anyone to see? "These clothes are warmer. Trust me, I'm fine."

She slid beneath the covers and turned her back toward him. He hesitated as he placed his arm around her, making sure not to snuggle up too close for fear she'd feel his erection. He didn't need to give her any encouragement in that department.

161

When he settled in, she grabbed his hand and held it against her chest, as if she was afraid he'd move or leave her. Within seconds, her breathing slowed and she slept.

He took in her scent and tried to relax, reciting, "She needs to sleep, she needs to sleep," over and over in his head.

And she would sleep as long as he held her. Problem was, could he ever let her go?

Chapter 18

His mother shoved her pudgy arms into her coat. "I can't believe that judge. He's been bribed."

Eddie exited the courthouse and braced for the impending storm. Snowflakes flew in the air and hit his face, but were nothing compared to the barrage of complaints ready to spew from Mom. "Just because he didn't see in our favor doesn't mean—"

"Sure it does. First he was able to see our case on such short notice. Then sat back while that bitch and her boyfriend lied. There were no fumigators, which means she broke the will."

"And why would she move out if she didn't think there were bugs? Admit it. It was a fruitless lawsuit and I should have never filed to begin with. Now no judge will take us seriously if she actually breaks the will." Eddie walked off toward the parking lot, wishing with all he had that she'd stay behind, say something stupid, and get arrested. But no. She followed him instead.

"You mean when. When she breaks the will."

"You don't know she'll do that. Especially if she finds whatever is in that house. Are you going to tell me what it is now?"

"No. It'd be just like you to go blab it to her in a fit of rage. Guess I have to take care of things on my own."

The only person he was mad at was her. But what was she talking about? He stopped and grabbed her arm. "Things? What things? What are you planning?"

She patted his cheek. "Now, now. Nothing to worry your head about. You let Mom take care of you."

Eddie nearly laughed. When had she ever taken care of him? Oh wait. When it suited her needs, that's when.

* * * *

Maggie rushed inside the restaurant and brushed the snow from her shoulders. Damn stuff was coming down harder. Following the instructions from Erica's text, she found her cousin sitting in a booth. "Thanks for meeting me for lunch."

"You're welcome, but did you have to schedule during the blizzard?"

Maggie slid onto the bench and shrugged out of her coat. "It's not that bad out there."

"Yet. If this keeps up, I might not return to work."

The waitress came by and took their order. The only thing that appealed to Maggie was the soup. She should be celebrating, but her stomach wasn't in it.

"Uh oh," Erica said. "I take it the suit didn't go well."

"Actually, I got lucky. Judge believed us. Man, if he ever found out we lied…"

"But you didn't lie. Dean said he'd take care of it and he did. So what if he was a little late? The important thing is that the fumigator didn't find anything. I don't think I could have stood another week with Mom."

Maggie leaned across the table. "He wasn't going to find anything. It was all a ruse."

"Did the judge ask you that? Of course not, so you're fine. Be happy he saw your case so soon. You could have been in limbo for weeks."

Erica had a point. Maybe the judge took pity on Maggie after all the grief Eddie and Gina had put her through. Probably figured it would be a short case, too.

"So, what did you want to meet for? You could have told me all this tonight."

"Since when can't I want to have lunch with my cousin?"

"Since I became your roomie. Oh I get it. You don't want the gho—" Erica shut her mouth and shrugged an apology. "I meant, Lindy to hear us, is that it?"

The restaurant was noisy and Maggie doubted anyone was eavesdropping, but still, it was probably better to keep their discussion low-key. Because it wasn't just talk of ghosts that she worried about.

"Something like that. I need your opinion and I don't want it getting back to Dean." Maggie's heart rate picked up. Spilling the beans was liable to get her ridiculed, but after three nights of sleeping with Dean so close but so out of reach, she wanted more. But how could she get more without spooking the poor guy?

"I thought you and Dean were sharing everything nowadays."

"Not really." With work and writing and going through Grandma's boxes, there hadn't been time for much else.

"Well, you're sharing your bed. That's pretty much everything."

"He's only sleeping in my bed to keep Lindy away." And it was working, too. She hadn't slept so well in weeks, or written so much. But the longer he stayed, the worse she felt. He should want to sleep in her bed, not feel obligated. Using him as an anchor wasn't doing her any favors, either.

"What?" Erica's eyes widened. "You mean you aren't..."

Maggie shook her head.

"How come? I could have sworn he was into you. Or are you the one pushing him away? And if so, why in the world would you do that?"

"We almost...did it...once. Then he found out something about me and it kind of changed his mind."

"Changed his mind? You got some kind of disease I don't know about?"

It was beginning to feel that way. Maggie leaned forward. "Yeah, and it's called being a virgin."

Erica choked on her soda. "What? You're kidding, right? You're on the pill."

Who kidded about that? Maggie leaned back and shook her head. "Actually, I'm not. I just let you believe I was."

"Why would you do that?"

"So you would think differently, why else?"

Of course, if her plan succeeded, maybe she *should* be on the pill. She made a mental note to call her doctor.

"Well it worked. Damn, girl. What are you waiting for? The right guy?" Erica's eyes widened followed by an eruption of laughter. "Oh I get it now. You freaked out Dean because he thinks you think he's the right guy."

"Is that what I did?" Except he was the right guy, it just wasn't the reason she'd waited. Being the loner that she was, and holing up each night writing, didn't exactly make her available to men. "How do I get him un-freaked then?"

"You could always take charge and initiate it. Do it in his office. I bet Bridget would turn a deaf ear. Or better yet, do it after she leaves."

"He won't have sex with me in bed, what makes you think—"

"Not sex-sex. Oral sex. Give him a blow job. He won't have taken your virginity then, well, except for your mouth. And if it turns out well, I'm sure he'd change his mind, then."

"Oh, and I'm supposed to just walk up to him and do that? I'm not even sure I could do it properly."

"You've got a mouth. You know how to suck. That's all he needs."

Their food arrived and Erica dug into her sandwich. Maggie could only stir her soup. Could she actually give Dean a blow job?

"I don't know. Shouldn't he be in the mood?"

"You touch him, he'll be in the mood." Erica dipped a French fry in some ketchup. "Now here's what you do…"

Maggie shook her head. Maybe telling her cousin hadn't been such a good idea after all. It all sounded so risky. But if she didn't take a risk now, she may never have the chance again.

* * * *

Dean shook the snow from his coat as he entered his business and found one pouting ghost and no sign of his assistant. The ghost he didn't care about. "Where's Bridget?"

Peter jerked his thumb over his shoulder toward the hall. "She's back in the bathroom. Why do you keep giving her work? She never has time for me."

"Because she works for me, not you."

"If you keep giving her work, how am I supposed to get out of your hair?"

"You could always stay on the roof. Or better yet, leave."

"You're mean, you know that?"

The toilet flushed and Bridget emerged from the bathroom. "Hey. How'd Maggie's case go? I didn't get a chance to ask her yet."

"Judge dismissed the suit." No thanks to Dean. It'd been pure luck to find a fumigator who could do a quick look-see on such short notice. "I have a feeling Gina isn't done yet. Something's not right with that woman. Should have seen the look she gave Maggie.

Guess I'll have to talk to them after all. I was hoping to avoid a confrontation."

Too bad he couldn't get any DNA samples from Eddie. Not that he believed Lindy's accusation. That ghost probably didn't know what the truth was anymore. But if by some strange chance she was correct, it would get that family off Maggie's back.

"That scary, huh?" Bridget asked.

"I'd rather face Lindy. By the way, any luck with her yearbook?"

She shook her head. "No one wants to talk over the phone. That's if they even answer it. You'd think I was some damned telemarketer. We might need to do a face-to-face investigation."

He'd been afraid of that. "Get addresses and we'll plan an attack later this week." Certainly wouldn't be tomorrow, even if the storm stopped in a couple of hours. "Snow's coming down pretty good. Why don't you call it a day?"

She beamed. "Thanks. I knew there was a reason I liked working for you." She wrapped a scarf around her neck and slipped on her coat. "Messages are on your desk. And Peter? Leave Dean alone."

As if that were possible. Dean nearly laughed. He entered his office and tossed his coat on the guest chair.

Peter popped into the room, blocking the way to Dean's desk. "You like Maggie, don't you?"

"Didn't Bridget just say to leave me alone?"

"You're not doing anything for me to disturb."

"Except existing."

Peter grabbed his chest. "Ouch. All the more reason to find the guy who killed me, right?"

Dean was not getting sucked into the same old conversation again. He walked around the ghost, although Peter nearly made it impossible without touching. Wonder what would happen if he touched Peter while he was hovering inside the desk? Maybe one day he'd find out. "Good bye, Peter. Go haunt someone else."

"Like Maggie?"

"No!" Shit.

"See, I knew you liked her. Otherwise you'd be billing her."

"You know who I bill?"

"I know everything about this place. What else is there to do?"

The front door buzzed, signaling someone had entered. Bridget must not have locked up behind her. Not that he'd told her to.

Whoever it was, they'd make the ghost disappear and give him some peace. He returned to the foyer to find the topic of Peter's conversation.

"Hey." Dean couldn't help but smile at Maggie. She'd been wreaking havoc on his libido, but sleeping beside her these past three nights had been the best in his life.

Maggie returned his smile as she stood by the entrance, removing her winter gear. Her cheeks were ruddy, but that was probably due to the weather. She hadn't spoken a word, though.

"What's going on? Everything okay?"

Her smiled faltered and she placed her coat on the reception desk.

All sorts of issues ran through his head. "Has Eddie—"

She raised her hand, stopping him. "Eddie hasn't done anything that I know of. I came to see...you."

"Me? Oh. Does Tom have another—"

She raised her hand again, shaking her head and stepped toward him. "Not for work."

Before he could ask another question, she stopped in front of him and placed her hand on his chest. "I feel like we don't have any time together, what with Erica and Lindy in the house. Is Bridget coming back?"

He stared down at her hand on his chest and his heart raced. How many times had he pictured her doing such a thing in bed? Too many. "No. Sent her home."

"Good. I was sent home, too, but thought I'd come here instead." The smile returned and she inched her hand lower, toward his belt buckle, and good Lord, he was getting hard.

"What are you doing?"

"Don't worry. I locked the front door. No one can see." She lowered the zipper and stuck her hand inside his pants.

Holy shit! He was more than hard now and damn, did she feel good. God, he wanted her. Had wanted her since he'd met her last summer. But what she was doing wasn't right. Not here, anyway. "Maggie, stop."

Thankfully she did. "Am I—Am I doing it wrong?"

"God, no. It's just..." While his dick had enjoyed her ministrations, he couldn't stand the thought that Peter was probably standing right beside her, watching it all. Except there was probably no probably about it, now was there?

"Just what? Is it still about my virginity, because last I saw, giving you a blowjob—"

"Oh God, stop. Don't say any more." To have her mouth on him… Man, if she kept talking like that he'd blow for sure. Like he needed any more grief from that ghost. Shit. He zipped up his pants, although his erection made it damn hard.

A frown marred her lovely face. "Why don't you admit you don't want me?"

"Ah, sweetheart, that's not it." Did she think all men got erections around women? Hmmm… Maybe she did. "That's not it at all. It's just…we're not alone."

She looked behind her. Then around him into his office. "I don't see anyone."

"And you won't."

Confusion flittered in her eyes. "You said Lindy could only go—"

"It's not Lindy." Dean rubbed his head. She already knew he could see ghosts, so what was the big deal? "Remember Bridget mentioning Peter?"

She nodded a split second before her eyes widened. "He's a ghost? How many do you know?"

"Too many."

"So there's no safe place," she muttered.

"My apartment's safe." Now why'd he go and say that? She would think he was really considering it. Okay, maybe he was considering it, but not one sided. No, no, no. If he were to actually succumb to her, he'd definitely reciprocate.

And he had to face it: he could easily succumb. The last few days had been a wonderful torture. He couldn't even jerk himself off before bed because Lindy kept popping up at the most inopportune times. And when he'd found some relief during his morning shower at home, it really hadn't been enough. Probably never would be, either. He wanted her.

"Your apartment?" Her voice sounded hopeful, but her face paled. She'd had that same expression with the ladder, too.

He would have laughed if he had an inkling she'd take it the right way. Then again, fear wasn't exactly a laughing matter to the fearful. "You're afraid of heights, aren't you?"

She lowered her head. "More like…concerned."

"Concerned?"

"Yeah. Concerned I'll fall."

"But you have stairs in your house. You don't seem all that concerned with them."

"That's because I can't see through them. And they're solid, my foot can't fall through. There's also a landing in the middle so I can't see all the way down." She shuffled over to a chair and plopped down. "I swear I've been cursed. Sure wish I knew what I'd done wrong."

He knelt before her. "You haven't done anything wrong."

"Oh? So you're saying, if it weren't for Peter, we'd be doing it right now?"

"I don't know." Probably. Oh hell, definitely. Didn't she know the power she had over him?

"That's what I thought." She stared at him. "I like you, Dean, and I love kissing you, but I want more."

And he wasn't giving it to her. Wasn't sure he could, either. Oral sex could easily turn into sex-sex. Maybe. He'd been able to sleep with her without sex-sex; he should be able to stop at oral sex. Especially if she got him off first. Yeah, that would do it. But he couldn't say that here. Not with Peter listening. "Let's go to my apartment and talk, okay? I'll make sure you don't fall."

"Talk?"

"That's all I can promise right now." Later, when he got her alone, he could tell her more. But Peter wasn't getting a show no matter what.

* * * *

Maggie slumped in the chair. He wanted to talk. She wanted sex. No, strike that. She wanted more than sex. She wanted him. All of him. At least he'd suggested his apartment. Of course, by the time she climbed up those steps—in the snow, no less—she'd be lucky to talk coherently.

Now why'd she go sneak some of Tom's whiskey before coming over here? Oh yeah. Because she'd thought she was going to give Dean a blowjob. Seemed smart at the time.

Amazing how the second helping hadn't burned nearly as much as the first.

She stood and the room only spun a little. Guess the booze was kicking in, what little good it was doing her now. "You must really think I'm crazy."

Dean smiled and she nearly melted. "Far from it. I'm the one who sees ghosts, remember? Go get your coat. I'll drive."

"But my car." Oh, why'd she bring that up? She was in no shape to drive, and admitting she drank for courage was more embarrassing than admitting she was a virgin.

"We'll pick it up later. No use both of us driving in that mess."

He went back to his office. She put on her coat and grabbed her purse. The storm hadn't let up one little bit and the steps up to his apartment would probably be treacherous covered in snow. *Don't think about it. Don't think about it.* He'd promised not to let her fall.

She'd think about being with Dean instead. Even talking would be better than nothing. They really hadn't been able to discuss anything with Erica and Lindy hanging around. Having some quiet time with him would be better than nothing. Actually, it would be a dream.

He opened the door for her and the snow hit her in the face. Three shallow steps led to the small parking lot, not that she could see them all that clearly. Even the footsteps she'd left behind earlier were obliterated. Okay, that couldn't be good. She turned to tell Dean that maybe tonight wasn't such a great night to go to his apartment when her foot dropped sooner than she'd expected.

Her ankle twisted and pain shot up her leg. She cried out as she fell into the fluffy snow, which really wasn't all that soft over the concrete walkway. She landed on her hip, then her elbow, finally her head.

"Maggie!" Dean rushed over to her. "How bad?"

She reached for her ankle as tears sprung from her eyes. "I don't know. It hurts."

She didn't want to cry in front of him, but it was hard holding back. Especially when he helped her up and she tried to put weight on her ankle. That was so not happening.

"Looks like we're taking a detour to the emergency room." He lifted her into her arms as if she weighed nothing. Not exactly the way she'd imagined being swept off her feet.

So much for getting some alone time with Dean. Regardless of what he said, she was cursed.

Chapter 19

Maggie lay flat on her back on probably the smallest bed ever constructed. Dean relegated himself to the small plastic chair in the corner, under an assortment of medical thingamabobs, and he'd done that after she told him he could leave. Was he the greatest or what? "Why are you all the way over there?"

Dean smiled, got up, and moved to her side. "This better?"

She would have nodded, but her head wasn't working so great. "Yeah. Did they tell you if it was broken?"

"Now, why would they tell me before they tell you? When they know, they'll tell you."

Yeah, maybe. She'd seen how the nurses looked at him. Like maybe he was in charge. Heck, she wouldn't mind him being in charge of her. To surrender to his every command. Of course, the bed would have to be a lot bigger than this one. Oh, why wouldn't he command her?

"How you holding up?"

She blinked. What? Where was she? Oh yeah, the emergency room. Because she'd hurt her ankle. An ankle which was currently the size of a football. She gasped. "Why is my foot so big? And it's cold. Oh my God. Are they going to have to amputate?"

Dean placed his hands on her shoulders. "Sweetheart, calm down. That's the ice pack."

"Oh." God, he must think she was dumber than a rock. Maybe she should have told the nurse she'd had some liquor before taking the pain pill. But then Dean would know what a chicken shit she was.

He slipped off his coat and covered her exposed toes. "How's that? Warmer?"

"Awww, that's so sweet." She leaned up on her elbows and the room spun. "Whoa."

"What's the matter?"

"Feel kind of wobbly." She fell back against the mattress. Whatever was in that pill they gave her might have made her loopy, but at least it made the throbbing stop. Heck, she wasn't feeling much of anything.

"Then it's a good thing I'm still around, huh?"

"It's always a good thing when you're around." Like now. And when he slept beside her at night. Especially when he did that. Now if she could only get him to do more than sleep. "Tell me. If I asked you to kiss me, would you?"

He brushed the hair away from her forehead and nodded.

"Anywhere?" When he perused her body with his eyes, she said, "I mean like anywhere public. Not anywhere on my body." Although she wouldn't mind the anywhere on her body bit. "Or aren't you into PDA?"

He leaned down close. "I'd kiss you anywhere, anywhere."

Oh yeah… Hopefully she'd remember he said that, too. "Would you kiss me now? On the lips?"

"Sure, sweetheart." His lips were soft and he kept the kiss gentle. "Feel better?"

"Mmmm… That was nice." She closed her eyes for a moment as she floated. He was definitely the best kisser. "Dean?"

He chuckled. "Yes, sweetheart."

He called her sweetheart. Again. She liked being his sweetheart. She wanted to be his sweetheart forever. But if she were really his sweetheart, why did he avoid having sex with her?

* * * *

Dean did his best to keep from laughing. Whatever pill the nurse gave Maggie really did a number on her. Her inhibition flew out the door. That, and maybe reality.

Amputation? Really?

But he loved the way she smiled when he called her sweetheart. Heck, he loved calling her sweetheart. What he didn't love was seeing her smile turn into a frown, and the tears that leaked from the sides of her eyes. Hopefully the doctor would return soon with some news.

"Hey, hey. What's this?" He cupped her face and wiped the tears away. "Your ankle bothering you?"

She shook her head. "I don't want to be a virgin anymore."

"Ahhh, Maggie." He rested his forehead against hers. Her mind was all over the place. "Now's not a good—"

The curtain was flung open, causing Dean to step back, and the doctor stepped inside their little cubicle. He rambled on about how she only sprained her ankle, would be given a boot and crutches, as well as some pain medication, and then left as quickly as he arrived.

Thirty minutes later, Dean was driving his precious cargo in the still-falling snow. Thankfully Maggie hadn't brought up their previous conversation. Maybe she'd forgotten all about it, but he really didn't think he was all that lucky.

Her street hadn't been plowed yet and he foresaw getting his car snowed under. The alley wasn't much better, but at least he could park the car in the garage and keep it clean. Of course, that meant getting it into the garage. Once he stopped, he could very well be stuck.

While leaving the motor running, he opened the garage door, found a shovel and cleared the snow leading to the garage. A cardboard box sat on the garbage can and he ripped off four pieces to shove under the tires. By the time he climbed back inside car, she had fallen asleep.

Within striking distance of Lindy.

Shit. Dean lightly brushed Maggie's hand in case the brat had decided to take charge and was faking it. Maggie never stirred.

She was so beautiful, sleeping there at peace. What was he doing with her, really? He could never be what she deserved, but he wanted her. Man, did he want her. And until this mess with Lindy was resolved, he couldn't leave Maggie. But the longer he stayed, the harder it would be to leave. And he had to leave her eventually. Didn't he?

Man, oh man, why couldn't things be different? Of course, if they were, he wouldn't be sitting here now. If that wasn't all fucked up, he didn't know what was.

He drove into the garage but left the car running. Dilemma time. Did he shovel a path to the back door and hope Lindy didn't mess with Maggie, or carry Maggie in the hope he didn't slip and fall, thus injuring her further? Guess he'd take his chances with Lindy.

The house was dark. Where was Erica? Oh yeah. She'd texted Maggie that she was stuck at her parents' and had asked for a ride. Dean had texted her back with Maggie's condition. While Erica had been glad Maggie wasn't seriously injured, she grumbled that she had to spend another night at her folks'. He pretty much grumbled, too. Without Erica around, his chances of seeing Lindy had multiplied significantly.

Dean grabbed the shovel and worked his way to the back porch.

"What happened to Maggie?"

He jumped at Lindy's sudden appearance. At least if she was here, she wasn't possessing Maggie. "She sprained her ankle. So don't try any funny business."

"I wasn't going to. I know I behaved badly and I'm sorry. Forgive me?"

"No." As if his forgiveness mattered. Maggie was the injured party. While he shoveled, he kept an eye on the ghost. Seemed he didn't have to worry. Lindy wasn't done talking.

"I've thought a lot about what you and Maggie said. I'm willing to let you, or that Bridget chick, help me move on. That's if you can. Or still want to."

"I'm not helping you get laid." Because that would mean Maggie would get laid and no one was touching her except him.

Oh crap. When had he gotten so possessive? And if he was to let her go one day, wouldn't someone else... Yeah, he wasn't going there.

Lindy shook her head. "That's not the help I meant."

"Really? Why the change in attitude?" Could he really have an honest conversation with Lindy? Highly unlikely. Before he would let her speak, he held his palm out. "You know what? I don't want to know. Right now my priority is to get out of the snow and get Maggie in the house."

Lindy looked up as if she hadn't noticed the snowflakes falling, and maybe she hadn't. It wasn't like she could feel anything. "I get it. But I just wanted you to know that you can trust me. I'll leave Maggie alone."

He threw a shovel of snow at her, not that it hit her. Got her to flinch, though, which was almost as good. "And why should I believe you?"

"I don't know. What can I do to prove it?"

Could he ever trust her? Maybe, in time. A lot of time. Still, she'd have to work her way there. "Stay away."

"What? You mean forever?"

Wow, there was a pleasant thought. One she surely couldn't accomplish, though. One step out of her boundary would land her back inside the house. "Tonight. Stay away tonight. Don't show your face around here until after sunrise tomorrow. Can you do that?"

"And then we'll talk tomorrow? You'll help me move on?"

There was no way he could talk to Lindy alone and gain any ground. "I'll have Bridget come over tomorrow and we'll see."

Lindy easily agreed and then poofed out of sight. But what if he was wrong? What if he couldn't help her move on?

Because he wouldn't just be failing Lindy, now would he?

* * * *

Maggie awoke on the couch. The movie was still playing, although a little farther along than she remembered. Her left hand still nestled comfortably in Dean's. He'd taken it when the movie started, much to her surprise and delight. But she'd been sleeping. Was he still afraid? "I thought you said Lindy promised to stay away until morning. So why are you still holding my hand?"

He paused the movie. "You ever think that maybe I just like to hold it?"

"Yeah?" Would he be up to more than that? No use in squandering any more of their time alone; they might never get another chance of having both Lindy and Erica gone. The liquid courage had left Maggie's system long ago, as did the pain pill, but neither had helped her all that much, and if she didn't take this opportunity she'd have no one but herself to blame. She lifted their joined hands, settled her head on his lap and hugged his hand close to her breasts. "Do you like this, too? Because I do."

She didn't really need him to answer. The growing lump under her head spoke for him.

"This is nice. How's your ankle?"

In dire need of another dose of medication, but she wasn't going to break the mood or fog her brain. She lifted her wrapped foot; she'd taken the boot off when the movie started. "Still attached to my leg. Apparently no amputation was needed."

Just how far out of it had she been to have actually thought that? No more mixing booze and pills again, if she ever touched liquor again. At least he laughed at her little joke, so maybe he didn't think she was such a doofus.

He shook his head, still chuckling. "What am I gonna do with you?"

She could think of several things, none of which he'd go for. Well, except for one. "Kiss me?"

"I can do that." He stopped part-way. Apparently a body could only bend so far. Using her free hand, she grabbed him by the neck for leverage and met him the rest of the way.

He was a drug, pure and simple. She could kiss him until the sun came up and it wouldn't be long enough. While he explored her mouth, she moved his hand over her breast. Instant nipple hardness. Now, if he'd only take the hint and explore the rest of her body like he was exploring her mouth.

Hot damn, he did. When he squeezed her breast and ran a thumb over her extended nub, the lower part of her body nearly combusted. If only she could make her clothes disappear.

He deepened the kiss and she sucked on his tongue. Forget the booze, his pleasurable groan gave her the courage she needed. She moved her hand down his hard, massive chest, and stopped at his groin. Oh, he'd gotten much bigger. And harder.

Another groan from him reverberated in her mouth and it was oh so sexy.

Yesss. Now it was his turn. He would take a turn, wouldn't he?

* * * *

Dean kissed Maggie. Ravished her mouth. Her lips had never tasted better and he'd never been this hard. For anyone.

And her breast. Oh, it was perfect in his hand. But her clothes…yeah, they had to go. Before he could suggest she lose the top, her hand landed on his erection and, for the second time that day, he nearly came from her touch alone.

God, he wanted her, but that wasn't going to happen. And while she'd been eager to please him earlier, that wasn't going to happen, either. He could rock *her* world, though. Just not on the couch. Even without the threat of an interruption, it didn't seem right. She deserved a better treatment.

"Okay if I take you upstairs?"

Maggie wrapped her arms around his neck. "Thought you'd never ask."

She was probably under the assumption that he intended to take her virginity. He'd have to make sure she wasn't disappointed. He lifted her with ease and finagled his way up the stairs without banging her foot. When he placed her on the bed, she reached for his shirt. He grabbed her hands. "No, sweetheart."

She turned those emerald greens his way. "No? But I thought—"

"I know what you thought. You trust me?"

She furrowed her brow and nodded.

"Then let's start with taking off your shirt." He lifted the hem and slipped it over her head. She nearly spilled out of that bra of hers and he caught his breath. What a bounty.

"What about yours?"

"Not now. Later. Promise." And he might keep that promise. Someday. But not now, no matter how much skin-on-skin action he desired. At least his promise seemed to placate her. "Now lay back."

His heart hammered. God, was he really going to do this? Was he going to survive?

Yeah, that was the real question.

She unbuttoned her jeans. "Should I take these off?"

"Let me. I don't want you to move." He made sure not to jar her injured foot in the process of removing her jeans. Her bikini panties barely covered anything and his dick twitched in his pants. This wasn't about his dick, though. It would just have to wait.

She sat up on her elbows. "You're not going to get undressed? At all?"

"No."

"But—"

"It's not up for debate. Now lay back. And don't move."

Her mouth imitated a fish a couple of times before she finally closed it and lay back. Her scent of arousal made his mouth water for her. The panties had to stay on, though. He'd never seen anything hotter in his life.

Being careful of her sore ankle, he straddled her and kissed her some more. Her half-naked body against his fully clothed one did nothing to slake his arousal. He might come in his pants after all. Hopefully she wouldn't notice.

He slipped one of the cups up and covered the exposed breast with his hand. Here was some skin-on-skin action he could savor. Playing with her hardened nipple elicited little moans from her. And more twitches from his cock. But he wasn't about to satisfy that body part.

She was willing to satisfy it as she ran her hand along his erection. About ready to explode, he shoved her hand away.

"What'd I say about moving?" He hated making it sound like a demand, but if she touched him again, he might not be able to control himself.

"But—"

"Maggie, I know you're curious. But if you don't do what I say, I'm gonna have to stop."

"No! I'm sorry. I'll be good." She smiled. "I'm all yours."

All his. Yes. And he would take damn good care of her, too.

He removed the pesky bra and laved one tasty nipple while he tweaked the other. Her breath sped. Her back arched. Nice reactions, but not good enough. He ran his hand along the curve of her waist and hip, her skin soft against his palm. When he reached her thigh, he turned toward the juncture and palmed her sex.

She jerked on a gasp. Getting closer. He loved her little reactions. Probably had more to do with him touching her where no man had touched her before than from any pain in her ankle.

He paused at that thought.

No man *had* touched her before. He was her first. He would always be her first. Maybe that wasn't so bad after all. He kissed her mouth and explored with his tongue while he slipped a finger inside her.

She moaned.

"You're so wet."

"Is that—"

"That's good, sweetheart. That's very good." And he couldn't wait to taste her.

* * * *

It took everything in Maggie to keep her arms by her side when she craved to touch Dean. Run her hands down his chest and up under his t-shirt. See if his nipples got as hard as hers. But he didn't want her touching him. Heck, he wouldn't even get undressed.

And what was up with that? Why not get undressed? Didn't seem all that fair, since she was practically naked. Well, she had wanted him to command her. Who knew her wish would come true so soon? Or be so frustrating?

He kissed her mouth like he owned her. Then he sucked her breasts like they were a lifeline. As he kissed his way down her body, he left a burning trail along her skin. When had kisses felt so sensual? So wicked? He bit into the waistband of her panties and she anticipated a rip. But no. Instead, he settled between her legs, and pushed them apart, being more careful of her right leg.

Now what? Did he just want a good view while he put his fingers inside her? And man, did she want his fingers inside her. When he'd touched her down there earlier, she thought for sure she'd come and he'd only ran his fingers along the outside.

He slid her panties to the side, exposing her. "God, you're beautiful."

She lifted her head to get a peek as he lowered his and slid his tongue along her clit.

"Oh good Lord." Closing her eyes, she threw her head back and gripped the sheets. Her finger had never felt this good. Heck, his finger hadn't felt this good.

How could something so soft and warm send her into another dimension? If possible, she would have floated from the wonderful sensations.

He stuck a finger in her and she jerked.

He stuck in another. Pressure built in her lower body. She was so close.

He rubbed her. Closer.

Sucked her. That did it.

Her world exploded on an orgasm greater than she'd ever experienced. She arched her back and nearly screamed in joy. What had he done to her? And would he do it again?

As she lay there shuddering, Dean crawled up along her left side and held her close. She was boneless. Simply, wonderfully, boneless.

Chapter 20

Maggie rolled over and pain shot up her leg. She gasped and then covered her mouth. Dean was still sleeping beside her. Under the covers this time. Up close and personal.

Her sigh of contentment died on another flash of pain.

Damn ankle. If it weren't for that, she might have woken up used and abused and loving every moment of it. Although with the way her ankle, hip, and elbow hurt, she was feeling pretty abused. Just not in a good way.

Time for another pain pill. Except they were downstairs, and her boot and crutches were way across the room. The clock displayed the ungodly time of 5:34. No way would she wake him up so early. Unless...

Last night he'd shown her what wicked things he could do with his mouth. Such tantalizing things. And he wouldn't even let her reciprocate. Didn't seem fair. She'd started it in his office and might have succeeded if not for the ghost.

Well, there wasn't any ghost now. If Lindy were smart—and she didn't seem stupid—she'd keep her promise to stay away until sunrise, giving Maggie plenty of time to give Dean the best wake-up call ever. Thank God he'd changed into his sweats before coming to bed. This might have been difficult if he wore his jeans. She rubbed her hands together, creating some warmth. Didn't need to give the man a start, or wake him before she got started. He might stop her then.

Slowly she lifted the waistband of his sweats and slipped her hand inside. Tiny hairs bristled against her palm as she made her way down to the prize. Ooh. He was all soft and warm. Well, maybe not so soft. She ran her hand along his penis and it was...growing.

Dean inhaled sharply.

Oh shit. No time to lose. She dived under the covers, freed his penis, and took the hardening length into her mouth. And damn, if that didn't get her all wet for him.

* * * *

Dean smiled as euphoria surrounded his dick. Best dream ever. Or was it a dream? He blinked several times and tried to focus, but the room was dark. As his boner grew, his eyes adjusted to the lack of light. Yep, there was a head over his groin.

And then lips around his cock.

Soooooo not a wet dream.

"Maggie?"

Calling her name only spurred her on. She sucked on him with the expertise of an experienced woman. Either she'd been holding out on him or someone had given her some good pointers.

Please be the second. Please be the second.

He reached for her head. He'd meant to stroke her hair, or even pull her back—eventually—but then she ran her wet, sloppy tongue all over his dick and he might have given her a shove instead. And damn, if she didn't take that as encouragement. She took him deeper. Sucked harder. He was on the verge of exploding.

After last night's activities, it had taken him several hours—or so it seemed—before he could go to sleep. His erection had refused to leave. But now, if she didn't stop, and stop soon...

"Maggie, you keep that up, I'm gonna come."

That was apparently the wrong thing to say. As she continued sucking him like a popsicle, she ran her finger along his nuts.

"Holy fuck!" The orgasm rocked his world as the spasm jerked his body. And through it all she continued sucking. He fisted the sheets as she drained him dry.

She adjusted his sweat pants and sat up. "Wow. That was fun."

Fun? Yeah, that was fun, all right. Most fun he'd had in months. Or maybe ever. After a few head-clearing moments, he turned on the bedside lamp. Had to make sure he wasn't mistaken. With her hair going every which way, Maggie smiled and her eyes sparkled. Was he the luckiest man or what? "Come here."

Slowly, she settled in next to him. "Good morning."

He pulled her into an embrace and kissed her deeply. What was this woman doing to him? She'd tilted his world and he wasn't sure he could straighten it. Soon he wouldn't be able to deny her anything. That's if the moment hadn't already arrived.

He broke the kiss and caressed her cheek. "Damn, sweetheart. Where'd you learn that?"

She blushed. The color was adorable on her. It also answered his question.

"Erica, huh?"

Thank God she nodded. Maybe he was her first for everything. He so badly wanted to be her only, but why dwell on the impossible. "Don't tell her I said so, but she taught you well."

Her smile melted his insides. He was goo with her. No doubt about it.

"Why didn't you want me to touch you last night?"

The truth or a stupid lie? Except he didn't feel right lying to her. "Because when you touched me...I was afraid I'd lose control, okay? I wasn't about to hurt you any further."

"You didn't hurt me at all."

"Tell that to your ankle. How is it?"

"Wishing it didn't get sprained." She snuggled against him and laid her head on his shoulder. A perfect fit. "You didn't make me fall, so stop feeling guilty. And you didn't hurt me this morning, either. So...I can touch you now?"

"I think you just did." And it'd been the best touch ever.

She laughed. "I guess that's true. How about see you, then?"

Good God, he'd created a monster. Albeit a cute one. "You didn't get a good enough view, is that it? Wasn't your face, like, right there?"

She slapped his arm, but smiled in the process. "Oh my God. You're impossible. What I meant was, you wouldn't take your shirt off last night. How about now?" She tugged on his t-shirt. "Can I see what's under here?"

Suddenly he was attacked by a case of the nerves. Which was silly. It was just a scar. A scar that led him to the truth. A scar that changed his life forever.

"Yeah, sure. But fair warning: it's not all that pretty." He sat up, removed the shirt, and lay back on the warm mattress.

"Ooh, you have a hairy ches—" Her smile faded as she got her first look at the line down his chest. She sat up. "What happened?"

"Heart surgery."

"From when you died?"

He nodded.

"Does it hurt?"

"No. It's all healed."

"But when Lindy…" Her eyes widened as her cheeks lost all their color.

He sat up and took her face in his hands. "Hey. Lindy didn't cause me to have a heart attack, okay? I'm fine. Really. Go ahead and touch it."

He released her and waited. She stared at the scar with concern, not repulsion, which eased his fears a little. She ran first her fingers, then her palm along the pinkish ridge. Her touch sparked a desire for her, not that he could do much about it.

"I'm glad you survived."

There was a point in his life when he hadn't felt the same, but now? Yeah, now he did. He would have missed out on knowing the most wonderful woman ever.

He lay back on the bed and pulled her down next to him. Time to change the subject. "I don't know about you, but I'm nowhere near ready to get up."

She glanced at the clock. "Oh crap. I'm not exactly speedy with this ankle and I don't want to be late for work. Would you get me my boot, please?"

As she slid toward the edge of the bed, he grabbed her arm and held her back. "What are you talking about? You're not going into work. You were specifically told to stay off the foot today."

"But I'll be sitting at a desk. How is that getting up?"

"I'm not driving you into work, so you might as well call Tom and tell him you're not coming in."

"If you won't take me, then I'll call Erica."

Before he could demand she stay home—and really, why was he getting so protective of her anyway?—Tom texted her and told her not to come in. Dean tried his best not to smile.

* * * *

Maggie huffed and itched to wipe that smug look off Dean's face. At least the reason Tom gave her for not coming in had to do with the snow and not her sprained ankle.

"Now that you don't have to get ready for work, come back under the covers."

Under the covers, beside Dean. Didn't have to tell her twice. She returned to his side and snuggled against him. "If I didn't know any better, I'd say you were in cahoots with him."

"But you know better. Hell, if it weren't for Lindy, I wouldn't even bother Bridget."

"Then postpone it. Surely Lindy would understand."

"Maybe, but I want this over with."

"Tired of sleeping with me already?"

"Ahh, Maggie. You're much too good for me."

"I highly doubt that. You're not the one getting possessed."

"And you won't be, either, once we get rid of Lindy."

Except, what if Lindy needed help? Maggie closed her eyes on an inhale and said the words that needed saying. "If you need my help, or rather, if she needs my help, I'm willing to let her use my body to do it."

Dean shook his head. "It won't come to that."

"But if it does—"

"It won't. What she needs to do is to come to grips with her death. Not possess you."

She took his hand. So big. So warm. So comforting. "Then if she can't move on, there's no use in my living here any longer. As much as I enjoy sleeping with you, I can't expect you to be here all the time. She's a threat. I'd never forgive myself if something happened to you because I stayed here."

"But you love this house."

Yeah, but she loved him more. "Doesn't matter. I don't want Lindy to be the reason you're sticking around. I'd like it to be me."

"Hate to break it to you, sweetheart, but I wouldn't be here if Lindy were possessing anyone else."

"Yeah? So you're saying you would have eventually asked me out?"

"Probably not. I was pretty content just seeing you during my runs."

His running, yes. She'd been pretty content watching him, too. At first. "Would you have said yes if I asked you out?"

"Truth? No."

"No?" Well, damn. That stung.

"It's not what you think." He ran his thumb across her knuckles. "Like I said earlier, you're way too good for me."

"Did you ever think that maybe you're perfect for me?"

"Maggie…I'm not perfect for anyone."

She couldn't believe that. Her heart wouldn't lie to her.

* * * *

Gina stared out the window. The rising sun cast long shadows along the pristine snow. Quite a bit of the stuff, too. What used to be shrubs and chairs were now pinkish-white lumps in the yard. Might have been a pretty sight if she were in the mood to enjoy it.

That son of hers meant well, but sometimes she wondered if he was right in the head. He'd had a whole week to break into that house, but he let some fake alarm sign stop him. And of course it was a fake. Why else would Maggie even need an alarm? It's not like she had anything of value.

That she knew of.

The judge declaring their case was unsubstantiated was the last straw. No one stole from Gina Steele and got away with it. Oh sure, the goods actually belonged to Eddie, but that boy wouldn't know what to do with the gold mine that was inside that house. And the fact her late mother-in-law had refused to hand it over after Ed died only confirmed the whole family had been against her. Linda Steele never did approve of Gina marrying Ed. Neither had his sister, Caroline. They both had the gall to blame Gina for Ed's death.

She had done nothing but love Ed. Took care of him. Fixed all his favorite meals. And when he'd gotten too big to have sex the normal way, she had gotten on top or used her hand. It was a heart attack that took her Ed. So how could those two have blamed her?

Well, she was through with being blamed for everything. This snow storm was a blessing. If there was an alarm, and she wasn't saying there was, it would take authorities a while to trek through the snowy mess. And if they came while she was there? Well, she had a key. She'd tell them Maggie had asked her to come over and she'd forgotten about the alarm.

Her only problem was Maggie. If the twit was actually home and let her in? There had to be something in this house to put Maggie out of commission.

* * * *

Lindy hovered in the living room. Wait, wait, wait. Seemed that's all she was good for nowadays. Wait for the sun to rise. Wait for those two to get their butts out of bed. And then wait on Bridget. Who knew when that chick would arrive? And why'd Dean need her anyway? Probably because the dumbass didn't know how to talk to a teenager.

Lindy snorted. Hated to break it to him, but she hadn't been a teenager for a long time.

Or maybe he had trouble talking to women. Of course, she wasn't really a woman, either. Not an experienced one. But seeing as how that little feat would never happen, she would settle with her other wish. And maybe Bridget would be the best in getting that. She at least seemed to care about other people, whereas Dean only cared about Maggie.

The steps creaked. Damn, he was even helping her down the stairs. He'd done nothing but wait hand and foot on Maggie since he brought her home from the hospital. Lindy sneered at the couple. Kevin had never treated her like that. Then again, he'd never really gotten a chance.

Dean had just settled Maggie onto the couch when his cell phone chimed. "Hey, Bridget. You and Rob on your way?"

Lindy moved in close to hear. Since Maggie was in the room, Dean wouldn't even notice.

"Rob had an emergency at work and he doesn't want me driving. Fiend even took my keys, like he didn't trust me."

Lindy groaned. Oh man. Just how much longer would she have to wait?

"Because you can't be trusted," Dean said.

"Very funny. I'm getting a cab. Just wanted to let you know I'll be late—"

"Are you kidding me? You'll be lucky if you can get one today. And didn't you say last night you had to stop at the office? I'll come get you."

"We can postpone. I'm sure Lindy would understand."

"Postpone?" Lindy wailed, not that anyone could hear her. "I have to wait some more?"

"No, I'm not postponing. I made a deal with her and she actually held up her end. I'll be over in a bit."

187

Wow. Maybe he wasn't so bad after all. Lindy could almost kiss the guy. Almost.

He completed the call and pocketed his phone. "Change in plans. I have to pick up Bridget. How about I bring some bagels or donuts back?"

Maggie stood. "I can fix breakfast."

He pushed her back down to the couch. "No. You're staying off your foot. If you can't wait until I get back, I'm sure I can fix you something."

"No, no. I can wait. I'll just sit in the dining room and work on the stuff from the attic."

"You're supposed to relax, not overexert yourself."

"Dean, the boxes aren't that heavy. I won't even lift them."

He shook his head and then raised his eyebrows. "How about writing? You sit on the couch. I'll bring your laptop to you."

"Fine. But bring me coffee, too."

He kissed her on the mouth, and not a little peck, either. "Thank you for humoring me."

Lindy popped into the office before she could witness any more of their sick sweetness. Those two would give her a stomach ache, if she got those things anymore.

He appeared in the doorway and then came to a sudden stop. "I'm working as fast as I can, but the weather will take me a while to get Bridget."

"I'm just impressed you're sticking with our deal."

"Unlike you, I keep my promises."

Ouch. Okay, maybe she had that coming. But she was a new ghost now. Hadn't she proven that to him by staying away?

He unplugged the laptop and carried it into the kitchen, where he proceeded to fill a mug with coffee. "Bugging me isn't going to make me work faster, so shut up."

"I'm not bugging you. And I'm being quiet. Sheesh." If anyone was bugging anyone it was him bugging her, being as slow as he was.

"Right."

After stuffing two sweetener packets into his pocket, he placed the laptop under one arm and picked up the mug. And just to prove her point, he walked as slow as he could possibly walk, wearing a smirk on his face. Damn man.

He set the mug down on the coffee table and pulled out the little packets from his pocket. "Here you go."

Maggie opened the two packets and shook the contents into her mug. "I should have asked for water for my pill, but I guess coffee will work."

Damn it! How long would it take the guy to get water now?

"Ummm, Maggie. Does it hurt that bad or can you wait until I return?"

"Wait? Why?" She looked up at him with confusion on her face.

"Yeah, why wait?" Lindy said. "Not that I don't want you out of here now."

"Because the pills make you sleepy."

"Of all the nerve!" She could have hit the man. Just how many nights would she have to stay away before the guy trusted her?

"How long do you think you'll be?" Maggie asked.

"Probably a couple of hours."

"A couple of hours?"

Maggie took the words right out of Lindy's mouth. Dean's portrait must be next to the definition of tormentor.

"That's if the roads are plowed. Will something over-the-counter work in the meantime?"

Maggie nodded. "I have some Tylenol upstairs in the bathroom."

Dean actually rushed up the stairs and returned with a bottle. Would wonders never cease? But he couldn't leave without giving Maggie another long and sloppy kiss. Lindy followed him to the car, but stayed out of sight. Why give him another reason to slow down?

* * * *

Maggie's ankle throbbed. That over-the-counter stuff wasn't working. Neither was her writing. The pain made it hard to concentrate. What she needed was something to distract her, and she knew just the thing. She placed the laptop on the couch beside her and picked up her cell phone from the table.

Even though he'd asked her not to, Maggie could no longer sit around and let Dean do all the work. This was her house. She should be doing something to keep it. But since she couldn't have a conversation with Lindy, she could talk with the other irritant.

Gina answered on the first ring. "What could you possibly be calling me for?"

"Well, good morning to you, too," Maggie said with a voice laced with as much syrupy goo as she could muster. She knew her aunt could be hostile, but gee whiz.

"I apologize. You surprised me is all. What can I do for you?"

Maggie sat up and her ankle throbbed in time with the faint pounding in her head. That prescription pain med was looking more and more tempting. "I was hoping we could talk about what it would take for you and Eddie to stop suing me."

"Really? You want to talk? Why now?"

Maggie couldn't fault her aunt's skepticism. If she hadn't learned of Lindy's possible meddling of the will, Maggie wouldn't even be calling now. Guilt was a great motivator, but in this case telling the truth was out of the question. "Does it matter? Just tell me what it is you want and I'll see if I can help."

"I'd rather not discuss this on the phone. Are you at work? I could stop by."

"No, I'm at home, but it's not necessary for you—"

"Even better. I'll see you in a bit."

"What's wrong with—" But saying any more was useless. Gina had hung up. Oh crap.

Maggie placed the phone back on the table next to her prescription bottle. Her head throbbed even harder. Damn it. She was taking her prescription. The threat of being possessed was the least of her worries.

* * * *

Making snow angels when she couldn't feel the snow or the cold just wasn't like she remembered. Forget that she couldn't actually *make* snow angels. Lindy rose from the unmarked snow as a beat-up old car pulled up to the curb.

A pudgy woman squeezed out of the vehicle, and Lindy could have sworn the car's tires rose. Large, ungodly squeaks echoed in the neighborhood as Tubbo struggled with closing the door. Once she accomplished that, she walked around the front of the junker and stopped, as if she hadn't seen the mountain of snow covering the strip of grass between the curb and sidewalk—thanks to the snow plow that had driven through earlier—when she drove up.

Lindy laughed. Surely Tubbo, whoever she was, would get back in her car and drive off. But nope. She opened the trunk and grabbed a shovel.

"Good luck with not getting a heart attack," Lindy said.

Tubbo went to work and shoveled a path. Well, not much of a path. The woman wheezed through the little bit of shoveling she did—surprise, surprise—uncovering just enough so she could walk on the snow without it coming up to her crotch. Once she reached the sidewalk, where the snow wasn't quite so deep, she skewered the shovel into the pile and trudged through the front yard toward the house.

Stomp, stomp, stomp up the stairs. She shook off what snow she could, then rang the bell.

Who the hell was she?

Lindy popped into the house just as Maggie grabbed her crutches. It took her a couple of tries before she could actually move on those things. After peering through the side panel, she unlocked the door. "Hi, Aunt Gina."

Tubbo was Gina? As in Ed's wife? What'd she do, eat a blimp? Or maybe she took over eating Ed's portions at the dinner table. Lindy hadn't seen her since the memorial service for Ed. What a fiasco that had been, too. Insults as well as food were flung that day. Mom and Caroline wouldn't have invited Gina at all if she weren't Ed's widow.

"I'm so glad you called." Gina breezed on through and didn't even bother shutting the door. Gee, what did Ed ever see in her?

"Make yourself comfortable," Maggie muttered with a roll of her eyes. She closed the door and hobbled back toward the couch.

Ever the observant one, Gina said, "Goodness, child. You're on crutches. What happened?"

"Sprained my ankle." Maggie plopped back onto the couch. "You really didn't have to come over here. We could have talked on the phone."

"Nonsense. Face to face is always better." Gina shrugged out of her coat and hung it over the chair, but kept hold of her purse. "Do you have coffee made?"

"Yes. It's in the kitchen." Maggie stood.

"Sit, sit, sit. You're in no condition to cater to anyone." Gina pointed to the empty mug. "Let me get you a refill. How do you take it?"

Maggie lowered back onto the couch and propped the crutches on the table. "Black with sweetener. But just bring me a few packets. They're on the counter."

Lindy followed Gina into the kitchen. Whatever was Maggie doing inviting this viper over? Did Dean even know? Probably not. He didn't like Maggie doing anything without him around.

Gina glanced back toward the living room, then skittered over to the coffee pot, hugging her purse against her blubbery belly. She placed the mug and her purse on the counter. After pouring a bit of coffee into Maggie's mug, she opened her purse and pulled out a baggie full of white powder.

"What the hell is that?" Lindy said. "Didn't she tell you the sweetener packets were on the counter?" Except she was pretty sure that bag wasn't holding sweetener.

Unaware a ghost was scolding her, Gina dumped some of the powder into Maggie's mug and stirred. More coffee. More powder. More stirring. She was sealing the bag when she shrugged and dumped the rest into the mug. After topping the mug with more coffee, Gina stirred and smiled.

"Oh, no you don't." Lindy swung a fist through the mug. Damn it. Hopefully Dean would return before Maggie drank that coffee. But the odds weren't looking so good.

Chapter 21

Maggie took a sip of her coffee. Ick. Bitter. Just how long had that pot been heating? No matter. She added another packet of sugar and took another sip. A little better. She couldn't afford not to drink the coffee; otherwise, the pain medicine would zonk her out.

Probably wasn't wise to mix it with the over-the-counter, but at least her ankle was feeling much better. Her head was another issue. But then that pain was caused by something entirely different.

Gina put her mug on the coffee table. "I'd like to go through Linda's, your grandmother's, things, to get something that was promised to Eddie."

So there was something of value in that mess. Maggie did her darnedest not to laugh out loud by taking another sip of coffee. "How about you tell me what it is and then I go find it for you."

"You're certainly in no condition to rifle through the attic. It won't take me but a minute."

Maggie almost said the stuff wasn't up there, but then how could she stop the woman if she decided to just start looking? "I don't think so. Besides the fact it would take you hours to go through the sheer amount of stuff Grandma saved, after everything you've put me through, I just don't trust you."

"*I* put you through? No, that was Eddie. I told him not to go through with it, but does he listen to his mother? Of course not.

He thinks he knows best, but he really doesn't. Still, it's not fair you get something that was promised to him."

"And it wasn't fair that he dragged me through court. Twice." Maggie gripped her mug and drank deeply. Losing her cool like that wouldn't solve anything. Certainly wouldn't get her crazy-assed family out of her life.

"And I am sorry for that. Truly I am. I feel it's all my fault anyway. Or actually Linda's. If your grandmother wasn't such a vindictive—well, she didn't like me so much, I guess that's not a secret. And after Ed died, well, she took out her disdain on Eddie, and he didn't deserve that."

Gina picked up her mug and continued. "I don't know what happened to cause her to change her will, since I left her alone like she asked. She told me at Ed's service that Eddie would get what was due him either after I died or after she died. I can only assume your mother talked her into changing it. She didn't like me none, either."

"But Grandma didn't leave the house to Mom. Mom wasn't even listed in the will."

"No, of course not. She was too smart for that. Instead, she talked your grandmother into leaving everything to you. Anything to keep it away from me."

"You mean Eddie." A yawn racked her body. Damn it. Why wasn't the coffee working? She couldn't afford to fall asleep. Not without Dean around. She took another long drink of the bitter coffee.

"No, I mean me. Your family seemed to think I would take it all from Eddie. Really, he is innocent in all this. He's always helped Linda. With the yard work and shoveling snow. He didn't have to do that."

Maggie's vision blurred and she blinked her eyes. Another yawn attacked her. Her last pain pill hadn't worked this fast, had it? And what was with her stomach? It was turning in knots.

Oh, God. Teach her to mix pain meds on an empty stomach.

* * * *

Lindy could only watch in horror as whatever Gina had given Maggie was taking affect.

"Are you okay?" Gina asked.

Maggie held her stomach. "I think so. I probably should have eaten something before taking my pills."

"Pills? What kind of pills?"

Lindy moved in front of Gina and gave her a blast of cold, causing the bitch to shiver. "Yeah, you should be concerned. If anything happens to her, it'll be your fault."

"Pills. For my ankle. Maybe…you…should…" Maggie slumped over on the couch.

What had Gina done? Had Maggie died? No, not yet. Her telltale glow burned brightly. Didn't mean she wasn't dying, though.

"What are you doing just standing there?" Lindy screamed at Gina. "Call 9-1-1."

"Maggie?" Gina whispered. When she got no response, she quietly headed up the stairs.

The bitch. All she cared about were the stupid contents of the attic. Good thing she wasn't observant or she would have seen the stacked boxes in the dining room.

The glow called to Lindy, as if it had a voice or a scent. Would she be breaking her promise if she possessed Maggie now? Who knew when Dean would return? By then it might be too late.

Lindy slipped easily inside, the rush going to her head. Dean hadn't been totally wrong when he'd said she was addicted. Who wouldn't love the feeling of such power? To actually feel alive again? Except this time the power fizzled out quickly and she nearly lost control. Whatever Maggie ingested had the same affect as the end of Lindy's two-day possessing stint.

No time to waste, then. Where was the phone? Ahh, the table. She picked it up and turned it on.

"Password?" Lindy clamped her mouth, forgetting she could be heard now. Shit. She placed the phone on the coffee table. Now what? Wait. There was a phone in the kitchen.

She stood, but her legs were uneven. Oh, the boot. She'd make a racket for sure clumping along with this thing on. She sat down and removed it, along with her shoe. Stood and pain shot up her leg. Ow, ow, ow. Forget about the boot making a racket, she might just scream. After a few deep calming breaths, she waited until the pain became bearable, then risked moving. Limping as quietly as she could, she snuck into the kitchen. Picked up the receiver. The line was dead.

Damn it. When had it become this hard to make a stupid phone call?

She couldn't very well traipse around the neighborhood looking for help, not with this bum ankle. On top of whatever Gina gave Maggie, the pain could very well cause Lindy to lose control and then what? Gina would win. Well, *that* wasn't going to happen. Guess the only thing left to do was to stop that woman from getting away. Then Dean could deal with her.

Lindy limped into the living room and grabbed the crutch. This would make an excellent weapon. Not to mention keeping her off the sore ankle. Slowly, she made her way up the stairs.

Gina was in the closet, squeezing that bountiful body of hers through the attic opening. As soon as her legs left the ladder, Lindy collapsed the thing and laid it on the closet floor. Gina wouldn't think of jumping down, she'd probably twist or break something, if she even had the nerve to begin with.

Gina poked her head through the opening and her eyes widened. "Maggie? What are you doing?"

"I should ask you the same thing. I don't know what you gave her, but you can tell the cops when they get here."

"Her? What are you talking about?"

Oh crap. "Me. I meant me."

Lindy's vision blurred. Damn. That had never happened before. If Dean had any chance of saving Maggie, he'd better get his butt here now.

* * * *

Dean came through the back door with Bridget behind him. Maggie wasn't where he'd left her and her boot was on the coffee table. What the hell? "Maggie!"

"Up here."

He rushed up the stairs and found her in the hallway. "What are you doing? Why aren't you wearing your boot?"

When he reached for her, she backed away. "Now don't be mad. It's me. Lindy. You need to call 9-1-1. Gina drugged Maggie and I'm losing control."

"What?" Maggie was drugged? "How bad?"

"Bad, I think."

Shit. He stuck his head down the stairwell. "Bridget! Call 9-1-1. Possible overdose." He stepped toward Lindy/Maggie. "Get out of her. Now."

"Okay. Just don't touch me." Lindy/Maggie sat on the floor. Moments later Lindy emerged and Maggie slumped over.

Dean caught her before she hit her head. "Maggie." He slapped her face. "Maggie. Wake up. Wake up!"

She blinked and moaned, but not much else. Oh God. Was she dying?

"What'd she drug her with?"

"I don't know. You could ask Gina, she's stuck up in the attic. She put a lot of powder in Maggie's coffee. Knocked her out pretty good."

Sleeping pills? No, not that. He picked up Maggie and carried her to her room. Slapped her face some more. "Come on, sweetheart. Wake up."

"That's not the worst. She'd taken her prescription medication before Gina got here. I think it's causing a reaction."

Bridget appeared in the doorway. "Paramedics are on the way. What happened?"

"I don't know, but I will soon." He stormed into the room containing the attic access. The ladder lay on its side and he was tempted to bash it against the wall. Or maybe against one fat woman. "Gina Steele!"

Gina's head appeared in the opening. "Oh, thank God. Would you let me down please?"

"What did you poison Maggie with?"

"Poison? I didn't poison anyone. I just gave her a few sleeping pills."

Exactly what he'd feared. "How many?" When the woman didn't answer, Dean yelled, "How many?"

"Just a handful. I don't know what the big whoop is about. I've given Eddie sleeping pills plenty of times and nothing bad ever happened to him. Now, would you help me down?"

A handful? Dean ran back to Maggie's room. "We have to get her up. We have to pump her stomach. We have to—" His legs gave out and he slumped to the floor. "Oh God. I can't lose her."

Before he could totally lose it, the paramedics arrived, as did the police. He let them take care of Gina, because if he'd gotten near the woman, he'd end up in jail for murder.

* * * *

Lindy smiled as the police ushered Gina out the door. Handcuffed, even. She certainly had enough to say about that. One of the paramedics bagged up the rest of Maggie's coffee. Then the two of them carried Maggie out to the ambulance on a stretcher. Dean followed as far as the door and watched.

Bridget touched his arm. "She's not going to die. Okay? The sleeping pills of today are nothing like Peter's time. She'll wake up."

He nodded, but didn't seem all that convinced. "I'll take you home on the way to the hospital."

"You go on. I'll stay and talk to Lindy."

"No. I won't leave you here alone with her."

"I'm not gonna hurt her," Lindy said, although she wasn't quite sure if they could see her or not.

Apparently they could. Dean glared right at her. "Forgive me for not believing you. I know you're behind this whole mess."

"Hey, I didn't give Maggie the sleeping pills."

"No. But you sure made it so someone would. I'm sorry you died young, but the world didn't owe you a perfect life. And it still doesn't." He turned to Bridget. "You're not staying here alone. I promised Rob I wouldn't leave you alone with *her*."

That last part stung. But at least he didn't call her an it.

"Hate to break it to you, but as much as I love the guy, he doesn't own me. Neither do you. But you go ahead and call Rob if that'll make you feel better. If you want to stay until he arrives, fine. But you don't have to. Lindy will not hurt me."

"You don't know that."

"Yes, I do. And you would, too, if you weren't so upset. You go follow Maggie. I'll be fine."

"You don't have to stay, Bridget," Lindy said, hoping against hope that if she sounded sincere, maybe Dean would trust her. "I kind of deserve it. I really hope Maggie will be okay. I only possessed her to get help. Honest."

"I don't want to hear any more," Dean said. "I'm tired of your lies. Let's go, Bridget."

He took her arm and headed for the back.

Lindy rushed after them. "His name is Kevin Tipton. The one you're looking for. In the yearbook."

Bridget smiled. "I'll see what I can find out."

Lindy really doubted they'd find anything, but at this point she had nothing left to cling to. She'd be lucky if Maggie even returned.

* * * *

Eddie sat in the waiting room while an attendant fetched his mother.

If it wasn't bad enough he'd spent a small fortune on lawyers to get a house he really didn't want, now he had to bail his mother out of jail. What the fuck was she thinking?

Mom came through the door smoothing her hair. When she spotted Eddie, she ran and wrapped him in an unwanted hug. "Oh, it was just awful in there. I can't believe that woman is pressing charges."

"Maybe if you hadn't drugged her, she wouldn't have."

"I didn't hurt her. Sheesh, you'd think she never took a sleeping pill before."

Eddie had heard it was more than just one, and that other medication had been involved. "It was enough to admit her to the hospital. Admit it, you were in the wrong here."

"I'll do no such thing." She walked over to a window to check out and collect her belongings.

She said that now, but surely she saw how futile her mission was. Jail had to have jolted some sense into her. Once she was in the clear to leave, they stepped out into the freezing air. He was so ready for this to be over with for good.

She grabbed his arm. "You need to go over there tonight, while the bitch is at the hospital. She's hidden the stuff somewhere because the attic was emptied."

"Are you nuts?" Silly question. Of course she was. He was the nutty one for believing otherwise. "I'm not going over there. Besides, what makes you think it's still in the house?"

"Because where else would she put the stuff? Maybe it's in the basement. Or the garage. Oh, I hope not. It could get ruined out there. You have to go and see."

"Mom, the only place we're going is home." Where a bottle of whiskey had his name on it.

"But my car—"

"Can wait."

"No." She stopped and opened her purse. "If you don't take me to my car, I'll just get a cab. And then I'll go through the house myself."

"Then you leave me no choice." He snatched the purse from her hands.

She reached for it but he held it away. "Give that back. What are you doing?"

"Making sure you have no money. Or a phone. And when we get home, I'll make sure the landline is disconnected."

"Oh, you horrible, horrible son."

"Would you prefer I give you sleeping pills?"

She narrowed her eyes at him, but at least it shut her up. Maybe later he'd slip her a pill or two.

Chapter 22

"I'll say one thing, I've never felt more rested." Maggie's attempt at humor fell flat. Dean only gripped the steering wheel harder as he drove them to her house. It was just as well. She'd been lying, anyway. Her head and ankle pounded, but if she'd said anything, he might have talked a doctor into getting her to stay at the hospital another day. At least she didn't have to go back to work until Monday.

"She could have killed you," Dean said.

"That's not what the doctor said." While Gina used several sleeping pills, there hadn't been enough to kill Maggie. Only put her out of commission for several hours.

"I asked you to stay away from them. Why did you even call her?"

She'd wondered when he'd bring that up. Never said a word at the hospital. But man, his face had turned red when he discovered she'd instigated the whole thing. "Because it's my house. You and Bridget are already doing enough. It's not fair I sit around and do nothing."

"I should have been there."

"Don't you think I can handle my aunt?" Okay, that might not have been the smartest question she could ask. Clearly, she couldn't. God, he must think she was a royal wimp. A wimp of the highest realm. That, or just plain stupid. She was feeling that, and more.

As if to reinforce her thoughts, he raised his eyebrow at her.

"Now that I know how low Gina will stoop, I'll do better next time."

His eyes practically shot out of his head. "Are you kidding? There will be no next time. If I have to carry you up to my apartment to keep you safe, I will."

"Dean, it's not your job to keep me safe."

"Well... Maybe I want it to be."

What was that supposed to mean? Job as in private investigator, or job as in significant other? And why did his protective nature turn her on? She should be furious and tried to sound that way. "You think stashing me at your place, basically wrapping me in bubble wrap, will keep me safe?"

"Bubble—" He took a deep breath and shook his head. "You wouldn't be a prisoner."

"Sure I would. You know how I feel about heights. How about I promise not to open the door to anyone and call the cops if I see Gina?"

He pulled over to the side, put the car in park, and covered his face. In all the months she'd known him, she'd never seen him break down. If that was what he was doing. His quiet unnerved her.

"Dean?"

He dropped his arms. "I know you're okay now, but you got to understand. I thought you were dying. After Gina told me what she'd given you... I nearly lost it." He took her face into his hands. "I love you, Maggie. I don't think I could bear life without you in this world."

She'd always envisioned this moment happening over a quiet dinner or an intimate evening at home. But when it came down to it, the atmosphere didn't matter. Only the words. For the words lightened her heart and filled her with joy. He loved her. She could be standing in a dump and still be smiling like a loon because he told her he loved her.

"Oh, Dean. I love you, too."

Her words didn't light up his face as she expected, but he kissed her. Tenderly at first, then thoroughly as he deepened it. He got her sex throbbing and nipples hard. If only they weren't in a car.

When he ended the kiss, he touched his forehead against hers. "So then you'll stay at my place?"

Disappointment in his change of tactic burned in her chest and she pulled his hands away. "Is that why you said it?"

"No. No, of course not. I meant every word. I don't want to lose you."

"You're not going to lose me if I live in my house."

"But, Maggie, it's not safe."

"Sure it is. Aunt Gina was stupid, true, but she wasn't trying to kill me. Lindy isn't trying to kill me, either, and she promised to be good. I'll be just as safe at home as I will anywhere else."

He shook his head. "That ghost doesn't know what good means."

"Then I'll chain myself to the house at the first sign of a yawn, okay?"

"Chain? If you think I'm leaving you alone—"

"You're not going to babysit me, so forget it. Besides, you have other cases, too."

"They can wait."

Not if she could help it. If she didn't stand her ground now, she never would. "Dean. Don't make me kick you out."

His eyes widened. "You'd do that?"

"I don't want to, but yeah, I'd do it. If that's the only way to get you to see reason."

He ran a hand through his hair and leaned his head back. "Damn it," he muttered under his breath. "You'll call me at the first sign of trouble?"

She resisted smiling, but relaxed in relief. "Promise."

Maggie was all set to face a nice, quiet-but-productive day when they returned home and Erica bombarded her.

Seemed she had a babysitter after all.

* * * *

Dean was driving to Eddie's place of business when his phone signaled Maggie's call. He clipped a snow pile in his hurry to pull over so he could answer the phone.

"What is it? Are you okay?"

Her laughter calmed him some. "Nothing's wrong. Just wanted to invite you to dinner."

"Is Erica cooking?" Although he knew the answer to that question was a big, fat no.

"No, of course not," she said with a chuckle. "I don't think she even knows how to use the oven."

Which was exactly what he'd thought. "I'd love to have dinner with you, but how about I take you out? I don't want you to overexert yourself."

"Nonsense. Cooking is easy. You be here at six with an appetite, okay?"

"Yes, ma'am."

"I love you."

It still pained him when she said those words. It was one thing for him to love her. He could do that from afar. But for her to return those feelings? She might expect more from him. More than he could give.

She deserved so much better than him.

"I love you, too." He disconnected the call, tossed the phone on the passenger seat, and pulled back into traffic.

Who knew falling could happen so fast? Those seconds when he'd thought she'd never wake up were the worst seconds of his life.

Man, he owed Rob an apology, big time. He now knew exactly what that man had gone through when it had been Bridget's life in danger.

While it was true he couldn't wrap Maggie in bubble wrap—but boy, wouldn't that be fun popping all those bubbles—he could make sure she was safe. Bridget was still working on the Lindy angle. Dean settled on the Eddie and Gina one. There had to be a way to get everyone to leave Maggie alone.

Dean pulled into the parking lot of Eddie's employer. Eddie worked in the IT department, which meant he was probably making pretty good money. He must be socking it away, though, or gambling it away, because his car was a rusting heap and his house wasn't all that flashy or big.

Could a gambling debt be what was motivating Eddie? He'd followed the guy to the Racino that one time, but never thought about checking his finances. Dean texted Bridget to do just that.

He walked into the reception area and flashed his private investigator's badge. Not that it really gave him any rights, but most people didn't know that. "Hi. My name is Dean Parker and I'd like to talk to Eddie Steele about a private matter."

The woman behind the counter was a petite young thing—if she was twenty he'd eat his badge—with a blonde pixie cut and blue eyes behind the pink frames of her glasses. Her eyes widened and she fumbled with the phone before righting it and dialing a number. Either the badge worked or it was just his size. He could look intimidating without even trying. Was that a trait he'd inherited from his biological father?

Shit. Like he needed to think of that bastard now. But he'd eventually have to tell Maggie. She deserved to know what kind of person she'd fallen in love with. It might change things for her. And wouldn't that be for the best?

Eddie walked through the door, saving Dean from barging into the unknown. "I know a place we can talk privately. Follow me."

Dean smiled. Well, that was easier than he'd thought. Then again, Maggie was pressing charges against Gina. That might be why Eddie was being so reasonable.

The conference room was small, but private. Almost claustrophobic. The only window was a tiny slit along the door. Just enough to show the room's occupational status. Eddie sat at the small, four-seated table. Dean sat across from him.

"What is it you want?"

No beating around the bush for this guy. "I'd like to know what your mother was hoping to find in Maggie's house."

"You mean my grandmother's house. And why should I tell you?"

"To end this mess? Do you really want to see your mother go to jail?"

"Do you honestly believe that will happen? She didn't do anything to warrant prison."

"You don't think drugging someone so you can rob from them doesn't warrant jail time?"

"She never would have resorted to that if Maggie had only let her go through Grandma's stuff."

"Oh, so it's Maggie's fault."

"She's the one who coerced Grandma into changing the will. Probably laid some sympathy trip because her mother died."

"Not possible. The will was changed before Caroline passed. Summer of 2000. August, to be precise."

Eddie paled. "What?"

Ah ha! Dean nearly pumped his fist. He knew Maggie and Lindy hadn't told the whole story. Something had happened and Eddie was part of it.

"That little bitch," Eddie mumbled. He shook his head and then frowned.

"Watch your mouth."

"Or what? You gonna hit me? Go ahead. I'd love to call the cops on you."

And he'd do it, too, of that Dean was sure. "What happened back then?"

"I'd tell you to ask Maggie, but I'm sure she'll lie to you like she lied to her mother and Grandma. You tell her unless she wants everyone to hear my side of the story, to stop fighting the contesting of the will and to drop all charges against my mother. Otherwise, you and everyone else will know what happened. There are two sides to the story and mine is the truth."

Dean gritted his teeth and fisted his hand. Now he really wanted to belt the guy one, cops or no cops. "Blackmail is a crime."

"So is extortion. But you don't see her in jail now, do you? Of course, that could change."

Extortion? Shit. What the hell happened that day?

Chapter 23

Maggie's foot itched. Again. Was there itching powder in the boot or something? She reached down and pulled the strap, making the loudest ripping sound ever. Then again, when was Velcro ever quiet?

Erica looked up from her stack of papers. The two of them were sitting in the dining room going through Grandma's stuff. Maggie's side of the table was neat with tidy piles of papers that may be worth a more thorough look, while Erica's side of the table resembled the top of Dean's desk. "What are you doing?"

"I'm thinking about taking a hike down the street. What does it look like I'm doing?"

"You're not supposed to take that off."

"And you're starting to sound like Dean." Maggie slipped the offending item off her foot and gently scratched her instep. Ahhh. Relief.

Erica dug into her box and pulled out more papers. "Maybe you should get one of those long hand-thingies. You know, like you use to scratch your back."

"A backscratcher?"

Apparently the term was too much for Erica as she scrunched her face in confusion. A moment later the light bulb must have lit and she smiled. "Yeah. One of those."

"Do you have one?"

"No. That's why I said you should get one."

"I think I'll stick with the easy way. You know, removing the boot. Since it's removable."

"You don't have to get all huffy. I was only trying to help."

"Then help me with another box. This one's empty." Maggie slid her foot back into the boot and strapped it up.

Ah. Snug as a bug in a—damn itchy foot. Okay, maybe a backscratcher would come in handy.

Someone knocked on the front door just as Erica stood. "Ahh, time to take a break. If I had known you were going to use me for labor, I'd have just gone into work. At least they pay me."

"You can always go in. I won't stop you."

"If I thought I could trust you to stay off your foot, I would." Erica turned toward the hallway.

"Make sure you look outside before—"

"Yeah, yeah. I know. Trust me, I don't want Gina around here, either." She disappeared into the living room and opened the door. "Hey, Bridget. Maggie's in the back."

"Actually, I came to talk to Lindy."

"Holy crap! You talk to ghosts, too?"

Maggie shook her head. Erica would probably start thinking everyone had some supernatural ability besides her. Heck, it seemed that way to Maggie, too.

"I thought Maggie told you." Bridget waddled into the dining room with Erica close behind.

Maggie smiled. "I didn't think that was my secret to tell."

Bridget hugged her. "That's so sweet of you. Thank you." She looked around the room. "Wow. Dean wasn't lying when he said there was lots of paper."

"And we'd probably go through it faster if Maggie wasn't such a stickler." Erica cleared a seat and offered it to Bridget.

"There's nothing wrong with being thorough. Grandma could have hidden whatever anywhere."

"And you're keeping those stacks of paper for what?" When Maggie didn't answer—because honestly, she had no real reason to keep them—Erica laughed. "I'm beginning to see a family trait between you and your grandmother."

"I am not that bad." At least most of her papers were filed electronically. As long as she had space on her hard drive, she'd never have to delete them.

"Reminds me of Dean's office before I worked there. It took me forever to sort that mess out and he didn't have near as much as this." Bridget nudged Maggie's shoulder. "So, how are you feeling today?"

"I'm fine, despite what Dean thinks. How's that baby coming along?"

Bridget rubbed her belly. "Charlie's been kicking up a storm. Probably can't wait to see the world."

"You're having a boy?" Erica asked.

"I don't know. We're naming the baby Charlie, after Rob's sister. Figured it would fit either sex and we wanted to be surprised."

Erica sat back at the table. "Wow. I bet she's happy."

"She would be if she were still alive. She died a little over a year ago."

"I'm sorry to hear that," Maggie said. "You said you came to talk to Lindy?"

"Yes. Is it okay if I go upstairs? I don't want to disturb you."

"Does Dean know you're here?"

"He will when he reads the note I left him at work."

"But Dean's not at... Oh, so that's how you do it." Maggie laughed. She'd have to remember that ploy. "Can you ask Lindy a question for me?"

"Sure."

Dean would probably blow his top again, but only if Bridget and Erica blabbed. Maggie took a risk they wouldn't. "Ask her how she knew she could possess me. Ask her how she does it."

"Is there some reason you need to know this?"

"Well...I'm kind of hoping you'll understand what she's saying and then...maybe...see if Peter can do the same thing. To me."

Bridget's eyes widened. "I don't know if that's such a good thing."

"Who's Peter?" Erica asked.

"He's the ghost at Dean's work," Maggie said.

"Holy crap! There's another—wait a minute. Are you nuts? Why would you want him to do that?"

Maggie fully expected Dean to react that way, not her cousin. "Because I need to know if it's me." She turned toward Bridget. "I know why Dean thinks it's not a good idea, but why do you? Is Peter dangerous?"

Bridget shook her head. "No, I don't believe he is. But Dean and I agreed he shouldn't know what other ghosts can do. That kind of knowledge might change him."

Maggie sagged her shoulders in defeat. "I understand. You can't take that risk. I just wish I knew another way to find out if it's me or if it's Lindy."

"What can other ghosts do?" Erica asked.

"Again, I'd rather not say."

"Because of Lindy? I don't feel her, so she's probably not—okay, correction. She's here. Dean and Maggie are so lucky not to feel the cold air."

Bridget looked at Maggie. "You don't feel her?"

"No. Dean thinks it's because she can possess me."

"Have you ever felt an unexplained chill at our office?"

No, she hadn't. Damn it. Depression sunk deeper as Maggie shook her head. "I guess that would be my answer, huh? If I can't feel them…"

"I'm sure there's another reason. It's possible he wasn't near you. Some people don't feel anything until they walk through the spirit. So don't go jumping to conclusions."

Kind of hard not to when the circumstances fit.

"Just how many ghosts are around here?" Erica asked.

"Don't know. I've officially met five."

"Only five? I would have thought there were more than that."

"Well, I've only had the ability to see ghosts for about a year. Lindy says a crazy one lives not too far from here, but don't worry, you're out of her zone. I've seen some at the hospital and some wandering on the roads, but it's not often I'm alone to see them." Bridget stood and grabbed her belly. "I swear Charlie is kicking me in the bladder. After my potty break, which room can I use for Lindy?"

"You can use mine," Maggie said. "It's—"

"I know which one." Bridget waved and headed out of the room.

Of course she knew which room that was. She'd been here with Dean when the paramedics arrived. Not that Maggie actually remembered any of it, only what Dean had told her.

Erica brought a box over and placed it on the chair Bridget had used. "I'm getting hungry. Do we have sandwich material?"

"You? In the kitchen?"

"Making a sandwich is not cooking, so don't get any ideas."

Oh, Maggie got ideas all right, and they all centered around Dean. Seemed her impromptu dinner invitation would turn out better than she'd planned. She'd actually get to enjoy a meal alone with him. Well, as alone as Lindy would make it. Maggie told her cousin where everything was located, then started in on the box. As she reached inside to pull out a stack of papers, her fingers touched something hard, like a book. No, not a book. Nestled under about an inch of statements was a photo album.

The pages were yellow and the edges kind of crispy, so she opened it carefully. Black-and-white photos of baseball players filled the pages. Some were taken over a hundred years ago. Could this have been her great-grandparents' book? One picture was taken in 1930, labeled "Edward and Leo Durocher." Holy crap. That was Grandpa when he was ten. And he was standing next to a man wearing a Cincinnati Reds uniform.

She flipped the pages carefully, marveling at the find. The last few pages were blank, or had used to contain pictures. All that remained were the photo corners.

Smiling, Maggie put the album to the side. Finally, something interesting. Once she was able to get around on her own, she would have the pictures framed, or at least put in a book that would protect them better. Especially the ones with her family.

Dean came through the back door. "Hey, Erica."

"Just in time for lunch. Want a sandwich? I'm making ham and cheese."

"Sure, sounds good. Thanks." He entered the dining room and Maggie couldn't help but grin. This guy loved her. "Still at it, I see."

"Yeah, and I found this neat—"

Dean's eyes bugged out and he backed away. "You need to cover those up. They're creeping me out."

Maggie turned around. The doll heads did seem to be staring in his direction. "Afraid they'll come to life?"

"Stranger things have happened." He returned with a towel and covered the box. "There. Better. Maggie, we need to talk."

"Well, that doesn't sound good." Erica came in carrying two plates, each loaded with a sandwich and chips. She placed them on the table. "Are you breaking up already?"

Maggie frowned as her heart fell to her feet. Talk about fleeting love.

"What are you talking about? Nobody's breaking up," Dean said. "I need to talk about when the will was changed."

Oh crap. Whatever he found out couldn't have been good. Maggie smiled at her cousin. "Erica, can you give us a minute?"

"More secrets? Really?" When Maggie didn't answer, Erica sighed heavily. "Fine. I'll just go in the living room and see what's on TV."

After moving the box to the floor, he took the seat beside her and held her hand. "I might have screwed up. Eddie didn't know the will was changed in 2000. He thinks you're behind it all. That you, or your mother, coerced your grandmother to leave you the house."

"That's ridiculous. We both know who was behind that."

"But what does Eddie think happened? How does he play into this?"

"Does it really matter?"

"Yes. He says he'll tell his side of the story if you don't stop fighting the contesting of the will and drop the charges against his mother."

"What?" Eddie had no side of the story. Not one that shed any good light on him.

"Maggie, what does he think happened? He couldn't have been that old."

Oh God. She should have known this day would eventually come. Embarrassment heated her cheeks. "Sixteen. He was sixteen. I was thirteen."

"So what'd you do? Burn something down?"

If only she had. She shook her head. Once Dean learned the truth, he'd never look at her the same. Because it was highly possible that Eddie was right.

* * * *

Dean hated grilling Maggie, but it had to be done. If not him, then Eddie would spew whatever he thought happened that day. Or worse, make something up. "Maggie. Please tell me. It couldn't have been that bad."

"He brought over some weed. And I experimented."

"He brought over weed for a thirteen-year-old? How could he think you're responsible for anything?"

"Well, he didn't exactly bring it for me. I found him with it and begged for some. He was probably just trying to shut me up or keep me from telling. So he shared and I..." She closed her eyes.

"You got a little high?"

She nodded.

"That's not so bad. I did that in high school. Why would he think—" Wait a minute. Maggie was high? "How out of it did you get?"

"A lot, I guess. I don't remember much."

"The events are foggy or you blacked out?"

"What I remember isn't foggy, but there is a block of time...gone. Does that matter?"

"Yeah, that matters." He'd bet every thing he owned that Lindy had taken over. "That little shit. What did she do?"

"Who are you talking about? You mean Lindy? How could she do anything? I wasn't asleep."

"I don't think she needs you to be totally out. You weren't the other day."

"But then..." Her eyes widened and she shook her head, causing a tear to escape. "No. No. Oh God. All this time I've been blaming Eddie. No wonder he hates me!"

"Maggie, please. You're killing me, here. What do you think Eddie did?"

"I thought..." She swallowed and wiped at another stray tear. "All this time I thought Eddie had removed my clothes. That he'd tried to rape me, or at least take advantage of my condition. When I came to and screamed 'rape,' he screamed 'tease' and said I was the one taking advantage of him." She covered her face as a sob shook her.

Could he murder a ghost? Because he'd certainly love to try. He took Maggie's hands and asked the question he wasn't sure he wanted answered. "How far did it get?"

"I don't think we had sex, at least I wasn't sore there. I just remember waking up, seeing him naked, and then screaming." She closed her eyes and lowered her head. "Oh, Dean. How could she do this to me?"

He cupped her cheek and lifted her head. "I don't know, but I aim to find out. You wait here."

As he went to stand, she grabbed his shirt. "Don't get her mad. Please? I want her gone. I want her to want to leave. And I don't want her to hurt you."

"You're asking an awful lot of me."

"Well, then consider Bridget's safety. She's upstairs—"

"What?" Dean rushed to the stairs, leaving Maggie's pleas in his wake. What the hell was Bridget thinking? How many times did he have to tell that woman to stay away from Lindy?

He stopped on the landing and took a deep breath. Must remain calm. As much as he would love to throttle Lindy, she was strong and could hurt either one of them, and without much effort.

Bridget's voice came from Maggie's room. He slowed his stride and took several more deep breaths. He could be calm. He could be cool. Yeah, he could be delusional, too.

The door was open a crack. He pushed it further and Bridget saw him.

She gave him that silly, oops-caught-me grin. "Hey, Dean. I was just getting more information on Kevin Tipton, since I'd hit a brick wall."

"Is that so?" He entered the room, shut the door, and turned toward Lindy. "What do you hope to accomplish with Kevin?"

She shrugged. "I don't know. I guess I'd just like to know if he meant everything he'd said to me."

"And knowing that will, what? Give you peace?"

"Hey, you're the ones who have been trying to get me to leave. I don't know what will give me peace."

"Do you think using a thirteen-year-old to have sex would have given you peace?"

Lindy's eyes widened.

"What are you talking about?" Bridget asked.

"Don't ask me. Ask Lindy. She knows exactly what I'm talking about. Don't you, Lindy?"

"I-I-I wasn't thinking when that happened."

"No, you were too juiced at having possessed Maggie, weren't you? What did you do? Maggie can't remember, but I'm guessing Eddie hasn't forgotten."

"Nothing. I was just having fun."

"Fun? She was thirteen! And he was your nephew. Would you have gone through with it if she hadn't woken? Would you?"

Bridget grabbed his arm. "Dean, I think you need to calm down."

He was through with calming down. He was out for blood. "Answer me."

Lindy lowered her head. "I don't know. But I know better now."

"You think that makes it okay? It doesn't. I want you out of her life. For good. Forever. Will this Kevin Tipton do that? Will he?" Because if he did, Dean would drag the man over himself. Somehow he'd fix this for Maggie.

* * * *

Lindy backed up as Dean advanced toward her.

"Well? Will he?" Veins popped out along his temples and his face was turning purple. "Answer me!"

He'd already suffered one heart attack because of her; she wouldn't be responsible for another. Without answering—because really, she had no answer for him—she popped out of the room and into Rhonda's territory. Maybe that crazy ghost could help.

Her first stop landed her in the pervert's place across the street. She'd been here numerous times out of some sick curiosity, back before she'd been banished to any area that did not include Rhonda.

"What are you doing here?"

Lindy turned around. Seeing Rhonda was both relieving and scary. The fact that she had hiked her nightgown up and was bouncing up and down on the perv's lap while the man was jerking himself off in front of a big screen TV where two men were doing it to a woman was merely disgusting.

"Can we talk in private?"

Rhonda laughed. "He can't hear us. Can you, stud?" She ran her face across his. He might have shivered a bit. That, or he was coming.

He moaned as his sperm squirted into the air. Guess that answered that.

"Whoa. Didn't know he had *that* in him. His talent is surely wasted." Rhonda moved away from the man. "Are you here to tell me when I can see this guy you can touch? It's been over a week."

Since Rhonda wasn't stepping away from the television, Lindy moved so her back was to the screen. Watching porn when you knew no one was watching was one thing, but Rhonda was liable to egg her on. "I know. But he doesn't like to deal with ghosts unless he thinks he can help them move on." Most likely a lie. Bridget seemed more into that than Dean, but whatever lie worked, Lindy would use. "So what should I tell him is keeping you here?"

"Move on? Who said I wanted to move on?"

"Oh, I don't know. Maybe all those cracks about being in hell. Are you saying you don't want to go to heaven?"

"Heaven? I didn't even know it was an option."

"Did you commit suicide? Is that why you're stuck here?"

"No. Nothing as glamorous as that. Wouldn't that have been a kicker, huh? Off myself only to end up in this hell hole."

"Then what's keeping you here? What did you want before you died?"

"To not have died?"

"You were killed?"

"Isn't that what I just said? Listen twerp, if you're not going to bring him over here—"

"Where are you buried? Dean could uncover your body and then the police would get involved and catch the killer."

Rhonda perked up at that. The most honest emotion Lindy had ever seen on the ghost. "He can do that?"

"I don't see why not. Just tell me where it's at."

"No. I want to tell him. If you're not lying and he can see me, then I'll tell him where. Why are you doing this anyway? You just trying to get your territory back? I already said I wouldn't zap you."

"I need to know how it works. I need to know if I have a chance to move on." Not that she deserved it any longer. She'd done some terrible things. Kind of hard to beg for forgiveness when she couldn't even communicate with the person she'd done wrong.

"Yeah? So what's keeping you here?"

"I wish I knew."

Chapter 24

"What the hell? Where did she go?" Dean spun on his heels, hands fisted into balls. The brat left. Figured. Probably a good thing, though. If Lindy weren't already dead, he wasn't sure she'd be safe in his presence. He'd never been so angry at another person. Maybe that's why she performed the disappearing act. Could it be she was actually afraid of *him*?

Bridget shook his arm. "Dean, you need to calm down. You're turning purple."

He laughed at that and loosened his hands. "Not a good look for me, huh?"

"I worry about you."

"So do I." Maggie had opened the door and was gripping the knob. "Are you okay?"

Was *he* okay? She was the one who'd been nearly raped, and by a ghost. "I'm fine. What are you doing without your crutches? And where's Erica?"

"I used the hand rail and I threatened Erica with bodily harm if she stopped me."

"Well, you shouldn't be on that foot." He went to her and offered her support. "Come on, sit down."

As he led her to the bed, she said, "So...did Lindy admit it?"

Would he ever have good news to tell her? "I'm afraid so."

Tears slid down her cheeks and she lowered her head. "All this time I blamed Eddie, when he was just as innocent as me."

Her misery gutted him and he wrapped her in a hug. "You couldn't have known."

"I'll leave you two alone," Bridget said.

"No," Maggie said as she sat on the bed. "You need to know what kind of ghost she is." She went on to explain while Dean sat beside her, holding her hand. Maybe she didn't need his reassurance, but touching her made him feel better.

"I'm so sorry," Bridget said. "But it's possible she changed. She seemed remorseful for her actions."

"You mean remorseful for being caught," Dean said. "I don't want you around her anymore. She's not safe."

"But she's never hurt me."

"Doesn't mean she won't. But right now we've got a bigger issue than Lindy."

Maggie looked up at him. "Who? Eddie? I don't care what he says. Let him tell people what he thinks a thirteen-year-old made him do. A thirteen-year-old he gave weed to. I'd rather get Lindy out of my life first."

He couldn't agree more, except Lindy would never cooperate, if she even returned. "With the way I scared her, maybe she won't come back."

Both women turned their beseeching eyes to him.

"What?" he asked.

Bridget smiled. "She'll be back and you'll have to be nice to her."

"Nice? Why nice?" He wasn't the one who did all those bad things.

"Because we need her cooperation in order to help her move on."

There was nice, and then there was *nice*. "There is no way I'm apologizing to her."

"I'm not saying you should. I'm saying she'll come to you to apologize and you should accept it."

He snorted. "And when she doesn't?"

"Why do you always have to be so difficult?" Bridget shook her head. "She *will* come to you because *I* won't be around. Unless you've changed your mind."

"No. That won't be necessary." He could suck it up if it meant getting rid of Lindy.

But being nice? To a ghost? He'd rather organize his office.

* * * *

Dean walked Bridget out with a promise from Maggie that she wouldn't go downstairs without his help. As if she were helpless. Well, she wasn't helpless. She could walk if she wanted. Hadn't she made it upstairs by herself? Just to prove her point, she stood.

Pain shot up her foot and she collapsed back onto the bed. Damn it. Probably would have made it if she wasn't due for another pain pill. Oh well, she'd promised anyway. Couldn't break a promise. She lay back on the mattress, closed her eyes, and breathed through the throbbing. It wasn't long before the stairs squeaked with Dean's footfalls.

"Maggie?" His voice was on the frantic side.

"I'm not asleep." She opened her eyes and smiled at his worried face. He wouldn't worry if he didn't care, and just that thought alone made her happy. She held her hand out for a help up. "Come on. Let's go have lunch. Then I can show you what I found."

He no sooner helped her sit up when his phone went off. He frowned at the display before placing it at his ear. "What is it, Greg?"

Dean moved into the hall. No one named Greg worked for Dean, so he must be family. Hopefully his mother was okay, but the frown on Dean's face said otherwise.

A few moments later, sitting turned to lying and she closed her eyes. The bed dipped. Dean took her hand.

She blinked up at him. Damn, how long had she been out? She may have told him she trusted Lindy not to possess her, didn't mean she believed it. But Dean's haunted expression wiped all those fears away. "Everything okay?"

He looked down at their linked hands and shook his head. "This is such bad timing."

She sat up. "Your mother."

He nodded. "I'm sorry. I have to go."

"For how long?"

"Probably just the weekend. She has a doctor appointment tomorrow and wants me there."

"Do you want company?"

He lifted his head and his eyes softened. "You'd come with me? What about Eddie and this house?"

There was no way she would let him face bad news alone. As for the house...he meant way more to her than it did. She

219

shrugged. "I'm beginning to wonder if it really should belong to me. If not for Lindy…"

"We don't know for sure what her part in this was. We may never know."

"You don't think she'll ever tell us the truth?" And would Dean believe Lindy if she did?

"I'm not sure she knows what the truth is anymore." He shook his head. "I can't believe I'm saying this, but if you want to maintain your residence here, you don't have to come with me."

"Do you want me with you?"

He nodded. "I'd like that. Yeah."

"Then I'm coming. I'll deal with the consequences if they occur."

He held her face and kissed her softly. "How'd I get so lucky to have you in my life?"

"I'm the lucky one. It's like you were born for me."

Pain flashed across his face for a moment.

She caressed his cheek. "I'm sure your mother will be fine."

"She has cancer. Greg's not sure she wants to fight it."

"I'm so sorry." Maggie kissed him. "I'm here for you. Okay?"

He smiled and stood as if nothing were wrong. "I've got some laundry to do before I can pack. I'll come back and pick you up. Don't even try and carry your suitcase. I'll get it. Okay? And please, don't go downstairs without Erica's help."

She saluted. "Yes, sir."

He rubbed his face. "Oh God. I didn't mean to sound so bossy. It's just that—"

"I know." She meant something to him and it felt…wonderful. "I was only teasing. Go on. I won't do anything stupid. Promise."

Maggie waved as he headed downstairs. She should feel sad seeing his mother under such dire circumstances, but her nerves started attacking. She was meeting his mom. More than that. She was meeting his family. Whatever was she thinking?

* * * *

Lindy popped into the kitchen just as Dean shut the back door. Damn it. Was he leaving? She floated through the door and rushed after him. "Dean."

No answer.

She continued calling his name as he trudged through the backyard to the garage, but he never responded. Either he was

220

ignoring her, or someone was watching. As he entered the garage and closed the door behind him she popped inside the semi-dark room.

"Dean?"

He jumped. "Shit."

"Sorry." Lindy backed up a bit, just in case he decided to take a swing at her. She wouldn't blame him if he did.

"I didn't expect you back so soon."

"Hoping not to run into me, is that it?"

He sighed. "No. Just surprised is all. Is there something you want? I have things to do."

"Yes, well, first I want to apologize. To Maggie. I'd do it in person, but…heh heh." Not a twitch flickered on his face. Okay, so he didn't think that was funny. "Would you tell her for me?"

He put his hand on his hip. "What are you apologizing for?"

"Everything?" Shit. She didn't mean for that to come out as a question.

"Everything. And you expect her forgiveness?"

"Well…not really. I've been kind of shitty. I know that. You don't know what it's been like, but that's not an excuse. There is no excuse for what I did."

He pushed a button and the garage door rumbled open, making the murky room all bright and sunny. "Fine. I'll tell Maggie what you said. I can't guarantee she'll forgive you, though. She shouldn't forgive you. But I have a feeling she will anyway. She's nice like that."

Damn it. Was he hoping someone was watching and she'd mist away? She'd better hurry, then. "I'm sorry for what I did to you, too. I could see you were really angry with me, so I poofed out. Didn't want you to have another attack. You know?"

"Whatever. Hate to cut our conversation short, but I have things to do before Maggie and I leave for the weekend. When I return, we'll work on getting you moved on." He opened his car door and climbed inside.

Lindy popped into the seat next to him, giving him a start. "You're going out of town?"

"Didn't I just say that?"

"Can you do me a favor?"

"Are you fu—" He rubbed his face and took a deep breath. "What kind of favor?"

Man, he was really trying not to lose it with her. "Well, I would like some proof you can actually help me move on. Could you help another ghost? That way I can figure out exactly why I'm still stuck here."

"You don't know why you're here? I thought you wanted to see Kevin."

"I thought I wanted to experience sex, but now that I know that won't happen, I'm still stuck here. I'm hoping seeing Kevin will be it for me, but what if he isn't? I just need to see it happen."

"Didn't you see your mother pass? I was told she died here."

"I wasn't in her room when she died. If I was, don't you think I would have gone with her?"

"I don't know. Would you have?"

Probably not, but he didn't need to know that. "I'm sure she would have talked me into it."

He shook his head and chuckled.

"What's so funny?"

"Oh, just that none of this would be happening if you'd been possessing your mother at the time of her death."

Telling him the truth again seemed pointless. He wouldn't believe her anyway. "Again, ewww."

"Right… So, I assume you have another ghost in mind?"

"Remember me mentioning Rhonda? Her."

"Rhonda? You said she was crazy."

"Yeah, but that could be because she was murdered. If I give you her information for you to confirm, would you be willing to talk to her?"

"Fine. But no tricks. We meet outside her circle."

Wow. That was easier than she'd thought. "That'll work."

She told him everything. Scowling, he wrote it all in his notebook. For someone who wanted her gone, he seemed awfully grumpy. Go figure.

Chapter 25

Maggie stared out the window as Dean drove them to Cleveland. So far, the trip had been wonderful. Just chatting about work and things of no importance. Like living in a fantasy world where she couldn't be possessed and he couldn't see ghosts.

Which wouldn't be such a bad idea for a book. She pulled the laptop from her backpack and booted it up.

"Won't that get you carsick?" Dean asked.

"Nope. Never has. Guess I have a cast-iron stomach. Or would that be a strong brain? I can never tell."

"And yet, you're afraid of heights."

"Okay, so maybe it's the cast-iron stomach. A strong brain could overcome that, right?"

"If you don't mind me asking, how did that happen?"

"Well, there was this tree house my dad built. Mom said it was too high. Dad and I disagreed. And it was great. Until I fell out of it."

"Ouch. Did you get hurt?"

"Broke my arm and leg. Lost that whole summer stuck in the house. By the time I healed, I didn't want near the tree house. But Dad never tore it down. He'd been so sure I'd change my mind. Fooled him."

She managed to get in a good thirty minutes of writing—her idea was forming up nicely—when Dean exited the freeway. "Where are we staying?" she asked.

He inhaled deeply. "I'd like to say a hotel, and I'll tell Mom that, but knowing her, she'll insist we stay with her. Will you be okay with that?"

"Sure, but I don't want to put her out if she's unwell."

"Trust me, she'll be more upset if she tells us to stay and we don't."

Staying at his boyhood home wouldn't be so bad. Maybe she'd learn some stuff about him. "How's the ghost situation there? I'm assuming we'll be in separate rooms and—"

"No ghost is going to bother you."

"Good to know." So much for forgetting about reality, but then the fantasy was just that—a fantasy. "Do you think I'll ever have a normal life again? One where I won't wonder what ghost will possess me next?"

"Maggie...how many times do I have to tell you? It's not you. It's Lindy. And the fact you're related. That's it. Once she's gone, your life *will* be normal."

"How can you be so sure?" Because if Lindy could do it, why couldn't other ghosts? And if *they* could... God, what was to stop them? She couldn't expect Dean to be around all the time.

"Because I'm right. Wouldn't you have noticed blackouts before moving into that house?"

"Maybe I wasn't living near any ghosts."

"You're working near one. And he hasn't mentioned anything about possessing you. And trust me, if he could have, he would have. And bragged about it, too."

"Peter." She'd forgotten all about him. And she had fallen asleep at work before. Maybe Dean had a point.

"Yeah, Peter. So please, don't worry about it. We'll get Lindy gone and it'll be over. Now, can we please not discuss ghosts this weekend? No one in my family knows I see ghosts and I'd like to keep it that way."

"My lips are sealed." She shoved her laptop inside her backpack.

"Frankly, I'm hoping I can convince Mom to let us stay in a hotel. Wouldn't mind having you to myself for a bit."

His smile warmed her where the heater vents couldn't reach. "You telling me you don't miss sleeping alone?"

"I've hated sleeping alone since the first time we slept together. Back at my apartment."

Wow. And here she'd thought maybe it'd been a hardship.

He pulled into a driveway. "Well, here we are."

Maggie stared at the small white house and her insides quivered. And to think it had nothing to do with the prospect of being possessed by a ghost.

* * * *

Dean hung the damp dish rag on the spout over the kitchen sink. Maggie was currently unpacking while Mom set up Greg's old room for her use. Dean would have preferred Maggie share his bed, but besides embarrassing Maggie or Mom, there really wasn't room. Heck, the twin bed barely held him.

He knew it'd been useless to hope he and Maggie could go to a hotel. Mom had nearly reamed him a new one for even mentioning that.

With Mom's upcoming doctor appointment looming over their heads, dinner had been quiet. The meal itself was great, though. Maggie had insisted on helping, as well as adding her own touches, proving she knew her away around any kitchen, even with that boot on.

Greg finished drying and put away the last plate. "Maggie seems nice. She got a sister?"

Dean laughed. He couldn't believe how easily he fell back into the family atmosphere. Except it wasn't family. Not anymore. "No, but she has a cousin who could pass as her sister."

"Oh? Maybe I should come down and visit more often. Especially if this cousin is anything like Maggie. Damn, I don't remember Mom's meatloaf tasting that good."

It hadn't. That was all Maggie. "I don't believe Erica cooks."

"Erica, huh? Well…cooking's not everything." Greg poked his head down the hall, which was empty. "Listen, I appreciate you coming down on short notice like this. Wish I could go to the appointment with you tomorrow, but I just can't get away."

"Don't worry about it. I don't mind taking her."

"Watch her, will you? I don't like the way she's been acting. It's almost like she's given up before the fight's even started."

"She's probably still in shock." Dean certainly was. Cancer was a scary word until the doctors told you differently.

"Maybe. Are you and Maggie serious?"

"What? Why?" Dean kind of expected the question from Mom, not his brother.

Greg shrugged. "Just thinking that maybe if you were, and then if you had a little Dean or Maggie floating around, it would give Mom something to live for."

"You do know you could do the same for her, right?"

"Yeah, but I haven't found anyone. Whereas you…"

"Forget it. Besides the fact we haven't been dating long, I don't want children."

"Every guy thinks that until they meet the right woman. Are you saying Maggie's not the right woman?"

"I'm saying butt out of my life." He didn't need his brother harassing him and making it seem all normal, like life used to be. He didn't need his brother to get too close and then realize why things had changed between them four years ago. He didn't need his brother to find out what happened to their mother. Because if she had wanted them to know, she would have said something long before now.

* * * *

Gripping her pill bottle, Maggie stood frozen in the hallway. Her heart sank at Dean's words. *I don't want children.*

True, she hadn't thought that far ahead, but was sure he was the one. And she'd always wanted a large family. Now to find out Dean didn't want any children, and worse, that maybe she wasn't the one for him… Disappointment squeezed her heart.

Is that why he wouldn't make love with her?

Dean barreled around the corner and came up short before he collided into her. "Whoa. You okay? I think you've been on that foot long enough. Where are your crutches?"

She couldn't help but smile as his expression morphed from surprise to concern in a beat of a second. Just as well, she certainly didn't want him to suspect she'd overheard his conversation. "I told you I don't need them. It's called a walking boot for a reason. I came to get some water for my pill."

"But if you need the pill, that means it's hurting. Come on. Sit down. I'll get the water." He not only helped her with the chair, he propped her foot up, too.

Clearly he cared for her, but in what capacity? Her chest tightened some more. Oh God, why'd she have to overhear his conversation? Being oblivious had its merits.

"You do look a little pained," Greg said.

Dean grabbed a glass from the cupboard. "She does, doesn't she?"

"I'm fine. Honest." Better to change the subject before she broke down and cried, although they would probably blame the tears on her ankle. "Are you two anything like my dad and uncle? They're always arguing about who's the big brother."

"I'm the big brother," Greg said.

Dean handed her the glass of water. "Being born twenty-five minutes before me doesn't mean shit. I'm four inches taller than you. Therefore, I'm the big brother."

"Hey, I don't make up the rules. I was born first. That makes me the big brother. Isn't that right, Maggie?"

She downed the pill, thankful for the distraction. "Well, see...that's exactly what my dad and uncle argue about. My uncle was born first, but Dad weighed more by a pound."

Dean turned toward Greg. "See? Size does make a difference."

"That's not what she said. Is it, Maggie?"

She held up her hands. "Hey, you two fight over it. I think I'll head to bed. It was nice meeting you, Greg."

She stood, but before she could ask Dean to accompany her, he scooped her up and carried her down the hallway.

"I wasn't asking for a ride." But she'd take it. Maybe she had spent a little too much time on that ankle. Not that she would admit it to him. He'd want to carry her all the time. On second thought...

"Well, you're getting one." He placed her on the bed. "You okay?"

No. Her ankle hurt and her heart hurt. It would just take time to heal them both. "Just tired. Your mom and brother are nice. Any other siblings?"

He crouched in front of her and loosened the straps on her boot. "Nope. Just the one. I think Mom was afraid she'd have twins again and didn't want to risk it."

"You were that bad, huh?" Cooler air hugged her foot when he removed the hot and sweaty brace. She slowly flexed her ankle and stopped at a twinge of pain. "Why didn't you ever mention you were a twin?"

He shrugged and reached for the button to her jeans. "Never came up."

His fingers against her stomach were heaven, but he couldn't be doing what she hoped he'd be doing. She placed her hands on top of his. "Have you changed your mind about us?"

"Changed my mind?" He stopped fiddling with her jeans and after a few moments his eyes widened. "Oh. No. I was just getting you ready for bed."

Of course he was. Anything more would have been in that fantasy world. "You don't think I can undress myself?"

"I think you can do anything. I just want to take care of you." He freed one hand and caressed her cheek.

Leaning into his touch, she closed her eyes. If only they could have stayed at a hotel, she'd be pushing him for more then, but the pained look his mother had given him when he suggested as much—

His lips touched hers and she gasped, giving him the opportunity to deepen the kiss. Desire swept through her and she wrapped her arms around his neck. Ahhh, to have all of him. But kissing wouldn't lead to more, and not just because his mother was down the hall. If she were truly the one for him, wouldn't he have taken her virginity by now?

He broke the kiss and nuzzled her neck. "God, I wish this bed was bigger."

If only he meant that for reasons other than sleeping. "So I won't expect you to sneak in here later?"

"Well...I didn't say that." He gave her a playful peck on the lips. "I love you."

And she believed him, but was he in love with her?

* * * *

Dean propped his feet on the coffee table. Two hours he'd been waiting for Mom to head for bed. Two hours of watching one stupid sitcom after another. At this rate, Maggie would be waking before he could slip into her room. "Shouldn't you get some rest? Doctor's appointment is at nine, right?"

"You waiting for me to go to bed so you can sneak into Maggie's room?"

His face burned. When had he ever been this embarrassed in front of his mother? "I don't know what you're talking about."

"Sure you don't. Well, I'm not a prude. I know you and Greg aren't innocents. I'd be worried if you were. You like her, don't you?"

"I love her."

Her eyebrows shot upward. "Does she know?"

"I told her, yes."

"Oh good. I was afraid maybe I raised a moron."

Dean laughed. "Well, the voting's still out on that."

"Thank you for coming up. And for bringing Maggie. I like her. And I'm so glad you found someone."

Found someone? Was she hoping he was headed to the altar? Because that would never happen. Or was Mom glad because... "Don't go thinking you're leaving us anytime soon."

"We all have expiration dates. Gotta live like it's coming tomorrow." She turned off the TV. "I think you're right. I will turn in. See you in the morning." She kissed his cheek and walked down to her room.

Ah, shit. He'd been hoping Greg was wrong, but now... Had she given up all hope for a cure? Or was she just being reasonable like always? The only time he'd ever seen her break down had been at Dad's memorial. God, was she just waiting to join him now?

He closed his eyes and leaned his back against the couch. Maybe he should turn in, too. And while he was tempted to actually sneak in Maggie's room and sleep with her in that tiny bed, he wouldn't. She was safe here and it wouldn't kill him to miss one night.

But what if he succeeded and Lindy moved on? Maggie wouldn't need him at all and then what kind of excuse would he have to sleep with her? Now, there was a depressing thought. Just because he wasn't right for her didn't mean he wanted to give her up.

He turned off the lamp and headed down the hall. He stopped at Maggie's door. Should he or shouldn't he? Oh hell. Seemed he had a serious addiction.

He opened the door slowly to keep the squeak to a minimum. Tomorrow he would WD40 the hinges so the next time he wouldn't have to worry. Because yeah, there would be a next time. Moonlight filtered in through the blinds, leaving slashes along the bed. He took two steps into the room when his ears crackled.

The ghost appeared in the corner near the window. An old man. Unfamiliar. Had he been one of Mom's friends? So why was he standing there staring at Maggie?

While Dean debated whether or not to let the ghost know he'd been seen, it leaned over Maggie and got sucked into her.

What the hell?

Maggie sat up and stared at her hands.

Dean rushed to the bed, his heart pumping wildly. "Lie back down, then get the hell out of her or heaven help me, I'll zap you back to your place of death."

Maggie-who-wasn't-Maggie stared up at him. Dean must have looked believable because he/she lay back down and the ghost slipped out of her body. "You can see me?"

Dean whispered, "What were you doing?"

"I don't know. I came over to say goodbye to Jenny and noticed the glow through the window."

"What glow?" Except for the moonlight, the room was dark. Maggie hadn't left any nightlight on.

"Her. She lights up this whole room. Then when she sucked me right in, I thought maybe she was the way, but apparently not?"

"What? She sucked you in?" Dean rubbed his head. Damn, that was exactly what Lindy had said.

"Felt like someone grabbed me by my shirt. I'm sorry. I didn't mean to cause her any harm. She's not hurt, is she?"

"No. You didn't hurt her." He, on the other hand, might be sick.

"Good. I gotta go find Jenny. Which way?"

Dean pointed to the room next door.

"Thanks. Again, I'm sorry." With that, the spirit floated through the wall.

Dean collapsed to the floor. He'd been so sure only Lindy could possess Maggie. So sure her troubles would be over once that ghost moved on. How could he tell her she wasn't safe anywhere?

He couldn't, that was how. But he could keep her safe.

"Maggie?" He brushed his hand across her cheek. She opened her eyes and jerked away. "It's just me. Dean."

"Something wrong?"

More than he was willing to tell her. "Am I welcome in your bed?"

"Sure." She lifted the covers.

He kicked off his shoes and removed his jeans and sweatshirt. He left his t-shirt and boxer briefs on as he slipped between the sheets. He adjusted her so she was lying partly on the bed and partly on his chest. "I'm not hurting you, am I?"

"I'm good. Everything okay?"

He kissed the top of her head. "Everything's fine. Go back to sleep."

He might not be good for her, but at least he could keep the ghosts away.

Chapter 26

Maggie snuggled against the warm boulder then blinked her eyes in confusion. Since when was a boulder warm? And when did it grow arms?

Ahh, not a boulder. Dean.

His left hand was currently resting against her boob doing…nothing. Just like every other morning. And while the other mornings they may have had a ghost spying on them, that wasn't the case here. He didn't even have to sleep with her. So when he crawled in last night, she had hoped maybe things would be different.

Nope. Still the same.

Well…just because he wasn't making the moves, didn't mean she couldn't. She hovered her hand over his stomach. North or south? She'd prefer south, but wasn't willing to risk a rejection right off the bat. She settled for north, ran her hand under his t-shirt, and aimed for something safer: his pec.

He opened his eyes and stared at her. His smile went straight to her heart. "Good morning."

Going north was the right choice. No objections so far.

"Did you sleep well?" She traced her finger around his nipple. While she grew wet from the action, his nub grew hard. Even better, he hadn't stopped her.

"I'm beginning to think I can sleep anywhere as long as you're there."

"How sweet." But she wanted more than sweet. More than sleep. Time to go for broke. She climbed over him and straddled his body. Her ankle might have protested a little at the movement, but she ignored it.

God, he was already hard. And she was over him just…so. A little rub brought moans out of both of them. Too bad his boxers and her pajamas were in the way.

"Jesus, Maggie. What are you doing?" he whispered.

Hoping to end the madness. "You love me?"

"Yeah, but—"

"Then let's make love. Now." She pulled down her pants, but straddling him made their removal difficult. Hmmm… Maybe she should have taken them off first.

He grabbed her by the hips. "No. Stop."

Of course he said stop. Not a surprise. But she wanted answers and she wanted them now. "Why?"

He blinked several times as if he were trying to think up something good. "Well, for one, my mother's probably awake."

A valid excuse, but not one she'd thought he'd use. Unless he thought she cared. Ha! Fooled him. At this point nothing but their relationship mattered. "Why else? We've been dating for two weeks and sleeping together for a week. I love you, Dean. And I want all of you. If you love me like you say, why else shouldn't we make love?"

And damn it, the man better give her a compelling reason.

* * * *

This was not the way he'd thought the morning would go. A little kissing, yeah. Some fondling, definitely. Making love? Not even close. And now she wanted to know why.

"I thought we discussed this."

"Before we started dating. This is a new discussion. I know you're interested." And just to prove her point, she sat on his erection.

He arched his back as a wave of desire washed over him. If she did that again, his willpower would falter for sure. But damn it, he wasn't ready to talk about the why of it all. "I'm not ready."

She jerked back onto his legs. "Not ready? Are you sore? Did you have a vasectomy?"

"What? Nooo. Why would you think—"

"Because you told your brother you didn't want children."

He rubbed his face. "You heard that, huh?"

"I didn't mean to eavesdrop, it just happened."

"I know. It's just…I figured we had some time before we needed to discuss this." Time, as in never. Why would it come up? Once she found out about him, the discussion would become obsolete.

"Don't you like children?"

He picked at the fuzz on the blanket. "It's not that."

"Then what is it?"

He took a deep breath. He wasn't ready to lose her yet, but he couldn't lie, either. Boy, the drive home was gonna be one long one if she dumped his ass now. "I don't want to spread his genes around."

"Whose? Your father's?"

"My biological father. Greg's my twin, but he has a different father. The one who raised us. I'm a product of rape. I shouldn't have been conceived."

There. He'd said it. Let the leaving commence.

Instead, Maggie caressed his cheek. "Dean, you can't think like that."

Maybe it hadn't sunk in her head yet. "How can I not think like that? I'm a constant reminder to my mother what happened that night."

"So is your brother."

"What?"

"But I'm guessing she doesn't see it that way. She loves you both. I can tell."

"I understand about unconditional love. Doesn't change the fact that Greg doesn't look like the man who raped her and I do."

"How do you know this? Did she tell you? Have you seen his picture?"

God, when did she turn into a psychologist? "No, and she doesn't know I know, so I'd appreciate you not saying anything."

"If you haven't talked to her, how do *you* know?"

"I didn't, at first. Not even when people asked if I was adopted, because I don't look like anyone else in the family. It took my near death, and the fact I had a different blood type than Mom and…Dad, to open my eyes."

She ran her hand along his chest. "Your surgery."

"Yeah, my faulty heart. Another reason I shouldn't be having kids."

"Then it's a good thing I'm not asking for children, huh?"

"But someday you might." And that someday would kill him. He didn't want to let her go, but what right did he have to keep her?

"I'm not looking at some day. I'm looking at now. You must have noticed I'm taking the pill now. Unless you have some disease I don't know about, we shouldn't even need the condom."

Knock-knock-knock on Maggie's door. *Knock-knock-knock* on the door across the hall. "Time to get up. Breakfast is almost ready!"

Dean had never been so happy to hear his mother.

"Thanks, Mrs. Parker. We'll be right out." Maggie leaned into his face. "This conversation isn't over."

No, but at least it was postponed. "You do realize you just told my mother that I'm in here."

"So now you know I don't care." She climbed off him and sat on the edge of the bed, nudging him aside to make room. "Just curious, but if you're so concerned about spreading his genes, why haven't you had a vasectomy?"

"Just because I don't want kids, doesn't mean I want a doctor to go snipping around down there."

"Okay." She stared at him for what seemed like forever, then leaned over and planted a light kiss against his lips. "Now, unless you want to see me naked, you might want to head to your own room."

He had to be the stupidest man in the whole world. Here was a woman who wanted him, probably as much as he wanted her, and here he was turning her away. If that didn't make her leave him, nothing would.

And for some reason that made him smile. He still grabbed his things and vamoosed it out of the room before she removed her pajama bottoms.

* * * *

Maggie sat behind Dean while he gripped the steering wheel of his car and drove back from the doctor's office. She didn't know what she could say to him. His mother's statement—*I don't want chemo*—had shocked her. She could only imagine what he must be feeling.

"You've been awfully quiet," his mom said, sitting in the passenger seat.

"Not much to say. You kind of made that clear." He glanced in the rearview mirror and stared at Maggie. She offered him a smile, but there was no joy behind it. How could anyone be happy in a time like this?

"What would you have me do? Waste what little time I have getting sick from treatments even the doctor said would probably do no good?"

He pulled into the driveway. "Probably. He said probably, only after you bugged him. Which means there's a chance they could work. But no, you don't want treatment. You're just giving up."

"I'm not giving up. I'm seeing reason."

"If that were the case, you would have seen a doctor long before now. Instead, you wait until you're in stage four, and only because I came up here and made you. Well, I'm not going to sit around and watch you die." He opened the door. "Come on, Maggie. We need to pack up. We're leaving."

Oh, no. He couldn't leave his mother like this. But what could Maggie say to make him stay?

"Jenny, Jenny, Jenny!" An older woman rushed across the yard and stopped at Dean's open door, keeping him from leaving. "Oh, sorry. Hi, Dean." Maggie wanted to laugh. If the woman was truly sorry, she would have gotten out of the way. Instead she poked her head inside the car. "Jenny, did you hear?"

"I've been out, Laura. Can this wait?"

"Ronald died. Can you believe it?"

Jenny clutched her chest. "Oh, dear."

"Who's Ronald?" Dean asked.

"He was her next-door neighbor. Her beau," Laura said.

Dean stared at his mother. "Beau?"

"He was no such thing," Jenny said. "He was a friend is all. How did he die?"

"We think it was a heart attack. Tim went over to get him for their fishing trip and found him in bed. He was just over last night and seemed fine."

Dean caught Maggie's gaze in the mirror. He'd gone pale. Why would Ronald's death mean anything unless... Unless Ronald's ghost stopped by. Was that why Dean wanted to sleep with her last night?

"Excuse me." After gently pushing Laura out of the way, he stormed up the steps and went inside the house.

"What's his problem?" Laura asked.

"He's a little mad at me."

"He just left you in the car."

As Maggie exited the vehicle, Laura walked around and helped Jenny out.

"You go and check on him," Jenny said, waving Maggie toward the house. "I'll be fine."

Maggie hobbled inside the house and headed back to the bedroom. She found Dean in the room he hadn't slept in, slapping and shoving clothes in his small bag. He looked up when she entered, but didn't say a word.

"You saw Ronald last night, as a ghost, didn't you?"

"Yeah. He was looking for Mom."

"Is he still around?"

"No, I don't believe so. He was in a hurry. I think he moved on."

"Then why do you want to go home?"

"Because it's pointless to stay."

"But she's your mother."

"And I'm her son. Yet that doesn't seem to matter to her, not that I blame her."

"Dean... You should talk to her."

He zipped his bag. "Do you need me to pack for you?"

"No, I can do it." She hobbled across the hall and proceeded to put back the clothes she had just taken out the night before. This whole thing wasn't helping with how he viewed his life, not with his mother basically giving up. But how could she convince him to talk to his mother?

He came inside the room with his bag, sat on the bed and watched.

"You can't leave like this. Go talk to her. About everything."

He shook his head. "Too late."

Not yet, but it could be. "You'll feel better if you'll just talk to her."

"Stop. Just stop, okay?"

She finished packing and zipped the bag. "Are you going to at least tell her goodbye?"

"I can't." Dean took both bags and headed down the hall. Maggie limped after him, hoping he'd change his mind and say something to his mother, but he just walked out the front door.

Maggie stopped and looked between the door and the living room, where his mother sat. Laura must have gone on home. "I'm sure once he's calmed down, he'll be back."

"I wouldn't be too sure of that. He gets that stubborn streak from me. I'm glad he's got you. You don't happen to have a sister or friend for Greg, do you? I'd sure feel better knowing I left them in good hands. Now go on. He needs you. I'll be fine."

Maggie sat on the couch and hugged the woman. "I'm very glad to have met you, Mrs. Parker."

"Now, now, you go ahead and call me Jenny." She grabbed a notepad and pen from the coffee table and started writing. "If you wouldn't mind, would you call or write me and let me know how he's doing?"

"Sure." Maggie took the paper and put it in her purse, then wrote her own address and phone number on the pad of paper. The car started outside. "Here's mine. I better go. I'll keep in touch."

She hated leaving like this, but this was Dean's family, not hers.

* * * *

Dean slammed the car door shut, the sound echoing through Maggie's garage and fueling his anger. An anger he welcomed with open arms. Because anger was a heck of a lot better than this overwhelming grief that threatened to take him down.

Was living really all that bad for Mom? Why couldn't she fight? If Dad were still alive, she would. Or was she tired of seeing the result of her worst day on Earth? He wasn't sure he could muster seeing a reminder of being raped.

Maggie climbed out of the passenger side. "If you're mad at your car, maybe it's time to get a new one."

Dean smiled. Maybe he should embrace humor, too. She knew exactly how to make him feel better. Just her presence in the car had been enough to keep him from totally losing it.

Maggie came around the car and hugged him. "You should have stayed up there."

He couldn't think of a worse torture than watching his mother die. After kissing the top of Maggie's head, he broke free. "You go on inside. I'll get the bags."

She walked to the door, stopped, and turned around. "I know you're hurting. I just hope you don't do something you regret. I'd have given anything to have more time with my mom."

He couldn't respond to that—her situation had been a wee bit different than his—but she left before he could say anything anyway. As soon as Maggie was out of sight, Lindy appeared.

He should have known she'd be hanging around. "Are you always eavesdropping on everyone?"

She shrugged. "What else is there to do?"

God, she sounded like Peter. "I can't believe I'm saying this, but I'm glad you're here. I had Bridget look up Rhonda's situation. Seems she's telling the truth about her being a missing person. You should have told me she died back in 1924. It's going to make my job a little harder."

"Holy crap. 1924?"

"You couldn't tell from her state of dress?"

"Ummm, not really."

Bags in hand, he closed the trunk. "Give me a minute to take these inside. Where can I meet this ghost and not get seen? Or touched?"

She gave him the addresses of two houses and told him to meet in the back alley between the garages. "Thanks for doing this."

"Just so we're clear, I'm not doing this for you." He trudged into the house. Now not only his time with Mom was limited, seemed his time with Maggie was, too. And if that didn't just suck.

* * * *

Lindy and Rhonda materialized at the designated meeting spot. As long as no one drove on the alleyway—and it being the middle of the afternoon made that highly unlikely—Dean should be able to see them.

With his head hung low, he strolled down the alley looking as if he'd lost his favorite pet.

"Is that him?" Rhonda asked. "You didn't tell me he was a hunk."

"Don't let his looks fool you. He's an ass." She knew he wasn't really helping her out of the goodness of his heart, but man, did he have to be a dick about it?

"So what does that have to do with him being a hunk? Lots of hunks are asses. Besides, he can't be too much of an ass. He's helping me out."

"For a reason." A reason by the name of Maggie. Lindy waved her arm. "Hey! Over here."

He looked up and then quickly turned around. "Jesus! Why didn't you tell me she was naked?"

"Naked?" Lindy looked over her shoulder. Oh God. Burn her eyes now. Sure as shit, Rhonda's nightgown had vanished.

"Well, what do you know? He *can* see me!" Rhonda said.

"What'd you do with your nightgown?"

"Oh, thank God," Dean said. "I was afraid she'd died that way."

"Neat trick, huh?" Rhonda misted away and reappeared, wearing that gossamer nightgown. She whispered, "You're wrong. He's not an ass. He's a prude."

No, he was a man who only had eyes for one person: Maggie. A love Lindy would never experience. Could that be what was holding her back? "You can turn around now. She's dressed."

He walked over and stopped when Lindy indicated he'd gone far enough.

Rhonda pouted. "You're not going to let me touch you?"

"No." Dean pulled out a little notebook and pen from his coat pocket. "What's the story?"

"You'll end up in my territory eventually."

"With someone who cannot see ghosts. Now, do you want my help or not?"

Lindy gave Rhonda the told-ya look.

"Fine. My dirty-rotten-no-good husband buried me behind our house. I'm underneath the flower garden in the backyard."

Dean confirmed her address. "Do you know why he killed you?"

"Because I refused to bow down and submit to his sexual needs."

"You?" Lindy said.

Rhonda shrugged. "I know, huh? I liked the kinky, but he was mean. And I told him if he couldn't be nice, I didn't want to do it anymore. Stupid me, I believed him when he apologized and I let him tie me up again. Only this time, he choked me. Told me it would give me a better orgasm."

"Shit."

"Yeah, that about sums it up. By the time he came, he was fucking a corpse. He did try to revive me, but it was too little too late. So he buried me in the garden and then reported me missing. I'd run off before, so everyone believed him. I don't know what happened to the bastard. He moved a few years later. I think he sensed me, you know? I certainly tried to make his life hell."

And she probably did a good job of that. She'd certainly made Lindy's life, death, whatever, hell, too.

Dean pulled out his cell phone. "After you'd been missing for seven years, he had you pronounced legally dead, although the missing person case was never closed. He married again and had three daughters. He died in 1964."

"That doesn't seem fair, now does it?" Rhonda said. "Do you think finding my body will help me out of this hell hole?"

"I don't know. I would have thought knowing this information would be enough. You can't get justice from a dead man."

"I think I want that case closed. I want my body found. I want a proper burial. My sister had some kids. They must still be alive. They must care about what happened to me." Rhonda gave him several names.

"I'll check the place out tonight, but I can't guarantee I'll be able to dig yet," he said.

"Tonight? Holy shit! You sure I can't hug you?"

"I'm sure." He turned and headed back to Maggie's.

Rhonda hugged Lindy instead. "I take back every nasty thing I ever said to you."

"But I haven't done anything."

"You've given me hope. Didn't realize until now how much I missed having that."

Hope. Now there was something Lindy didn't have. Because even if she did manage to see Kevin, he wouldn't be able to see her. He wouldn't know she was real. Not unless Bridget and Dean had some tricks up their sleeves. She wouldn't put it past them to keep quiet about such things.

Chapter 27

"Not exactly how you expected to spend your Saturday night, huh?" Dean said to Rob as he pulled up to the curb and killed the engine.

"Oh, I don't know. I've never gone grave hunting before. Could be fun."

Luckily, Rhonda's house was for sale. As were several houses nearby. Most likely she made it intolerable for anyone to live in the neighborhood.

Night wasn't Dean's ideal time to dig a grave, but doing it in the daylight might cause some nosey neighbor to call the cops and he really didn't want to get them involved. The less he had to explain to someone, the better.

"Is this even a quarter-mile from Lindy's point of death?" Bridget asked as she climbed out of the backseat with a little help from Rob.

Leaving the car running, Dean climbed out and helped Maggie from the rear. "Just barely. Lindy said she can make it to the garage. Please stay in the car unless we call for you, okay?"

"Yes, boss," Bridget said as she climbed into the driver's seat.

"I was talking to Maggie. She can make the ghost disappear. You can't." He failed to tell either woman that Maggie was actually watching Bridget, a requirement for Rob's help. He hated leaving his wife alone when she was so close to giving birth.

Maggie climbed into the front passenger seat. If it weren't for her ankle, she'd sit in the driver's seat, not that Dean expected they'd go anywhere without him. "You sure we won't get in trouble?"

"I got permission from the owners to check the place out."

"Yeah, but they don't expect you to go digging, do they?"

"They don't care. They just want to sell the house. I'll call you if Rhonda becomes a problem." After making sure the women were settled in the front seats where they would stay warm, Dean met Rob at the trunk and proceeded to remove the metal detector.

"Why do you need that?" Rob asked as he pulled out the pick and shovels.

"Insurance. If someone should happen to see us, it'll be an excuse. She *was* buried with her ring on."

"Like that thing will pick it up."

"Hey, I don't know that. Come on. Let's go see what we've got. I'm sure Rhonda's waiting."

The houses here were similar to Maggie's, where the garages were in the back, accessible via an alley. They walked around the house.

Rhonda hovered near the back door. Thanks to the security light next door, Lindy could be seen hovering beside the garage. He wasn't too thrilled with the light, but it did make their job a little easier. As for Rhonda, he could only hope she behaved; otherwise he'd have to call Maggie.

Rhonda grabbed his hand and became solid. "Holy shinoli. That girl was right."

Dean shrugged free. So much for hope and not wearing his gloves. He pulled them out of his pocket and yanked them on. "If you want my help, don't do that again."

She looked at Rob.

"Don't touch him either."

She crossed her arms and pouted. "Thought you were bringing someone who couldn't see me."

"I did. She's in the car. You gonna make me get her?"

"Anyone ever tell you you're no fun?"

"All the time. So, where are you buried?"

Rhonda pointed to the snow-covered area alongside the back of the house. Old bricks, stacked four-high, surrounded what was probably a flower garden.

"Are you in it or under it?"

"If I were in it, wouldn't someone have found me before now?"

Dean shook his head and grabbed the pick. "I'll start. Keep an eye out for her."

"Lindy was right. You are an ass. Don't you trust anyone?" Rhonda asked.

Sure he did. They all just happened to be living.

* * * *

Gina pulled up along the curb a few houses back from Dean's car and quickly doused the lights. So far it didn't appear she'd been spotted.

It had taken a couple of days, and plenty of nagging, to finally get Eddie to relinquish the keys to her car. She wouldn't have had to wait that long if the boy had only left the keys at home when he went to work. But noooo, he had to take them to work with him. The brat.

Once she'd obtained her freedom, she had planned to just drive by the house and see if that P.I. was still there. Instead, she stumbled upon him and Maggie leaving, with two other people, even. Didn't mean they would be gone long, or that her cousin had also left, so Gina had followed them. With any luck, they were going to a restaurant on a double date and would be gone for hours. Instead they drove a short distance to another neighborhood.

When Dean and that other fella pulled out shovels and stuff from the trunk and then carried it around to the back of a house, Gina smiled. About time someone else ended up in jail. It certainly wouldn't be her. She called 9-1-1 and reported a break-in, and damn, if she didn't sound convincing. Finally, her high school drama classes came in handy.

Leaving those four to their destiny, she drove back to the house. If Erica was out as usual, Gina would finally get what belonged to her and none of them could stop her.

* * * *

Maggie turned down the radio. "They've been gone a while. How long does it take to dig up a body?"

"Are you asking because you think I should know?" Bridget said.

Maggie laughed. "Sorry. No. Completely rhetorical. Just thinking we should have brought books to read or something."

"Then we wouldn't be good lookouts."

"Is that what we are?" Shoot. Maybe she should have been paying more attention to the traffic then. "You do this often?"

"Nope. First time." Bridget held her belly. "Okay, Charlie. Calm down. I swear, the baby is practicing gymnastics."

"You're not going into—"

"No, no. Don't worry. I've got a couple of weeks yet."

"I'm surprised you even came. I could have sat here by myself." Or even helped dig, after the ghost had told them where she was buried.

"Are you kidding me? Rob's afraid to leave me alone. I'm sure he told Dean he wouldn't help unless you watched me. As if I won't have enough time to call him or my mother if I go into labor. He's going to be so disappointed when he realizes labor for a first baby takes hours."

Flashing lights bounced off the windows and illuminated the street. Maggie pointed. "Is that the—"

"Police," Bridget finished. "Shit. We need to go warn the guys."

Maggie pulled out her cell phone to do just that when Bridget climbed out of the car.

* * * *

Dean wiped the sweat from his brow while Rob hacked at the garden. Digging through the top portion hadn't been all that bad. But when they'd reached ground level, the work began. And not just because the ground was frozen. Damn clay. It could have been worse, though. Rhonda's husband could have used cement.

"You're not going to hurt my remains, are you?" Rhonda asked.

"What does that matter? The goal is to find them, not preserve them."

"I suppose."

Rob stood and Dean shoveled the loosened dirt. They'd gone down a good six inches and still nothing. Or maybe not. What was that white piece? *Please don't let it be another rock.* Dean stuck the shovel into the pile of dirt just as his phone indicated an incoming text message.

"Hold on. Something's up." He pulled out his cell and read the text from Maggie. Police? "Shit!"

"Rob. Dean. Police. Coming. Silent." Bridget said between pants. She grabbed her stomach. "Oh shit."

"What's the matt—" Rhonda misted away, cutting off her words.

"Bridget, honey?" Rob dropped the pick and ran to his wife just as Maggie came limping around the corner holding her phone.

"What are we gonna do?" Maggie looked at the mess. "Oh wow. You found her?"

"Police. Hold it right there."

Dean took a deep breath. He was prepared for this scenario. Trick was to not look guilty. He turned and faced the cop. "I can explain."

The police officer took one look at Dean and raised his eyebrow. "What the hell are *you* doing here?"

Dean relaxed at seeing his friend, Danny. But before he could say anything, Maggie's phone blared.

"Someone's breaking into my house," she said.

"Dean?" Danny said accusingly.

"This isn't her house," Dean said. "She lives over on Demphle. The security system at her house just went off. You need to get someone over there quick." This couldn't be a coincidence. First the police here. Then the alarm at Maggie's. Someone must have followed them. He'd bet his money on Eddie.

Danny raised a hand. "Hold on." He called in the alert for Maggie's house. "Now do you mind telling me what you are all doing here?" He shined his flashlight toward the garden. "And is that a bone?"

* * * *

Gina flipped on the dining room light and rubbed her hands. God, she was freezing. She'd parked down the street just in case some nosey neighbor recognized her car, and her coat wasn't near warm enough for the walk to the house. But she was here now. Finally, she'd get what was hers.

After determining that Erica was indeed gone, Gina had used her key only to discover it no longer worked. Damn witch, Linda. She probably changed the locks the day after Ed died. So instead of walking through the house like any normal person, she'd been relegated to breaking the office window and crawling through. As if she were a thief or something. Good thing she hadn't cut herself on the glass.

She'd been heading for the stairs to the basement—thinking that's where Maggie had moved the attic contents—when she'd noticed stacks of boxes in the dining room. Bingo! The light confirmed it.

She rummaged through several boxes until she came upon the photo album. Yes! She opened it up and thumbed through several old photographs. They were here somewhere. Maybe toward the back? But the pages were empty. Only the little black photo corners remained. "The bitch! What'd she do to them?"

"Put the book down and exit the room. Slowly."

Gina turned around to find a cop pointing a gun. At her.

"You don't understand. I only came to get what was mine."

"Put it down. Now. And come here."

Gina looked between the photo album and the box. What could Maggie have done with them? Maybe they had just fallen out. Or maybe this wasn't the right book. Gina placed the album on the table and reached for the box.

"Ma'am. Don't make me ask again."

"Or what? Are you going to shoot me? I'm unarmed."

"For all I know you're reaching for a gun. Out. Now."

Damn it. She straightened up. Maggie would so pay for this.

Chapter 28

"Dean, you got an explanation for this?" Danny squatted by the hole and shined the light on the skeletal hand.

Well, at least they'd found Rhonda. And while Dean would love to chat with his friend, Bridget wasn't looking all too well. Rob sat her down on a picnic table that looked ready to collapse.

"She okay, Rob?"

The little shake of Rob's head wasn't so much an answer on Bridget's condition, but more like on his. "I need to get her home."

Danny turned around and saw Bridget. "You brought a pregnant lady to a break-in?"

"I'm not breaking in. We have permission to be here."

"It's all my fault," Maggie said. "We're just looking for Rhonda's grave."

"Who's Rhonda?" Danny asked.

"I'm guessing she is." Dean pointed to the grave. "Dead since 1924. You gonna arrest me for that?"

Danny stood. "I'm not arresting anyone until I figure out what you're doing here."

Maggie stepped forward. "Well, see... I was doing research for a book. My grandmother told me about Rhonda Tremain. How she was a missing person case. Except Grandma believed Rhonda was killed and buried in the backyard. I wasn't sure whether to believe Grandma or not, but what if she was right? So I asked Dean to do a little investigation. He was able to pinpoint the possibility of a grave from the metal detector. We were going to report it if we found any evidence of a body."

Danny rubbed the back of his neck. "Research for a book?"

Hopefully Maggie's story would fly—and man, if that woman couldn't think fast on her feet!—but he wasn't taking any chances. "Yeah. Her pen name is M. L. Detrick. She writes horror novels."

"You're M. L. Detrick? Well, hot damn! My wife is reading your latest. Think I can get your autograph later? You know, for her."

"Can you do this without us?" Rob asked. "I need to get my wife home to lie down."

"I can call an ambulance."

"I'm okay," Bridget said. "I ran when I shouldn't have. I don't need an ambulance."

She just didn't want to go to the hospital. The local ones had their share of spirits. One of the reasons he'd never left Maggie's side when he'd taken her to the emergency room. That, and the fact he just didn't want to leave her side.

Danny pointed at Dean. "You better not be lying to me."

"I'm not. I swear." At least, not in the way it counted.

Danny agreed to let Rob and Bridget leave after getting their names and address. Dean tossed his keys to Rob. "Go on. Put the keys in the glove box. We'll get a cab."

"You don't have to get a cab," Danny said after Rob and Bridget had departed. "I can give you a ride. Need to make sure everything is clear at her house anyway. Right?"

"Thanks. I appreciate that." Dean ushered Maggie to the picnic table and wrapped his arm around her shivering shoulders. Hopefully they wouldn't be detained much longer. Some hot chocolate sounded good right about now.

Danny crouched beside the dug-up grave and shook his head in disbelief. "Now tell me, why didn't you just contact the owners of the house?"

"I did," Dean said. "You want to call them?" *Please don't.* He sent that mental command to his friend several times as if it would make a difference. While he'd told Maggie the owners wouldn't care, he wasn't so sure himself. Digging a hole in the yard wasn't exactly covered in getting permission to view the property, now was it?

* * * *

"Can you believe it?" Rhonda said. "He actually found me. I really didn't think it was possible."

Lindy looked out over the fence at the commotion in Rhonda's yard. "So why are you still here?"

"Because that cop doesn't believe it."

"Yet."

"Yeah. Yet."

"Nervous?"

"A little. I'm going to see what they're talking about."

"Sure. Go on."

Rhonda popped back to the scene. What would it take for her to move on? A wish, a desire, or the definite proof that her body had been discovered?

Lindy would love to listen to the conversation, too, but they weren't talking loud enough and another step would pop her back to the living room.

Funny, she'd been hoping that Rhonda would leave ever since she'd met the ghost, and now when it seemed imminent... Well, maybe she wouldn't leave. Maybe nothing was keeping Rhonda here just like nothing was keeping Lindy here and Dean was one big fat liar.

A light shown down on Rhonda, like a spotlight from a helicopter. But there wasn't any helicopter in the air. In fact, the place was eerily quiet. Rhonda looked up—although no one else had—and smiled. Just as quickly as it appeared, the light disappeared and Rhonda vanished.

What was that? What happened? Where'd she go?

"Rhonda?" Lindy yelled out for the ghost several more times. Nothing.

She remained near the scene of the uncovered grave until everyone left. Still no sign of Rhonda. No sign of any ghost. Lindy didn't know whether to cheer or cry.

* * * *

Huddled inside her coat, Maggie swept the last of the glass onto the dust pan. "I can't believe she broke my window. It'll take forever to warm this place up."

"Be glad they nabbed her before she had a chance to grab anything." Dean held a roll of duct tape and some plastic garbage bags. "This was all I could find. If the window repairmen can't come tomorrow, I'll get some wood."

Regardless, her new wallpaper would be ruined. Just another expense to add to the total. Damn it. "This has got to end. I'm going through every box and won't stop until I find whatever it is she's looking for. Then I'll just wave it in front of her face and tell her she can't have it."

"Start in the morning, okay? You look like you're about to crash."

She collapsed onto her chair. "This has been a long day, hasn't it?"

Coming home to find that Gina had broken in the house had pretty much topped it off. All she wanted to do now was go to bed and snuggle against Dean. Heck, maybe more than snuggle.

"That it has." He unrolled a strip of tape and tore it off. "I should have postponed the grave-digging. Then maybe I would have noticed being followed."

She held the plastic bag up while he applied half the strip to one end. "Hey, no one saw her. We all just want this over with. At least you knew the cop."

"I'll say. If anyone other than Danny had shown up, we'd be downtown explaining ourselves. And that story you told about it being research and all? Good thinking. Now I just have to get rid of Lindy and then you'll be home free." He took the taped bag and secured the top edge to the wall above the window, then taped the other edges to the wall. It wasn't perfect, but at least it would keep the wind from blowing inside.

"What's next in your plan to help Lindy?"

"Bridget found her boyfriend. Thought I'd go talk to him."

"Do you need my help?"

"Help? Like how?"

"I could pretend I read Lindy's journal and want to know more about her. Oooh… Do you have any spy cameras in your arsenal?"

He chuckled. "I do, actually. Wouldn't call it an arsenal, though. Why would you need a camera?"

"To record the conversation. Actually, it would be better if Lindy had some questions I could ask for her. Which means…"

"Yeah, I know. I gotta talk to Lindy." Dean groaned.

She stood and hugged him. The contact instantly warmed her. "Ahh, you're the best. Why don't we go upstairs and get ready for bed?"

"You go on up first. Let me get this conversation with Lindy over with." He pulled away, but took her hand and led her out through the kitchen into the living room.

She'd love to tell him not to bother, to just come upstairs, but she still had questions that needed answering. "While you're at it, would you please ask her how she discovered she could possess me?"

He coughed. "Maggie… Do we have to go over this again? Once Lindy is gone, you're safe."

So he kept saying. "Safe where? In my house? That's fine now, but what if someone else nearby becomes a ghost? What if—"

He grabbed her by the shoulders. "Stop. You're obsessing over something that's not going to happen."

"But you don't know that, do you?"

"You don't have any other family members floating around here."

"If you're so sure it's family related, then why won't you ask Lindy how she knew?" She yanked herself free and limped to the stairs. "Never mind. I'll have Bridget ask her."

"And risk her going into labor again?"

Maggie stopped on the first step. She hadn't thought of that, not that Bridget had actually gone into labor. Still, it was probably enough for Rob to keep her at home. "Then I'll ask Rob. He sees ghosts, too, right? And if he won't do it, then I'll ask Lindy, let her possess me—"

"Are you high?"

She hated manipulating him, but he left her no choice. "If you don't like those ideas, then you ask her."

He ran his hand through his hair. "Fine. But I won't guarantee what she says is the truth."

"Why would she lie about that?"

"To scare me. To scare you. Who knows? We're a game to her and she's having way too much fun."

Maybe so, but Maggie wanted, no, needed to know everything. This was her life, not his, and Lindy was the key. When she finally moved on, her information would move on with her. If only Maggie could see and talk to ghosts. Didn't seem right that she couldn't.

* * * *

Dean paced in the living room while Maggie went upstairs to get ready for bed. Surprised Lindy hadn't materialized as soon as Maggie was out of sight. At least their conversation had been private. Like he needed to be scolded by a ghost.

Why couldn't Maggie just drop the possession bit? He couldn't tell her the truth. It would freak her out. Hell, it freaked him out.

He scrubbed his head and plopped down on the couch.

"Well, I guess it worked," Lindy said.

Dean opened his eyes to the ghost. "What? Almost getting arrested or installing the security system?"

"Neither. What happened with the security system?"

"Gina broke in. Didn't you know?"

"No. I was too busy watching you all uncover Rhonda. That's what I meant, by the way. She left."

He sat up. "Left? Are you sure?"

"Pretty sure. Saw a light come and go from the sky and haven't seen Rhonda since. Looked everywhere for her, too."

"Well, I'll be. So why aren't you happy? You have your whole territory to yourself now."

Lindy shrugged. "Yeah, I guess."

She seemed kind of in the dumps. Maybe now she would be more inclined to move on and leave Maggie alone. "Maggie would like to talk to Kevin for you. Figures she could find out his intentions by wanting to know more about you."

"Yeah? Would she be willing to let me possess her so I could talk to him myself?"

God, if Lindy only knew how close that could come to happening. Dean just stared at her, though.

She shrugged. "Yeah, I didn't think so. Can't blame a ghost for asking."

"Listen, since you've just gained a large piece of territory, check and see if any of the occupants glow. Then see if you can possess them."

"What? You believe me now?"

"I might have reason to do that, yeah. Pay attention to those individuals who are more likely to be virgins."

"You think she glows because she's a virgin? Hmmm...hadn't thought of it like that. Wouldn't that be a kicker, huh? If I had succeeded with Eddie..." Her words trailed as Dean glared at her.

"Hey, you could always do it with her and then I can see if she still glows."

The thought had crossed his mind, but that wasn't any reason to have sex with Maggie. Although, he was about ready to cave in as it was. One more attempt from her and he'd be a goner. Maybe he should pick a fight with her so she'd stay away. He'd have to do it eventually because she deserved so much better than him.

But if she glowed because she was a virgin, and that glowing was what caused her to be possessed... God, the thought gave him a headache.

"Just check your area, okay?"

"Sure. But I should tell you that once I knew what to look for, I looked, you know? I haven't seen any of them glow."

"But you haven't checked everyone."

She shook her head. "I'll get back to you in the morning, but don't get your hopes up. If there were any out there that glowed, Rhonda would have surely said something. She liked to brag."

Hope was all he had left, and even that was getting pretty thin. His only option was to get Lindy good and gone. With enough time, Maggie could forget about ever being possessed. Because really, what were the odds another ghost would appear within reach of her house?

* * * *

Eddie placed his cell phone on the nightstand and plopped back against his pillow. Jail? Again? When would she ever learn?

Parker would definitely call him on his bluff now. He'd really had no intention of letting his wife know what happened that summer, but had hoped the threat would deter Maggie from pressing charges.

Ronnie snuggled against him. "What happened? Is your mother okay?"

"I should have never given the keys back to her."

"Oh, God, Eddie! Did she have an accident?"

"No. No accident." Nothing as normal as that. No, he had to have a mother who liked to perform B&Es. Maybe a night in the jail would cure her. Then again, maybe not. Even a dog would continue to chase his tail after catching it several times. "She got caught breaking into Grandma's house. Again. And needs me to bail her out."

"With what money? Listen, I love your mom and all, but maybe it's time to cut the cord."

This was news to him. He'd thought Ronnie and Mom were tight. "What do you mean?"

"What would happen if you didn't help her this time?"

"She'd probably spend the whole weekend in jail. And then when she got out, chew my ass." Or cut off his dick. He wouldn't put that past her.

"Unless you stood up to her. Told her she wasn't welcome in our house if she continued to break the law. Could you do that?"

Could he? Hell, yeah. But he'd never even attempted that because of what Ronnie would think. Her opinion always meant the most to him. "You're okay with me letting her stew in jail?"

Ronnie caressed his cheek. "She won't learn otherwise, now will she? And we'll have the place to ourselves. All weekend."

It was that moment when Eddie realized what a gem he had for a wife. He picked up his phone and texted his mother's lawyer. Mom was his problem now. Eddie then kissed his wife, which led to love making, which led to the best night of sleep he'd ever had.

* * * *

Maggie stared at the book in her hands. She must have been on this page for the past fifteen minutes. Somehow reading wasn't doing it for her tonight.

She should have never snapped at Dean. The unknown was getting to her and she'd taken it out on him instead of Lindy, who she really wanted to strangle. She hoped to God that talking to Kevin would do the trick in getting rid of the ghost.

Her door opened and Dean entered, sending her blood pressure up-up-upward. Suddenly, living in oblivion became a whole bunch more desirable than knowing the dangers.

He sat on the edge of the bed. "Rhonda's gone."

"Really?"

"Lindy can't find her anywhere. Thinks she saw her move on."

Maggie sat up and placed the book on her nightstand. "That's good, right? That means Lindy knows it can happen. Did you ask her about me?"

"She found out by accident that she could possess you. Got too close when you were high and got sucked into your body."

Sucked? Maggie shivered. What was she? The vacuum for ghosts? "She ever possess anyone else?"

"She's tried, but now with Rhonda's territory open to her, she said she would try again. Doesn't mean anything if she does or doesn't. It could still be her. Rhonda never mentioned possessing anyone and according to Lindy, she would have."

"That still doesn't eliminate it being just me."

"But you don't remember any black-out periods before you lived here. I really wish you'd stop worrying about it."

He made a valid point. One she should just accept. "Thank you. I know you don't like talking with her."

"Can't be helped. I want her gone so you'll be free."

Free? Free from ghosts, or free from him? She didn't want to be free from him. She wanted to keep him forever. She rose to her knees and caressed Dean's face. "Lindy is basically busy tonight. Right?"

"For a little while. You want to sleep alone? I can wait to come to bed."

"It wasn't sleep I was thinking about." She kissed him and pushed him down to the mattress. Then she ran her hand down his chest, to his stomach, to his—

He grabbed her wrist, stopping her exploring. "You're killing me here, Maggie."

"And what do you think you're doing to me?" She sat up and yanked free from his grasp. "You make me feel like I'm a freak."

"Ah, Maggie. There's nothing wrong with you. You're perfect."

"I can't be that perfect if you don't want me."

"That's not it, and you know it. I can't give you what you want. What you deserve."

"Says you. I say differently."

He shook his head and rose from the bed. "I think maybe tonight I'll just stay downstairs."

"If you go downstairs, you might as well keep on going."

"What do you mean?"

"Exactly what you've been telling me. You don't want to be with me, then don't. Just go home."

"But what about Lindy?"

"I still have the chain." If she decided to wear one at all. "Besides, it's almost over anyway, right? I talk to Kevin, show the video to Lindy and poof, she's gone. Your job will then be over. Right?"

"If that's what you want."

Far from it, but she wasn't going to beg for his company. "It is."

"I'll come by and pick you up tomorrow then."

That wouldn't work. Just being with him would hurt. "I don't want you to come with me. I'll get Erica to go. You give her the camera and information and she'll call you when we're finished."

"Okay, then." He walked out of her room and silently closed the door behind him.

Damn him! He didn't even fight for her. She fell into her pillow and cried.

Chapter 29

Sitting on Maggie's couch, Dean punched the ignore button on the incoming call. How many more attempts would it take before Greg gave up calling and drove back to Dayton? Dean knew he had to talk to his brother, but some things were more important. Like patching his relationship with Maggie.

He'd only meant to create some distance between them, not shove her away completely. What an idiot! He should be shot for even thinking that fighting with her would be good. Last night was the most miserable night of his life.

And the misery continued. She hadn't even come downstairs since his arrival. Erica had let him in and then promptly departed. Not without giving him the evil eye first. Something he fully deserved.

"Whatcha got there?" Lindy asked. "You're not going to watch porn, are you? 'Cause if you are, I'm outta here."

He'd been plugging the laptop into the television and jumped at her sudden appearance. "I'm not watching porn. Why would you think that?"

"Because that's what the perv across the street does when he's jacking off."

Eeww. Okay, that was TMI. "If I'm lucky, this is your ticket out of here."

"You talked to Kevin already?"

"Not me. Maggie." He sat on the couch and turned on the TV. As badly as he wished for Maggie's company, it was just as well she wasn't around. This way he'd know if Lindy moved on or not. Or at least he'd pass out when she left. According to Bridget and Rob, that would happen if he was alone with Lindy. "Are you ready?"

She held out her hand. "Not yet. Aren't you interested in what I discovered last night?"

"Let me guess. No one glowed."

"Not even those so-called virgins. Did you really need that as an excuse to have sex with Maggie? Doesn't seem fair to her."

"Since when do you care anything about Maggie?"

"You might not believe it, but I've grown a conscience since our little conversation about me so-called raping her. I really didn't think I was hurting her. She was a way for me to get out of this house. A way for me to do what I couldn't when I was alive—you know, live. So… You gonna tell her the truth?"

"The truth? That's a good one coming from your mouth." And what would the truth do? Make Maggie paranoid? She didn't need to live that way. Besides, once Lindy moved on, the possessions would stop. There wasn't another ghost floating around.

"Hey, just because you don't trust me doesn't mean I've been lying."

Damn it. He hated it when she was right. Since he'd accused her of raping Maggie, he hadn't caught Lindy in a single lie. And he'd tried. Boy, had he tried. Maybe he could trust her after all. "I'm sorry. You didn't deserve that last remark. I know you just want some answers. Maybe this video will help."

Dean clicked on the PLAY icon. He had yet to see the recording and was as curious as Lindy.

Maggie turned toward the camera. "You got that thing on?"

"Yes, ma'am," Erica said. "So knock on the door, already."

Maggie knocked. An older man answered. "Hello. Mr. Tipton?" When the man nodded, she held up Lindy's yearbook featuring a sixteen-year-old Kevin Tipton. "Is this by any chance you?"

Kevin grabbed the book from her hands. "Oh my God. Where did you find this?"

"Stop, stop!" Lindy said. Dean paused the video and the screen froze with Kevin's face. "That's Kevin?"

"Seems so. Should I continue?"

"He's gotten so old."

"As we all do while we're alive."

"Hmph. How were you able to film this without his knowledge?"

"Trade secret." When Lindy put her hands on her hips, Dean continued. "Small camera in Erica's glasses, okay?"

"Really? Cool. Go on. Play some more."

He pushed the play button.

"So I take it that's a yes?"

"Yes. Yes, that's me. Sorry. I haven't seen this yearbook in ages. Mine got lost in a fire. Is this about a reunion or something? You two seem rather young."

"My name is Maggie Russell. I'm Lindy Steele's niece. This is my cousin, Erica, from the other side of my family."

"Oh my God. Lindy's niece?"

"I ran across her journal and you were mentioned. I thought maybe you could talk about her with me."

"Oh. Sure. Sure. Come on in. Would you like something to drink? I have some coffee."

"We don't want to put you out."

"Nonsense. It will only take a moment." Kevin stepped out of view.

"Where were you?" Lindy asked.

"I had something else I needed to do."

Maggie stuck her tongue out at Erica, who was probably making faces first.

Lindy hovered close to the screen. "It looks like she's been crying."

God, it did look like she'd been crying. Or maybe she just hadn't slept. And he'd done that to her. What the hell was wrong with him?

"I also noticed you didn't spend last night here. You two have a fight?"

"Shut up and watch."

Kevin returned with three filled mugs, creamer, and sugar.

"What would you like to know? If you have her journal, I would think you know a lot about her already."

"She really didn't write a whole lot. Mostly about fights with her sister and her mother. Teenager stuff. How long did you know her?"

"We met in the ninth grade. I was smitten at first look."

"So you were her boyfriend?"

"Eventually. Took a lot of convincing. On my part."

"She didn't like you?"

"No, I don't think that was it. I think she was scared. Because of the leukemia. At the time we met, she was in remission, but still scared. I guess she had reason to be, huh?"

"Were you with her at the end?"

"No. I feel bad about that, too."

"Why? Did her parents stop you from coming over?"

"If they had, then I wouldn't have felt so guilty. You see, she got so bad there at the end I couldn't bear to see her die. So I chickened out and just stopped coming over to see her."

"What?" Lindy screamed. "He promised. Why would he do that? I thought he loved me."

Dean paused the video. "You think he didn't love you because he didn't want to watch you die?"

"How did he think I felt? I was the one dying. Then Mom told me she forbade him to come back. Why would she say that?"

"To spare your feelings?"

"I was so mad at her. I never could forgive her. Told her she was ruining my life, when it was Kevin all along. Why couldn't they just tell me the truth? Why? Why did everyone lie to me?" She looked at the paused video. "Keep playing."

Maggie said, "Hey, you were young. It's understandable."

"No, it's not. I promised her...something. I'd never broken a promise to her before. It was the biggest mistake of my life, not spending every last minute with her. I could have made her last days happy. Instead, she spent them being miserable, hating me."

Kevin's words sparked something inside Dean. Would he regret not spending every last minute with his mother? Maggie thought he would and now Kevin wishing... Shit.

"She didn't hate you," Maggie said.

"I didn't hate you," Lindy said at the same time as Maggie. Lindy turned toward Dean. "I need to talk to him."

Dean stopped the video. "And how do you expect to do that?"

"Ask Maggie if I could possess her."

"No. No way," he said as he shook his head vehemently.

"But she wants to help me."

"That may be so, but you're not possessing her. And that's final."

"Then I'm sorry."

Before he could figure out what she was sorry about, she hit him with an upper cut.

* * * *

Dean collapsed to the couch.

Damn. Lindy thought for sure she'd break her knuckles, but her hand didn't even sting. God, she didn't kill him, did she? She felt for a pulse and breathed a sigh of relief when she found it. Guilt pinched her heart at having to hurt the guy, but there just wasn't any other way she could get to Maggie without him interfering.

Of course, if Maggie were awake, then it wouldn't matter. Lindy popped into the bedroom. Hot damn! Luck was on her side. Maggie was on the bed, laptop on her lap, nodding off. Green light softly surrounded her. Lindy hovered close enough to get sucked inside.

That rush of pleasure flowed through her and she leaned her head against the wall. Man, she'd missed this. No time to dawdle, though. Dean could wake up and she still had to figure out a way to get to Kevin's. She stood, turned around to straighten the bed, and stopped.

What the hell? This is where a habit got her. Even Maggie's habit. What did it matter if she made the bed? It wasn't like she needed to be stealthy any longer.

Lindy took two steps toward the hall. The stupid boot on her foot made it impossible to walk any distance. But maybe she could drive. She rushed downstairs and hunted for Maggie's purse.

Ah, car keys. Even better, Kevin's address. Thank God it was a street she recognized. She grabbed Maggie's purse and headed to the garage.

Lindy had gotten as far as taking driver's training, but had never gotten her license. Stupid leukemia returning had put a stop to that. She removed the boot and hoped she could do this and not cause any damage to Maggie's ankle. She didn't exactly want to feel the pain.

And it wasn't too bad until she had to step on the brakes. Maybe she could brake with her left foot instead, provided she didn't get pulled over for crazy driving. Thankfully the car was an automatic.

She stayed under the speed limit and stuck to the side streets. Kevin didn't live all that far away, a couple of blocks from his parents, so that wasn't too difficult. When she pulled up along the curb—or more accurately when she drove the tires up over the curb—she turned off the engine and just stared at the house.

Kevin lived here. Did he have a wife? It never occurred to her to ask and one never showed on the video. Oh well, too late to worry about that now.

If everything Dean said was true, that getting closure would mean she'd move on, then she should at least apologize to the two of them. She rummaged through Maggie's purse and found a pen and a small pad of paper. She wrote one note to Dean and another to Maggie and then shoved both notes inside Maggie's purse. Maggie would most likely give Dean his. If Dean found these, he might not give Maggie hers.

She put the boot back on her foot, exited the car, and hiked the purse on her shoulder. She climbed the steps to the porch and knocked on the door. Her heart beat a bazillion times a minute until Kevin opened the door. Then it went up to a gazillion.

"Hello, Maggie. Did you change your mind about leaving me the yearbook? I could pay you for it."

The lump in her throat turned into a desert. She couldn't swallow. "I'm not here for that. Can I come in for a moment?"

"Sure, sure." He opened the door wider and let her pass. "You okay?"

"Yeah, fine," she said with a raspy voice. Sweat broke out on her forehead. Sure, she got moisture there, where she didn't need it. She sat on the couch and rubbed her sweaty hands on her thighs. "I've got something to say—"

Her throat seized and she coughed.

"Let me get you some water." Kevin left, giving Lindy time to compose herself.

When he returned with a full glass, she downed the contents. Ah, much better. "Thank you. You always were such a gentleman. It's one of the things I loved about you."

He furrowed his brow. "Excuse me?"

Oops. Too much too soon. "As I was saying, I've got something to say that will sound a little crazy, but it's the truth. And the truth is, while you're seeing Maggie in front of you, and you spoke to Maggie earlier, I'm not Maggie right now. I'm Lindy."

"Excuse me? Is this some kind of sick joke?"

"No. No. I'm not joking. It's me. Lindy. When I died I became a ghost and I just recently discovered I can possess Maggie's body. Just let me prove it to you before you kick me out on my ass, okay?"

"How do I know whatever you say to me wasn't something you read in Lindy's journal?"

"Oh please. Like I would have kept a journal? I was dying, for Pete's sake. Who would I have written it for?" She got up and paced. This wasn't going like she thought it would. Not that she gave it all that much thought. "Ask me something only Lindy would know. Better yet, remember the summer after ninth grade? At the lake? I saw what your brother James did."

Kevin turned pale. "What are you talking about?"

"You know. He pulled your swimsuit off when you were climbing back up on the dock. Got a nice view of that butt of yours. And maybe a little more when you turned around and jumped back in the water."

"But you said you didn't…"

"You were embarrassed enough. I know how you hated being the youngest. James would have hounded you forever if I admitted to witnessing that."

"Oh my God. Lindy?"

Yes, finally. She plopped back onto the couch. "Why did you promise we'd lose our virginity together when you didn't mean it?"

"I did mean it when I said it. Then you got sick again. It just didn't seem…right."

"So instead of talking to me about it, you just stopped coming over?"

He lowered his head. "I was sixteen. And I was losing you. I thought it would be less painful. For both of us. Instead, it was the worst decision I'd ever made. If I could relive that, I'd do it differently."

"Did you even love me?"

Someone pounded on the door. Lindy groaned. She couldn't suppose he'd just ignore that, could she?

* * * *

"Dean?"

He opened his eyes. He was sitting on Maggie's couch and a man was standing in the living room. Not just any man. Damn, had he been driving down here during all those texts? "Greg? How did you know where to find me?"

"I'm not Greg, son."

Son? Dean jumped to his feet. "Dad?"

"That would be me."

264

"No, that's not possible." Dean stepped forward. This couldn't be his father, the man who'd raised him, but it sure looked like him. "You died miles from here."

"That's true, but I'm not an earthbound spirit."

"Not an—wait a minute. You don't seem all that surprised I can see you."

"That's because I'm not really here. And you're not really awake."

Dean rubbed his temples. "What the hell is going on?"

"Your mother is dying."

"I know that—wait. You mean now?"

Dad held his palm out. "No. But soon. Her body is giving out."

"You mean she's giving up."

"Your mother is a fighter, but she's also reasonable. She knows the end is near. You need to talk to her. If you don't, I'm afraid she won't move on."

"Talk to her about what?"

"Dean, I think we both know about what. Talk to her. You'll help her and yourself."

Something invisible shook his shoulder and his father disappeared.

"Wait! Come back!"

"Dean? Are you okay? Did Lindy move on?"

He opened his eyes to Erica. What the hell? And why was he lying on the couch? Had he been dreaming? He sat up and pain seared his head. Rubbing his tender jaw, he remembered what happened. "Damn it. Lindy hit me."

"Why? What'd you do?"

Her tone stung. He might deserve it where Maggie was concerned, but for Lindy? He pointed to the television. "I showed her the video, so cut the attitude."

Erica smirked. "And she didn't like what she saw?"

"No, she…" Shit. Not good. "Where's Maggie?"

"Upstairs?"

He'd bet his last dollar she wasn't. "Go check. There's only one reason Lindy would have knocked me out."

Erica looked at the squiggly lines on the television. "Ohhh. Oh shit." She raced upstairs and a moment later she barreled back down. "She's gone and her bed's not made."

That right there told him Maggie hadn't left of her own accord. "I need to go to Kevin's. I'm sure Lindy took Maggie there."

"I'll go get her. You've done enough, don't you think?"

He didn't blame Erica for being angry with him. Hell, he was angry with himself. But he couldn't let her go alone. "And you can make Lindy leave Maggie's body?"

That stopped her. She put her hands on her hips and let out a breath. "Fine. *We'll* go get her."

"I can live with that." He stood and the room tilted. Or maybe that was just him.

Erica grabbed his arm. "Easy, big fella. I'm not so sure I could keep you from falling. And I'm certainly not going to be your pillow. Guess this means I'm driving."

"That might be wise." Because he couldn't even keep the room from swaying. After what seemed to take forever getting their coats, they finally made it outside. Man, he thought his car was small. He wasn't even sure he could fit in it. "What's this thing called?"

"Smart Car. Gets great gas mileage."

"Nice. Remind me not to get one."

"Haha, smart ass."

He managed to squeeze his body inside the tin can. Thank goodness Erica knew where Kevin lived. The address had flown his mind. Might've had something to do with a possible concussion.

As Erica drove, Dean played the dream over in his head. It was a dream, wasn't it? Except with his dreams, they faded as minutes passed. Yet, he remembered this one as if it had actually happened.

"You hurt my cousin. You know that makes you a jerk, right?"

He lowered his head. "Yeah. I know."

"Are you going to make it up to her? Or remain a jerk?"

"I'm not so sure if I do make it up to her that I'm still not a jerk."

"In that case, you better just get rid of the ghost and don't say a word unless Maggie wants you to." She pointed up ahead. "Seems you were right. There's her car. Nice parking job, Lindy."

The car straddled the curb. And while that was appropriate parking in some neighborhoods, it wasn't in this one. The curb was rather high. Surprised Lindy was able to drive at all. She'd never done that in the past. That she admitted to, anyway.

Erica pulled in behind and Dean struggled out of the little box. As soon as he got to his feet, dizziness struck again and he leaned against the door. Crap. Well, like his football coach had always said, he should "suck it up, buttercup." He took a deep breath, found his bearings, and walked up to the porch. Knocking would be too...calm. He pounded on the door.

Chapter 30

Kevin stood to get the door and Lindy grabbed his arm. "Please don't get that."

"Kevin!" Dean yelled from outside. "If Maggie is there, please open the door."

"Who is that?" Kevin asked.

"That would be Dean. Maggie's boyfriend. Don't answer. Please."

The pounding became insistent.

"I don't need him breaking down my door." Just as Kevin turned the knob, Dean barreled his way inside.

Lindy held her hands out to ward off Dean. "I'm sorry I knocked you out. But please don't touch me. I'll leave as soon as I'm finished talking with Kevin."

"*You* knocked *him* out?" Kevin asked.

"Shocker, huh? But if he touches me while I'm in Maggie's body, I'll pop back home and then I won't be able to come back here."

Dean glared at her. "You told him who you are?"

"She said she was Lindy," Kevin said. "Should I not believe her?"

"I am Lindy. God, Dean. Could you just give us another minute?"

"You did not have permission to use her body," Dean said.

"I asked you. You're the one who didn't ask her for me. So what choice did I have?"

Erica pulled Dean away. "Is that true? Did Lindy ask for permission?"

"Whose side are you on?" he asked.

"Maggie's. And I believe Maggie would have wanted to help Lindy."

Dean shook his head. "Not by being possessed."

"Well, how would you know if you never asked her?" She grabbed his arm. "Come on. Give her a few minutes. She doesn't appear to be hurting Maggie any."

"I'm not!" Lindy smiled. Was this for real? Would she get her time?

Dean pointed his finger at her. "We'll be on the porch. You have five minutes." He then looked at his watch and walked outside.

"Nice to meet you, Lindy," Erica said as she followed Dean out.

"Wow. I guess there's no denying it now," Kevin said. "You really are Lindy."

"Yeah. I'm just one lousy ghost possessing someone without their permission." But at least she got her time. Hopefully five minutes would be enough.

"Maggie did seem like the kind of person who would want to help. Just like you were."

"I'm a far cry from that girl now, though." She looked up at Kevin. "But did you love that girl? The girl I used to be?"

"I did, Lindy. I really did. And I'm so sorry I wasn't there for you. Can you forgive me?"

Her heart lifted. All she really wanted was the truth. "Yes, I forgive you."

A light shown above. Mom. Dad. Caroline. Ed. She could see them all and they were smiling. Lindy cried out and sat down on the couch.

"Lindy? What's the matter?"

"My family. I-I can see my family." She turned toward Kevin and kissed him on the cheek. "I love you, Kevin. I always have, but it's time for me to leave. Be sure to tell Maggie I won't be bothering her anymore."

But how would she get there? If she left Maggie's body here, she'd pop back at that house. Would they follow her?

As if Mom had read her mind, she said, "Just raise your hand. We'll get you, baby girl."

Lindy did just that and her hand became wrapped in warmth while she floated upward. As soon as she reached her family, her feet hit solid ground and they wrapped her in hugs.

Home. She was finally home.

* * * *

A gentle-but-persistent shaking woke Maggie. Lately nothing good came from being shaken awake. Maybe she should just stay asleep for once. Although her pillow was rather lumpy.

"Sweetheart, wake up," Dean said.

Had he finally come to his senses? Was he willing to fight for her now?

"She was looking up one moment and then fell over the next. Should I call 9-1-1?"

Kevin? What was he doing in her room? She opened her eyes. Not her room. Kevin's house. And her head wasn't on any pillow, but Dean's lap. "What happened?"

He helped her sit up beside him on the couch. "You fell asleep and Lindy took advantage. She brought you to Kevin's."

"She said she wouldn't bother you anymore," Kevin said.

"What are you talking about?" Dean asked.

"She said she saw her family and that she had to leave. That's when she passed out. Or you passed out. Which is it?"

Maggie grabbed Dean's arm. "She moved on?"

"It would seem that way. How are you feeling?"

Better than she had all month. She turned to Kevin. "The tape worked? Is that why she used me? To talk to you?"

"Yes, she was sorry about that."

"I don't care. Doesn't matter." She hugged Dean. "She's gone. She's really gone."

"See?" Erica said with a punch to Dean's shoulder. "I told you she wouldn't mind."

"What are you talking about? Mind about what?"

"Lindy had asked Dean for permission, but he didn't want to ask you."

"Ahh, Dean."

"I didn't trust her. I was only thinking of your safety."

"I would have been safer if you were with me, though, huh?" Still, she couldn't bring herself to be mad at him. Maybe now that Lindy was out of their life, they could concentrate on their relationship. She found her purse on the floor and picked it up while she stood. "Why don't we go home and celebrate and give Kevin his house back."

"It's not been a hardship. I'm glad everything worked out."

Dean held out his hand to Maggie. "If you give me your keys, I can drive your car back."

She was about to ask why her car was there, but then why wouldn't it be? How else had Lindy gotten there? Oh great. Maggie was almost afraid to see what kind of damage Lindy had caused her ankle.

"You sure you can drive?" Erica said. "Lindy really whopped him one."

"I can drive fine."

That explained the makings of a bruise on his jaw. She kissed the reddened area. "To think, if you had asked my permission, she wouldn't have had to resort to that."

"Moot point. Let's go."

Maggie reached into her purse to grab the keys and found two folded pieces of paper. "What's this?" One was addressed to her. She handed over the other one with the keys. "This is addressed to you."

She unfolded hers and read it.

I'm sorry for possessing you this one last time, but I just had to speak to Kevin. Know that I never meant to hurt you. It was your magnetic glowing that made it possible for me to possess you, which I believe any ghost can do if they're around you when you're sleeping. Dean doesn't think you should know this, because he thinks you'll freak out, but I know now that keeping secrets doesn't do anyone any good. I'm sorry I wasn't a better aunt for you and I hope you'll come to forgive me for taking advantage like I have. Just know that even if I do not move on, I won't ever possess you again. At least, not without your permission.

~Aunt Lindy

Tears formed in Maggie's eyes as a stinging sensation filled her chest. It all made sense now. Why Dean had acted so strange when his mother's neighbor mentioned the passing of their friend. And to think she'd trusted him to tell her the truth. She looked up at the man she thought she loved. "Were you ever going to tell me?"

* * * *

Pain flashed across Maggie's face and her eyes shone with unshed tears.

"Tell you what?" Dean gripped his unopened note. Only one person who could have written them. Only one person who had a bone to pick with him.

"That any ghost can possess me? It's true, right? That ghost you saw at your mother's. He possessed me, didn't he?"

"What?" Erica said. She looked at Dean. "Is that true?"

Oh shit. Thanks a lot, Lindy. "I saw it happen one time. One time. So I don't know if it's totally true *any* ghost can possess you, and as for telling you…well…I just thought it would be better if you didn't know."

"Except you don't have that right to keep this kind of information from me. Information I've been asking for. God, I trusted you."

She then turned toward Kevin. "Sorry for the drama. We won't be bothering you again."

"Not a problem. My life could stand a little drama."

"Come on, Erica." Maggie stormed out of the house.

"Dean, Dean, Dean," Erica said, shaking her head as she followed Maggie outside. Probably thinking he was a first-class jerk, now.

Kevin clapped Dean on the shoulder. "If you want my advice, don't give her more than a day to cool down. If you care for her, fight for her. Apologize. Might not hurt to give her flowers, either."

It would probably take more than flowers. Groveling. Lots of groveling. But first he had something else to take care of. "Did you mean what you said? That you regretted not spending every last minute with Lindy?"

"Yeah. It's why I made sure not to repeat that mistake when my mother became ill. Life's too short, you know? Got to savor every day."

"It didn't bother you to watch her die?"

"No. It gave me joy knowing I made her last days happy. And maybe if I had done the same with Lindy, she wouldn't have been stuck here all these years."

He thanked Kevin and walked out onto the porch. He played with the letter. Why had Lindy told Maggie? Couldn't she just leave things be? He unfolded the note.

If this works and I move on (and you'll know I've moved on if you don't see me in the living room at 8 tonight—be there or be square!), I have you to thank. I'm sorry it took punching you out and possessing Maggie to do that, though, but I just didn't know how else to go about this. I need to talk to Kevin.

And if this doesn't work, you have every right to hate me. Not that you don't hate me already. I know you do. Especially now, since I told Maggie what you refused to do—how I came to possess her. Face it. She deserves to know.

But know this: if I don't move on, I promise to leave Maggie alone. Although right now I'm sure my promises mean shit. At least you have it in writing!

In case I do move on, you should know that I had told Mom, while possessing Maggie, that Eddie had kissed me and said it would be okay if we had sex because we weren't really related. That I was adopted (I thought it was better to say it that way since Eddie didn't know about his parentage—I still say he's not Ed's). I asked her if that were true. She assured me I (Maggie) was not, that what Eddie did was wrong, but that she would get to the bottom of it. I don't know who she talked to, probably Caroline. But to seal the deal, I made sure to leave a journal entry behind detailing what had happened in the garage. Of course, I made it sound like Eddie had forced Maggie to smoke the weed, and that he wanted me (Maggie) to take some pills, too, but that I had refused. It was awful of me, I know, but at the time I didn't think I'd ever see Maggie again. I wanted her to have the house. I wanted to possess her again. Anyway, it was because of me the will was changed at all. Just thought you should know that in case I can't tell you in person. Tell Maggie or not tell Maggie. I'll leave that to you.

Sorry again for that punch. But boy, did you go down in a hurry. Never knew I had that in me. Probably just as well, too. Huh?

~Lindy

Dean rubbed his tender jaw. He'd screwed up royally. He might not be able to fix his relationship with Maggie, but he could do something about the rest of his family.

He pulled out his cell phone and called Greg.

* * * *

Maggie pulled the last batch of cookies from the oven. She probably shouldn't have bothered—it wasn't like she needed the calories—but she needed to do something comforting after snapping at Dean the way she had.

Although, he had it coming to him, didn't he? Still didn't make her feel any better. And again, he just ignored her. She'd thought by now he'd have at least called and seen how she was. But nope. Not a peep.

The doorbell rang. Could it be? Her heart leapt for joy as she rushed as fast as her booted foot would let her. But when she opened the door, Dean wasn't standing on her porch, rather Bridget and Rob. Disappointment stung and then fear set in. "Is Dean okay?"

"Hello, to you, too," Bridget said with a laugh. "Dean's fine. Can we come in?"

"I'm sorry. Hello. Come on in." Maggie led them into the living room. "It's just that I kind of hoped you were Dean."

Bridget slowly lowered her body, with a bit of help from her husband, onto the couch. "That's why we're here. Lindy told him in her note that if she hadn't moved on, she'd see him in the living room at eight tonight. He had to go up to Cleveland so asked us to do that for him."

"Cleveland? Is his mother okay?"

"As far as I know, she is. He said he needed to talk to her."

Maybe there was some hope for Dean after all. That was a huge step for him. "I'll leave you two alone, then. Do you need anything? Water? Soda? Cookies?"

"Cookies?" Rob said. "I thought I smelled something good."

Bridget smacked her husband good naturedly. "Hey, if I can't have them, you can't either. Thanks, Maggie, but we're good. Just let Erica know not to come in here."

"Not a problem. She's on a date."

"Good. We won't be long, then. It's almost eight."

So it was. Only ten minutes to go. Maggie left them alone and headed to the dining room. Her heart wasn't really in searching through Grandma's papers, but then neither was it into sleeping without Dean. Damn, when had she become so used to having him around?

Probably around the time she'd fallen in love with the guy.

Fifteen minutes later, Bridget poked her head into the dining room. "Good news. No sign of her."

"You think you waited long enough?"

"Yeah. She's nothing like Peter. He thinks it's fun for me to look for him, and this from a ghost who *wants* my help."

"Are you trying to help him move on?"

"I don't think he can, but I am trying to give him closure. Doesn't seem likely now. I had to tell him that his friend was in the hospital and most likely won't be coming out. He had hoped to be able to see him, but it doesn't appear that's going to happen."

"That's too bad. Can I help him?"

"Help him how?"

"Is Peter nice? Do you trust him?"

"I guess I trust him as much as anyone I'm acquainted with. Why?"

"Just wondered if he used my body—"

"What? You *want* someone to possess you?"

"Well, not really. But if it brings him peace, why not? I would have helped Lindy if I knew what she needed. What's the harm, if you're with me?"

"Probably nothing, but let me ask Dean about this first, okay?"

"Dean doesn't own my body."

"No, but he controls my paycheck and I kind of like having them. And then there's Peter to consider. First, we don't even know if he can possess you. Second, I'm not sure we'd want him to know if it's possible. If he can possess you he would probably look for others. Or you, if you happened to take a nap at work. Might turn out...bad."

"Well, when you put it that way, never mind. It was just a silly thought." A thought that wouldn't go away, though. If Bridget and Dean could help ghosts move on, why couldn't she?

Chapter 31

Dean parked alongside his brother's car in Mom's driveway. As he climbed out, Greg was storming his way. Maybe he should have suggested they meet in a coffee shop. Then there would be witnesses if Greg decided to kill him.

Greg punched him in the shoulder. "I can't believe you left without saying anything to me."

"I was going to call you." Dean rubbed the offending spot. At least his brother hadn't hit him in the face. His jaw was still quite tender.

"Yeah? When? Next week?"

"Does it matter? I'm here now."

"Damn it, Dean. She's not telling me anything." Greg ran a hand through his hair and turned his head. Light from the porch shone in his eyes. He was near tears.

Dean lowered his head. His selfishness had done this to his brother. "She's refusing treatment."

"What? And you left her alone?"

"I was mad, okay?"

"And of course, it's all about you. What the hell happened to your heart? Ever since your surgery, you've been different."

"You mean since I died. I *died*."

"Well, you're not dead now, are you? So...what? Did you cross over and see something you wished you hadn't?" Greg's eyes widened. "Did you see Dad?"

"Why would you think I saw Dad?"

"I don't know. I've heard stories of people coming back from the dead."

"Do you believe those stories?"

Greg shrugged. "I don't know. Maybe."

Holy shit. Dean leaned against his car. Could he actually confide in his brother? He could use that as the excuse why he'd stayed away all these years. But if he was going to spill the beans to Greg, he might as well spill them to Mom, too. But before he could answer, she stepped out onto the porch.

She hugged the white, fluffy robe around her. "You two plan on jawing out there in the cold or are you going to come inside?"

"How mad is she?" Dean asked Greg.

"Not as mad as I was."

"Was? Not anymore?"

"I'm still mad."

Dean followed his brother and mother inside the house. Again, the heat blasted him as he shut the door. Who cared if he was uncomfortable? If it helped her any, that was all that mattered.

She came up to him and hugged him tight, certainly not the sign of an angry woman. "Thank you for coming back. No Maggie this time?"

"I thought it would be better if I came alone." Which wasn't a total lie. Maggie's presence might have made it difficult for him to hash out what needed hashing. Of course, he'd never know for sure since he'd screwed up their relationship. First things first, though.

Mom turned toward Greg. "I know you want some answers, and I'll give them to you, but I need to talk to Dean alone. Can you come back in an hour?"

"You don't think I have a right to be here?"

"This isn't about my appointment."

Greg pointed at Dean. "You better be here when I get back."

Mom grabbed Greg's face. "He will. I promise."

Even though his mother's promise irked him just a tiny bit, Dean nodded to reassure his brother. Greg hugged her and left.

Dean crossed his arms and plopped down on the couch. "You're pretty confident I won't bolt again, huh?"

"I'm going to boil some water for tea. Want some hot chocolate?"

Apparently more than confident. "Sure." He followed her into the kitchen. "What did you want to talk about? About what an ass I am? Because you didn't have to send Greg away to do that."

Not even a chuckle. Hmmm… Maybe Greg was right about Mom being mad. After filling the kettle and setting it on the stove, she slid a plastic container across the countertop. "I made some cookies. Want some?"

He nodded. First the hot chocolate. Then the cookies. Was she trying to make him feel miserable? It was working. "I'm sorry about yesterday. I shouldn't have left like I did."

"You were upset."

When the kettle whistled, she busied herself with getting their drinks ready. He grabbed the container of cookies and took them to the table. "Ohh, chocolate-chocolate chip. My favorite."

"I know. They were supposed to be last night's dessert."

Crap. Nothing like Mom laying on the guilt. Yep. She was mad.

She brought the drinks over and sat in the chair beside him. Several silent minutes went by while he munched on a cookie. Or two. Or maybe three. Okay, four. The quiet was so unlike her. She was usually a fountain of stories. Finally, he couldn't take it any longer.

"What's with the silent treatment? Thought you wanted to talk." Although he had no idea what it was she wanted to talk about, if not her disease. Except she'd told Greg it wasn't about that.

She looked up from her tea. "When did you find out?"

No, no, no. Not now. That small part inside him that said he was ready for this discussion suddenly buried itself inside his chest. And it hurt. He needed more time. "Find out what?"

"Oh, don't bullshit me, Dean Richard. You know exactly what I'm talking about. I first thought you stayed away because Dad died, but then during your last visit, you were so distant."

Damn it. There was no avoiding the conversation, it seemed. "I just thought it would be better if I stayed away."

"Better for who? You?"

"No. You. After my surgery I put two and two together."

"Seems like you added wrong. If anything, I needed you more."

"How can you say that? If not for me, Dad would still be alive."

"You didn't cause his accident. That drunk driver did. I never blamed you."

"I don't see how that's possible. I'm not a good reminder of him. I'm a reminder of someone else, aren't I? Are you going to tell me who my real father is?"

She slapped his face, bringing tears to his eyes. Her scorn hurt more than Lindy's uppercut. "You know damn well who your real father is. I don't want to hear differently from your mouth."

"I'm sorry." And he was. He'd never meant to sully the man who'd raised him. "My biological father, then."

"No."

"Because you can't or because you won't?"

"I didn't cheat on your father."

There had been a tiny part of him that had wondered and he didn't know whether or not to feel relief, because if there wasn't an affair, then that meant she'd been abused. But she hadn't answered his question. "Did you know him?"

"Yes."

"God, Mom. Why didn't you report him?"

"I probably should have, but I was younger, weaker then. Wasn't sure what your father would do. Leave me? Kill him? Nothing good ever came to my mind. So I didn't tell him. I just wanted him to love me so I could forget about the ugliness. When I found out I was pregnant, I knew I could no longer keep quiet."

"So he knew?"

She nodded. "He knew I was raped, not who did it. I still saw no sense in telling him that. And when Greg was born with that dark hair, I'll admit it, I was relieved. But then you were born. Fair-haired. I never thought it was possible that I could have twins from different fathers. I loved you regardless, but wasn't sure how your father would take it. I needn't have worried. He just smiled and said, 'He looks more like a Dean Richard than a Scott Matthew, doesn't he?' We hadn't picked any family names to give you two, thought it was better to keep it generic, but he wanted you named after his father. And himself. All this, knowing he wasn't your biological father."

"Why not tell me? Don't you think I have a right to know?"

"And what will that accomplish?"

"What if I have siblings out there? I could be related—"

"He has no other children documented."

Documented. She started to sound like him. The bastard could have raped several women who went on to bear his children, though. Something hard to prove. "What about for medical reasons? Maybe I wouldn't have nearly died if—"

"That hole in your heart was not hereditary."

"What?"

"I made it a point to get your family medical history and there was no mention of heart disease. For him or his family members. What happened to you was just a fluke."

A fluke. Just like her rape. Just like his birth. "How can you stand to look at me?"

"Stop it. You're my son. You could have been born with pox all over your face and it wouldn't change a thing. I love you."

"But to be reminded—"

"You only remind me of what a wonderful husband I had. He loved you, Dean. He raised you as his own, because in his heart you were his. Don't ever forget that."

To hear those words brought tears to his eyes. "Then why do you want to leave me?"

"You really think I want to leave you and Greg? I'd give anything not to have this cancer. To see you two get married and have kids of your own."

"Kids? No. I'm not about to spread that guy's genes around."

"Ah, Dean. Please don't think like that. They're my genes, too. If there are other reasons you don't feel like you could be a father, fine, but don't let your ancestry be the reason. You are nothing like that bastard and neither will your children be."

He so badly wanted to believe that, but without a name, without the history, how could he?

* * * *

While sitting in the dining room, going through another useless box of papers, Maggie stifled a yawn and glanced at the clock. 10:30. Her plans to experiment would have to be postponed if Erica didn't get home soon.

The front door opened and shut. Oh, thank God. Maggie abandoned her search and headed for the living room.

"What are you still doing up?" Erica asked as she unbuttoned her coat. "Missing Dean?"

Maggie purposely ignored the question, even though she missed him very much. "Keep your coat on. I need you to drive me to work."

"Can it wait 'til morning? I'm beat."

"I gotta go now." She was on the verge of falling asleep now and there was no way she could stay up all night.

"Then call a cab."

"I need you, too."

"Me?" Erica narrowed her eyes. "Why?"

"I'll tell you when we get there, but it's something I have to do now. And I need your help."

Erica sighed as she re-buttoned her coat. "Why do I feel like I'm the getaway driver?"

"I'm not stealing anything. Honest." Maggie grabbed her coat and purse and together they went out the back to Erica's car.

The garage only held one vehicle, and Maggie being the owner of the house got dibs on that, forcing Erica to park outside, next to the garage. But with the temperature below freezing, the windows on her car were covered in a sheen of ice. Erica wasn't in the mood to scrape and Maggie wasn't in the mood to argue. She handed over the keys to her car.

A few minutes into the drive, Erica said, "I can't believe Tom couldn't wait until morning."

"This has nothing to do with work." And before Erica could question that, Maggie changed the subject. "Good news. Lindy has officially moved on. She told Dean in her letter that she'd be at the house at eight if she hadn't moved on, and she didn't show."

"Oh?" Erica raised her eyebrows. "Why didn't you say Dean came over? Did you two make up?"

"He didn't and we didn't. Bridget and Rob came over. Dean had to go to Cleveland on family business."

"So, you going to forgive him?"

No. Yes. Maybe. "I don't know."

"You know he loves you."

"I just wish he'd stop trying to protect me all the time."

"I think it's kind of sweet. I wish someone wanted to protect me."

"Even if they lie to do it?"

"Well…when you put it that way, probably not. But Dean didn't really lie, did he? He just withheld information."

"I don't see how that is any better. He knew what I was looking for, he found out what I wanted to know, and he didn't tell me. If not for Lindy, I'd still be in the dark."

"Has knowing made you feel better?"

Maggie refused to answer. If anything, the knowledge made her more paranoid. Just how safe was she when she fell asleep? But if she told Erica that, she'd only get an I-told-you-so look. Aww, crap. Apparently her silence was just as bad as an answer.

Erica gave Maggie the I-told-you-so look. "That's what I thought. Knowing hasn't done a damn thing for you. And I'm guessing that's why Dean didn't tell you. Plus, it probably freaked him out."

"Because I'm an actual freak?"

"No. Because he doesn't know *how* to protect you. Once he's had a chance to think about it, he'll apologize. For the omitting bit. I believe his heart was in the right place."

"Doesn't make it right."

"Maybe not, but can you honestly say you never want to see him again?"

Maggie wiped a tear from her eye and shook her head. She wanted to see him now, even though he'd put a stop to her plans. All that protection crap and stuff.

Erica pulled into the parking lot and killed the engine. Maggie climbed out of the car. "Peter? Are you here?"

"Who you talking to? No one's here." Erica waved at the empty lot. "Wait a minute. Are you calling the ghost?"

Maggie let her silence be her answer. She unlocked the door to her work and let Erica in first. "Let's go to the copier room where it's warmer."

Erica leaned against the supply cabinet. "Why are you calling the ghost? You know we can't see him."

"I know." Maggie turned on the light and shut the door. The small room was perfect. No windows, so no drafts. "I want to conduct an experiment. Tell me when you feel a blast of cold air, would you? Peter, touch Erica, please."

"Blast of..." Erica shivered and rubbed her arms. "Oh shit. Why do you need a ghost? And why do you need me?"

"Because you can tell if he's here. Did you feel him?"

"I felt something."

"Peter, keep touching Erica so I know you're here."

"What? Wait. Damn it. Okay, okay, I feel you. Stop. You better explain yourself pronto or I'm out of here."

Maggie pulled Lindy's letter from her purse and handed it over. "Read this."

Erica unfolded the note and read. "Eeww. She was sucked into your body? That just sounds gross. But what does Peter..." Her eyes widened. "Oh no. You want him to possess you?"

"It's not like that. I want to help him get closure. Bridget told me his friend is in the hospital. I'd like Peter to visit him before the man passes away."

"Even if this is a good idea, which it isn't, the hospital isn't going to let you—him in tonight."

"I know that. But I need to know if Peter can do it first." Maggie turned and faced the empty room. "Peter, I'm going to go into Tom's office and sleep. If you can possess me, just have a little conversation with Erica, tell her who you are, then leave. Could you do that for me, please?"

Erica placed her hands on her hips. "You're asking someone who can't answer you."

"Good point. If the answer is yes, please pat Erica's face."

"No!" Erica jerked away and placed her hand against her cheek. "Damn it, that's cold. Are you sure you can trust him?"

"According to Bridget, he's nice. Why wouldn't I trust him?"

"I'm sure Lindy was nice at one time, too. What does Dean think about him?"

"We all know what Dean thinks about ghosts."

"But he should be here."

"Right. Because he's going to let me do this."

"Then Bridget."

"I'm not going to ask Bridget to come here tonight. Once I fall asleep, he'll be in and out. Won't you, Peter?"

"Again, you're asking someone who can't answer you. What happens if he becomes as obsessed with possession as Lindy was? Then what? Without Dean or Bridget, you have no one here to pop him out of you."

"You saying you can't shake me awake?"

"You saying that would work? What if it doesn't?"

Maggie slumped to the floor. She hadn't thought about that. "Damn it."

Erica sat beside her. "I know you need some answers and I know you want to help. Maybe when Dean returns—"

"How many times do I have to tell you? He's not going to go along with this."

"He will if I say I'm helping you. And I'll be here, too, to make sure it happens. But you need him in case Peter doesn't cooperate." Erica looked up as if she could see the ghost. "No offense, okay?"

"Okay, okay. Damn it. I'm sorry, Peter. We'll do this after work on Monday, then. If Dean isn't back, at least Bridget will be here." She'd have to remember to bring sleeping pills. Or maybe just stay up all night writing. That would work, too.

Erica wrapped an arm around Maggie's shoulders. "That sounds good. Thanks for being reasonable."

Reasonable. Yeah, that was her middle name. For once she wouldn't mind being a little reckless.

* * * *

"Wow, my brother's a Ghostfacer," Greg said from the other side of the dining table.

Dean shook his head. After convincing their mother to give chemo a try, he'd finally confessed to seeing ghosts after his death. Telling them had lifted a great weight from his shoulders, especially when they didn't shy away. But maybe he needed to watch this 'Supernatural' show just to get the reference. "I'm not a Ghostfacer. I just see them."

"And talk to them. And touch them. And help them on their way."

"So glad you see the fun in this." He may have said it sarcastically, but in a way he *was* glad. Glad they could joke about something that used to scare the pants off him.

Greg sipped at his hot chocolate. "They're just spirits. They're harmless."

"They're harmless to you. Me, not so much."

Mom put down her tea. "What do you mean?"

Dean rubbed his jaw. "Let's just say they're strong."

"That bruise was caused by a ghost? How big was he?" Greg asked.

"She. The ghost was a she. And she was sixteen."

His brother tipped his head back and laughed. "A little girl popped you one. That's priceless."

"Now, Greg. I don't think this is funny." Mom examined Dean's chin, looking a little sad in the process. Probably because of the slap she'd handed him earlier. "Do you need ice?"

"Naw. It's fine."

Greg grabbed a cookie, leaving one behind. "Is that why you didn't bring Maggie? Because she doesn't know?"

Dean's fingers itched to snatch the last cookie. If he kept his mouth busy, then maybe he wouldn't have to answer. Of course, that wouldn't stop his brother from continuing to ask. So maybe he'd just answer the second part and hope for the best. "She already knows."

"And she doesn't think you're a freak?" Cookie crumbs sprayed every which way.

Dean nearly laughed at Greg's expression. Their mother didn't think it was so funny, though.

"Greg! What are you? Seventeen? Clean this up. And Dean is not a freak."

He got up and grabbed a rag from the counter. "I didn't say he was. But some people might think that."

Touché, brother. Touché. "It's okay. It's not something I hadn't thought myself."

"Well, I think it's rather noble that you can help confused spirits." Mom patted his hand. "If you're here when I die, I'll certainly seek you out."

"Hey!" Greg said. "You promised you'd fight this."

"And I will. But that doesn't change the fact that I *will* die someday. That fate awaits us all."

"Yeah, but I don't necessarily want that day to come anytime soon, okay? So don't scare me like that." Greg tossed the rag in the sink and kissed Mom on the cheek. "I'm gonna head on home. I'll see you two tomorrow?"

Mom insisted he come over for breakfast, but Dean nixed that. He offered to take them both out to Mom's favorite restaurant for brunch. After Greg agreed to meet them, he left. Dean picked up the mugs and carried them to the sink.

"I saw the look on your face when Greg mentioned Maggie. Are you going to tell me what's going on with you two?"

"And you wonder why I don't come over more often."

"Don't be a smart ass. Tell me what happened."

He sat on the chair. "I might have screwed up. Maggie found out I'd been keeping something from her. She's kind of mad."

"Might have? Kind of?"

"Okay. I did and she is."

"Was there a reason you withheld this information?"

"I thought she might…take it wrong." More like freak out, but the less he said about it, the better. If Maggie wanted Mom to know what ghosts could do to her, then she'd have to be the one to say.

"And did she?"

"Hard to tell. She was too busy yelling at me."

"Are you sorry she found out or sorry she didn't find out from you?"

"Is there a difference?"

"Were you ever going to tell her?"

"Eventually. After I figured out some things." Like how he could protect her. How could he dump that kind of information on her without knowing all the answers?

"Is her life in danger?"

"I don't know. That's just it."

She shook her head. "You don't think she could help you figure that out?"

"I didn't want to worry her needlessly."

"Instead you've gotten her mad *and* worried."

"Right." Ah, the hell with it. He took the last cookie and bit into it.

"If you're sorry she didn't find out from you, apologize. Then ask for her help."

"You know, this is strange advice coming from you, especially since you won't tell me who my biological father is."

"There's a difference. Your life isn't in danger from not knowing. It's in danger from knowing."

"What? You think I'm going to go beat him up or something?"

"That's something I don't wish to discover. Or to have to explain to Greg. You don't plan on telling him, do you?"

Dean shook his head. "But Maggie knows."

"Why did you tell her?"

"Because she wanted to know why I don't want children."

"And? Did it make a difference to her?"

He shook his head.

Mom smiled. "I knew I liked that woman. Greg's right. Don't lose her. Go home tomorrow. Give her flowers. Give her candy. Give her whatever she needs. And apologize. Life is too short not to spend it with the person you love."

Yeah. He was beginning to see that now.

Chapter 32

Sunday afternoon and Maggie tossed another stack of papers in the recycle bin. Had she even made a dent in the boxes? Didn't seem like it. Going through Grandma's stuff was taking longer than she'd thought possible. Maybe if she had some help, but Erica had a family event to go to—one where her mother threatened bodily harm if she didn't attend—and Dean was…well, not around, now was he?

In fact, he was eerily silent. Even after she'd sent a text saying she hoped everything was okay.

Maggie wiped her stupid leaky eyes. She'd always wondered if Dean would stick around after Lindy left. Guess she got her answer. Just as well. He wouldn't have gone along with her experiment anyway. Now she could do it without his scorn.

She got up from the table and stretched. If she looked at another receipt she'd scream. Time to exercise her brain and get some writing done. She'd let it go for too long now. Plus, her foot was aching. How that was when she'd been sitting all afternoon was beyond her. As she limped into the kitchen to get another pill, the doorbell rang.

Tempted to ignore it—it was Sunday-freaking-afternoon—she gave in to curiosity and opened the door. Her heart thumped wildly.

Dean stood on the porch, holding a bouquet of some kind of pink flowers and a huge bag of M&M's. "Hey. You alone?"

She resisted the urge to run into his arms. Pride might have had a lot to do with that. "For now. I heard you went up to Cleveland. Is your mother okay?"

"She's good. She decided to give chemo a try."

"She decided or you two strong-armed her?"

He shrugged. "Does it matter?"

"No, I guess not. I'm glad she's fighting it. For you. So what's that for?" She pointed to his bundle.

"Well, I was told you bring flowers and candy to apologize to a loved one, and since I wasn't sure what kind of candy..." He held up the bag and grinned. "Who doesn't love M&M's, right? Can I come in?"

His grin—and the fact he'd called her a loved one—warmed her insides and gave her hope. And the M&M's. He was giving her M&M's. Best candy ever. She nodded and stepped aside. "You came to apologize?"

"I know I should have texted you back, but I didn't want to do this— Aw, gee, Maggie. Don't cry."

Cry? Oh. Guess her face was a bit wet. Stupid eyes were leaking again. Except this time they were from happy tears. "You're apologizing?"

"Yes." He put the flowers and candy on the front entry table, then pulled her in for a hug. "I'm really sorry I didn't tell you sooner. It's just that I had hoped to have all the answers first. I don't want you to worry."

She buried her nose against his chest and took in his scent. Enjoyed the embrace of his strong arms. But again, he was trying to control what she should and should not know. Backing away was the hardest thing she'd ever done. "I know you mean well. Truly, I do. But I don't like being kept in the dark. How would you feel if I didn't tell you I asked another ghost to possess me just to see if they could do it because I didn't want *you* to worry?"

His eyes widened, just as she suspected they would. "You didn't? Did you?"

"That's not the point. Should I keep something like that from you so you don't worry?"

He shook his head. "I get it. I do. I'd rather know so I could help. But please tell me you're just hypothesizing."

Help. He wanted to help. Hopefully his attitude wouldn't change when he learned the truth. "Thank you. You don't know what that means to me. And no, I wasn't hypothesizing. I went to see Peter yesterday."

"Aw, gee, Maggie. You let him possess you?"

She shook her head. "I wanted to but didn't go through with it. And you can thank Erica for that. But I want him to try and I'd like you there in case something goes wrong."

Dean paced the entryway a couple of times, then turned and headed for the living room. He practically fell to the couch. "I'm glad you told me, don't get me wrong, but why? Why do you need to do this? Isn't it enough you know it can happen?"

She sat beside him. "I just need more proof, I guess. Plus, I want to help him. Bridget said his friend is in the hospital. I thought maybe it would give Peter closure to see him before the man passed."

"That's not Peter's friend, it's his lover. Or rather, former lover. He's why Peter committed suicide."

"You think he wants revenge?"

"No, I never got that vibe from him. He's probably still in love with the man."

"Then all the more reason to do it."

"You think if Peter possesses you, everything will be peachy? Do you really think this man will talk to you? Remember, he won't see Peter and he'll probably think you're nuts to say you're him." Dean scrubbed his face and growled. "This is giving me a headache."

"That would be Peter's problem, not mine. But I want him to at least try."

"I can't believe you want to do this."

At least he hadn't forbidden her. That was certainly a change, and one for the better. Still, she would like his okay in the whole matter. "I want to help as long as you're around to put a stop to it if Peter decides he doesn't want to give me up. Please, Dean. I'd like to think I'm the way I am for a reason."

* * * *

The anguish on Maggie's face was too much for Dean. Maybe it was time he started to trust more people, even ghosts. Because if he didn't, he might lose Maggie, and he wanted to have something with her. Whatever she was willing to give him.

"I'm not okay with it, I doubt I'll ever be okay with it, but if it's that important, I'll help you."

"Oh, Dean!" She practically flew onto his lap and hugged him. "Thank you."

"I'd do anything for you, Maggie. I love you." And he did. More than anything. He held her tight. No one had ever felt so good in his arms, or his lap. That sweet ass of hers was making him hard. "God, I've missed you. I swear, I'll never keep anything from you again."

She pulled back and held his face. The kiss she gave him was only a peck, but did nothing to lessen his hard-on. If anything, he got harder. "Well, little secrets are okay, else birthdays and Christmases wouldn't be much fun."

He closed his eyes and shook his head. That she could joke after everything he'd done to her. His love for her grew so much his chest ached. "Then I promise not to keep big, important secrets from you."

"And I promise to do the same." She wiggled to get off him, but he was having none of that and locked his arms around her.

"There's something else I have to say." When she stilled and stared at him with curious eyes, he released his hold and caressed her face. Ran his thumb across those luscious lips of hers. "I'm sorry for pushing you away. I want you, Maggie. All of you."

She blinked several times. "Are you saying what I think you're saying?"

He was, but the time for words were over. Cupping her face, he planted his lips against hers and consumed her. When she opened her mouth on a whimper—and damn, he loved the sound of that—he plunged in and devoured her. Sweet and spicy, she tasted like home.

She ran her fingers though his hair and sucked on his tongue. He nearly popped out of his jeans.

Gathering his willpower, he pulled back. "I know you've told me before, but are you sure? Really sure?"

She touched his cheek, her fingers like silky feathers against his face. "I've never been surer of anything in my life."

He would never deserve her, not in a million years, but he would do his best to be everything she needed. Holding on to her, he stood and carried her to her room. Laid her out on her bed. She was his and would only be his. So why couldn't he move?

She sat up. "You're not changing your mind, are you?"

"No, sweetheart." He sat on the bed and took her hand. "Just a little nervous. I don't want to hurt you and yet…I will."

"I can handle a little pain." She nibbled on his ear and whispered, "Besides, I hear it gets better after." She pushed him to his back and lifted his shirt. Sucked on a nipple and rubbed against his erection. Holy shit. She made it difficult not to blow his load right then and there.

"God damn, Maggie." Everything in him wanted to rip her clothes off, followed by his own, and then mark her as his own, but he needed to slow down, get her more prepared. Of course, slow wasn't exactly in her head at the moment since she was in the process of unbuckling his belt. He grabbed her hands and kissed her, slowly rolling them so he was on top. "Let me savor you, okay?"

"Savor? I like the sound of that."

He slipped her sweatshirt over her head and was met with…bare skin. His eyes nearly bugged out of his head. "You're braless."

"I wasn't planning on going out today. Is that a problem?"

"Hell, no." If anything, it saved him time. Cupping the wonderful mounds, he latched onto one breast and started savoring.

* * * *

Maggie was in love with Dean's tongue. Heck, she was in love with all of him, but right now her focus was on his tongue and his lips and what they were doing to her breast. Savoring her. God, yes! Had her nipples ever been so hard?

She tugged on his shirt. "Am I going to get to savor you, too?"

His chuckle tickled her skin. "I'm not the one needing to be prepped, but maybe next time, okay?"

Prepped? Oh. Was he still afraid of hurting her? "It would help me to feel your skin against mine, then."

He lifted his head and raised an eyebrow. "You just want to rush this."

"You have to admit, I've been waiting a long time."

"Yeah, you have." He licked a nipple and then sat up. One fast move, he jerked his shirt over his head. "Better?"

Oh yeah, much better. But she was greedy. "No. The pants, too."

Stacy McKitrick

"So demanding," he whispered as he stood and unbuckled his belt. His pants and boxers were history and her heart nearly stopped. His penis stood out long and proud. Yeah, she'd seen him before, but not like that. Maybe he had reason to worry about hurting her.

"Your turn now." After removing her boot, he slid off her jeans but left her panties alone. "Not commando, I see."

"It's one thing not to wear a bra…"

"But could you?" He slid up beside her on the bed and propped up on an elbow. "If I took you to a dark restaurant and you wore a skirt? I could play with you." He slid her panties to the side and ran his finger over her sex.

She arched into his touch and moaned. God, that felt wonderful. But what he was suggesting, it was just a fantasy, right? "You would do that? In a restaurant?"

"Well, I'd probably have to do this to keep you quiet." He kissed her, his tongue demanding entrance and she obliged. While he explored her mouth, he inserted his finger and explored her more. He'd have to stop touching her if he wanted her quiet. Each moment was pure ecstasy. "On second thought, I like you noisy."

After leaving kisses and nibbles down her body, he ended back at her sex, where he feasted on her. She rode a wave to somewhere great with that magical tongue of his. But should she come? Was that what he wanted?

He stuck one finger. Then two. "Come for me, sweetheart."

That third finger was a charm. She broke into a million pieces. Or maybe she just turned into goo. Whatever, she'd never felt so wonderful.

* * * *

Every sound Dean managed to entice from Maggie warmed his heart. The moans. The cries of ecstasy. He practically ripped the damp panties from her body and reached for the condom he'd left on the nightstand, keeping those encouraging sounds in his thoughts.

"May I?" she asked as she held out her hand.

If he said no, she'd take it the wrong way for sure. If he said yes and lost it, how disappointed would she be? Well, he'd just have to not lose it. Thank goodness he wasn't a teenager and had some control. Emphasis on the some, because he wasn't sure exactly how much control he did have. He placed the foil packet in her hand.

With a little guidance from him, she slid on the rubber. Her fingers were an erotic kind of torture, but he kept it together. Turned out he had more control than he'd thought.

"I never knew putting a condom on you would be so hot."

Yeah, neither had he. He settled over her and smiled. His heart belonged to her and it always would. "I love you, Maggie."

"I love you, too." She cupped his face and kissed him.

He slowly entered her, letting her adjust to his size, trying to make it easier on her, but going slow wasn't going to break that barrier. He mentally counted to three then thrust. She winced and he stopped. "I'm—"

"Don't," she said. "Don't apologize and don't stop. Just keep going." To prove her point, she grabbed his butt and pulled him closer.

He leaned down and kissed her. "Anything for you, sweetheart."

Once she adjusted to all of him, he paused for a moment to enjoy all that hot tightness. "God, you feel so good."

"So do you," she said.

He picked up a decent rhythm, still trying to be easy on her, but everything in him wanted to rut her. Mark her. Claim her. He'd never felt so possessive in all his life. She just felt...right. Like home.

Her breathing picked up and she grabbed his biceps. A couple more thrusts and she cried out. Damn, he got her to come again. Her spasms around his dick were all it took for him to follow suit.

God, if she could accept him, warts and all, he'd be the luckiest man on the planet.

* * * *

Maggie lifted her arms over her head while Dean did his best to keep his weight off her. Sunday was now officially her most favorite day. Sure, she was sore, but damn. That orgasm—or was it two?—more than made up for that. Dean was hers and she couldn't be happier.

"We're definitely doing that again," she said.

He chuckled. "Yeah, but not today. I bet not tomorrow, either."

"It takes you that long to recover?"

"Uh...no." He kissed her. "I was talking about you. You've got to be sore."

"Not that sore. So, you're not sorry you're my first?"

"No, sweetheart. I'm glad." He rolled off her and snatched a tissue from the box on her nightstand, his presence, his warmth, instantly missed. "I really don't deserve you."

"Stop it. You make it sound like I don't know any better." After he tossed the tissue-covered condom in the wastebasket, she snuggled next to him to get some of that warmth back. "And I know plenty. I love you, Dean. Please take what I'm giving because I give it freely."

"You're right. I'm sorry." He pulled her in close. "This is nice. Just being alone with you. No Erica. No ghost. Which reminds me..."

"What about?"

"The note Lindy left me. She told me she was responsible for your grandmother changing the will. She just used you to do it." He sat up, crawled to the edge of the bed, and pulled a piece a paper from his jeans. "Here. You can read it."

She did and her heart sank at the words. "So the house doesn't belong to me?"

"It does. No one's going to believe the truth."

"But Eddie—"

"Doesn't need to know if you don't want him to. Besides, Lindy was pretty sure Gina cheated on your uncle and that Eddie was the result. So just think on it awhile. Come on." He hopped off the bed and held out his hand. "Let's go take a shower."

She placed the note on the nightstand. "Together?"

"Hell yeah, together. There's no ghost here anymore and I gotta clean you up properly."

Ooh, she was really loving this being free of a ghost thing.

* * * *

Dean slid Maggie's boot onto her injured foot while she was sitting on the bed, leaning back with her elbows. The sex had been great—okay, better than great, more like mind-blowing—but the shower...sheer bliss. He didn't have to fight himself any longer. Touching her was allowed, and he touched her, all right. All over. He'd made sure she stayed off that foot and took delight in soaping her up. All that soft, slippery skin. And then when he rinsed her off, sampled everything she could give him. Damn, he was getting hard again reliving it in his head.

"You know, you're going to spoil me if you keep this up," she said, bobbing her foot.

He tightened the last strap and patted her knee. "You deserve to be spoiled."

And he would spoil her forever, but was he the right one for the job? Even after the discussion with his mother, he still didn't feel right about having kids. And to lead Maggie on just seemed wrong.

"Hey." She sat up and tapped his hip with her good foot. "Where'd you go?"

He hugged her, buried his face in her belly. Prayed it wouldn't be the last time he could touch her. "I love you. More than anything. But I haven't changed my mind about fathering children."

"Dean." She tugged on his arms. He hated to let her go, to even face her, but did as she wished. She lowered to the floor and cupped his face. "Hey, I'd be lying if I said I wasn't disappointed, but I understand your objections. I love you. And all I ask in return is for you to love me back."

"I do, Maggie. More than you could know." His eyesight blurred and he blinked back impending tears. "How'd I get so lucky?"

She kissed him. "Nah, I'm the lucky one. My boyfriend likes to spoil me. But now it's time for me to spoil you. What's your favorite meal? I'm cooking."

"Oh, no you're not." Although the thought of eating one of her meals sounded heavenly. "I saw how swollen your ankle is still. You don't need to be on your foot. I'll take you out. In fact..." He stood and scooped her up. "I don't want you walking at all."

Her laughter accompanied a playful slap to his chest. "What? You plan on carrying me all day? We'll see how long you last."

Oh, he could last a good long time. Nothing felt better in his arms. He carried her down the stairs and when he reached the bottom, the doorbell rang. "Are you expecting anyone?"

"No, but if you let me go, I can find out who it is," she said.

"Not yet." Carrying her, he walked to the door. "Do me a favor. If it's Gina or Eddie, don't answer it." There might come a day when he wouldn't worry about unexpected guests, but today wasn't that day. Gently, he put Maggie down.

She inched the curtain back from the panel window. "Not Gina or Eddie," she whispered and opened the door.

An older gentleman with salt-and-pepper hair stood on the porch. "Hello. My name is Zane Grey. Are you Maggie Russell?"

"I am. How can I help you?"

Intrigued, but still cautious, Dean moved closer to Maggie and slipped his arm around her shoulders. "Zane Grey, like the author?"

When Mr. Grey spotted Dean, his face lit up. "Yes. My dear mother was a fan and couldn't resist naming me after him. Are you Dean Parker?"

The man's familiarity was seriously freaking Dean out. "Okay, who the hell are you and how do you know us?"

"Dean! Be nice."

"That's quite all right. I understand. Could I please come inside? Besides being chilly out here, I really do not wish to have this conversation out in the open."

Dean didn't wish to have the conversation at all, but Maggie moved, giving Mr. Grey room to enter. She shut the door on the cold air. "Okay, what's this about?"

"This is about the body you found the other night."

Man, news sure traveled fast. Especially unusual news. How many more people would fall out of the woodwork? Hopefully the gentleman was only a relation, but before Dean could ask, Maggie beat him to it.

"Are you related to Rhonda Tremain?"

"No, I'm afraid not. What I wondered was…which one of you saw Mrs. Tremain?"

An uneasy feeling came over Dean. "Saw her? If you read the news then you know she died long before we were born."

"Right. Right. I meant her spirit, but I think you already knew that, Mr. Parker. So let me put your mind at ease. I can see spirits, too."

"And what? You want a medal?"

"Dean!" Maggie hissed.

"That's quite all right, Ms. Russell. Most people don't want to admit their gift. And it is a gift, Mr. Parker, despite what you might think. Otherwise, why did you bother to help Rhonda? I assume she moved on when you discovered her grave."

A gift? More like a curse, but he wouldn't admit anything to this stranger. "What do you want?"

"I'm here to tell you about our organization. I am the founder of HeSMO, which stands for Helping Spirits Move On. That's what we do."

"Are you fucking kidding me?" Geez. If Bridget got wind of this, he'd never hear the end of it.

"Dean!" This time she didn't stop with the reprimand. She elbowed him in the stomach. "Do you have people in your organization that can be possessed, too?"

"Maggie, no."

Zane's eyes lit up. "Are you saying ghosts can possess you?"

Dean moved Maggie behind him. "She's saying no such thing."

"Dean," she said, shoving him out of the way. "What did we discuss earlier?"

"We don't know who this guy is."

"A valid point," Zane said. "I understand you are a private investigator, so investigate me. You'll see I'm fairly harmless. A retired businessman from Chicago who suffered a near-death experience over thirty years ago. I'm a widower; my wife passed last year."

"I'm so sorry for your loss," Maggie said.

"Thank you, my dear. It has been a difficult road. If not for HeSMO, I'm not sure I would have survived it. What you won't find in your investigation, Mr. Parker, is HeSMO, or the fact I can see spirits. I keep that part of my life very private, as you apparently do, too. I'm not here to harass you. If you'd like to join my organization, you're more than welcome to. I just wanted you to be aware of its existence." Zane withdrew a card from an inside pocket and handed it out to Dean. "My e-mail address and phone number. I do hope you'll take the time and consider joining. It's a wonderful support system. We not only help spirits, but each other."

Dean took the card. The guy had a point. The day Dean discovered he wasn't alone in the ghost-seeing business had been one of the best days of his life. But if he joined this HeSMO thing, he'd probably be required to actually find ghosts. God. Just the thought gave him a headache.

"So, do you?" Maggie said. "Have people in your organization who can be possessed?"

"My late wife was one such person. I haven't been fortunate enough to find another one. Until now, I assume?"

The look of joy on Maggie's face set Dean's teeth on edge. Seemed he'd have more than Bridget to contend with.

Chapter 33

Gina sat in the backseat of the cab, fuming. She couldn't believe Eddie had abandoned her in her time of need. Instead of posting bond, he'd left her to rot in that cell and made her wait for her lawyer to do it instead. On Monday.

Then, when she'd gotten her phone back, she found the battery dead. Thank goodness she had enough money for cab fare; otherwise she might have had to rely on her sister, and that was one person Gina did not want to depend on. Tammy was beyond bossy. As if being older really meant something. It only meant she was older.

The cab driver dropped Gina off at her car and she wasted no time driving home. After a nice, warm shower, she would confront her traitorous son at his work. Well, maybe after a good meal, too. Veronica would make sure to fix her something good. That woman was a saint, and easily manipulated.

Gina rushed up to the house and turned the knob. Door was locked. She fished inside her purse and found the key, but when she tried to unlock the door, the key wouldn't turn. What was it with her and keys lately? It was the right damn key, too. She huffed, sending a plume of fog in the air, and rang the doorbell. When that didn't get an immediate response, she knocked. Loudly.

What was taking Veronica so long? Gina jumped up and down, trying to generate some heat. Finally, her daughter-in-law opened the door. Gina moved to enter the house. "About time. I'm freezing out here."

Veronica blocked her way. "Eddie's at work."

"What does that have to do with the price of beans? Let me in."

"No."

"What do you mean, no? I live here."

"Not anymore. Goodbye, Gina." Veronica started to shut the door, but Gina stuck her foot in the way of it closing.

"Wait. What happened? Why are you treating me this way?"

"You happened, Gina. You and your obsessions." Veronica kicked Gina's foot away and shut the door.

"It's not an obsession if you're trying to right a wrong!" Gina jiggled the door knob. Locked. "Just wait until Eddie hears how you've been treating me. Then we'll see who's in and who's out." Of all the nerve. She stomped to her car and drove over to Eddie's work.

Eddie was scowling as he stormed into the reception area and dragged her outside. "What are you doing here?"

"You don't have to be so rough with me. And I'm here because for some reason your wife won't let me in the house."

"That's right. You're not welcome there anymore. Your stuff is back at Aunt Tammy's. Didn't you get my message?"

Oh God. Not that. Anything but that. "I haven't had a chance to look. My phone is dead. Why are you doing this to me?"

"I'm not doing anything to *you*. I'm liberating myself. I still don't know how it is you weaseled your way into my home, but it stops now. This last trip to jail woke me up. You're never going to change and I have a life to live with my wife. Not you."

"You can't treat me like this. I'm your mother!"

"And I'm your *son*. But that never really mattered to you, did it? It was that house. It's always been that damn house."

"Your grandmother ripped me, I-I mean you off. Don't you know I've only been trying to help?"

"Yeah? Well I don't need your help. Maggie called this morning. She's willing to sit and discuss the matter. With *me*. Not you. And after what you've done, I've a mind to just drop the whole thing."

"You can't do that. Maggie is a thief—"

"Enough! I'll do what I damn well want. Goodbye, Mother." He walked off, leaving her alone.

How did this all turn out so bad? What had Maggie said to him to make him turn on his mother that way? Well, that bitch wasn't going to get away with it. No siree.

* * * *

"I'm running a little late," Erica said. "Don't go without me."

"As if I would," Maggie said. Regardless of what Dean had said, she still wasn't sure how patient he'd be with Peter possessing her. Erica would have a calmer head about her. Well…maybe. "But I'm getting ready to lock up now. I'll just meet you at Dean's, okay?"

"I'm so glad you two worked everything out."

"Me, too." And maybe if Peter actually moved on with her help, lunch time could be more…recreational. Dean had a bed over there. Anything could happen.

"So, thirty minutes. Tops. See you there. And don't go making out on the couch. My eyes can only take so much." The phone cut off in the middle of Erica's laugh.

Maggie had to laugh, too. Wasn't her fault Erica had decided to sneak in last night. Maybe if she'd made more noise, she wouldn't have caught the make-out session in the living room. Thank goodness no one had been naked.

The computers were off, the main lights were off—a little one by the door stayed on 24/7—and Maggie shrugged on her coat. All she had left to do was dump the trash and then she could walk over and give Dean a big kiss. Oh, he'd probably object with Peter in the room, but she didn't care. She hadn't seen him all day and needed a fix. With a smile, she slung her purse on her shoulder, picked up the bag of trash and headed for the exit.

At first, the thought of falling asleep at five p.m. seemed impossible without intervention, but she hadn't gotten much sleep last night—thanks to Dean, not that she was complaining—and had been yawning for the better part of the afternoon. A nap sounded good about now. After the kiss, of course.

As she stepped outside, the frigid air snuffed any yawn she might make. Stupid groundhog predicted an early spring weeks ago, so where was the warmer weather? Instead, she suffered with temps in the twenties and the threat of more snow. The sun still had another hour before it set, but nothing was getting through the dark, grey clouds. She locked up and walked around the plowed snow piles to get to the dumpster.

It could be worse. She could be alone and cold. Tonight called for snuggling in front of a roaring fire. And maybe even a little celebratory wine. Regardless if Peter moved on or not, he'd get closure. That had to be worth celebrating.

Two extra cars sat in the shared parking lot. Rats. Guess there wouldn't be any kissing for a while. Not until Dean got rid of his clients.

She tossed the bag of trash into the dumpster, turned around, and ran into Aunt Gina. Maggie's euphoria took a nose dive. God, would she ever be rid of this woman? "What. Now?"

"Bad enough you took what was rightfully mine, you turned my boy against me."

"*I* turned Eddie against *you*? Oh, that's rich. Just like you not to take the blame. I'm sure you blame me for getting arrested, too, huh?"

"It *is* your fault."

"Right…" No use arguing with a crazy woman. "Why don't you just tell them that in court? Until then, leave me alone." Maggie might have bumped into Gina on her way to Dean's. And she might have bumped her hard. Unfortunately, not hard enough to knock her to the ground.

Gina grabbed Maggie by the arm and shoved something into her stomach. *Zap. Zap. Zap.*

Maggie's gut lit on fire. She grabbed her stomach and doubled over. "What the hell was that?"

"Damn it. Stupid coat." Gina jabbed the device into Maggie's neck.

The cold metal was followed by a searing burn. The zapping sounds exploded in her ear. Pain greater than anything she'd ever felt took her breath away and had her crumpling to the ground. She couldn't control her movements, but she could sure feel. The freezing asphalt scratched her face but that was nothing compared to the fire racing through her body. Gina grabbed her under her arms and dragged her. By the time Gina stopped at a car, Maggie regained some control.

The trunk popped open. She managed to slip free and stand, but another zap to her neck sent her to the open trunk. Tears burst from her eyes. Gina shoved the rest of her inside the trunk and zapped her again. Maggie tried to cry out, but no sounds came from her mouth.

Gina slapped tape over Maggie's mouth, then secured her hands behind her back. Her purse landed beside her head with a thunk.

"I'm taking you to your house where you can then give me those cards you hid. You don't cooperate, then maybe I'll just shoot you and your boyfriend, and maybe even your cousin, and end the whole thing. And don't think I won't. I have a gun in my car. It's not like I have anything else left to lose now that you've turned Eddie against me."

Gina slammed the trunk closed and Maggie's world turned dark.

Cards? What cards? And how would she ever be able to warn Dean and Erica? Right now she could barely move at all. Damn stun gun.

* * * *

Dean shook his new client's hand in front of Bridget's empty desk. "I'll start work on it first thing in the morning."

"Thanks. You don't know what a relief that is." He shrugged on his coat. "Hope you get that heat issue fixed. Got downright drafty in your office."

"I'm sure it's nothing." Nothing, except one pesky ghost. As the man left the building, Dean smiled at Erica's arrival. Perfect timing. Now Peter couldn't bug him. Although, he'd rather it was Maggie walking in, but hey, he'd take whatever he got.

"Hey, Dean. Glad to see you upright."

He shook his head and chuckled. Maybe if she hadn't had squealed when she found them, it wouldn't have been so funny.

Erica followed him into his office. "Where's Maggie?"

"At work?"

"Huh. I didn't even look. When I told her I was running late, she said she was on her way over here. That was thirty minutes ago."

"Yeah, well, I wasn't exactly ready, either. It's possible she saw me with a client and returned to her work." Too bad she hadn't said anything, or popped her head in. He certainly would have cut the interview short.

Erica pulled out her phone. "That's possible, I suppose." She held the phone up to her ear. "She's not answering. Must be in the bathroom. Hey, Maggie. I'm at Dean's. Get your butt over here. We're both ready now." She dropped her phone into her purse. "I'm surprised Bridget isn't around."

"Me, too, but she wasn't feeling well. I think she's still recovering from that little jog she did Friday night. I offered to postpone it, but she didn't want to do that to Peter." Dean was beginning to hope the possession worked after the stunt Peter pulled with his last client. The ghost was going off the deep end. Why antagonize the people who were willing to help?

Erica shrugged out of her coat and settled on the couch. She rubbed her arms. "Hi, Peter. I'm assuming it's Peter. You only have the one ghost, right?"

"Yeah. Just the one. Ignore him. He's been going crazy since I agreed to this possession. You'd think he won the lottery or something."

"Maybe to him he has."

He supposed Erica was right. Not that Peter had it all that rough being a ghost. Dean sat on the other end of the couch. "I want to thank you for stopping her the other night. I'm not saying Peter wouldn't have behaved, but I know Lindy had a hard time staying away. Maggie was like a drug to her."

"Well, if this works, it won't matter, will it? He won't be around to become addicted."

"We can only hope." Man, to actually work here without a ghost around? When Bridget went out for lunch, Maggie could come over. He did have that extra bed…

"Maggie tells me you have a brother. Only his name is Greg, not Sam."

Erica's question pulled him out of dream-land. And it was such a nice dream, too. "Yeah, so?"

"Is he married?"

"I thought you had a boyfriend."

"Who? Trevor? Nah. He's just a friend with benefits. Okay, only one benefit. But I could never live with the guy. We would totally kill each other. At least, I would end up killing him."

"But yet you continue to have sex with him."

"Only until someone better comes along. So is he? Married?"

"No. He's single."

"Cool. Think you can hook us up?"

"You do know he lives in Cleveland, don't you?"

"So? It's not like I have a career here." She rubbed her arms again. "Okay, Peter. I'm sure you're a nice guy, and I get you're excited, but would you please stop the freeze? Maggie will get here soon."

Dean stood. "Okay, that does it. Stop it now or there will be no visit to Alan."

"Dean?" Shivering, Erica looked at him with widened eyes. "He's not stopping. Maybe he's trying to get your attention?"

"He's been doing that all day. Wait here. I'll go see what he wants this time." He no sooner shut the door to his office when Peter grabbed his arm.

"Finally. Maggie's been kidnapped."

"What are you talking about? Who would kidnap her?"

"Her Aunt Gina?"

And as Peter relayed the events that happened in the parking lot, Dean's blood ran cold.

* * * *

Maggie's head cleared during the drive. Feeling returned to her extremities and the searing pain abated, but she could use a little heat. Stupid trunk was freezing. She was determined not to get zapped again, but for that to happen she would have to disarm her aunt. Kind of hard to do that with the way she was bound.

Zip ties. The woman had used zip ties and they cut into Maggie's skin. Bracing for the pain, she'd tried to bring her hands around in front, but either her arms were too short or her butt was too... Well, whatever, her hands were going nowhere.

She still wore her boot. Could she smack Gina in the face with it? She'd have to open the trunk eventually. One swift kick in the face with that thing, she just might go down.

The car stopped, then moved in reverse. Parking it so she could make a quick getaway? Or hoping no one would notice a woman coming out of the trunk?

Maggie lifted her booted leg and stretched it as far as space allowed. She could do this. Even trussed up and injured, she could move better than Gina. Might've helped if she'd taken some kind of self-defense class, but how hard could it be to kick someone? Especially if they weren't expecting it?

Silence came hard as the engine died. The trunk popped open and red light streamed inside. Either Gina hadn't turned off the lights or her foot was still on the brake. Whatever, she was up front and the driver's door remained closed. Forget kicking. Maggie wasted no time. She rolled and swung her legs out the opening. As soon as her feet touched the ground, she high-tailed it toward the alley. But the never-melting snow drift and her boot didn't get along and she landed face first into the crusty stuff.

Shit! Shit, shit, shit!

Gina pulled Maggie up by the zip ties, causing the plastic to cut into sensitive skin. "Did you really think you'd get far? Silly girl. Now don't make me shoot you."

Maggie's heart froze, the pain in her wrists forgotten when Gina pointed an actual gun at her face. She hadn't believed her aunt owned the weapon, but there it was. Pointed at her.

"Let's go." Gina waved the gun, indicating Maggie should return back to the car. Gina grabbed the purse and shut the trunk. "Go to the back door."

Probably to ensure Maggie wouldn't run off again, Gina held onto the zip ties. Maggie walked around the other side of the garage, where the ground was more manageable. When she reached the back door, she stopped.

Gina came around and pointed the gun at Maggie's stomach. "I'm going to remove your tape. You yell out, it will be the last thing you yell. Do you understand?"

Maggie nodded and then braced herself for the rip. Gina didn't disappoint. Maggie's face burned from the release of tape, but at least she could open her mouth and breathe easier.

"Now, I'm going to unlock this door and you're going to give me the code to disarm it. Because if anyone, *anyone*, shows up I'll shoot them, then I'll shoot you. Do you understand?"

God, Gina had really gone off the deep end. Maggie nodded, afraid to even utter a peep.

Gina found the keys in Maggie's purse, unlocked the door, then shoved Maggie inside. The display was flashing in the darkened room. Maggie almost uttered the distress code, but she didn't want Gina going around shooting anyone, so she gave the correct one. Once Gina punched in the numbers, the flashing light stopped.

Gina turned on the kitchen light. "Sit."

Maggie sat at the kitchen table. First step in escaping had to be getting her hands free. Better yet, get Gina frustrated enough to leave. Unfortunately, her frustration could come out in bullets. That wouldn't work out so well.

"Now tell me what you did with the cards."

"What cards?"

"Oh, don't play dumb with me. You know damn well what cards. Only you could have hidden them."

"I swear, I don't know what you're talking about."

"Baseball cards! Baseball cards!" Spittle flew from Gina's mouth and Maggie winced as it hit her face.

"I haven't seen any baseball cards."

"Don't lie to me." Gina grabbed Maggie's elbow, yanked her out of the seat, and proceeded to drag her into the dining room where she pulled a book from a box. "Here. They were in here and now they're gone. Give them to me."

Not a book. The photo album. "There weren't any cards in there when I found it. Maybe they fell out." Or someone took them, but why put thoughts in Gina's head? Gina just might shoot her out of spite. "Or Grandma stored them somewhere…safer. In a protective case or something." Yeah, that was it. "She probably didn't want them ruined. I haven't been able to search through all the boxes yet. It could be in one of them."

"That makes sense. Fine. Start searching."

"How?" Maggie turned and lifted her bound hands.

Gina went to the kitchen and grabbed a knife from the butcher block. "If you try anything funny—"

"I know, I know. You'll shoot me." Maggie braced for a slip of the knife, or even a jab out of spite, but Gina managed to cut the ties without incident. Free. She was free. She rubbed her tender wrists.

"Go on." Gina pushed Maggie toward the boxes. "What are you waiting for?"

Maggie opened the flap to the box closest to her when her phone went off. Dean or Erica? Did it matter? She needed to get her aunt out of the house. Now. "You do know eventually someone is going to come looking for me. So you don't have to shoot anyone, why don't you just take the stuff and go. I'll even help—"

Gina threw the album at Maggie. Maggie dodged, but not quite quick enough. The corner of the album struck her temple before hitting the wall. Pictures fluttered to the floor.

"I didn't ask for your opinion! Now quit stalling and get to work. Because I won't hesitate to shoot anyone who walks through that door."

She rubbed the offending spot, thankful she didn't get her eye poked out. The last thing she wanted to do was stall. If she didn't get Gina out of the house before Dean arrived—and she was fairly certain Peter let him know she'd been abducted—his life would surely be in danger. But searching through those boxes? It would take forever, and she didn't have but twenty minutes at the most. Even in her frenzied state, the mess on the floor called to her. As she picked up the album, an envelope slipped out from inside the back cover. *Oh, please, let it be the cards.*

Her name was scrawled on the front in familiar writing. If the cards existed, they weren't inside, though.

"What is that?" Gina asked. "Could it be a map?"

Maggie could only hope. She opened the envelope. "It's a letter from Grandma and a printout of some kind."

"Read it. Out loud."

Seeing Grandma's handwriting nearly brought tears to her eyes. And she might have outright cried if the circumstances were different. She cleared her throat and read.

"Dear Maggie. I just want you to know I never told anyone what happened that summer. I would have if I thought for one second you weren't okay, but the next morning you woke up as if nothing had happened. And then years went by without another incident, so I believed everything was okay. However, I did run a—"

No, no, no! That printout was DNA results. Would Gina shoot her now?

"Why'd you stop? Keep reading."

Maggie quickly scanned the letter, praying she wouldn't have to read it out loud, and hit pay dirt. "Oh here. It says she put the baseball cards in a tin can and stored them in my old tree house."

Gina narrowed her eyes. "What aren't you telling me?"

"Nothing. Why don't you go on over to Dad's and get the cards? The tree house is in the backyard. He's in Florida right now, so no one will bother you."

"I don't think so. Give that to me." Gina snatched the letter from Maggie's hands.

It wouldn't take long for Gina to read what Grandma had discovered. That Uncle Ed wasn't Eddie's biological father. Appeared Lindy was right. Maggie swallowed hard. At least Grandma hadn't implicated her, as if that mattered to the crazy woman.

"Nooooooooo! That bitch had no right!"

What nostalgia hadn't done, fear did when Gina raised her gun. Tears threatening to fall, Maggie stared at the weapon. "Please don't shoot me."

Gina crumpled up the letter. "Damn them! How did she find out? Ed said no one would know. We made sure and found a sperm donor that matched his description. No one should have known. How did they know?"

"Wait. You're saying Uncle Ed knew Eddie wasn't his?"

"Of course he knew. I didn't cheat on him! But he wanted a child and he didn't want his family to know he couldn't father any because he was sure they'd blame the lack of babies on me. I swear, if your mother and grandmother were alive, I would shoot you. In front of them. Let them feel the pain they've caused me all these years. The pain they're causing me now." She clutched her chest with her free hand. "But killing you won't give me any satisfaction."

She meant yet. Maggie could almost hear the word uttered from Gina's brain. Why else would she keep waving that gun around? She would have stuck with using the stun gun.

Gina smoothed the letter, folded it with the test results, and shoved them in her coat pocket. "Come on. You're driving."

Maggie caught the keys that were thrown her way. "Driving? Aren't you just going to tie me up here?"

"And have someone find you? No way. Besides, I need you to get the cards."

"Me? But...they're...in...the...tree house." The tall tree house. The tree house she fell out of when she was a kid. The tree house of her nightmares.

"So the letter says. But I'm not stupid. For all I know you set this whole thing up as a trap."

"You think I wrote the letter?" When Gina just stared at her, she shook her head. "I'm not going up there."

Gina waved the gun in the air. "You think I'm kidding with this thing?"

She'd die going up that tree, or rather, going down. That's if the thing could support her weight to begin with. "You're going to kill me anyway. Why wait?"

"I'm not going to kill you if you get me my cards. But since you don't seem to believe that, how about: you don't go up there, I shoot your boyfriend. In fact..." She grabbed a paper from the box and pulled a pen from her purse. "Just to motivate you to move faster, I'm leaving a note here telling him where we are. If he's coming here like you said, you'll have at least fifteen minutes to get me the cards. If you don't, or they're not there, boom! He's dead."

Seemed she was climbing a tree house, because watching Dean die wasn't going to be on Maggie's agenda.

* * * *

Dean pulled up in front of Maggie's garage as snow started to fall. The phone tracker still indicated Maggie's phone was in the house, but Gina's car was nowhere in sight, neither in the front nor back of the house. Either she had driven them away or…

Oh God. Please don't let it be the or.

Erica stared out the window. "Are you sure we shouldn't call the cops? If Gina has a gun—"

"And what would I tell them? That a ghost told me she'd been abducted by her aunt?"

"We could say I saw it all."

"So why didn't you go after her? Why didn't I go after her after you told me what you saw? Too much time has gone by and I don't need the police stalling us. Besides, we're not even sure if Gina has a gun. Peter said she claimed there was one in the car. Could have been a scare tactic." A scare tactic he took seriously. "I need you to stay here. But if you see Gina, get out of sight and call 9-1-1. You hear?"

She nodded. "Please be quick. I'm scared."

So was he. This was Maggie. She was his life now. If he lost her… No, he couldn't think like that. She was okay. She had to be.

Dean ran toward the house, slowing as he approached the porch. Making as little noise as possible, he climbed the stairs and tested the back door. Unlocked. Slowly he pushed the door open. The kitchen light was on and the alarm deactivated. Silence filled the house.

Maggie's purse sat on the kitchen table. He checked each room downstairs, upstairs, and the basement. At least he didn't find her body, so not the or. Just a minor relief at that. He wouldn't have total relief until he held her living body in his arms.

He texted Erica it was all clear. Moments later she appeared in the door.

"No one's here," he said. "Any idea where they went?"

"No." Erica covered her face. "Oh God. What if Gina decides to kill her?"

"Hey. Don't think like that." He was doing enough of the worst-case scenarios in his head as it was. "We'll figure it out. She had to have left a clue, right?"

"Right!" She spun around in the tidy kitchen. "But where?"

"I was thinking more along the lines of the dining room." But that room was almost as clean. Cut zip ties and a few photos littered the floor. An old photo album sat on the table. Fear re-settled as he began to have doubts of finding her. Period.

Erica walked over to the table. "I know where they went. She left a note. Well, not Maggie. This isn't her writing. Gina?"

Sounded like a set-up to him. But at least Maggie was still alive.

Chapter 34

Big, wet snowflakes splattered on the windshield as Maggie pulled into the driveway of her childhood home. Since she was forced to drive, she'd made sure to replace her boot with an actual shoe. Could she make a break for it now? Find a neighbor and call to warn Dean? She didn't limp all that much. But with the snow falling and the way Gina was pointing her gun, one slippery move could find both her and Dean dead, as well as innocent bystanders. Best to wait until Gina's focus was on something other than Maggie. Like the cards. If they even existed.

"Are you going to put that thing away or do you want the neighbors to call 9-1-1?"

Gina shoved the gun inside her purse, her hand still gripping the weapon. "Don't go getting any ideas of running. I'm sure this purse won't stop the bullet none."

No, it wouldn't, but Gina's actions might still cause a neighbor to call 9-1-1. Maggie wasn't about to say anything, though, and she was sorry she'd said anything before. But *seeing* a gun pointed at her just made her more itchy than *knowing* one was. Who knew?

With Gina poking the purse into her back, Maggie limped into the backyard, the lawn a patchwork of white and green. Even though she'd grown since the fall, the tree house seemed higher than Maggie remembered. Her stomach lurched at the memory.

"Go on," Gina said. "Hurry it up. Clock is ticking."

The hand-built ladder steps didn't look all that safe for an adult. Were they ever? Keeping her focus on the rungs and not the ground, she planted her uninjured foot onto the first step and lifted. She repeated the motion with the same foot. So far, so good. Her ankle wasn't screaming in pain—more like a moan—and the steps miraculously held her weight. Too bad they didn't do anything for her heart. It raced as if she'd been watching one of those slasher flicks.

Possible material for a book. If she survived to write it.

Three long, agonizing steps later, Gina yelled up at her. "Will you move it? For someone who doesn't want me to shoot their boyfriend, you're slower than a sloth."

Maggie froze. Was Gina behind her? She risked a look behind. No such luck. Not that she wanted the extra weight on the steps, but it would have been a good time to smack that woman in the face. "I'm going as fast as I can. My ankle, you know?"

"Your ankle-schmankle. Just hurry it along."

Doing her best to ignore her aunt, Maggie climbed the remainder of the steps at her sloth-like pace. She'd love nothing more than to hurry and end this whole disaster, but somehow she didn't think falling would benefit anyone. When she reached the top she practically hugged the creaky floor. Not that it was any better up here. Weather and time had done a number on many of the boards and she could see down to the ground in some places. Big mistake. Looking forward, she crawled on the few solid boards over to the hidey-hole she'd made as a kid.

The pink paint had faded over the years, but she could still make out the words on the little door: SECRET HIDING PLACE. She'd labeled it as such because she had wanted her tree house to be her Bat Cave and Batman had labeled everything.

Maggie tugged on the rope handle and the door popped off. A tin can sat inside and she sighed in relief. "Oh, thank God."

"Give that to me."

Maggie jumped at Gina's voice. When had she climbed up the ladder? The boards creaked and cracked as she walked across the rotting floor. Maggie prayed, *fall through, fall through*, but her prayer went unfulfilled.

Gina grabbed the tin can from Maggie's hands and opened it. "Yes. Thank God that woman had sense enough to protect these from the elements."

Maggie sat in the corner, away from the edge where she'd fallen all those years ago. "You got your cards. Now go."

When Dean finally found her quivering body, he'd be able to help her down. Or at least call 9-1-1 for the fire department.

"How do I know you're not going to tell Eddie about his parentage?"

Oh shit. Would this day end in her death after all? "Because I already knew and hadn't told him anything. It's not for me to say."

"But you could, that's the point. Maybe I should just shoot you here. It'd probably take a few days, if not weeks, before someone found your body."

"You think no one will hear a gun shot?"

"People will only think a car back fired. No one wants to believe a gun went off. Only one problem with that. The note I left. Guess I'll just have to shoot the boyfriend after all. Now, let's see. How could I do that?"

While Gina mused, anger stirred inside Maggie. This would only end if she grew a spine. Now was the perfect time to make a move. If she died in the process, at least Dean would still be alive. That's all that mattered.

She charged. Gina's eyes widened, and before she could raise the gun, Maggie tackled the woman. With a sickening crunch, the floor gave way as the gun went off.

* * * *

Dean drove as fast as he dared through the neighborhoods while Erica leaned against her seatbelt and drummed the dash with her fingers.

"Can't you go any faster?" she said. "God, I hope we're not too late."

They were already too late. Too late in getting to Maggie's house. Too late finding that note. Although without it, they'd still be searching for her.

Dean was reading the house numbers through the falling snow when Erica squealed.

"There it is!" She pointed at the house across the street. "And there's Gina's car. That's a good sign, right?"

A good sign that Gina hadn't left, yes. That Maggie was still alive? Not so much. He pulled alongside the curb and left the engine running. Grabbing the gun from the glove box, he said, "If I don't text you in five minutes, call 9-1-1 and park down the street. If Gina really does have a gun, I don't need her shooting it at you."

"I don't need her shooting at me, either. Hope you don't have to use that."

He hoped so, too. But as he climbed out of the car, a gun shot reverberated through the neighborhood and his heart stuttered. He looked back at Erica climbing over the console.

"I'm calling. I'm calling," she said.

Gun held down to his side, he rushed to the fence and peeked through the gate. Gina was lying on the ground, unconscious. Where was Maggie?

He barged through the gate. "Maggie!"

"Dean? Watch out. She has a gun!"

Relief at hearing her voice squeezed tears from his eyes. She must still be in the tree house. The weapon lay a few feet from Gina. As he went to pick it up, Maggie's legs came into view. Okay, Maggie wasn't *in* the house, but hanging from a hole in the flooring. She struggled to regain her hold. He stowed the guns in his coat pockets and grabbed her legs. "I got you, sweetheart. Let go."

She slid down his body as he loosened his hold. When her feet hit the ground, she hugged him around his neck. "I thought I was dead. Oh God, I thought I was dead. But…is she dead?"

"No. Only unconscious. But it's over now." He overcame the urge to hold her tight, afraid of hurting her. The gun *had* gone off. "Are you hurt? Did she get you?"

She shook her head. That was all the confirmation he needed. He held her face and kissed her. Long, hard, and deep. All that pent-up fear was erased as she melded to his body.

Sirens sounded in the distance. The cops could take care of Gina. Right now, he only wanted to take care of one person. And he planned on doing that for the rest of his life.

Chapter 35

"Can't I have any privacy?" The words came from Maggie's mouth. And Maggie's body was standing before Dean in the hallway of the hospice. But Maggie wasn't in control.

He had asked her to wait another day, but she wouldn't hear of it. Said Peter had waited long enough. One shot of whiskey was all it had taken for Maggie to relax enough for Peter to slip into her body.

If Dean had needed any proof that Lindy got off on possessing Maggie, he got it seeing Peter's reaction on Maggie's face. Pure, unadulterated bliss. It was all Dean could do not to touch Maggie's body and force Peter back to his point of death.

"I'm making sure you don't use Maggie to do something stupid. Like kill the guy."

"I'm not gonna kill anyone."

"Yeah, just like you weren't going to commit suicide."

"Enough," Erica said. "Are you two always like this?"

"He is always like this," Maggie/Peter said. "I've always been nice."

Dean snorted. "Yeah, right."

"Behave, the two of you. I'm here to ensure you, Peter, don't abuse Maggie, and you, Dean, don't zap poor Peter too early. Got it?" She punctuated by pointing at each person's chest.

Peter moved Maggie's arms to her hips and stared at Dean. "I like Maggie, okay? She's doing me a huge favor. I won't spit on that and abuse her in any way. I never realized how short she was, though. I don't think I like looking up at you."

And it wasn't as if Peter had been a tall man. He just made sure to hover at eye level.

Erica stayed between Dean and Peter/Maggie as they entered the room. An old man, named Alan Baker, lay on the bed. Dean still couldn't believe Bridget had managed to track the man down. Of course, he might be the wrong Alan Baker.

"Is that him?" Dean asked Maggie/Peter.

Maggie/Peter inched over to the bed. Peter had been instructed not to touch anyone except Erica, since they couldn't tell if someone had the ability to see ghosts.

"Hello," Alan said. "I was told I had some visitors, but I don't know you."

Cancer was eating the man. Dean hated to think his mother had the same fate awaiting her.

"Hi, Alan," Maggie/Peter said. "Do you remember Peter McDermott?"

"Peter? Now there's a name from the past. Not a day goes by that I don't think of that young man. Died much too young. Are you a relative of his?"

This was where Peter was supposed to follow the script. Pretend to be a relation who had found Peter's diary and a letter addressed to Alan. Instead Maggie/Peter stared at Dean for a moment then turned toward Alan. "I'm sorry."

Alan furrowed his forehead. "What could you possibly be sorry for, dear girl?"

"I'm sorry for not respecting your wishes. I'm sorry for not giving you the time and space you needed. I'm sorry for disrupting your life. And I'm sorry for taking my life when I didn't get my way."

Dean shook his head. He knew it. Peter's insisting he'd been killed was all a lie. And now this poor old guy was going to think Maggie had gone insane.

"Excuse me?" Alan furrowed his forehead. "I don't know what you're talking about. And you seem very much alive to me."

"This woman before you is just a vessel. She's asleep inside so that I can use her to see you again. I have to say, you've gotten rather old."

"Peter, don't be rude!" Erica whispered.

Rude was the least of Dean's worries. Peter was blabbing everything. So much for planning a script.

"Peter?" Alan's eyes widened. "Oh my. You didn't move on?"

"Wait," Dean said. "What do you know about that?"

Alan glanced at Dean and Erica. "Which of you sees ghosts?"

"I don't believe it," Dean muttered. "How many freakin' people see ghosts?"

"Oh, I don't see 'em," Alan said. "But I had a friend who did. Never knew ghosts could possess anyone, though."

"Maggie is special," Maggie/Peter said.

"I suppose she is."

"I know I don't deserve to know, but if you had answered my call, would you have come and saved me, or was I too much of a drama queen?"

"You called?" Alan ran a hand down his face. "Oh God. I hadn't known."

"So you would have saved me? We would have been together?"

"Ahh, Peter. Of course I would have saved you. I loved you. But no, we wouldn't have been together. You know how life was back then. I was tired of living the double-life, cheating on my wife. I loved her and our children just as much as you, but they deserved all of me. I'm so sorry you felt suicide was your only way out."

"No, it was my fault. My head was messed up. I blamed you. I blamed your wife. I thought a drastic move on my part would make you see how much you loved me. I only wish I had taken the pills after I made the phone call. But I wanted to sound realistic. And then when you didn't answer... I took it as a sign. It was too easy to give up. I just loved you so much. I couldn't imagine life without you." Tears ran down Maggie's cheeks. "And now I'm stuck like this forever."

"No, you're not."

"What?" Maggie/Peter and Dean asked together.

"But I committed suicide."

"All you have to do is ask for forgiveness and mean it." Alan looked at Dean. "Why don't you know that? Don't you belong to the group?"

"You know about HeSMO?"

"I told you. I had a friend."

"Can I hug you?" Peter asked.

Alan spread his arms as wide as the tubes attached to him allowed. Maggie/Peter sat on the bed and gently hugged the frail man. After a few moments of whispering, he/she kissed Alan's cheek and went limp.

"I think Peter left."

Dean rushed over and pulled Maggie from Alan. If Peter hadn't moved on, he'd be gone from her body now. "Maggie? You okay?"

She blinked. "I'm fine. Got a little dizzy is all."

Dean chuckled at their practiced excuse. At least she hadn't forgotten. "Don't worry. Mr. Baker knows."

"Please, it's Alan. That was a nice thing you did for Peter."

"Did it work?" she asked. "Did he move on?"

"I'd like to think he did. But if you find him at home, please don't tell me."

They thanked him for his time and left the hospital. Dean had one place he wanted to stop before he took Maggie and Erica home.

He walked into his office and shut the door. "Peter?"

Silence. That's all the place held. He'd always wanted the ghost out of his life and now he had his wish. He'd just never thought he'd end up missing the guy.

Chapter 36

"If I had known you could move fast in that boot, I'd have taken it away. Would you slow down before you get hurt?" Erica said.

Maggie practically trotted down the hospital corridor, her boot clunking against the linoleum. So much had happened in the past forty-eight hours. Gina was in jail. Peter had moved on. She'd met with Eddie. Now Bridget had given birth. Going slow was not an option. "I can't believe he didn't tell me the sex of the baby."

"Yeah, Dean's a big meanie, and he'll be even meaner if you get hurt. Slow down."

Maggie stopped, but not because of Erica. She arrived at the elevator and hit the up button. "What? You afraid of Dean now?"

"Hey, he said he'd introduce me to his brother. Gotta stay on his good side, you know?"

Erica had done nothing but talk about Greg for the past two days, grilling poor Dean with questions. He'd probably only agreed to the meet to shut her up.

The elevator doors opened and Maggie rushed inside. "Oh, so it's not my well-being you're concerned with. It's yours."

"Don't go putting words in my mouth. You know you're my number one cousin."

"Your number one cousin who happens to let you live rent free?"

"Hey. Don't go there. I offered. You refused."

"You gonna be okay living there if Dean moves in?"

"What? You mean he's not living with us now?"

320

Maggie chuckled. He was over a lot. And even spent the night. But he still left too early in the morning to go to his own apartment. Once life quieted down, she planned on asking him to make it official. Even move his big bed over so there would be more room for him. Not that she minded the snuggling. God, he'd still snuggle, wouldn't he?

"I'm okay with it," Erica said, "if you're okay with me living with you two. I don't want to crowd you."

"But if you're dating Greg, will we even see you?"

"Hmmm... Good point."

The doors opened and Maggie went back into rush mode, stopping abruptly at the doorway to Bridget's room, causing Erica to bump into her back.

"There's the hero!" Bridget said.

"Hero? What are you talking about?"

"You helped Peter move on. I call that being a hero. I'm sure gonna miss him, though."

"It'll pass." Dean kissed Maggie, his lips lingering and causing her insides all sorts of commotion. Those lunch-hour quickies only seemed to make her yearn for him more, not less. "You got here fast."

"Blame her," Erica said. "She wouldn't stop pinching my arm unless I ran a few red lights."

"You didn't run any red lights. So, where's this baby?"

Rob brought a bundle over. "Here's Charlie Deanna."

"A girl? You had a girl?" Maggie took the sleeping infant. "She's so tiny. And beautiful." She sat on the chair Rob offered to her.

"So how did the meeting go with Eddie?" Bridget asked.

"Pretty good, actually. Before I had a chance to even mention the house, he told me he was dropping the suit. Apologized to me for his mother's behavior. He never really cared about the house. Sure made giving him the baseball cards easier. Felt sorry that he'd been disowned by Grandma all because Uncle Ed wouldn't admit he couldn't father any children."

"Wow. But weren't the baseball cards worth a lot?"

"Certainly nothing worth killing over. Eddie and I looked up some of them online. He could probably get a couple thousand for a few of the cards. The rest could garner a hundred bucks or so each. I didn't recognize any of the players, but I guess some of the cards were rare. I'm sure Gina will be disappointed to learn they aren't the cash cow she'd come to believe they were. That's if Eddie ever speaks to her again."

The baby stirred and Maggie looked down on little Charlie. What a sweetie. Might as well enjoy holding other people's babies, since she would never hold Dean's. And surprisingly, she was okay with that. Dean was hers and he loved her. And he was all that mattered to her. Tonight she would ask him to move in officially. Why wait? She couldn't imagine life without him.

* * * *

Dean smiled as Maggie rocked the baby. She was a natural. And here he was denying her children. There was always the route her aunt and uncle had gone. But could he stomach Maggie pregnant with an anonymous sperm donor?

"You want to hold her now?" Rob asked.

"No, that's not necessary."

"You haven't held her yet?" Maggie stood and walked over. "Come on. You gotta do it at least once."

She placed the baby in his arms. So light and fragile. Damn, he was going to break her or something.

"Just pretend she's a football," Rob said.

"Don't tell him that," Bridget said. "Don't go puntin' my baby." Everyone snickered at that, except her. She gave him the evil eye.

"Take it easy. I'm not going to hurt her." He hoped. Man, she was small.

Maggie snuggled beside him and stuck her finger into Charlie's tiny hand. The baby gripped tight. Maggie laughed. "Isn't she the sweetest thing?"

No. The sweetest thing stood beside him. With her arm around his waist and her face glowing at the baby. He couldn't stomach her carrying an anonymous sperm donor because he only wanted her carrying his children. Somehow it didn't feel so wrong. In fact, it felt right. Righter than he'd ever thought possible.

"I want this," he said. "With you."

Maggie looked up. "What?"

"Marry me. Have my kids. Grow old with me."

"Are you asking her or telling her?" Bridget asked.

"I was going to say the same thing," Erica said. "Some proposal."

Maggie's eyes shone. "But... I thought you didn't—"

"I was wrong. I love you, Maggie. I want everything with you. Do you want everything with me?"

The smile on her face lit him up. "More than anything."

He kissed her to the sounds of cheering. His Maggie. She would always be his Maggie and he would love her forever.

Epilogue

Dean sat at his mother's kitchen table and toyed with the envelope. After months of refusing to tell him who his biological father was, Mom had left him that information in an envelope. To be opened or not opened upon her death.

She'd died two days ago. Even knowing the end was near, it had still come as a shock to Dean. He would miss her terribly.

Maggie came up beside him and rubbed his shoulders. "Still haven't opened it, I see."

He kissed her rounded belly. Baby Jenny was due to arrive in a couple of months. At least Mom had known she would be a grandmother. He'd given her that. But could he throw the letter away without opening it? She hadn't wanted him to know.

Yet, she'd come to him after she died, just like she said she would. Told him where he could find the envelope. Kissed him, told him she loved him, and then moved on.

He shoved the envelope into his coat pocket. "Ready to go?"

He drove them to the funeral parlor. Bridget and Rob arrived. They'd left Charlie at home with Bridget's folks, but had wasted no time in starting another. Their second—sex unknown since they liked being surprised—would be born a month after Baby Jenny.

Greg arrived with Erica in tow. Guess cousins marrying twins ran in Maggie's family, or it would once those two tied the knot in a few months. Mom had left this world knowing both her boys wouldn't be alone. Probably what made it easier for her to let go.

The funeral service was nice. Greg said a few words. Dean said a few more. Then they helped carry Mom to the hearse, where she'd be taken to lie beside Dad.

A limo drove him, Maggie, Greg, and Erica to the cemetery. Dean kept toying with that envelope. Maggie grabbed his hand and squeezed.

"I saw your book, '*I Was Possessed by a Teenage Ghost*,' in the store," Greg said to Maggie. "Cool story, by the way. I never read anything so fast. Told the clerk I'm related to the author. He wanted to know if it was a true story."

"What?" Dean's heart nearly stopped. His brother wouldn't be so stupid as to say anything. Would he?

"I know, right?" Greg winked. "Some people don't understand fiction, huh?"

Maggie laughed. "No, I guess they don't."

They arrived at the cemetery. More words were said. Flowers were placed on the casket. Dean asked Maggie for a moment as he stood by the grave. He still fingered the envelope.

"I'm sure gonna miss her," Greg said as he approached. "What you got there?"

Dean looked up at his brother, who wiped a tear from his eye. They shared the same mother. They were raised by the same father. That's all that mattered. "It's nothing. Just some instructions. Ready to go have that toast for Mom?"

He ripped up the envelope and tossed the papers in a nearby trash can.

I love you, Mom.

ACKNOWLEDGMENTS

Special thanks to Maria Zannini for putting up with me when it came time to create the cover for this book. I may not know what I want, but I know what I don't want. I just wish I could have saved her some grief and explained that all better. She managed to do a great job despite me and I couldn't be more pleased with the end result.

To Piper Denna for jumping in and offering her editing services. She not only did an outstanding job, she saved me a lot of angst in trying to find someone short notice.

And lastly, to my daughter, Stephanie, for being my first reader as well as my copy editor. As always, I added a little something in this story from one of her favorite television shows to show my appreciation.

ABOUT THE AUTHOR

Stacy McKitrick always had stories in her head; she just never knew what to do with them. Then one day she decided to give writing a try and discovered the passion she'd been looking for all her life. She waived goodbye to accounting and now spends her time writing romance featuring vampires, ghosts, and aliens. All with happy endings, of course. Born in California, she currently resides in Ohio with her husband. They have two grown children. You can learn more about Stacy at her website www.stacymckitrick.com.

Thank you for purchasing this book

Sign up for Stacy McKitrick's newsletter to receive new release announcements, sneak peeks of future books, and bonus content. She sometimes even give away stuff.

http://eepurl.com/-Auwz